By Earl Emerson

Vertical Burn
Into the Inferno
Pyro
The Smoke Room
Firetrap

The Thomas Black Novels

The Rainy City
Poverty Bay
Nervous Laughter
Fat Tuesday
Deviant Behavior
Yellow Dog Party
The Portland Laugher
The Vanishing Smile
The Million-Dollar Tattoo
Deception Pass
Catfish Café

THE
SMOKE
ROOM

A NOVEL OF SUSPENSE

EARL EMERSON

BALLANTINE BOOKS • NEW YORK

2006 Ballantine Books Mass Market Edition

Published in the United States by Ballantine Books, an imprint of The Random House Publishing Group, a division of Random House, Inc., New York.

BALLANTINE and colophon are registered trademarks of Random House, Inc.

This book contains an excerpt from the forthcoming hardcover edition of *Firetrap*. This excerpt has been set for this edition only and may not reflect the final content of the forthcoming novel.

Originally published in hardcover in the United States by Ballantine Books, an imprint of The Random House Publishing Group, a division of Random House, Inc., in 2005.

ISBN 0-345-46291-2

Cover design: Carl Galian
Cover photograph: © Lightworks / Alamy

Printed in the United States of America

www.ballantinebooks.com

OPM 9 8 7 6 5 4 3 2 1

What good is happiness? It can't buy money.

—HENNY YOUNGMAN,
comedian

Be good and you will be lonesome.

—MARK TWAIN

1. HOWLING IN THE DEEP BLUE TWILIGHT

Experts estimated the pig fell just over 11,000 feet before it plunged through Iola Pederson's roof.

The lone witness had been snitching cherry tomatoes from a pot on his neighbor's front porch when he looked up and spotted the hog as it tumbled through the deep blue twilight. Whether the hog had been howling because he was delighted with the flight or because of the rapidly approaching earth, nobody ever knew. Ultimately the critter pierced Iola Pederson's roof with the sound of a man putting his foot through a rotten porch.

The pig's demise pretty much signaled the end of all my ambitions.

My name is Jason Gum. Just call me Gum.

At the time, I was twenty-four years old and had been a Seattle firefighter just under two years but was already studying to take the lieutenant's examination in another year. I was aiming to be chief of the department. It was ambitious, I know, but the way I figured it, you need goals if you are going anywhere in life—goals and a straight and narrow pathway.

Engine 29 runs out of a sleepy little station in a residential district in West Seattle. Four people work off the rig: an officer, a driver, and two of us in back. On the day we got the call to check out Iola Pederson's roof, I was working a rare turn on B shift. Stanislow had less time in than I did, and I could tell she was looking to my lead as we raced toward the scene of what the radio report said was a rocket into a house. I knew not to get too worked up until we'd evaluated the scene ourselves.

"I wonder if it's an accidental firing from the submarine base across the water," said Stanislow. "Christ."

"It's probably nothing," I said.

As we sat in the back of the crew cab watching the streets unfold behind us, Stanislow and I slipped into our MSA harnesses. They'd also dispatched two more engines and two aerial ladders, a chief, a medic unit, and probably an aid car; yet even with all that manpower, Stanislow and I would be first through the door. Life on the tailboard. Cash money couldn't get a better seat to every little bizarre extravagance of human behavior.

The address was on Hobart Avenue SW, a location drivers from stations outside our district were going to have a hard time finding.

Siren growling, Engine 29 moved through quiet, residential streets until we hit the apex of Bonair Drive, where we swooped down the hillside through a greenbelt that was mostly brown now—Seattle enjoying the driest August on record.

The slate-blue Puget Sound was spread out below us like a blanket. West over the Olympics the sunset was dead except for a few fat razor slashes of pink along the horizon. A hawk tipped his wings and bobbled on air currents over the hillside. Above us a small plane circled.

The house was the only single-family residence on a street of small apartment buildings. The lieutenant turned around and said, "Looks like smoke. I want you guys to lay a preconnect to the front door."

The driver placed the wheel blocks under the rear duals and started the pump, while I jumped down and grabbed the two-hundred-foot bundle of inch-and-three-quarters hose preconnected to an outlet on the rig and headed toward the house, dropping flakes of dry hose behind me. The officer busied himself on the radio, giving incoming units directions to our location. Because the driver on this shift was noted for filling the line with reckless speed, I moved quickly, not wanting the water pressure to knock me down the way it had Stanislow at her first fire.

In front of the house a man with one of those ubiquitous white Hemingway beards you see on so many old guys sat cross-legged on the turf, covered in blood. Behind him, the living-room windows were broken out, pieces of plate glass littering the lawn like mirrors and reflecting distant city lights, a twilight sky. The roof had a hole in it the size of a duffel bag. All I could think was that the man on the lawn had been burned and wounded, possibly in an explosion.

"Anybody inside?" I asked.

"My daughter," he gasped. "My daughter's in there! I *think* she's in there. God. I'm confused."

Stanislow stooped beside the victim. "What happened?"

"I'm not sure. It might have been a bomb."

"A bomb," Stanislow said. "Did you hear that, Gum? What if there's another one?"

"You got any explosives in the house?" I asked.

"Just a few bullets. But *I* didn't do this. It came from up there." He pointed toward the sky.

Powdery material that might or might not have been smoke drifted out of the hole in the roof. Later we determined it was creosote dust being distributed by the kitchen fan. The broken window frames were draped in a wet substance that appeared remarkably similar to entrails.

As I neared the doorway and the cotton-jacketed hose started to harden at my feet, I clipped my air hose to my face piece and began inhaling compressed air. Stanislow caught up with me but stopped near a gore-festooned window frame. "Jesus. Look at that."

I pushed the front door open with my boot.

"You think that's his daughter?" Stanislow asked. "You think that's her guts?"

"Only one way to find out."

"There's no telling how bad he's bleeding. I better stay out here and take care of him."

"Okay. I'll go in. You take care of him."

I picked up the nozzle and went through the front door, keeping low the way we'd been taught, not crawling but not standing, either. When I switched my helmet light on, hundreds of thousands of black motes wafted in the yellow beam. I could see maybe ten feet through the nebula.

It had been close to 90° Fahrenheit when we left the station, and experts estimated that under normal working conditions the microclimate inside our turnouts was nearly 150°. It was probably higher tonight, which kept me sweating profusely in the heavy, all-encapsulating turnout clothing.

It didn't occur to me until I entered the structure that I'd been listening to howling for some time now, the noise obscured by the roaring of Engine 29's motor and pump. The noises might have been coming from an animal. More likely it was a second victim. Most of the ceiling in the main room was on the floor, plaster and broken boards underfoot. I moved through the blackness, at times forced to feel my way, dragging the hose even though there was no sign of heat or fire.

"It's okay," I said. "I'm here to help."

She was hunkered on the floor. The black ink in the air had settled on her like broken spiderwebs. The floor was gooey, and as I reached her I slipped to one knee. When I tipped her head up and peeked through the blood and the black residue covering her face, I was greeted by the most startling blue eyes I'd ever encountered.

"You all right?"

She blinked but did not move.

"What happened? Are you all right?"

"There's a head over there."

"What?"

"A head."

"How many people were here?"

"Just me and Daddy."

"So whose head is it?"

"I don't know. Maybe somebody came in the back. All I know is, he was huge."

The furniture had congealed into vague, elusive lumps swathed in plaster and rubble. On the floor in front of the kitchen sink I found a large animal's head. It took a moment to ascertain the head had belonged to a hog and the material surrounding it was an animal cadaver, half-empty, the entrails spewing this way and that like grotesque Halloween ornaments strung up by a lunatic.

"Am I going to die? Please don't tell me I'm going to die."

"You'll be okay." My Emergency Medical Technician training taught me to start with what we called the ABCs: airway, breathing, and circulation. She'd been making noise, so she had an airway and was breathing. As far as the circulation and bleeding went, she was covered in gore, so I had no way of knowing whether she was bleeding or not.

Speaking into my portable radio, I said, "Command from Engine Twenty-nine, team B. No sign of fire. There's light smoke in the structure. We've got a second victim inside. I'm bringing her out."

"What happened?" she asked, as I took her arm and stood her up. "Who did this?"

"I don't know. Let's get you out of here. Can you walk?"

Apparently not, I thought, as she sagged against me.

One arm under her shoulders, the other under her knees, I lugged her through the ravaged interior of the house. As it turned out, she was a full-grown adult, almost as tall as I was—five-eight—and while I wasn't the strongest firefighter in the department, I managed to get us out the doorway and onto the lawn without either of us falling on our butts.

Outside, Stanislow and our earlier victim were gone.

I set my victim down on the lawn away from the broken glass and got my first good look at her in the twilight. In addition to the blood and guts, she was covered in soot. I took off my helmet, shut down my air supply, and removed my face piece.

"Oh, God," she said, holding her arms stiffly away from her body. "Can't you do something? Oh, my God. This is disgusting. Get it off me."

I yarded the hose line out of the house and cracked the nozzle until water poured out in a limp, silvery stream. "Here."

She cupped water in her hands and splashed it on her face, picking at her hair. "Oh, God. Just pour it over my head. It's all in my hair. It's everywhere."

"It's going to be cold."

"I don't give a damn. Get this off me."

I opened the nozzle on flush, giving her what amounted to

a cold shower. Underneath the gore and soot she wore a T-shirt and jeans. The cold water emphasized the fact that she wasn't wearing a bra.

"Is Daddy all right?" she asked, after we'd sluiced the last of the blood and soot out of her hair. "Have you seen Daddy?"

"He's over by our engine. Anybody else in there?"

"Just that god-awful head."

As I turned the Task Force nozzle around and screwed up the pressure to knock the crap off my rubber boots, she looked up at me, suddenly bashful. "I must look hideous."

"No. I think you look terrific."

Her name was Iola Pederson, she was maybe twenty years older than I was, and although I didn't know it then, she was the first nail in my coffin.

2. THE FIVE F'S

As firefighters and police investigators dissected the wreckage, the mechanics of the destruction were slowly unraveled. Contrary to expectations, we found no bombs, no exploded water heaters, no downed rockets, and no fallen airplane engines. Clear and simple: an animal had fallen out of the sky, later identified as a breed of hog known as a Chester White. The hog had penetrated the Pederson homestead, punching through the roof, the attic, and the second floor, and then had exploded against the concrete subfloor under the living-room rug.

Accompanied by his owner and his owner's brother, the animal, having just won two ribbons at a county fair on the Olympic Peninsula, had been returning home to Ellensburg, a small college/farming town east of the Cascades. The pig's owner had modified his Cessna 210 to transport livestock, altering the door, removing the last four seats, and jury-rigging a wooden pen in the rear of the plane. The floor of the pen was lined with straw, old blankets, corncobs, rutabagas, and stale doughnuts to keep the hog occupied during the flight. Despite the fact that their passenger tipped the scales at 947 pounds, total weight for the three of them was still under the allowable payload for the plane.

During the originating flight from Eastern Washington, the hog had become airsick and thrashed about in his pen, his movements tipping the plane from side to side. Fearing another bout of airsickness on the return flight, the pilot laced a bucket of apples with Stressnil and fed it to the creature. If he'd been paying attention, the pilot would have seen the hog spit out the tranquilizers, ingesting just enough to doze off after they prodded him into the plane, but not enough to keep him asleep.

Because he'd already weakened the slats of his pen on the initial flight, it took only a minute of thrashing about before he broke the enclosure.

Without hesitation the hog rushed forward and nuzzled the back of the pilot's seat in a desperately friendly move, thrusting the pilot up against the yoke. The weight shift sent the plane into a shallow dive, which prompted the pilot to shout at his brother, "Goddamn it. Help me here. I've got half a ton of pork crawling up my ass."

"I'm trying," said his brother, whose seat was also rammed up against the instrument panel. Despite their efforts to discourage the airsick hog, the plane's dive grew steeper.

"Open the door!" said the pilot.

"Are you kidding? He'll jump. You know how hard it was to get him in here."

"Okay, then you jump!"

"Are we crashing?"

"What do you think? Open the goddamned door!"

They plummeted almost 5,000 feet before the pilot's brother got the door open, before the cabin filled with cool air and scraps of flying straw, before the hog seized his opportunity and, with a snorking sound, heeled around and dove into the evening sky, all four legs splayed out, headed for Iola Pederson's roof.

It was one of those misadventures that got picked up by wire services around the country, the kind radio personalities wore out and schoolkids embellished and reenacted for one another on the playground.

What our officer had mistaken for smoke turned out to be creosote-impregnated soot that had accumulated in the attic over a period of thirty years and disgorged into the house when the pig went through the rooms and broke the conduit for the kitchen fan. On final impact in the living room, the animal exploded, plastering the main room of the house in animal matter.

Amateur psychologists talk about the fight-or-flight response, but it's not an either/or situation. Behaviorists have determined that when threatened, all mammals respond in five predictable patterns, the five F's: fight, flight, freeze, fidget, or faint.

The man we found sitting on the lawn, having gone for his gun before staggering outside, had run through three of them: fight, flight, and fidget—the latter being just another name for confusion. Iola had limited herself to one reaction. Freeze.

Despite the media flurry over the event, Iola and Bernard Pederson declined all requests for interviews. Iola explained it to me weeks later when she turned up at the station with a plate of cookies.

"It's not a question of being camera shy," she said. "It's a question of whether you want your worth defined by the fact that a pig destroyed your home. We're not about to be painted by the media as the latest freak-accident victims."

The flying pig was my first but not my last brush with celebrity. A firefighter who's lucky gets one surefire story among the thousands in his career, a nugget of liquid gold he can spin at parties and bars and standing in the sunshine after church; a tale that entrances at the same time it hypnotizes; a yarn he can tell in his sleep and not screw up; one he can hand strangers the way a rich man pushes five-dollar bills at panhandlers to surprise and delight them; a story that is so certifiably unbelievable it simply has to be true.

The falling pig was the beginning of such a tale for me, yet in the end it was a tale I dared tell no one.

3. READING WOMEN UPSIDE DOWN

In early September, three weeks after the pig punched through her roof, Iola Pederson showed up at the fire station. Just as August had been, the month had launched itself with a warm, dry spell, although from time to time the temperatures dipped into the forties at night.

Iola Pederson wore heels and a skirt and blouse, with her auburn hair shoulder-length. She wasn't exactly what you'd call beautiful, but you couldn't deny her calculated, raw-boned sexuality, either. Vivacious and well spoken, she soon had Tronstad and Johnson eating out of her hand. Even the sober Lieutenant Sears appeared to be entertained, and when she turned those amazing blue eyes on me, my mouth went dry.

"You were so wonderful that day," she said. "There I was, covered in that god-awful . . . I don't even want to think about it . . . and you were so cool and collected."

"That's our boy," Tronstad said, grinning.

Iola said, "Gum, you promised me a tour of the station."

"Yeah, give her the tour, Jason," said Johnson, his cheeks tightening into knots as he smiled.

"Your first name's Jason?" she asked.

"Just call me Gum," I said.

"Juicy Fruit is what we call him," Tronstad said, elbowing Johnson on his way out of the room with the plate of cookies Iola had brought. "Come on, Robert. Ms. Pederson wants to be alone with the boy wonder."

As Lieutenant Sears left to take a phone call, Iola Pederson's fingernails dug into my arm like talons. You almost would have thought she was as nervous to be alone with me as I was to be with her.

"Gum. That's a funny name," she said, her face so close, I was afraid to breathe, the combination of perfume, touch, and proximity intoxicating. For some reason I'd always been a sucker for older women.

"We're related to Judy Garland, whose real name was Frances Gumm. Except they spelled it with two m's. My mother's family changed the spelling."

In the apparatus bay I told her about the firefighters on my shift, Ted Tronstad and Robert Johnson, as well as our officer, Lieutenant Sears. I explained that the battalion chief was also stationed here.

Johnson was African American and the driver on Engine 29. He had a paunch now, but he'd played football in high school and nearly every day mentioned the glory years. A devoted family man, with a wife and daughter, he was also the station philosopher and had opinions on everything from how the department should be run to the snazziest Motown tunes of all time.

Ted Tronstad had been working on Engine 29 for seven years and was, as Johnson had once declared in a moment of bitterness, "descended from a long line of poor white trash." Tronstad had a reputation around the department for being funnier than a couple of toddlers giving each other haircuts. He was tall, wiry, and nervous, a man who lost weight at the drop of a hat, continually gobbling meat to keep flesh on his bones. He had black circles under his penetrating brown eyes, a result no doubt of his propensity for burning the candle at both ends, and he went through women at about the same rate he went through beer. He'd recently divorced for the third time. His life revolved around his Harley-Davidson motorcycle and talking women into the sack. He and Johnson amused themselves by playing an endless stream of practical jokes on each other.

I found it ironic that behind his back Johnson accused Tronstad of being a lecher, while Tronstad was irritated that

Johnson managed to coerce every female visitor to the station into a full-body hug. Tronstad believed Johnson had an unfair advantage, in that he could leverage women's fear of being accused of racism into physical contact. To my way of thinking, Tronstad and Johnson were like an old married couple who'd assembled a long list of gripes about each other, which they each confided to the neighbor over the back fence—in this case, me.

Lieutenant Sears had been with us for four months, and I still wasn't completely comfortable working under him.

"So," Iola Pederson said, "you have the driver. You have the officer. But why do they call the two riding in the back *the tailboard guys?*"

"There used to be a shelf on the back of fire engines called a tailboard. Firefighters rode back there, standing on the tailboard and holding on to a metal bar. About twenty years ago a woman firefighter in town fell off, cracked her head, and died. Now we sit in a crew cab behind the officer and driver, but we still call it *riding the tailboard.* Just like they still call it *the hitch* when the bell goes off at zero seven hundred, because that was when they used to size up the harnesses for that day's team of horses."

Iola remained intensely focused on me in a way that made my skin flush with embarrassment. We'd only known each other ten minutes, but I couldn't shake the feeling that she had the hots for me. Tronstad could work that sort of magic with women, but I was a stumblebum when it came to the opposite sex.

As it turned out, Iola Pederson's forte was focus. Her attentions aligned on me like a searchlight that burned bright and hot and left me feeling cold and desperate when she turned away. Despite all the effort I invested in making myself immune to her ministrations, despite the fact that I told myself she was old enough to be my mother, I couldn't get enough of her as we walked through the station.

Surrounded by a tidy little lawn we mowed and watered every Saturday, Fire Station 29 sat on a small triangle of property between two residential streets in a quiet little neighborhood of single-family homes in West Seattle.

Except for its small basement, Station 29 was built on one level, constructed around a barnlike apparatus bay with a single roll-up door in front and an identical door in back. We exited through the east door with red lights and siren blaring and came home quietly through the west door, which accounted for why homes on the east side sold for slightly less than homes on the west. We had a fifty-foot hose tower for hanging our cotton-jacketed fire hose to dry. In addition to Engine 29, our apparatus bay housed the Battalion 7 chief's buggy, as well as a spare engine. On the north side of the apparatus bay were bathrooms—male and female—a bunk room, and a small TV room. On the south side of the apparatus bay were the watch office and front door, our radio scanner, our computer printer, and our watch book, into which everything of note concerning the rig and station was entered. At night, one crew member was assigned to "night watch" and slept on a rollout bunk in the middle of the room.

Violating department protocol, I took Iola into the bunk room on the other side, showing her where we slept, showered, and changed. "Women sleep here, too?" she asked.

"Sure. There's a woman on the other shift."

"She sleeps here with the guys?"

"With one other person."

"You mean it's just her and him? Over here alone all night? Aren't there ever any—you know—romantic complications? It would be so easy to slip into somebody else's bunk."

"Stanislow's gay."

"All the women in the department can't be gay. There haven't been any romances?"

"Sure there have, but not here."

"I've always wondered about men and women working together in the fire station. It must be tempting."

"Not with Stanislow, it's not."

"What if I worked here?" She gave me a long look. I could

feel something beginning to happen here, and it frightened me almost as much as it excited me.

A minute later on the apparatus floor, she had me strap her into one of our MSA backpacks, where it was a monumental struggle to ignore the way the shoulder straps accentuated her breasts. As we walked around the station, she kept finding excuses to touch me, and I found myself beginning to perspire. At one point she excused herself to use the "powder room" and returned with an additional button undone on her blouse, exposing the top of a lacy black bra. "This is just so charming. I've always wondered what the inside of a fire station looked like. It must be so sexy living here."

"I've never thought about it like that."

"How can you not? You can almost smell the sense of adventure in these walls. I've always loved adventures."

We descended the stairs to the windowless basement, where we kept the pinball machines, weight benches, and stationary bicycle. Iola tested the bicycle and then had me spot her on the weight bench, where she managed to bench-press sixty pounds. As she lay on the bench, recovering from her efforts and looking up at me past the weight bar, I began to get the feeling I was headed for trouble. Her skirt was hiked up her thighs, and her auburn hair was splayed out and falling off the bench almost to the floor, and from above her where I stood, I had an unparalleled view down her blouse.

Looking at her upside down, I got the crazy notion she wanted me to kiss her. It was cracked, I know, because I'd known her less than twenty minutes by then and she was much older than me, and I had enough trouble reading women right side up. It was hard to know what made me do it because I'd never done anything quite like it before, but I leaned over slowly, and as I attempted to kiss her, she raised herself up and kissed me back, our faces upside down against each other. It was funny, because I really thought I would get my face slapped, which was going to happen later, much later. Instead, I got an erection.

"How's your father? Was he okay?" I asked.

"My father?" She lay back down, trying to suppress a

smile, which was of course, from my point of view, a frown. People look outlandish upside down, their features all scrunched into this little space, their foreheads huge.

"When we were at your house you called him *Daddy*."

"He's doing fine. He had a black eye for a week. Are you changing the subject? Have I embarrassed you? You're not embarrassed, are you? Haven't you ever kissed a woman before?"

"Pardon?"

"Come here."

She grabbed my fire-department belt buckle, pulled me down, and kissed me again, once again upside down. "I'm on duty. There are people here."

"That's part of the fun of being naughty. Or haven't you figured that out? I thought you guys were supposed to be brave."

"How about if I meet you tomorrow?"

"Tomorrow will be a different day. Tomorrow it won't be naughty. In fact, tomorrow it won't happen."

"But—" We kissed again.

"Have you ever done it in a fire station?"

"What?"

"Have you ever fucked in a fire station?"

"Uh, not recently."

"Well, then, here's your chance."

"I'll see you tomorrow. What do you say?"

"You're not listening. I have this fantasy about doing it in a fire station. That's why I came here."

"No, come on. Tomorrow night."

When she sat up and began rearranging her skirt, I realized I was facing an ultimatum. Say good-bye forever, or bow to this insane whimsy of hers. We looked at each other for a minute under the dim basement lights. I'd never been faced with a choice quite like this and had no reference points for making a decision. The proper course of action, obviously, was to take her upstairs and send her packing.

I wasn't sure if having sex on duty was an offense punishable by termination, but if not, it should be. On the other hand, it was almost ten o'clock at night, the chief was out, and he wouldn't return until late. Lieutenant Sears had retired for the evening, and I'd seen Johnson heading for the bunk room earlier. Tronstad had the night watch and would be rat-holed for hours in front of the television. I could most likely get away with this.

In college I'd walked in on my roommate while he and a girl he picked up at a party were humping; she'd had the same listless look in her eyes Iola Pederson had right now. Tronstad called it *the doggy-fuck look,* because it was what you saw on a couple of rutting dogs, the look you'd see in your own eyes if you were to look at yourself in the mirror during sex.

As compliant as a schoolboy, I let her unbuckle my pants and pull my shorts down, burying me in her face. For about one second it was clinical and weird, but then it turned into something only a major earthquake or another hog falling out of the sky could halt.

"Hey, you two," Tronstad called from the top of the stairs. "You going to be screwing around down there all night?"

A frog in my voice, I said, "We're just talking." Iola's mouth was full or she might have said something, too.

"Don't do anything I wouldn't do, Doublemint," he said, closing himself inside the beanery.

One would think, after that wake-up call, that I would come to my senses, but it didn't happen.

Some minutes later when the bell hit, Iola and I were coupled like rabbits, my trousers bunched around my ankles, her dress pushed up to her waist, a pair of deflated panties on the floor.

The station alerter was still going when Tronstad rushed out of the beanery, stopped at the head of the stairs, and yelled, "Hey, Gum! We're rollin'." I heard Lieutenant Sears emerge from his office above us, and it was at that point that I did exactly the wrong thing: I hesitated.

The thing about being on a fire crew is that you have to be ready to jump on the rig and dash out the door at the spur of the moment. Without complaint or reluctance, we get up from meals, out of the shower, off the phone or the shitter, or out of bed, and onto the rig. Some crews are faster than others, but since Sears had come on board four months earlier, we'd become one of the fastest in the city. We *raced* to the rig and we *raced* to the locations. If we didn't, we got chewed out by Sears. We'd begun to take pride in it, timing ourselves, looking down on crews who took even five seconds longer than we did.

I heard the apparatus bay doors open. I heard the apparatus fire up. And I faltered again . . . still moving, still straining against the woman on the weight bench, as if it were possible to finish what Iola Pederson and I were doing and still make the rig before it pulled out of the station. As if the bell had caught me drinking a glass of water instead of copulating. I'd been abducted by the most primal of biological imperatives.

"I gotta go," I said finally, trying to extricate myself from her while she kept her legs wrapped around my waist. Her eyes still had that doggy look. She must have thought this was some sort of game, because she wasn't going to let me go. We wrestled until we uncoupled with a horrible sucking sound. As I sprinted for the stairs, she lay flat on her back on the weight bench, clothing in disarray, hair mussed, face flushed, bare breasts melting against her ribs, white thighs squashed on either side of the bench.

Upstairs, I stomped down the narrow corridor to the apparatus bay and emerged into the garage just as the engine roared out of the building, leaving me in a cloud of diesel exhaust, Tronstad staring back at me from the darkness of the crew cab.

They were gone and I was not.

I felt like vomiting.

I'd screwed up a couple of times in my short career, but I'd never come close to anything like this. I didn't know the official punishment for a missed alarm, but numerous unpleasant possibilities sprang to mind. I'd heard stories about people in my predicament, and in those stories the miscreants were invariably the butt of crude firefighter parody and ridicule. My name would be forever appended to that sorry list.

For the longest time I just stood there staring at the empty apparatus bay, and then, as the timed house lights went off, I got the dry heaves and rushed over to the slop sink. The radio in the watch office had been spewing information on the alarm, so I knew they were headed to a confirmed house fire. Fully involved. Flames showing. Trapped occupants.

Fully involved.

Engine 29 didn't get a call like this but once every couple of years.

Dashing into the watch office, I ripped the computer print-out from the machine and scanned the response information. The fire was on Arch Place SW, only blocks from the station.

It couldn't get any worse. I was going to have charges written on me. I was going to get a month off without pay. Chief Abbott might even try to take my job.

On the apparatus floor I spotted my bunking boots and trouser combination where I'd left them, and next to the boots, my coat and helmet—which I routinely left in the crew cab, but which Tronstad must have offloaded, along with my portable radio.

A fierce glimmer of hope struck me as I realized what Tronstad had in mind. I could don my gear and drive to the fire in my own car. It wouldn't absolve my infraction, but it might diminish the punishment.

4. MAD DOG GUM BECOMES THE DEPARTMENT LAUGHINGSTOCK

As I scramble into my gear, Iola Pederson materializes from the basement, and although I don't notice her until she speaks, she is furious. "What the hell do you think you're doing?" One of her breasts is hanging out of her blouse, and I notice her panties bunched in her hand. The fact that I've noticed any of this bothers me. It bothers me a lot. Even now I'm thinking about sex.

I brush past her and flee the building through the personnel door next to the large roll-up apparatus door at the rear of the station, squeezing in my bulky turnout clothing into the Recaro seat, clumsily working the racing-style clutch and brake pedals of my Subaru WRX with my fat rubber boots.

As I swing out of the driveway behind the station, I catch a glimpse of Iola watching me like an abandoned puppy. I pray she has the good sense to vacate the station before we get back. Things will be incomparably worse if Lieutenant Sears finds out I missed the call because I was banging some woman in the basement.

With adrenaline and guilt saturating my bloodstream, none of this is easy. I am sweating and trembling and on the verge of messing my britches. I feel as if I've been punched in the stomach, as if my pounding heart is skipping every third beat.

My WRX is basically a rally car, and I drive it that way now, running stop signs and red lights, zipping around what little traffic there is on the roads at this time of night, sliding through corners and working the short-throw shifter I've installed. Throughout it all, I am unable to catch my breath. More astonishing than anything else is the fact that my fall from grace had taken less than ten minutes. I'm thinking, *This is the worst fuckup of my life.*

Everybody's bloodstream takes on adrenaline during alarms. You want to do well. You want to be safe. You don't want to get hurt. You don't want to see other people hurt, firefighters or civilians. Time is limited, and you are always in a hurry. People are watching. You have a split second to make decisions upon which lives depend. There exists the very real possibility of getting injured. Or killed. Tonight it is more than adrenaline, however.

Tonight I am crazy with fright. Fright that Tronstad will go into the fire without me and end up maimed. Fright that people will die because of my absence, that Sears will hound me out of the department. Fright that I will become the department laughingstock.

Sears is a no-nonsense, by-the-book officer who does not tolerate screwups, and this is the pièce de résistance of screwups. A week after he met me, Lieutenant Sears said something that still sticks in my craw. "Gum, you mean well, but you make mistakes. Most of them are small ones, but every once in a while you pull a doozy." He arched an eyebrow at the word *doozy*. "Watch yourself." At the time I'd considered his words a huge insult, but I've since proved him right.

I switch on the portable radio and stuff it into the chest pocket on my bunking coat, each transmission making me more frenzied than the last.

The dispatcher says, "Engine Twenty-nine. This is a report of a house fire. Several callers have stated the occupants may still be inside."

Lieutenant Sears announces over the radio that he is at the location on Arch Place SW. "Flames showing from the first floor of a two-story wood-frame building approximately forty by fifty. No exposures. We're laying a preconnect and establishing Arch Command. Engine Thirty-six, lay a supply and a backup line. Engine Thirty-two, you'll be the RIT team. Ladder Eleven, split your crew. Do a search and rescue, and ventilate."

Sears is good on the radio. He hasn't been at 29's long enough for us to judge how he will react on the fire ground, but around the station he talks a good fire, and tonight his radio voice is accelerated but calm, just the way it should be.

Because of a preponderance of oversized trucks and SUVs parked on either side, the streets around Arch Place are even narrower than usual. When Engine 29 stops, it effectively plugs the thoroughfare so no other vehicles can get past.

The house is on the east side of the street, flames boiling out a picture window on the near side, heavy black smoke pouring from the front door. I swerve into a tight space between two colossal SUVs and pop out of my Subaru like a cork out of a bottle, rolling onto the pavement. I pick myself up and sprint up the shadowy street, toward Engine 29.

Highlighted by flames, a silhouette in a helmet and bunking coat walks through the yard in front of the house. From his military bearing I know it is Lieutenant Sears, who oddly enough has never been in the military. Johnson will be working the pump panel on the engine. Tronstad's job will be to take the nozzle, lay out all two hundred feet of hose, and go inside.

I don't see any sign of Tronstad, but I spot an inch-and-three-quarters line stretching from the rear of Engine 29 across the yard and inside the front door of the house. Normally, Tronstad and I would be together on the end of that hose line, pushing it into the house until we find the seat of the fire, partners to the end. That is our contract. In the fire department you have a partner and you remain in contact with him or her throughout a fire, a shared system of responsibility the Seattle department adopted subsequent to a series of firefighter deaths years ago.

Because of me, Tronstad is alone.

When I climb into my seat in the crew cab to get my air mask and backpack, Robert Johnson is on the catwalk in front of me working the pump panel. I slip on my MSA backpack, put my face piece on, activate the bottle, and hook up the air.

Inside the house, flames lick a window to the right of the front door.

The hose line snakes through the smoky front doorway, but there is no sign of Tronstad. No indication water is being applied to the fire. The smoke is black and hot. Through it I can see only part of the house and the front doorway. For all I know, he's already tits up.

As I race across the yard, I bump into a large man in a bathrobe and slippers, hitting him so hard, we both tumble in the grass. We've been told not to run on the fire ground, and this is one of the reasons.

"You see another firefighter go inside?" I ask as I get up and head for the front door. "Is this your house?"

"I live across the street. The Ranklers live here."

"You see a firefighter go inside?"

"A while back."

"Was he alone?" God, what a stupid question. Of course he was alone. There is only one rig at the scene, and I've already spotted two of the three firefighters on it, Johnson at the pump panel and Lieutenant Sears in the yard. "Did they get out? The people who live here. Have you seen them?"

"I don't know. The man's in a wheelchair. They're—"

"Two people?"

"Yes. A man and his wife."

I heel around and race toward the front door, trying not to trip over the hose. To my surprise, I cross paths with Lieutenant Sears on the porch and almost knock him over. I am out of control.

"Where's your line?" Sears yells. "Don't come up here without a line. And where's your partner?"

Without answering, I crawl through the front door, where the interior of the house is as dark as the inside of a nut. When you're in a house that's on fire, the rest of the world ceases to exist. You have no friends, no family, no past, and no goals except to do your job and get out. You maintain concentration because if you don't, the fire will spank you. I've never been in a good house fire and been able to think about anything but the here and now, never wanted to think about anything else. Afterward, probably because you've been closer to death than at any other time, you realize you've never been more alive, either.

The doorway is dark with rushing hot gasses and smoke that looks thick enough to ride a surfboard on. I squat low under the heat and follow the hose line to the left. I'm moving like a mad dog. A mere five feet inside, I bump into a man and knock him against the wall. I know it is Tronstad by the way he curses when my plastic helmet smashes against the hard air cylinder on his back. I've never been so hyped. Not at a fire. Not the time my mother and I went to San Francisco and got mugged. Not the time I fell off a cliff when I was eleven. If I wasn't twenty-four years old, I would think I was having a heart attack.

"What the hell! If that's you Engine Thirty-six fucks, you can just get out of my face." Tronstad's angry voice tugs me back to reality.

"It's me."

"Who the fuck is 'me'?"

"Gum. How much have you searched?"

"I got turned around. I'm in here alone, man. I been alone fuckin' forever."

"The neighbor thinks there's somebody in here. Where have you searched?"

My helmet light is on and I have the feeling Tronstad's is on as well, but there's so much smoke, I can't see his light or the beam from mine. It's been a while since I've been in a good house fire where there isn't a truck company ventilating, but because they aren't there to ventilate, I can't see ten inches in front of my face.

We hear flames in the rooms to the right of the front door. The fire is beginning to lap over our heads with a soft crackling sound, and I can feel the heat increasing. We don't have long. When you open the door on a house fire, you give it additional oxygen, which causes the fire to build, and if you don't get water on it right away, it grows like a son of a bitch.

"How much have you searched?"

When he doesn't reply, I crawl over him like a halfback swimming through a sea of linemen for a touchdown. I don't have time to wait for his answer. I head into the living room.

I know what the layout of the house probably is from having been in so many of these remodeled prewar houses on aid calls. Somewhere between me and the kitchen will be a stairwell leading up.

Like a madman I search the rooms at a breakneck pace. I am stronger, faster, smarter, and crazier than a slaughterhouse rat, and more focused than I've ever been in my life. I crawl on my hands and knees, performing a frantic left-wall search of the rooms, knocking over lamps and chairs and anything that gets in my way, plunging through rooms like a burglar hyped on methamphetamines.

To the left of the doorway is a corridor, which is where I've met and trampled Tronstad. Next is a living room filled with furniture I identify only by touch: couches and coffee tables. After that I encounter a small dining room, then the kitchen. I storm through them all on my hands and knees. It is far too hot to stand up. Toward the rear of the house, off the kitchen, I encounter a closed door.

When I try to open it, the door jams against an object.

The house is clean and tidy, so I don't expect any doors to be blocked. I stand up in the heat and ram my shoulder into the door, breaking it apart. As I lever the door open, I am barely able to squeeze in. Blocking the entrance is a wheelchair with a man in it, unconscious, slumped over, his head and neck forming a wild distortion of normal human body mechanics.

I pull the chair back, kick the door out of the way, and wheel him through the smoky house the way I came in. We bump into objects in the smoke, but after about a minute of crashing into furniture, I manage to trundle the heavy wheelchair and its cargo across the hose line in the hallway and outside onto the porch. His white hair is combed straight back and is neat enough for a portrait.

Behind me in the house I hear somebody opening the bale on a nozzle, and water strikes the ceiling hard. I recognize Tronstad's style—Tronstad, who'd been a firefighter in the Air Force before joining the Seattle department. We are taught to dispense just enough water to put the flames out, never to drown a fire, especially when working inside. A cubic foot of water turns into 1700 cubic feet of steam, and the steam smothers the fire—thus you put the fire out without causing water damage. Dry floors after a fire signal you've done your job correctly.

There are more crews on the scene now, and one of the firefighters in the yard sees me and heads toward the wheelchair while I duck back through the smoke. The neighbor said there were two people inside. I have to find the other one.

Even though the house is as dark and smoky as it was on my first traverse, I make a beeline for the bedroom where I found the man, moving with more confidence now that I've been through these rooms once.

There is no one else in the bedroom.

I get lucky and locate stairs at the back of the house. The air in the house grows hotter as I climb the carpeted steps. The smoke is denser, if that is possible. I've been sweating since before I left the station, but now I feel the heat radiating off my equipment as my gear begins to grow hot. Against my neck, the collar of my bunking coat feels like toast just out of the oven.

At the top of the stairs, I swing my arms in a wide swath but find only carpet. I turn right. The first door I come to is closed. It turns out to be a closet. I find a window and break it with my portable radio. The glass panes splatter on the rooftop outside like falling crystal. I now hear Engine 29's pump outside. I am sweating in my gear, growing weaker with each passing moment.

I turn and begin working my way down the hallway, past the stairs. On my right I find a doorway; inside, there's a body on the floor, a woman, tiny and dressed in nightclothes. Shaking produces no results. She is out cold. I lean over to listen for breathing but hear nothing. It is hotter up here than it was downstairs, and my helmet and gear are so hot I find myself wriggling around inside the suit to avoid skin contact with it.

Still on my knees, I pull her outside the swing path of the door. I haul her a few feet, then, working like a grizzly dragging a fresh kill, move forward, drag her to my new position, then move forward again. Her backside is going to be raw, but I am alone and it is too hot to stand up.

"Ted!" I yell. "I need help. Ted! I've got a victim."

Tronstad does not reply, and if there are other firefighters in the house, I cannot hear them.

As I drag her toward the stairs, my head fills with stupid

thoughts: that this is the strangest thing in the world, to be dragging a woman I've never seen out of a burning house. That I've been trained for just this event and after two years of waiting I'm now doing a genuine rescue. That she will not survive. That I should have been here five minutes sooner, and that if I had been, Tronstad and I would have saved her life.

Striving to protect her neck and spine, I drag her down the stairs. Her body thumps on each stair. I'm not sure she is breathing, but it makes little difference to this process. Alive or dead, I will get her outside.

Downstairs near the front door, Tronstad sees my victim, drops the nozzle, and takes the woman's legs. I take her arms from behind, locking her wrists in front of her torso, and together we carry her into the yard as three firefighters in full bunkers and MSA bottles charge up onto the porch.

We carry her to the center of the lawn and lay her down. Tronstad drops her feet and rips off his helmet and face piece and yells, "Somebody bring a vent kit! Gum's got another victim here."

Twenty feet away an empty wheelchair sits beside a team of firefighters doing CPR on the man I brought out earlier. One of the CPR team is the neighbor I knocked down—a local doctor, I learn later—nose still crusted with blood from our collision.

We begin working on the woman. She isn't breathing, and neither Tronstad nor I can find a pulse.

When you do CPR on somebody, it's not like on TV where they have a shirt on. The first thing you do is bare the chest. Then there's the electrodes, one under the right clavicle and one below the left nipple, on the ribs. Tronstad rips her night-gown open and begins ninety seconds of CPR, the current protocol.

Somebody brings vent kits, and we hook her up to the electrodes on the Physio-Control Lifepak. I get out the plastic bag mask and begin pumping air into her lungs, working in sync with Tronstad, two breaths after every fifteen of his compressions. Eventually more firefighters and a medic assist in the resuscitation effort. Tronstad continues the chest compressions. I stick with the bag mask, forcing oxygenated air into her lungs.

Under the direction of the Seattle fire paramedic, we shock her three times, beginning CPR anew after each shock. Johnson spells Tronstad on the chest compressions while I shrug off proposals of relief. As I kneel over her and use the bag mask, I try not to drip sweat onto her.

A pretty woman, she looks to be in her early sixties.

We shock her again, but she doesn't come around. Across the yard they aren't having any better luck with the man.

This is my fault. I saw off a piece of ass, and my negligence kills two people.

These two citizens have done nothing more than entrust their lives to the city. I've been hired by the city to fight fires and save lives. I've been trained and sworn in, and while my duties and responsibilities on the tailboard are minimal, my failure has resulted in this fiasco. I deserve to be jailed. Buggered. Hanged. You name it. They can't devise a punishment severe enough for me.

Finally, after what seems like hours but what I later learn is twenty minutes, after several firefighters have offered to spell me with the bag mask and I have refused each, our patient is pronounced dead by a medic, confirmed by a doctor on the phone, and we are told to cease CPR.

Somebody takes the Laerdal bag mask out of my hands and speaks gently.

"She's gone, man. You did your best."

Eventually I stand and remove my MSA backpack. I am in another space. Another time. For a few minutes I am as disembodied and removed from this world as the woman at my feet.

It is hard to imagine any more crap falling out of the sky anytime soon.

5. GET OUT THE UMBRELLA, PAL

Across the yard they are packing the man from the wheel-chair onto a gurney and running him down the street, to the rear of Medic 32, one firefighter following along doing chest compressions, another at the head with the bag mask.

It turns out only Engine 29 and Engine 36 have responded directly to the address. Engine 32, Ladder 11, Medic 32, and Battalion 7 have all gone wrong and arrived late. One of many bad addresses in our district, this Arch Place is located about seven blocks from another Arch Place, and the two aren't directly connected. Most of the response, including Chief Abbott, who'd been at Station 32 when the alarm came in, followed the relief driver on Engine 32 to the wrong location.

To make matters worse, the other Arch Place is a narrow, contorted street that once populated with oversized fire apparatus becomes a nightmare to navigate. The mistake costs the bulk of our incoming response units between six and ten minutes in lost time, which explains why we had no help inside.

Unbuttoning my bunking coat until I feel the cool night air kissing my wet shirt, I walk over to Engine 29 and sit on the step below our crew cab. The motor is still roaring. Firefighters from Ladder 11 have set up a powerful gasoline-driven fan in the doorway of the fire house, quickly clearing the rooms of smoke. The fire had been tapped while we were outside doing CPR. Engine 36 is doing mop-up.

Through the side yard between the houses, I note an iri-descent slice of downtown Seattle lit up like a ten-year-old's birthday cake. Trying to hypnotize myself into a better frame of mind, I focus on the city until it becomes a blur of light. Having started off as arguably the best night of my career, this has rapidly segued into my worst, and possibly my last.

While I languish on the sideboard of Engine 29, two fire-fighters from Aid 14 lift the dead woman onto a gurney and wheel her away into the darkness.

Civilians are walking across the lawn, gawking at the broken-out windows of the house, ogling the bodies. Ogling me. Somebody needs to put up some fire-scene tape.

From across the yard, Tronstad watches me. Later in the rehab area he begins gabbing and joking with firefighters from the other units. It doesn't help my spirits to see him so carefree and lighthearted. But Tronstad is a me-me kind of guy and can be incredibly blasé about somebody else's misfortune.

While the rooms at the south end of the house continue to smolder, two investigators from Seattle's Fire Investigation Unit show up and, after twenty minutes of poking around inside the structure, determine that the origin of the fire is a discarded cigarette near the front door. It seems that the man in the wheelchair had a history of careless smoking, and that we had in fact been here a year earlier for a small fire. Throughout the first floor of the house, cigarette burns stain various pieces of furniture and the floor. Neighbors tell us the man's wife routinely complained that he was going to burn their home down with his carelessness.

One of the fire investigators, a tall, ungainly man named Holmes, comes over to me and says, "You mind showing us where you found them? We're going to have to go over this with SPD."

"Sure."

Wordlessly, I walk them through the house under the hard glare of the string lights Ladder 11 has set up. None of us are masked up, although we should be since the ruins are smoldering. The walls are coated in soot, but the actual fire damage is limited to a couple of downstairs rooms to the right of the front doorway.

I show them where I found the man in the wheelchair, and then we climb the narrow staircase to the second floor. The woman smelled smoke or heard the crackling of the fire or the pinging of the smoke detectors, woke up, and did the worst thing possible—leaped out of bed and stood tall. That first inhalation cauterized her lungs with superheated air that was probably close to a thousand degrees. Had she rolled out of bed and crawled along the floor, she would have had a chance, although a slim one.

Nobody says much until we are outside and past the racket of the gasoline-powered ventilation fan in the doorway. Holmes gives me a lugubrious look. "These your first fire victims?"

I nod.

"Tough, huh?"

I shrug.

"Everybody goes through it. You'll be okay. It'll take some time, is all. You'll bounce back."

Resuming my position on the side step of Engine 29, I watch the firefighters in the rehab area. You don't go wrong on an alarm and lose a fire victim, with another one in critical condition, and then stand around and yuk it up. Nobody is laughing except Tronstad; but then, Tronstad is the kind of guy who would tell dirty jokes at his own mother's funeral—and did.

I can't help noticing Holmes, the fire investigator, talking to Lieutenant Sears across the yard. After a while, Chief Abbott joins their enclave and all three steal looks at me. Five minutes later Lieutenant Sears approaches and kneels in front of me, touching my knees with both his hands.

Sears worships the fire department and everything it stands for, knows the operating guidelines like the inside of his pockets, and is one of the most personable people I've run across. In his early forties, he has been in the department seven years, has recently taken the captain's exam, and will soon be leaving Station 29 when he's promoted.

Sears is a short, stocky man, maybe an inch shorter than my five foot eight. He has sandy hair that, had it not been cropped short, would have been a mess of curls. He has to shave twice a day and has thick, muscular arms that are so hairy Tronstad once looked at them and said, "Nice sweater." He loves counseling people and was a teacher before he got sidetracked into the department. He has an undemanding sense of humor, and despite all the grousing Johnson and Tronstad direct at his leadership abilities, I like him.

From under the brim of his red lieutenant's helmet his brown eyes bore into mine. His eyes are sunken, his brow heavy and even darker than normal, his heavy mustache twittering in tune to his breathing. In the dark he presents a rather simian appearance. Sears is insanely proud of the job he does, which is why my conduct must disgust him. He squeezes my knees through the thick turnout clothing.

"Listen," he says. "Bad things happen. You learn to roll with the punches."

"Not like this."

"This is something . . . well, it's definitely not good, but hey, there'll be flowers in the morning, and the sun will rise, and you'll get past this. It might be ugly for a while, but you'll move past it. I've had things like this happen . . . well, not like this, but . . ."

"What are you going to do?"

"Frankly, I haven't decided. I'll have to talk to Abbott about it. Listen, Gum. You need advice, come to me. Anytime. Day or night."

"Yes, sir."

"And don't call me *sir*. At least not tonight. Tonight I'm just Sears."

"You really think I'll get past this, Sears?"

He stares at me for a moment, then glances at the still-smoking structure. When he turns back I see the beginnings of tears in his eyes. He is as thoroughly empathetic as Tronstad is thick-skinned, and even if he won't admit it, he knows what they are going to do to me.

"I wish I could replay this whole night," I say.

"You and me both."

"Can you tell me what's going to happen?"

"What do you mean?"

"What they're going to do to me."

"They're probably not going to give you a medal, if that's what you're getting at."

"I wasn't expecting a medal. I was . . ."

"What?"

"I don't know."

Sears leaves.

Tronstad is watching me, cookies from the fire buff's table in one hand, a paper cup of Gatorade in the other. He's a self-confessed sugar junky who claims a bowl of ice cream after four in the afternoon revs him up so much, he can't sleep. God knows why he is eating cookies at this time of night.

Two men in plainclothes march over to him and lift up their sweatshirts to reveal badges on their belts. I assume they are from the Seattle Police Department. They speak to Tronstad for a few moments.

A minute later the SPD men come over to me. "Mr. Gum," says the black police officer.

"Yes, sir." He lets out just the hint of a smile at the fact that I've called him *sir*.

"SPD," says the white officer. "We understand your actions were integral to what happened here."

"Yes, sir."

"Can you lay it out for us?" asks the white officer.

"From the time the bell hit?"

He smiles. "Maybe from the time you went through the front door."

"The front door of the house over there?"

"That's the one." He looks at his partner and rolls his eyes.

As we speak I decide to peel my turnout pants down so some of the sweat can evaporate. When I shrug my shoulders out of my suspenders and pull my turnout pants partially down, I realize the white material around the zipper of my uniform trousers is coated with what e. e. cummings would have called *fuck dust*. I pull the turnouts back up.

"What were you saying?" I ask.

"Were either of them conscious when you got to them?"

"No, sir."

"The man was downstairs? The woman was up?"

"That's right."

Dancing around my culpability, they ask more questions

about the house, the fire, the victims. When they start to leave, I stutter, "Uh . . . what's . . . what's going to happen now?"

"What do you mean?"

"Well, uh, you know . . ."

"There'll be a further investigation. We'll get the ME's report on the woman. Contact the relatives. It's pretty much routine."

"I mean, what's going to happen to me?"

"You?" I am weeping in front of these two heavyset cops. I've screwed up beyond imagination, and I am blubbering. "Well, son. Maybe you can see the department chaplain. Or your own minister. You can get some counseling is what you can do."

"Because of jail?"

"Do me a favor."

"Sir?"

"Before anything else happens, get yourself some counseling." He catches up with his partner, who's met with the two fire department investigators. Moments later all four glance over at me.

When Chief Abbott approaches, I grow still. I don't like Abbott, and I'm pretty sure he doesn't like me. From the beginning of my tenure in the 7th, he's treated us as though he had a vendetta against Station 29—in particular, the members on our shift: Robert Johnson, Ted Tronstad, and me. Johnson and Tronstad dislike him even more than I do, although around the station we feign a stilted camaraderie.

Abbott is a short, rotund man who wears heavy glasses, teaches management classes at one of the local community colleges, and doesn't fit anybody's idea of what a firefighter should look like—not even his own, for he often makes self-deprecating jokes about it.

Around the station Abbott is a man with a million outspoken opinions about where the department should be headed, but downtown he sits on his ideas and is known as the biggest ass-kisser around. His round head is almost entirely bald, and when he isn't at the station, Tronstad and

Johnson call him *Chief Spalding,* after the ball company, since all of his visible body parts are round enough to warrant it.

"So, young man," Abbott says, stumping through the darkened yard toward me. "I understand you're having problems."

The obvious concern in his voice brings the tears back. If a man as obtuse as Abbott is concerned, my predicament is on the underside of bad.

"Tell me what's bothering you. One of my boys gets into trouble, my first instinct is to help. I mean that, son. Start from the beginning. By the way, the man's dead, too." He sniggers and the slovenly snort brings me back to my senses. Abbott's instinct is *never* to help.

"It's the alarm," I tell him.

"It sure got him into a lather, Chief. A real lather," says Ted Tronstad, interrupting with the saucy rudeness he is known for. As usual, he speaks quickly and spits his words like a machine gun spits lead. His mind works quickly. It is a rare moment when Tronstad gets an idea and waits to fit it into a conversation with the deference to other speakers most people take as a matter of course. Childlike, Tronstad blurts out whatever is on his mind, no matter who he is cutting off. He gets away with it because he is funny and, underneath the brash exterior, charming, and because everybody knows he is Ted Tronstad, *comic extraordinaire.* He can be crude, but for a variety of reasons—primarily having to do with how prickly he gets when criticized—you don't correct him. At least *I* don't.

"Glad you came over, Chief," Tronstad says. "I was about to have a heart-to-heart with Gum myself. You know, tell him about the birds and bees and dead people and suchlike." He makes small talk for another minute until Abbott leaves, and I realize this is the first chance I've had to speak to Tronstad alone. "I hope she was a good piece of ass, Gum."

"I'm in so much trouble."

He gives me a look that is equal parts amusement and condescension. "Not unless you opened your trap."

"They're talking about me over there, the cops are."

"Jesus, you didn't tell anybody what happened?"

"I—"

"Because nobody knows you weren't on the rig when it left the station. Nobody but you and me and Robert."

"What do you mean?"

"I mean, when you fuck up, you keep your lips zipped. That's the first rule of fucking up. What did you tell them?"

"I'm not sure."

Tronstad looks across the yard at Lieutenant Sears. "I know you didn't tell *him*. He'd be dancing a jig."

"He's not that way."

"Oh, yes, he is."

"How could he *not* know I wasn't on the rig?"

"Sears had his head up his ass the moment he heard 'trapped victims.' He doesn't know about you. Trust me. Did he say he was going to write disciplinary charges?"

"No."

"Trust me. He was scared shitless."

"So was I."

"You? Jesus, kid, you were ferocious. You ran over me like I was roadkill."

The more I think about it, the more Tronstad's words make sense. When I bumped into him on the porch, Lieutenant Sears said, "Don't come up here without a line. And where's your partner?" It hadn't made sense to me at the time, because our line had been underfoot, but he'd been talking about a *second* line. A second line would only come in with a second unit. Despite the big E-29 designator on the front of my helmet, he thought that the firefighter who bumped into him on the porch was from another unit and that I was inside.

Tronstad says, "I know and Robert knows, and *we* ain't talkin'. You know, and *you* ain't talkin'. Nobody else has a clue, least of all our firefighter-of-the-year lieutenant. Keep your yap zipped, and it'll stay that way."

"What are you going to do if they ask?"

Tronstad makes an exaggerated gesture that implies he'd rather die than blab. I look across the yard to where Robert

Johnson is talking to one of the other drivers, and Johnson gives me a twinkly smile and a thumbs-up signal.

"I should confess."

"Don't be an asshole. You going to miss another alarm?"

"No."

"There you go. What would be the point of getting punished for something that's never going to happen again?"

"I owe you, Tronstad."

"Let's go pick up some hose. And by the way?"

"What?"

"You got enough guts to hang on a fence, kid. I never thought you had particularly big balls, but between rattling that woman in the basement and what you did inside the house here . . . you're my hero."

"Shut up."

6. THE PERFECT SETUP

The next morning the front page of the *Seattle PI* sported an article about our victims, Fred and Susan Rankler.

Fred had been sixty-two, formerly an attorney with a prestigious law firm in downtown Seattle; Susan, fifty-eight, a flight attendant with Delta and the mother of three grown children. Fred Rankler had run for city council; Susan had been homecoming queen at Central Washington University. One of their daughters was living in Hollywood, studying to become a movie actress. One son worked for a Chicago law firm, the other for Microsoft.

Fred had been retired almost a year when another driver mangled him in a car accident and put him in a wheelchair. Susan retired soon thereafter to care for him.

I was thinking about the family as I was leaving for home the morning after the fire. I'd just bumped into Robert Johnson in back of the station, next to his black BMW 3 Series sedan, a car he washed and vacuumed each shift. "Robert?"

"Eh?"

"About last night."

"Hey, that was a nice rescue. You pulled two people out. Even if they didn't make it, a save like that will cancel a hell of a lot of other dirt." He gave me a meaningful look.

"Robert—"

"Have a nice four-off."

"Thanks."

Half expecting my car to be staked out by the police, I walked the eight blocks to where I'd parked my Subaru on Arch Place and drove home without incident.

I lived in a single-story, side-by-side duplex on Genesee, directly across the street from the Delridge Playfield. I rented the east unit, which included a garage just large enough to accommodate my WRX. The whole place was maybe eight hundred square feet: two bedrooms, a living room, and a kitchen, with electric wall heaters you could stand in front of on a cold winter morning, toasting your backside—1960s kitsch. Out back was a covered patio, along with a patch of lawn that was mostly brown because we'd been admonished to conserve water during the drought.

The previous night had been one freak show after another. Iola Pederson with blue eyes as big as hen's eggs. Her unbuttoned blouse and the enormous ice floes she called breasts. Our hijinks in the basement, the feel of her silky skin under my hands, the warmth of her soft naked belly against my hard stomach. Her rigid nipples. Her sharp, ratlike teeth gnawing my lower lip.

I almost wished I'd been caught. At least the matter would be concluded. The way things stood, I would forever carry the vague unease that I would be unmasked at some future date. I read once that a secret can only truly remain a secret when it's known by only one person. Tronstad and Johnson were friends, but neither had the same investment in this I did.

I would never break another department rule. Ever.

I wasn't sure why Ted Tronstad and Robert Johnson had remained silent on my behalf, whether it was esprit de corps among mates or the desire to put something over on Sweeney Sears, but I was thankful.

After we got back to the station that night I slept like a drunk, my narcosis fueled by the release of tension. The effect was transient, because the next few nights I was wracked with insomnia, and when I did manage to snag rack time, I found myself battling through a series of degenerate sex dreams involving Iola Pederson and the dead woman, the two females I'd seen bare-breasted that night. Nothing was more perverse than dreaming about sex with a corpse.

What made it almost unbearable was the very real possibility that the Ranklers would have survived had I not missed the rig. During the next few days I thought about it every waking minute.

I thought about transferring to another station. About confessing. About resigning from the fire department.

After I'd tortured myself enough, I began to look at it from a different angle. If you were a veterinarian and fed the wrong medication to a prize horse and the horse died, it didn't mean you were going to kill a nag a week for the rest of your career, did it? In fact, it didn't mean you would ever kill another nag. The truth was, you'd take particular care *not* to kill another horse, wouldn't you? And if the animal's owners didn't realize why the beast was dead, it would be pointless to tell them.

Still, no matter how much I rationalized, I continued to feel physically ill for the first twenty-four hours, weak and listless thereafter. I knew I was going to have to wear my guilt for the rest of my life. What I didn't know was how I would accomplish that—for I didn't have Tronstad's capacity to blow off setbacks and blame things on other people, or Johnson's ability to rely on the Lord Jesus Christ.

I was raised by a single mother who always treated me like an adult, spoke to me as an adult, and had me call her *Judy* as well as *Mommy*. I suppose I'd been trying to act the part of a self-possessed adult since I was six, and more than once I'd been told I talk and act older than my years; but now I was feeling more like an incompetent, clueless little boy than when I actually was one.

The evening after the fire I took my mother to the Seattle Aquarium, and we spent an hour watching the new sea otter pups. I could tell she knew something was wrong, but she didn't press me. As was her habit, she took dozens of pictures with her digital camera and then had bystanders take photos of us together. I did my best to look carefree, but I don't think I pulled it off.

Two days after the fire my doorbell rang.

When I answered the door, Iola Pederson breezed into my small duplex without invitation.

"How did you know where I live?"

"The other night I found your address on the desk, under the glass."

"I wish you'd called first."

"I do things on the spur of the moment. It's the kind of girl I am. How have you been?"

"Surviving."

"That good, huh?"

It was late afternoon. I was in sweatpants and a fire department T-shirt, my hair mussed. Looking at her, all I could think about was the sex dreams I'd been having. There'd been a lot of TV footage from the fire, and this morning's paper carried another piece on the grieving family, so I figured that was why she'd shown up. If my crew wasn't going to rat me out, perhaps she was.

"Well, well, well," she said. "So this is where my little boy toy lives."

She did a walk-through of the kitchen, eating area, and living room and then sat heavily on my couch. Much of my paycheck went to the car out in the garage, so my furniture was mostly castoffs and hand-me-downs. Iola gave me that look—the same one that started things back at the fire station. She picked up a pair of my mother's walking sandals from the floor next to the coffee table. "Girlfriend?"

"No."

"Tiny feet, whoever she is."

"About the other night—"

"I've always fantasized about making love to a fireman in a fire station. I still get goose bumps when I think about it. The thing is, in the fantasy my partner doesn't get up and run out before we're finished."

"The bell hit."

"I don't see any bell here."

She got up, walked to the end of the hallway, pushed my bedroom door open, and strolled in. Articles of clothing began dropping off her limbs like autumn leaves. Nude, she jumped between my sheets and pulled the covers up until only her head and auburn hair peeked out.

I went into the bathroom, half closed the door, and brushed my teeth, staring at myself in the mirror. Just looking at her brought back all the trauma of the night of the fire, and for a moment I considered tossing her out. On the other hand, there would be no consequences this time. And maybe being with her would erase some of the earlier memories.

"What'd you do the other night after we left?" I asked from the bathroom.

"Went home. Watched TV."

"You watch the news?"

"I never watch the news."

"You read the papers?"

"I read memoirs." She didn't have an inkling of what had happened at the fire.

Tronstad called it *DSB:* deadly sperm buildup. I'd been thinking about her all day—when I wasn't thinking about dead people—and the tantalizing glimpse of her backside and heavy, swinging breasts as she leaned over to peel back the covers on my bed moments earlier had aroused me, just as she knew it would.

I slipped off my shirt, my sweatpants, and my socks and climbed under the covers.

It was nearly five o'clock when she gathered up her clothing and scurried into the bathroom. When she emerged, I was at the kitchen sink washing lettuce for a salad.

"See you later, darling."

"You're leaving?"

"Got to."

"I'm fixing dinner. Enchilada soup."

"I have to get home. I've got something going on tonight." Uncertain of the etiquette involved, I stood facing her in the kitchen, mute and embarrassed. Kissing her good-bye seemed redundant, probably because we'd already done so much kissing that my lips were sore.

"Can I have your phone number?"

"I'll be in touch," she said.

"What if I want to call you?"

"Oh, don't look so pitiful, honey. I just prefer you not to call."

"Could I drop by? Would that—"

"Don't *ever* come to my house!"

I must have looked sadder than a broke-dick dog, because she closed the distance between us and kissed me on each cheek, my forehead, and the tip of my nose. "Don't take everything so seriously. You really need to lighten up, sweetie. Anybody ever tell you that? Look, I'm in between phones now and we've got workmen in the house all day, so you don't want to show up there. You really don't."

"Okay."

"You *do* want to see me again?"

"Yes."

"You don't sound too sure."

"I'm sure."

I watched her drive away in a brand-new Toyota Land Cruiser that cost easily twice what my car had.

After that we saw each other several times a week, and each time she left me feeling physically trashed and mentally bewildered. She quickly became verbally abusive, which I ascribed to her personality, assuming she was like that with all men. Perhaps because of the age difference, I tolerated it. As the number of our meetings increased, the manner of our first sexual encounter in the basement of Station 29 receded further from my thoughts and more into the forefront of hers. She never tired of talking about it, using the story almost as an aphrodisiac at each of our liaisons. It seemed to be the high point of her autumn, that evening in the station.

We fell into a disturbing pattern.

She showed up unannounced, parked out of sight around the corner on the potholed side street, blew in as if I were expecting her, and within minutes swept me into the bedroom, where we tore each other's clothes off and went at it. After a while we started having sex on the sofa, on the floor, in the shower, or parked in her Land Cruiser in various locations around West Seattle. She was as randy as I was. She'd show up at lunchtime, or midafternoon. Only once did she arrive after supper.

When I suggested we take in a movie or go out to eat, she invariably declined. What she wanted was sex, pure and simple, and she made no bones about it. She called me her *boy toy*, her *little fireman*, and *the nonstop sex machine*. I didn't much care for the way our relationship was evolving, but her visits were spaced far enough apart that any notions I had about talking her into a real date dissolved by the time she showed up: DSB. Tronstad called it the perfect setup, sex with no entanglements. "Unload your nut sack without having to take her out in public." Aside from him and Johnson, I told no one.

We never discussed the fire or the deaths, and I hardly thought it possible she didn't know about them, yet she didn't seem to.

A week after Arch Place, the battalion held a post-fire review, where talk circulated among the troops that I deserved an award for dragging the two civilians out. Chief Abbott dismissed the idea out of hand, creating general outrage, but I told everyone I didn't want an award. What I wanted was to replay that night and get it right. Probably because it was heartfelt, the sentiment endeared me to all who heard it.

7. CADAVER IN THE CAT HOUSE

Charles Scott Ghanet was one of our regular customers, a man every firefighter in the station knew by name. In fact, at 29's we didn't even call him *Ghanet* but referred to him less than affectionately as Charles Scott.

Typically he called 911 somewhere between two and five A.M.

Our crew believed his complaints were mostly fictitious, that he called because he was a hypochondriac and because he was lonely. Viewed in one light, he was sadder than a lost orphan in a bus station. On the other hand, getting up at three in the morning because some clown needed a warm body to talk to got old fast.

Ghanet, who was sixty-eight but looked younger, routinely complained of stomach ailments, headaches, and pains in his joints and had several times hinted that he might commit suicide, a theme he abandoned after he was told the SPD automatically responded to suicide threats.

Despite our mixed feelings—and the fact that his house reeked of cats—we tried to treat Ghanet with the same courtesy and regard we gave each of our patients.

It was a Sunday night when we got the call. Charles Scott Ghanet lived near Schmitz Park in an area of dry yards and treeless avenues, in a house that was small and nondescript. When we rolled up, I got off and collected the aid and vent kits while Tronstad grabbed the Lifepak. On the sidewalk, Lieutenant Sears spoke to a Latino man in jeans and an unbuttoned plaid shirt, then filled us in as we marched up to Ghanet's front door. "Neighbor said he's worried. He hasn't seen any lights for a couple of days."

"Charles Scott didn't call this in himself?" Tronstad asked.

"The neighbor."

"Don't you think this asshole might have called at noon instead of three in the morning?" Tronstad muttered. "Is this whole neighborhood retarded?"

"Settle down," said Sears.

We banged on the barred door, and Lieutenant Sears called out loudly, "Charles Scott? Fire department! You okay? Charles?"

"Maybe he had a stroke," said Johnson, who had a theory about everything. "My aunt had a stroke."

Tronstad headed around the house with a flashlight, attempting to peer through the windows. Lieutenant Sears looked at Johnson and said, "Why don't you go with him?"

"A black man peeking in windows at three in the morning? I don't think so."

I left Sears and Johnson glaring at each other. Together, Tronstad and I circled the house, pushing through knee-deep weeds. The blinds and drapes were pulled tight on the other side of the barred windows. Behind the house Ghanet's fifteen-year-old pickup truck sat in the garage.

"Fuckin' Fort Knox," said Tronstad. "I always wondered what he's hiding in there."

"He got burgled once."

"*I* got burgled once, but I don't live in a fuckin' vault."

When we returned to the front door, Sears gave us a grim look.

"What?" said Tronstad.

Johnson said, "Take a peek through the mail slot."

Switching on my medical flashlight, I propped open the mail slot with two fingers and swept the beam across familiar stacks of old newspapers six feet tall and the backside of a piano half buried by storage. A distinctive odor wafted out the slot. Without waiting to be told, I went back to the rig and retrieved the Halligan tool and flathead ax we carried for forcible entry. It took a minute to get the heavy steel door open. Inside, the smell was worse—a lot worse.

"Hey, yo," Sears said. "Charles Scott? You in here?"

Ghanet was a pack rat, one of those old-timers who hoarded every newspaper, article of clothing, coupon, magazine, book, car battery, camera instruction booklet, and canceled check he'd ever touched.

Tronstad forged ahead, plowing through the piles of garbage as if on an Easter egg hunt, while I jumped in front of Lieutenant Sears. After the Arch Place fire Sears had treated me gingerly, thinking I'd been shaken because of the deaths. This would be my chance to prove corpses didn't bother me.

"Jesus. I wonder where the cats are?" Tronstad said as something dark and furry shot between my legs and out into the yard. A second feline shadow followed.

It was a three-bedroom house, and if there hadn't been garbage piled higher than our heads everywhere, we might have searched it in thirty seconds. As it was, it took our little train over a minute to reach the nook in front of the flickering television, where we usually met Ghanet. He was nowhere in sight.

Like hamsters burrowing into tall grass, we continued our search. Tronstad went into the bathroom, while Sears made his way into the master bedroom. I explored the kitchen. A minute or two later, we met in the cramped pathway Ghanet had carved in the litter between the kitchen and the living room. "He's not in there," I said.

"Not on the shitter," Tronstad said.

"Back East they lost a body in a situation like this," said Sears. "Somebody found her a year later. She'd turned into a mummy."

"That isn't going to happen here," said Tronstad, with uncharacteristic resolve. "We're not leaving until we find him."

Tronstad was already making his way to the second bedroom. Because of the junk in disorderly rows along both walls, we couldn't see any of the hallway, or Tronstad, but we knew from past visits that except for the master bedroom, the other bedroom doors were padlocked.

When Sears heard Tronstad forcing the bedroom door, he said, "Hey, Ted. What are you doing?"

"He might be in here."

"The door's locked from the outside, isn't it?"

"Home invasion. They break in and lock him inside. We

go away and he turns into a mummy. You going to leave without taking a look?"

The bedroom door burst open and Tronstad disappeared inside as if falling through a trapdoor. Sears followed, while I edged my way through the stacks. We found a neatly made queen bed, a bedside table, and a dressing stand, no disorder whatsoever. Gauging by the layers of undisturbed dust, there'd been no visitors in years. Tronstad opened the closet and pulled out a woman's dress on a hanger, dangling a brassiere off one finger.

"This is like Miss Havisham's," Sears said, peering under the bed.

Tronstad exited the room. "Who's Miss Havisham? Some patient you had when you worked at Thirty-one's?"

"The old maid in *Great Expectations*," I explained. "Charles Dickens. Miss Havisham wore her wedding dress until it was rotting on her."

Tronstad stuck his head back in the doorway. "Charles fucking Dickens? You need to get a life, Juicy Fruit."

Within seconds Tronstad had cracked the door frame on the second bedroom and was stepping inside. I followed. Unlike the first bedroom, this one was a total mess. As we looked around, the lieutenant shouted from the other end of the house. "I found him. Code green the search. I found him."

I followed Sears's voice to the bathroom, where the tub was stuffed with a large, swollen corpse, his head huge and bulging, as were his limbs and stomach, testicles the size of baseballs. All of his skin was black, and he looked like a blimp. "Where's Charles Scott?" I asked.

"This *is* Charles Scott."

"But Charles Scott isn't black."

"He's been dead a few days. This is what they do sometimes. Ted searched in here. How did he miss this?"

"I don't know."

"Geez, he's ripe. I'll call for a C and C. Tronstad! We found him. Code green the search."

Lieutenant Sears and I made our way through the junk to

the front door and stepped outside into the cool night air. Sears keyed the mike on his portable radio and asked for the police and medical examiner. I took several deep breaths of clean air, but the stench seemed to have permeated my nostrils.

When the neighbor Sears had spoken to came out of a house two doors down, Sears walked over and met him. As they went inside, I climbed into the officer's seat next to Robert Johnson. "You find him?" Johnson asked.

"Oh, yeah."

"Was it bad?"

"No."

Johnson cradled the steering wheel and stared at the empty street through the windshield, his eyes drowsy. Five minutes later I felt somebody bouncing the rig and turned around to see Tronstad standing on the tailboard with a large black plastic garbage bag in his hands. A moment later Tronstad jogged to Ghanet's house and disappeared inside and was still in there twenty minutes later when the police car arrived. Then as Sears and the SPD officer went through the front door, Tronstad sneaked out of the back, carrying another plastic bag.

"What do you think he's doing?" I asked, but Johnson was asleep.

Obviously we weren't supposed to touch the dead man's belongings, yet on two previous alarms I'd seen Tronstad remove items from dead people's homes, in one instance four commercial pornographic tapes. He claimed he was doing the dead man a favor by removing them so his loved ones wouldn't be shocked. On another alarm with another DOA, he hooked a small picture frame. None of the items were of much value; it was almost as if the nature of the event required him to snitch souvenirs.

Moments later, as Tronstad climbed into the crew cab, I said, "What's in the bags?"

Tronstad peered past me toward the dark house. "The place was full of old papers. Nobody's going to miss them."

"Newspapers?"

"Yeah. Papers, man. It's nothing."

"Well, you'd better put them back anyway," I said.

"Hey, man, don't get your panties in a knot."

"You guys ready?" asked Sears, climbing into the rig.

Five minutes after we got back to the station, I discovered Tronstad and Johnson arguing in the bunk room.

8. BEARER BONDS

Tronstad and Johnson were squared off in front of Tronstad's clothing locker, at their feet three bulging black garbage bags. "You can't keep this," Johnson said, shaking his head.

"It's just junk."

"It's not *your* junk. You can't keep it."

"Watch me." I'd seen them bicker before, Tronstad a man who could get contentious about something as inconsequential as whether to have peas or green beans with dinner—afterward acting as if the squabble never occurred. "You just watch me."

"It's not right and you know it."

"Oh, yeah? And it's right to go bad on one alarm out of four?"

"I don't go wrong on one out of four."

"The hell you don't."

I stepped into the bathroom at the west end of the bunk room to use the urinal. Before Sears galvanized them into a posture of unity, these two had quarreled almost daily. Tonight their tone was more malicious than usual, especially Tronstad's, as if the months of holding back had built his grievances to the point of bursting.

Even if these two didn't, I knew we'd never quite worked together as a unit until we found ourselves united against Sears, who liked to think *he'd* brought us together through his authority and unyielding leadership. In reality our unification was a rebellion against his inflexibility. Personally, I liked him as an individual, but I stood with the others in my dislike of his stubbornness. It was always his way or the highway.

"What do you think, Gum?" Johnson was standing in the bathroom doorway watching me in the mirror, giving me the smile he used when he was furious. Lately, I was beginning to see the multiple layers of angst buried beneath his cheerful exterior. His gambling, for instance: he believed with a conviction equal to his belief in God that it was his destiny to win millions of dollars, that he would pick the right numbers and it would be handed to him, that every time he lost he was getting personally screwed out of what was rightfully his.

"What?"

"Gum? You and I have to take a stand on this. Ted needs to turn in those bags."

"Of course he does. What's in them?"

Johnson handed me a slip of official-looking paper about twice the size of a dollar bill, replete with intricate script and seals. The print on the front claimed it was worth a thousand dollars to the holder and that it had been authorized by the Bank of Alfalh.

"What is it?" I asked.

"Says it's a bearer bond for a thousand bucks."

"What's a bearer bond?"

"I don't know."

Johnson and I walked into the bunk room, where Tronstad was cramming the last of the three plastic garbage bags into his clothing locker, forcing the door shut, and locking it. They barely fit. "If they're not worth anything, what do you need them for?" I asked.

"Yeah," said Johnson. "If they're not worth anything, what do you need them for?"

"I want to play a joke on my brother-in-law."

"You have to tell Sears you took them," said Johnson. "Tell him it was an accident. We'll back you up, but we have to get these back where they belong."

"It's not like he's got any relatives to inherit that junk.

Some real estate speculator will buy his house from the government for a song, and then he'll get a Dumpster and hire a crew of beaners and they'll gut it. This stuff was headed for the scrap heap. I'm not going to hand it to Sears so he can write me up. No way, José."

"Gum, tell him he's gotta give it back," said Johnson. "You know I'm right."

"I'm beat. I have to go to bed."

"You're not squirming out of this, Gum," Johnson said. "And don't think if you go over there and go to sleep, you won't be making a decision. It'll be the wrong decision, but it'll be a decision."

I turned to Tronstad. "It says a thousand dollars. What if it's real?"

"The Bank of Alfalh? Gimme a break. It's play money. Trust me, man. You want me to burn one? Will that prove it to you?"

"Burn it all. That'll prove something."

"Tell you what. I'll hold it, and if his family shows up, I'll turn it over to them. They'll throw it away, but I'll give it to them. Does that satisfy you?"

"No way," Johnson said. "You turn it in tonight."

"You want me to lose my job over a bunch of junk?" Tronstad turned to me. "You're not going along with him after what I did for you at Arch Place?"

Mention of Arch Place was like a blow to my solar plexus.

Tronstad glowered at me. His hair was black and thick, pulled into a ponytail barely legal by department standards, and his bulky eyebrows and mustache were menacing under the best light. When his deep-set eyes fixed on you, the weight of his look was almost palpable.

"We can take it back to the house in the morning," I said. "I want to go to bed now."

"Hey, buddy. You ain't voting against old Tronstad, are you? You and me have an arrangement. I don't tell on you; you don't tell on me." He smiled and bobbled his eyebrows comically.

"That's dirty pool," Johnson said. "You ain't going to tell on Gum, and you know it. Anybody could miss a call."

"Not the way Gum missed it."

As far as Johnson knew, I'd been in the bathroom the night of Arch Place, but now, spurred by Tronstad's remark, he looked at me curiously.

"Okay," I said. "We can't take it back tonight because we don't want to tell Sears. You're right. He'll try to fire you. But we have to take it back in the morning. The three of us."

It was disquieting that I seemed to have the power here. Of the three of us, I was the youngest by ten years and had only two years in the SFD, while Johnson had eleven and Tronstad eight. Robert Johnson had served in the Navy, where he'd once seen a man decapitated by an exploding truck tire. Ted Tronstad had done a tour in the Air Force, where he worked as a firefighter at various air fields around the world and had once witnessed a man incinerated in a jet fuel accident. I'd gone to community college. Next to theirs, my worldly experience was limited.

We went to bed, and in the morning when I walked over to the bunk room, I found Tronstad making up his bunk. Johnson was in the TV room, in front of one of the station computers, a single bearer bond on the desk next to him. Across the apparatus bay Sears was making his bunk and Chief Abbott was brushing his teeth loudly in the officers' washroom.

"Hey, Gum," Johnson said, smiling brightly. "There's been a small modification to our plan."

"What do you mean?"

"I looked up bearer bonds on the Internet. Tronstad has bonds from the Bank of Sierre Leone. From Deutsche Bank. From companies in Europe I never heard of. Mostly from the United States government. There's a lot of stuff in those sacks."

"A lot of stuff we're going to give back."

"We should think this over before we do something we'll regret."

"Robert . . ."

"Here. Read this. Just read this part right here." On the

computer screen, he pointed the curser to an open page of text. *"Bearer bonds and bearer certificates belong to the bearer. Possession is a hundred percent of the law with a bearer bond. Bearer bonds aren't registered anywhere, but they can be stolen, which makes them ideal for anonymity. While the U.S. government no longer issues bearer bonds, they still honor bonds issued in earlier years. Millions of dollars' worth of bearer bonds are outstanding."*

As Tronstad would put it, Johnson was happier than a dead pig in the sun. "We got bearer bonds in there from all over the world, but the majority are from the U.S. government. There's no way to trace them. Those sacks might be worth a million each, Gum."

"There's no way a pack rat like Ghanet had that much money lying around. That's junk paper."

"How about four million each?" Tronstad said, when he came into the room. "I stayed up last night and counted them. Just over twelve million total."

"Whoo-hoo," Johnson said. "The beauty of it is that this ain't money. It's paper, and it ain't stolen. I don't know where Tronstad got those sacks. Do you?"

"We were going to make him take it back," I said, more convinced than ever the paper was worthless. If it had been worth a few thousand, I might have believed Ghanet had squirreled it away for a rainy day. But millions? The man lived on macaroni and cheese. His truck barely ran. His TV was fuzzy on every channel.

Johnson gave me a long, slow look, as if trying to convince himself. "We were like family to Charles Scott. He would want us to have it."

I could see they'd closed ranks and become a team, the two of them against me. They knew that I knew if I turned them in, I would be turning myself in for missing the alarm on Arch Place—and for lying about it over the course of the past three weeks. How could I get them fired over three garbage sacks full of worthless paper they thought was Aztec gold?

"You in?" Tronstad asked. "Or are you going to walk over there and cost us our jobs? Your choice, pal."

"You just said it was worth—"

"Nothing, probably. Your choice."

"What choice?" Lieutenant Sears opened the door from the apparatus bay in time to catch Tronstad's last words. Despite our bad night, he looked military and shipshape.

"The choice is ice cream," Tronstad said. "Gum owes us ice cream for his first DOA in a tub."

Sears knew we'd been talking about something else—you could see it in the tilt of his head and his questioning brown eyes. "Is that what you guys were talking about?" Lieutenant Sears asked, looking at me.

"No, it isn't," I said. "We were talking about . . ." Tronstad's veins began bulging. Johnson stood up. ". . . about a surprise gift for somebody when he gets promoted."

The lieutenant's look softened. Rumors were flying around that he might soon be transferred to a captain's position in the fire marshal's office, so the lie had come easily.

Before he left, Sears, striking like a snake, snatched the bearer bond out of Johnson's hands, then examined the gaudy colored ink and toy-money look. "This smells like cats," he said.

You could have heard a pin hit the floor.

"I sure hope this didn't come from where I think it came from," Sears said. "Any time a firefighter removes something from the scene of an alarm, it's a crime. I hope you boys know that." He stared at us each in turn.

I could hear Johnson's Timex ticking.

"I've got a safety committee meeting this morning at zero eight-thirty, and then Heather and I are heading out of town. But . . ." He held up the bond. "I'm going to keep this, and if it came from where I think it came from, somebody's in trouble. I mean that."

"Give it back," said Tronstad. "You don't have any right to take that."

"Is it yours?"

"Well . . ."

"Then I'll keep it." Pausing in the doorway, Sears said, "This is potentially a serious offense." He sniffed it again. "Oh, boy."

"Hey," Tronstad said. "Give it back. It's mine. I brought it from home. Swear to God. It's my sister's. I gotta give it back to her this morning or she'll be hot." Tronstad held out his hand. They stared at each other for half a minute, and for at least part of that time I thought Sears was going to return it.

"We've got a four-off. If your explanation holds up in four days, I'll apologize. Otherwise . . . you're in a heap of trouble, buster. All of you."

"At least keep it confidential," said Tronstad.

"Why should I?"

"Because charges are supposed to be confidential. I ain't saying we done anything, but if you're thinking of writing charges . . ."

"Confidential it is."

"Thank you," I said.

Sears had been on his way out the door, but when I spoke he stopped and looked at me. He had heart. I had to give him that. He was hoping I wasn't part of this. I could see it in his eyes. He liked me more than the others, probably because I was young, moldable, listened to his lessons, and tried to learn from him. "You're going to hang, too. You know that, don't you? If you're part of it."

"I'm not part of anything," I said.

"I said, you know that, don't you?"

"I know."

After he left, Tronstad turned to Johnson. "If we can get it out of his locker on this four-off, he'll never know the difference."

"He'll know the difference," Johnson said.

"Maybe, but he won't be able to do anything about it."

"What makes you think he's going to leave it in his locker?" I said.

"How are you going to get in?" Johnson asked. "It's got a padlock the size of an alarm clock."

"I can get into anything." It was true. Tronstad routinely picked locks around the station for fun.

We wiped down the chief's buggy and Engine 29 without talking, and then one by one the members of the oncoming shift showed up and relieved us.

Minutes later, when I went outside to the small parking area on the west side of the station, Tronstad and Johnson were waiting for me. The three black plastic bags sat at their feet. I clicked the remote key to unlock the doors on my WRX, then opened the rear hatch. I threw my gear bag inside next to my skates. "What?" I said.

"This isn't going to work," Tronstad said.

"It's going to work unless you want to start throwing punches," said Johnson, angrily. "You think one bond is bad, try to explain three sacks of them when Sears and Abbott come out to stop our fight."

Tronstad jumped as if on a pogo stick: small, comical movements, clenching his fists at his sides like a cartoon boxer. I had the feeling that in a fistfight he would be both hilarious and deadly, and I didn't want to be around to see it. He was over six feet and wiry, while Johnson was five-ten and over two hundred pounds. They could probably make a fight last for a good long time. I closed the hatch on my Subaru and stepped between them.

"What's going on?" I said.

"He wants to take them home," said Johnson.

"Three sacks of worthless paper, for God's sake," said Tronstad.

"Oh, that's funny," Johnson said. "A few minutes ago they were worth twelve million, but now it's three sacks of worthless paper. If it's so worthless, let me have it."

"Not on your life."

"Why not?"

"For one thing, it's mine."

"We're in trouble, too. Me and Gum. And you're not sandbagging me. Let Gum take it. I trust Gum. *You* trust Gum. *Gum* trusts Gum. Hell, he was going to turn himself in at

Arch Place. Look at him. He's a choirboy. He holds it, or we fight right here. I swear."

"Bullshit!"

Johnson put his fists up and started advancing on Tronstad. I'd never seen him so angry or resolute.

Tronstad looked me in the eye. "Okay, okay. You keep this for us?"

"Why don't we take it back to Ghanet's right now?"

"No way," they said in unison.

"Then I don't want it."

"Then we're fightin'," said Johnson.

"I'll take it, but only because I don't want to see you two fighting over garbage. If I find out it's worth anything, I'm turning it in. Agreed?"

"Agreed," Johnson said.

"Agreed," Tronstad said.

Even so, I had misgivings when I opened the rear hatch of my wagon once more and heaved the three plastic bags inside—Tronstad had secured each with a knot at the mouth of the bag. I fired up my ride and drove away, revving the engine so the throaty, turbocharged roar woke up any neighbors who hadn't already left for work. Sears had warned me about making noise in the morning, but I wanted to show my wrath to Johnson and Tronstad for dragging me into this.

When I peered into my rearview mirror, they were standing dismally on the sidewalk like a couple of freshmen who'd just been pantsed by an upperclassman.

I thought about Sears as I drove away. Of the three of us, I was the only one who actually liked our new lieutenant. Don't get me wrong. I wanted him to transfer out as much as the others, but I admired him as a person, and I had to admit some of the changes he'd instituted were for the better.

It was common knowledge that Chief Abbott had shipped in Sears to flog us into shape. Before Sears's arrival we'd had one stand-in officer after another, and none had tried to reform us, probably because they all knew they were temporary. During the first four weeks he worked with us, Sears drilled us three or four hours every shift and frequently had us doing some idiotic project until ten at night. Unable to stand the sitting-around part of being a firefighter, Sears filled the cracks in our days with busywork, piling nonsensical chores on top of our regular duties, alarms, equipment maintenance, station housework, and regular diet of fire department classes. He never seemed to fatigue and didn't understand it when others did.

Once, before Sears was officially appointed lieutenant, he ordered his crew outside to lay hose in the rain in the middle of a Seahawks playoff game. Despite their protests, he ran them through two and a half hours of wet hose evolutions and caused them to miss the entire game. The following morning, crew members threw a tarp over his head and tied his feet together. When the next shift arrived, they found Sears wrapped in a tarp, hanging upside down in the hose tower. He'd stopped screaming long before.

9. SKATING

California Avenue took me down a steep, winding hill through a greenbelt of madronas to Harbor Avenue, where I headed north for half a mile along the west side of Elliott Bay before parking at the Duwamish Head, the northernmost point in West Seattle. From there a paved path ran south about a mile along Harbor Avenue, a second leg stretching three more miles southwest alongside Alki Avenue and what was arguably the best beach in the city—the closest thing to a tropical paradise Seattle had to offer.

Alki Beach attracted volleyball players, sunbathers, beachcombers, joggers, in-line skaters, and all manner of showoffs. On summer afternoons traffic jams stretched for miles, though on this early September morning tranquillity reigned.

The promontory didn't have much in the way of amenities—some parking spaces and an expansive view across Elliott Bay, for which people in the condos across the street paid upward of a million dollars. Across the bay lay the entire vast panorama of downtown Seattle: skyscrapers, hospitals on the hill, the Space Needle, and as a backdrop, the Cascade Mountain Range running north and south as far as the eye could see. State ferries scudded across the Sound from the downtown terminal. On a nice day, which this was, you could see snowcapped Mount Rainier looming in the southeast.

To the northwest you could look directly up the Sound until your eyes surrendered to the distant gray-blue haze between sky and water. Behind me at the foot of the treed hillside were condos, apartments, and here and there a small beach cottage, valiantly holding its own in the shadows of a steamroller economy that wanted to tear down the old and build anew everywhere. Iola Pederson lived above the first layer of housing on the steep hillside.

The pavement along the beach ran for a total of four miles and at this time of the morning attracted a meager assortment of walkers, bikers, and women pushing strollers. I skated whenever the weather allowed, and some days when even the walkers bailed out. For variety, I skated the Cedar River Trail out of Renton, the three-mile path around Green Lake, the Burke-Gilman Trail out of Gas Works Park, and downtown at Myrtle Edwards Park, but most times I came here. On Thursday nights during the summer a loose group of us got together and skated at midnight through downtown Seattle, up sidewalks and down hills nobody in his right mind would attempt. When the weather was bad, I skated in parking garages with friends, in local pedestrian tunnels, and, when we got desperate, at local indoor rinks.

My skates of choice were a pair of Solomon TR Magnesiums with 80 millimeter racing wheels I'd hopped up with ABEC-8 bearings, lighter axles, and a superlight oil I'd discovered. Although they were four-wheel skates as opposed to the five-wheelers racers used, they were almost as fast as my five-wheeled Miller Pros. I hadn't been born with many gifts, but one of them was a pair of lungs equal to a quarter horse and quadriceps like steel. The guys at work could lift more than I could in the weight room, and in drill school I'd had some bad days carrying ladders, but on skates I was headed for mythic territory.

This was where I retreated when I was frustrated or worried, where I felt most at home with the universe.

With my legs hanging out the driver's side of my WRX, I laced and buckled my skates, then locked the Subaru and took off, zipping around four women walking side by side. I would do the first eight miles at cruising speed and then start blasting.

The temperature was in the low sixties, perfect for hard exercise. On the beach side of the street, sunshine poured down, while across the road morning shadows swallowed the houses and condominiums along the hillside.

Two years before, when I signed up with the department, I had no clue how much of my identity would be tied up in being a firefighter. I had no relatives who were firefighters. One day I simply decided it was the right career move and began taking entrance tests for various departments.

Until I was twenty-one I lived at home, attending Bellevue Community College after high school. After receiving my AA, I found temporary work at a janitorial firm, cleaning office buildings between eight at night and four in the morning, polishing floors, scrubbing out crappers, plunking ice cakes into urinals—not a profession I yearned to revisit.

I'd come to think of Station 29 as a second home, the people who worked there as brothers and sisters, and the job as inextricable from my life as a lung or a kidney was inextricable from my body. I'd joined a community, a select and special community.

Firefighting was a job that made you tense. You never knew what was going to happen on an alarm, and you never knew when you were going to get one. Although the last firefighter death in Seattle had occurred four years earlier, the department had scraped through several close calls since then, and each gave me pause for thought. Somewhere in the country a firefighter got killed every day.

For weeks I'd been trying to push the deaths of Fred and Susan Rankler out of my mind. Skating helped. Much as I hated to say it, climbing into the sack with Iola Pederson helped, too. I wasn't exactly sure what I was doing with Iola. It was possible our relationship might grow into something more than just a sex-fest, but it was equally possible she would simply fail to show up one day and that would be the end of it.

It was surprising how much I still didn't know about Iola. I didn't know where she was born, where she worked, or anything about her past or present life other than her appetite for sex. I didn't know her religious or political persuasion or her taste in music. I'd told her everything there was to know about me, but all I knew about her was she'd been married once and worked part time in a office somewhere south of Qwest Field, the Seahawks' stadium.

I'd managed to glean a few facts about her education, probably because she was vain about it: that she had a master's degree in art history, had attended the University of Heidelberg, spoke German and Dutch, and had traveled and lived in Italy and France. At times while we were making love she would murmur Teutonic ciphers to me, and each time I imagined she was saying something like, "Ride me, you big fireman stud," but when she translated one it went more like, "Oh, little boy. You drive so fast, but you never go anywhere." Not what I had in mind.

I savored the sex enough to overlook everything that was wrong between us, which was just about everything, including the twenty-one-year age difference. I'd sneaked a peek at her driver's license. She was forty-five. I was twenty-four and had more than once been pulled over in my Subie by cops who didn't believe I was old enough to have a license, and here I was involved with a woman four years older than my mother. I didn't know what to make of it.

Skating in the early-morning sunshine, I thought about the three bags in the back of my Subaru. It was probably garbage, but on the off chance that it was not, I would be in real trouble. The question in my mind was, why would a pack rat like

Ghanet have twelve million in bearer bonds lying around his house?

People got terminated for theft. Tronstad could lose his job and might even go to jail. *I* could lose my job. Now that I thought about it, I could go to jail, too. I should have confessed to Sears back at the station.

The thought occurred to me that even now I might drive downtown to the union office and wait for Sears to finish his safety meeting, tell him the whole story, turn over the garbage bags, and throw myself on the mercy of the court. If I turned the swag in now, there was good reason to believe I would be regarded as something other than a co-conspirator.

But then, if I spoke to Sears, I'd be putting Robert Johnson in jeopardy as well. Tronstad had stolen the bags. Whatever came down on him was deserved, but Robert and I had been sucked into this by accident.

Still, we'd lied to Sears. All of us.

What it boiled down to was, I didn't want to turn Johnson in and didn't have the balls to send Ted Tronstad to jail, especially after he'd covered for me at Arch Place. I'd had weeks to think about Arch Place and now realized missing the rig on a call wasn't the most egregious crime anybody ever committed. Over the years plenty of firefighters had missed the rig, albeit most likely not for the reason I did. But some of the blame would fall on Sears, who was supposed to make certain everybody was on board before the apparatus left the station. Odds were, I would have kept my job had I been forthright.

If the truth came out now, however, it would look terrible, because I'd been lying for three weeks. I'd lied to Lieutenant Sears and Chief Abbott. I'd even lied to the chief of the department, who'd phoned to commiserate over the fire deaths. And now I'd lied to Sears about the bond.

I kept telling myself that I didn't have any choice, that Tronstad had blackmailed me with Arch Place, that it was out of my hands. But that was a lie, too. You always have a choice.

After sixty minutes of skating I changed out of my skates,

fired up the Subaru, and drove up the hill. I would put the bonds back where Tronstad found them. The drive took less than ten minutes, Ghanet's neighborhood squatty and dry in the morning sunshine.

My plan was scotched when I saw that Ghanet's front door was open and there were two sedans and a Ford Expedition in front of the house. From their license plates I knew the cars belonged to the city, police detectives probably. I'd only been to Ghanet's house once during daylight hours and was surprised at how shabby it looked.

I drove past the house and kept going.

I'd been hoping I might be able to stuff the bonds through the mail slot or toss them into the garage in back, but that wasn't going to happen with all those people around. It was about then that I realized I was being followed. It was Tronstad, in the old pickup truck he'd inherited from his father. I knew he was following me so he could get the bonds back. It was going to cause a major blowout between him and Johnson, but more than that, if they turned out to be worth something, I would never be able to retrieve them to turn them in.

Downshifting, I cornered hard and floored the accelerator. Let him try to follow me. Even a new truck wouldn't have a chance. He was in my rearview mirror for a block and a half and then he was gone.

Once I was sure I'd lost him, I drove back down the hill to the water and past the lighthouse at Alki Point, following the route I'd skated earlier. I couldn't go home with the bags in the car: Tronstad knew where I lived and would be waiting for me. I had to hide them. I detoured off of Alki, knowing Tronstad could reappear in my rearview mirror at any moment on this long strip of road. Driving up the hill, I found myself in Iola Pederson's neighborhood and slowed to a crawl in front of her house. This was the first time I'd been there since the pig plunged through her roof, and the house looked as good as new.

There were no cars on the premises and no signs of life. Off to the right of the house, a detached garage served as a storage shed for lawn mowers, bicycles, and ski equipment.

If I hid the bags there I could pick them up in a few days and return them—sometime when I knew Tronstad wasn't on my tail and official interest had died off at Ghanet's house.

I parked in the driveway, popped the rear hatch, grabbed all three bags, closed the lid with my elbow, walked over to the outbuilding, and pushed open the unlocked door with my shoulder. Inside, I found an old black sixties-era Volvo. Beside the car was an upside-down canoe. I opened the rear door of the Volvo without difficulty. Depositing the three black garbage bags on the floor in the back, I closed the door and peered through the windows, finding the bags nearly invisible.

When Iola Pederson pulled up, I was in the driveway.

"Hey, dumbbell," she said, leaving the motor of the Land Cruiser running as she ran toward me. "What did I specifically say to you about coming here?"

"Nice to see you, too."

She wore an old sweatshirt and sweatpants, and although she'd put on at least one layer of makeup, under the oblique precision of the September sunshine she looked older today. "What are you doing here?"

"I was in the neighborhood and thought I'd stop by to see how the house looked," I lied.

"Christ. You didn't talk to anybody, did you? My God, you're a moron." She moved close and kissed my cheek coldly. "Get the hell out of here."

"When am I going to see you?"

"When do you normally see me?"

"When I see you."

"That hasn't changed."

She stared at me, peeking out from under a mop of auburn hair. "Get out of here before one of the neighbors tells Daddy. My life is complicated enough. Go. Shoo!"

"I wouldn't want your dad mad at you," I said, walking toward my car. When I looked back, I thought I saw an apology lurking behind her blue eyes, but I'd waited in vain for apologies from her before and wasn't about to waste my time.

I roared up the hill, the sound of the boxer engine echoing against the hillside. It would piss her off, but I *wanted* to piss her off. No woman in my life had ever treated me as shabbily as Iola. Mind-bending sex or no, I was starting to get fed up.

10. WHAT DID THE SEVEN DWARFS DO AFTER SNOW WHITE WOKE UP?

I parked in the sunshine outside my duplex, but before I got through the door, Ted Tronstad emerged from behind the honeysuckle bush next to the garage and poked his nose up against my face. I started laughing.

"The fuck's so funny?"

"What were you doing in the bushes?"

"Waiting for you."

"I just saw you at work. And you were following me, weren't you?"

"Why'd you go past Ghanet's?"

"I was going to put the bags back."

"You little bastard. I knew you couldn't be trusted, Mr. Goody Two-shoes." He walked over to my car, and after trying two of the doors and the rear hatch, cupped his hands to his face and looked into the rear window. "Jesus, Spearmint. Get over here and open this up. For Christ's sake, I ain't got all day."

"We had a deal. I was going to hold them."

"I'm canceling the deal."

"Does Johnson know about this?"

"Fuck Johnson. This is my shit. Hand it over."

"Fuck who?" I hadn't seen him show up, but Johnson was sitting in his car in the middle of Genesee, driver's window rolled down. He drove over to the curb and jumped out. "Fuck Johnson? Fuck you, too, Tronstad," Johnson said.

"Hold on, you two," I said.

"Fuck *you*," said Tronstad, addressing me. He turned back to Johnson. "And stay away from me. I'll fuck you up."

"I'll fuck *you* up," said Johnson.

"Fuck you, Robert."

"Stop it," I said.

"Fuck *you*. Those bags belong to me," said Tronstad. "Fuck you both. Hand them the fuck over, or you'll wish you had."

"You threatening me?" I asked.

Johnson said, "Fuck you, too, Ted. Fuck you and fuck your . . . your . . . grandmother."

"Fuck your sister," said Tronstad.

"Fuck your . . ."

"Aunt's hairdresser," I said, laughing.

"Yeah," said Johnson. "Fuck your aunt's hairdresser."

"Fuck your cat," said Tronstad.

By now I was laughing so hard, I could no longer contribute to the insanity. Johnson was spluttering, unable to come up with any more pets or relatives to have intercourse with, and then, seeing me, he began laughing, too.

Finally, Tronstad broke down and chuckled. "Ah, hell. Let's just take it inside and divvy it up. There should be plenty for each of us."

"You didn't come here to divvy up anything," said Johnson. "You came here to screw me out of my share."

Tronstad turned to me with a folded Buck knife in his fist. "Open the car, or I swear I'll break the window."

I used the remote key fob in my hand and unlocked the doors. In an instant they'd pulled open the rear hatch.

"They're gone," said Johnson.

"No shit." Tronstad strode toward me. "Where did you put them?"

"I hid 'em. If we have to turn them in, I want it all accounted for."

"Well, crap," said Tronstad. "Fuck this shit." He turned on his heel and walked ten feet. "What if something happens to you? What if you hit your goddamn head and forget where you put them?"

"Then you're shit out of luck, aren't you?"

Moments later he came roaring out of Twenty-fifth in his truck and passed us without a glance.

"I knew he'd try to snatch it," Johnson said.

"You think he would really turn me in for Arch Place?"

"I wouldn't put anything past him. Think about his first wedding. How many people you know left a bride standing at the altar?"

Ten years before, when he was in the service, his wedding had been scheduled for one o'clock in San Diego. At ten o'clock, Tronstad got into his tuxedo and had another soldier drive him two hours into the desert while he sulked in the passenger seat swigging whiskey and thinking up excuses not to go through with it. By twelve-thirty they were 150 miles from the church, Tronstad was drunk off his ass, and it was too late to get back for the wedding. His actual first marriage, by Tronstad's own admission, had been a calamity of his own making. He'd started off by seducing one of the bridesmaids two weeks before the ceremony. He secretly videotaped himself having sex with his bride several times during their year and a half together, and after the breakup, in a fit of pique over the fact that she'd rejected him, he played the videotape repeatedly for his biker friends—and, rumor had it, for certain firefighters on duty. His third marriage was annulled after the bride's father put a private detective on him and learned he was trying to sleep with the bride's sister two weeks after the honeymoon, which, incidentally, the bride's father had paid for. There was another marriage in there somewhere, but it went sour so fast, we couldn't get the details out of him.

Tronstad was self-centered to a degree you saw only in a small child; fickle, and possessed of a need to avenge any perceived slight. Thinking about him in this light, it was hard to believe we were friends, although around the station he was personable and funnier than heck in a way that was hard to explain to somebody who'd not seen it in person. It was the way he moved and reacted to things, his herky-jerky body language. Until now, he'd always treated me like a brother. Not that any of us were going to buy land with him or let him babysit our kids.

After they left, I went inside, took a shower, and packed. I grabbed a small pack, a sleeping bag, and the tent, though I'd allotted enough cash to buy a room for one or two nights. I packed the car, locked the front door to the house, and was walking around to the driver's side of the WRX when a figure stepped across the parking strip and pushed me against the car, hands flat on my chest. It took me a few seconds to realize it was a woman.

She was tall and slender and strong. She bounced me off the car, then pinned me against it by my collar. I could hear the material of my shirt tearing. I might have fought her off except for the surprise.

"Your name Gum?"

"Who are you?"

"I'm asking the questions, pardner."

"My name is Gum. What is it—"

"Just settle down. I'll do the talking." She was cute in a fierce sort of way, her hair in a pixie cut, her eyes pale blue. "You're seeing a woman a couple times a week."

"What's it to you?"

"It's gonna stop, you hear?"

"I don't see how this can be any of your business."

"That's where you're wrong." She threw me against the car again and stepped back onto the grass, where she took a moment to look me over. She was an inch or so taller than my five-eight, her wide, bony hips pushing at the denim material of her jeans, her small breasts barely making a bulge in her black T-shirt and white fleece vest. Her golden-brown hair looked almost blond in the sunshine, and her face was clean, its lines sculpted. She had a dimple in her left cheek, her only visible hint of vulnerability.

"You're going to leave her alone, and you're not going to call again."

"And you are?"

"Sonja Pederson."

"That doesn't mean anything to me."

"Iola's my stepmother."

"Oh." Iola had never mentioned a daughter. "You don't want me to see Iola?"

"That's what I said. Want me to write it out for you, or do you think you can remember it?"

"Why do you care?"

"You think about it for a while. You'll figure it out. Jesus, Iola really robbed the cradle this time."

She'd looked familiar all along, but now it came to me. "Have I met you before? I've seen you down on Alki."

The statement and change of subject surprised her. "I . . . What?"

"I've seen you skating. You show up around lunchtime. You have an older pair of K2s. Seventy-millimeter wheels that need rotating. I could fix those for you."

"I know you think you're a hotshot. But leave Iola alone or I'll make things happen you won't like."

"This is a joke, right?"

She pushed me against the car again. "Don't piss me off."

"I don't fight girls, but if you keep this up I might break that rule." I'd barely finished the sentence before she had my thumb in her fist and was levering me until my knees were pressed into the damp sod. For a minute I thought she was going to break my thumb.

"Okay," I said. "I get your point. Geez. Let go, girlie."

She dropped my hand and stepped back. "Don't call me *girlie.*"

"Girlie, sir. I still don't understand what this is to you," I said, working my hand to get the blood flowing.

She proceeded toward a small car parked in front of the house next door. "Just remember what I told you. Tick me off, Gum, you'll be sorry."

"I'm already sorry."

I thought about Sonja Pederson while I drove up the hill to California Avenue and the West Seattle Junction near Station 32. So Sonja was Iola's daughter. Three generations living in one house.

One of the few things Iola had told me about her father,

whom she had called *Bernard,* was that he was a gun nut and
that he'd trained her to use just about every weapon ever
made. For her birthday once she'd asked for a necklace but
he'd given her a twelve-gauge shotgun instead. He must have
given Sonja her share of guns, too. In addition to martial arts
training.

By the time I got to my mom's apartment house at the
Junction, she had been standing on the sidewalk with her
bags for forty-five minutes. As usual, she had a complete set
of maps, routes, and plans. "What do you want?" she said,
asking the question she'd been asking my whole life.

"Whatever *you* want."

"Well. Yes. But what do *you* want?"

I wanted my mother to be well, but that wasn't going to
happen. "How about we drive up to the mountain, follow
whatever route you pick, and see what we can?"

"Sounds good to me."

It had always been just the two of us, but Mom and I were
closer now than ever. When we first got the diagnosis, I cried
for two days, but Judy Gum took the news like a trooper,
rolled up her sleeves the way she'd been doing her whole life,
and went on about her business—in this case, the business of
wringing the most out of what little time she had left.

We followed Highway 410 out of Enumclaw, driving the
two-lane road higher and higher through forested foothills,
every once in a while catching a glimpse of the volcano we
were ascending. As usual, Mom, who wanted to see every
last scrap of the planet before she left it, had me stop at every
viewpoint and lookout, and as usual, her enthusiasm was in-
fectious. We had four days to explore Mount Rainier National Park and environs, or until Mom got tired, whichever
came first. Four days before C shift worked again and I had
to be back at Station 29. Four days in which to forget my
troubles, in which to evade Iola and her fruitloop daughter.
Four days in which to ponder the situation with Tronstad and
Johnson and the bearer bonds.

We camped at the White River Campground the first
night, and though it was cold in the two-man tent, we made

it through to morning, when I started a campfire and heated up some hot chocolate. Over a breakfast of scrambled eggs, Mom told me a joke she thought I could take to the guys at work. She'd always been fond of jokes, but I noticed as she got sicker, so did her jokes.

It went like this: What did the seven dwarfs do after Snow White woke up? *They went back to masturbation.*

It was ironic, because before her illness, Mom wouldn't have told a raunchy joke if her life depended on it. Now maybe she thought it did.

During breakfast we got out the binoculars I'd bought surplus at the Army/Navy store in downtown Seattle and searched the east face of Emmons Glacier for climbers, finding two parties moving like ticks on a sheet in the sunshine. After spending the morning in the camp, I packed up and Mom drove my WRX up the mountain to Sunrise while I hiked the three uphill miles to meet her in the parking lot. When I got there she was leaning against the hood in her blue fleece jacket, basking in the sunshine. We were going through one of the warmest periods in Northwest history, and temperatures on the mountain climbed into the seventies during the day. No wonder the glaciers were wasting away.

We did some easy hiking above Sunrise, then drove around the mountain to Paradise, stopping along the way at Panther Creek and taking in small portions of the Wonderland Trail, Mom clicking pictures all the while. We'd already explored every beach and mountain in Oregon and Washington and camped in almost every campground from California to British Columbia. We'd said good-bye to each other a hundred times without ever once putting it into words.

11. GHANET'S SECRET HISTORY

Infused with a dystopian premonition that when Sears showed up the cracks of hell were going to start showing below our feet, I drove to work an hour early on Friday. In the silent beanery bordered by the wall of food lockers, the sheer familiarity of my surroundings instilled a calm I hadn't felt on the pacific slopes of Mount Rainier, where I'd become more and more worried about the bonds.

During our trip, I'd spent an inordinate amount of time trying to dissect my two-year relationship with Johnson and Tronstad. In one sense we were family, I the little brother they'd tutored and protected since my first day in the company. Yet in another sense we were a triangle of interwoven secrets and hidden grudges.

In public Johnson was all smiles around Tronstad, who played endless practical jokes on him, many of them later repeated in reverse by Johnson. It was funny to watch, partly because Johnson was so good-natured about it. It was also good not to be part of it, because I'm not sure I would have been so good-natured if I found my food locker stuffed full of packing peanuts every shift for a month. Or if I had a digital camera and a notebook for recording interesting alarms and then one day downloaded a picture I hadn't taken of the notebook clenched between somebody's hairy butt cheeks. Johnson got his licks in, too: a condom stretched over the trailer hitch on Tronstad's truck, loaded with liquid soap so that it looked as if it'd already performed its function; a water balloon inside Tronstad's helmet that burst over his head when he put the helmet on.

It was as much a concession to my personality as anything else that I wasn't included in their endless rounds of practical jokes. While I thought the gags were funny, they didn't suit my temperament the way they suited Johnson's and Tronstad's, who were both capable of absolute silliness.

At the station Johnson and I remained friendly and often engaged in long dialogues about the oddities of life, dialogues I looked forward to. Johnson made a habit of analyzing various personalities in the department, sometimes successfully, more often through a lens of wishful thinking and half-baked conjecture. It was amusing when he got it right and even more amusing when he didn't.

"I'm interested in what makes people tick," Johnson said. "For me that puts the spice in life."

I was interested in what made *Johnson* tick but had not quite figured it out. He was less a man who'd accrued a bank of knowledge over his thirty-seven years than one who was still in the process of identifying the basic structure of the world around him—a wandering soul who never tired of trying to puzzle out life in the same way that a hopelessly untalented but determined skier or softball player never tired of striving for skills he couldn't achieve.

As far as Ted Tronstad went, I liked him and for the most part thought he liked me, but the truth was, he and I had more of an alpha male thing going. I'd pondered this a lot, because the way it started was so typical, especially for firefighters, most of whom tend to be aggressive personalities to begin with. Not that I was particularly aggressive. In fact, I considered myself a relatively timid person who was capable of displaying streaks of bravado when required.

Tronstad had been a hockey player in his youth and continued to play ice and roller hockey on city teams, hitting the trail on in-line skates three or four times a week, usually with a hockey stick and a ball.

Early in my tenure at 29's he brought his skates, and one morning after shift we drove down to Alki, he in his new truck—which was repossessed several months later—and I in my new WRX—which I bought after getting my first paycheck. He'd talked all shift about how I wouldn't be able to keep up with him, but once we started skating I could see he didn't have the wheels or bearings to maintain the kind of speeds I routinely hit. After playing with him for a while, I skated away while he chased futilely. He never got over it.

Sometimes friends break something small and seemingly unimportant between them, and at the time it seems like a scratch on the paint job of their relationship, when it's actually closer to a blown engine. Most days I didn't feel any spite between us, but other times the alpha male bullshit separated us like a tidal pool. It didn't help that I got all that recognition for bringing the victims out of Arch Place when he knew I should have been disciplined for missing the rig.

Because of the stolen bonds, all three of us had our necks on the chopping block. I hadn't thought so at first, but four days on Mount Rainier had given me time to think. We'd lied to Sears—*I'd* lied to Sears—and if the bonds were worth anything, we would certainly be ejected from the fire department and sent to jail. It was hard to see a way around it or to know how I'd gotten into this pickle. I would have gone nuts if I hadn't been so confident the bonds were worthless.

In the Seattle Fire Department you could cheat on your EMT exams the way Tronstad and Johnson routinely did, and they would look the other way. You could do drugs and plead chemical dependency—they would get you therapy. You could screw up and plead stress—they would transfer you to a quieter station. You could get contentious and plead personal problems—they would get you counseling. But the minute you stole anything you were terminated.

Maybe I should have turned Tronstad in a long time ago, but how do you justify causing a friend to lose his job because he swiped a picture frame worth five dollars?

It was quarter to seven when I tiptoed down the hallway to the dark beanery and turned on the coffeemaker. I was scanning the newspapers when Hampsted came in and headed for the coffee machine. Hampsted, a B-shifter, was a tall, sleepy-eyed man who seemed to take life in stride. He'd been a stock-car racer before joining the department, an adrenaline junky in a department full of adrenaline junkies.

"You seen this?" he asked, keeping his voice low so as not to wake the sleeping officers and the night watch down the hallway.

"What?"

He nodded at a newspaper clipping on the bulletin board, an article topped by a photo I suddenly recognized as Charles Scott Ghanet, taken twenty-five or thirty years ago. No doubt Hampsted tried to engage me in conversation over the next few minutes, but if he did, I didn't hear a word.

Death of Local Man Spurs FBI Investigation

BY ROB HARDING
Seattle Times staff reporter

When King County Medical Examiner investigators began searching a local man's house after his body was found there late Sunday night, they made a startling discovery.

For twenty-seven years Charles Scott Ghanet, sixty-eight, who died of natural causes, was known to his neighbors as a retired longshoreman and deck hand from San Diego. Investigators have discovered, however, that the man neighbors knew as Charles Scott Ghanet was actually George S. David, whose name has been on the FBI's Most Wanted list since 1976, according to Fred Hagerty, agent in charge of the FBI's Seattle office. David used various aliases during his lifetime, including Brian Wilson, David Geiger, and Renee Whipple.

At twenty-three, David received a four-year sentence at Missouri State Penitentiary for armed robbery and assault. After his release, he is alleged to have committed a series of robberies of gem dealers, private gold collectors, and armored cars in the Midwest. In 1978 David fled Ohio just minutes in front of an IRS raid that could have put him behind bars for close to half a century.

Dozens of bank robberies by a lone gunman in Minnesota, North Dakota, and California were eventually linked to David, and a fingerprint taken from a stolen car he used in one of the robberies tied him to the murder of a confederate, though he was never apprehended for these crimes. David has been proclaimed one of the most successful armed robbers in United States history.

Wells Fargo and a consortium of Midwest banks eventually posted a reward of $300,000 for David's capture, a reward that has never been collected.

As of Monday, local police, FBI, ATF, and Treasury agents were combing David's house in West Seattle for clues to what he might have done with some of the more than six million dollars he is thought to have stolen over a fourteen-year period. In addition, agents are looking for money David might have earned after putting large amounts of the stolen funds into legitimate investments.

The last robbery attributed to David took place in Lake Oswego, Oregon, in 1981, where a local bank was robbed of $87,113 by a gunman who escaped on a stolen motorcycle.

Neighbors in West Seattle said the man they knew as Charles Scott Ghanet was a loner, a quiet neighbor who kept to himself and had frequent medical problems.

FBI agents say David's home was piled with junk and that it would take a week or more to sort through papers and documents in order to track down any remaining funds.

"Who would have thought that old guy was an armored-car robber?" said Hampsted, sipping his coffee. "This the first you heard of it?"

"I've been out of town."

"But you guys found it? Right?"

"We didn't find anything."

"You didn't find his body?"

"Oh. Yeah."

"You know they're tearing that house apart board by board. They're even digging up the backyard with a Bobcat."

"They find the money?"

"Not that we heard."

"Why would a guy with millions of dollars be living in that little house with all that junk?"

"You met him. He was nuts."

The odds of our bonds being phony had dwindled to practically nothing. There were hundreds of slips of paper in each sack, thousands altogether. It was easy to believe Tronstad's assertion that the three bags combined were worth twelve million dollars.

I couldn't believe I'd hidden them in Iola Pederson's garage as casually as if they were discount coupons for margarine.

My throat went dry at the prospect of how much trouble I was in.

12. CASH ME OUT, BABY, I'M BLOWIN' TOWN

"You talking to yourself?"

Lieutenant Sears breezed into the beanery and deposited a sack lunch in the refrigerator. His wife, Heather, got up in the morning before he left for work and put together a couple of sandwiches and a pile of sliced veggies, with a small bag of raisins for dessert. It seemed out of character, because according to Sears, she ruled the roost in their household and dominated their decision making. Although she didn't have a job and he was often tired from having worked a twenty-four-hour shift, he ran all the household errands, did the chores, and did virtually all the shopping and cooking. Her sole concession to domesticity was the sack lunch. Johnson said it was because she knew we would see it.

We all thought the way she made him dance to her tune was funny, considering what a ball buster Sears was inside the department.

"You were talking to yourself," Sears said. Hampsted had left the room.

"Was I? I guess it was this article."

"What article's that?"

"The Charles Scott Ghanet thing."

"Charles Scott made the paper? I'll have to read it when I get time."

I got up and walked across the bay to the firefighters' quarters and my locker, changed into my uniform, and inspected my face in the bathroom mirror. I only needed to shave every two or three days, but I ran the electric shaver over my face anyway.

The news about Ghanet had hit me like a falling house. If

Sears didn't nab us, the local gendarmes would, and if the local gendarmes didn't, the FBI would, and if the FBI didn't, some tenacious reporter would do it for them—all of which didn't even take into account the treasure seekers who were bound to show up. I could turn myself in right now, but at this late date I couldn't see how it would make any difference.

My only consolation was that we hadn't made bigger targets of ourselves by indulging in conspicuous binge spending. If you were going to be a criminal, you'd better be a smart one—like Ghanet. Look poor; act poor. Keep your money where nobody will find it. Avoid ostentatious displays of wealth.

I relieved my man early—actually, my woman, Stanislow—and busied myself in the apparatus bay doing normal morning maintenance in the hope that keeping busy would stave off my mounting anxiety. I half expected Tronstad and Johnson to call in sick, but they showed up at their normal times, Ted at 0729, one minute to spare, and Robert six minutes later, at 0735. Sears and I were the only ones who routinely came in early. The drivers on the other shifts resented Johnson, who came in precisely five minutes late every shift. Whenever he needed somebody to trade shifts or stay over a half hour, he got stiffed, a fact he attributed to racial prejudice, when in fact it was due to his chronic tardiness, a habit that, ironically, several others unfairly attributed to race.

If Johnson and Tronstad knew about Ghanet, they didn't let on. Tronstad was bouncing on the balls of his feet and grinning ear to ear, and Johnson moved about the apparatus bay whistling as he checked the lights on the rig, the fuel level, and the water level in the tank, looking over the hose beds and equipment and glancing at his watch periodically.

Johnson approached the workbench, where I was running the Lifepak through the morning tests. "You see the newspapers?" I asked.

"I saw." He grinned, his teeth white and even. "We got the real deal. Think about it. No taxes, either. We're rich."

"We're not rich, Robert. We're in trouble."

"How do you figure?"

"To start with, there's a thousand cops looking for what we have. And Sears doesn't know about Ghanet right now, but once he does, he's going to figure out what that bond was all about. I wouldn't be surprised if the chief of the department and the police show up for roll call."

The permanent frown lines in Johnson's forehead deepened into trenches, as if this was the first time he'd considered the bonds a liability instead of an asset.

"I think we should turn it in right now. Tell them we thought it was worthless. That Tronstad took it and we would have given it back earlier but we thought it was junk."

"No way in hell. I'm not doing it."

"What if I turn it in? I'm the one who has it."

"I'll tell them you stole it."

"You wouldn't do that."

"Try me."

"Jesus, Johnson. You're losing your marbles here."

"*You* are, if you think I'm giving back twelve million dollars."

"You two having another lovers' quarrel?" said Tronstad, grinning as he passed us on his way to the watch office for eight o'clock roll call.

As usual, Sears had typed out a schedule for us. No other officer I'd heard of was as meticulous, or as obsessive.

"Listen," Sears said after we'd gathered in the watch office for roll call, "I've been out of town at a women's rugby tournament with Heather, so I haven't had time to think about this—" He pulled the folded bond out of his shirt pocket and tapped it against his mustache. "—but I know something is going on." The shaved stubble on his face caught a shaft of sunlight coming through the window on the front door. I liked him. I couldn't help it. He was going to write charges on us and probably put at least one of us in jail, but I liked him. He was a man who tried to do the right thing. "I don't know what you three are up to, but I'm going to get to the bottom of it before the day is out."

He looked at each of us in turn. "I hope this isn't what I think it is, because I'm so proud of you guys," Sears said.

"You're the best-drilled company in Battalion Seven. You know, when I first got here, you were a joke, but now you work together like Chinese acrobats."

"Thanks, Lieutenant," said Johnson.

"Yeah, thanks," I said.

"How'd the rugby tournament go?" Tronstad asked.

Sears handed him the list of chores he'd printed out and said, "You just worry about today. I've got a union meeting, but I should be back around suppertime. Maybe a little after. You'll be acting lieutenant. The chief is sending somebody up here from Thirty-two's to fill in your spot."

"Yes, sir," said Tronstad, saluting smartly. In the fire department we didn't salute our officers unless making a joke or mocking them. Sears gave him a withering look.

The three of us walked down the hallway to the cramped beanery, where the television was tuned to one of the national morning shows. The interviewer was quizzing the attorney of a murder suspect. Johnson turned the sound up to cover our voices and said, "Gum thinks we're in trouble."

"Don't be an ass." Tronstad slapped me across the shoulders and grinned. "What trouble?"

"How about a bunch of FBI agents combing through Ghanet's house?" I said. "We gotta give them back."

"They don't even know Ghanet had the bonds. You don't think I left any lying around, do you?"

"How would you know in all that junk?"

"And how're you going to explain the one Sears has?" Johnson asked.

"I can explain anything."

"Maybe we could make an anonymous phone call and tell them where the bonds are," I suggested.

"Oh, yeah," said Tronstad, playing with his mustache. "That would be brilliant. They'd be on us like stink on shit. Go ahead and make the call, if you want to get jailed for grand larceny and obstruction of justice."

Johnson looked at me. "He's right. We're in this and we can't get out. It's like when you're a kid on a sled going down a fast hill with a lot of rocks around. You ride it out, because if you bail, you're going to get hurt. The sled keeps going faster and faster, and your only chance is to ride it out."

"Yeah," said Tronstad. "Unless you want to go to jail and deal with a bunch of butt pirates. Pretty boy like you would be wearing lipstick and eyeshadow by the end of the first week."

"Geez, Tronstad," I said. "Don't talk like that."

"Don't talk like what?"

Tronstad and I had both been aware that she was coming through the patio door, but we'd kept talking, the way you do sometimes when you're caught up in a conversation.

The lieutenant's wife was tall and athletic in a gawky sort of way, with thick, tattooed ankles and a mane of blond hair that was a chronic mess. The cargo shorts she was wearing showed off rugby bruises on both legs. She spoke to us as if she were one of the guys, and I liked that about her. Heather Wynn—she'd kept the last name of her first husband, who'd died in a car wreck. "You guys look like you're having a meeting."

"We don't have any secrets from you," said Johnson, stepping forward for the obligatory hug. "What brings you here on this fine sunny day?"

"I need to speak to Sweeney for a few minutes. Whose new truck is that out there?"

"That'd be mine," said Tronstad.

"You bought a new truck?" I blurted.

"There's a new Cadillac SUV out there, too. Whose is that?"

I turned to Robert Johnson, who at least realized the insanity of what he'd done and looked chagrined. "It's actually . . . kind of a demo thing. We'll probably take it back. I'm not really sure we can afford a new car right now."

We all knew the finance company had repossessed Tronstad's original Ford F-350 for nonpayment. Since then he'd done the forty-five-minute commute from his apartment in Kent on his Harley. Most people who had as much time in the department as Tronstad had bought a house by now, but Tronstad fiddled away while Rome burned.

"And what's this?" Heather took Robert Johnson's wrist and pulled it toward her. "*Longines?* This must have cost a pretty penny."

"I got a deal on it," said Johnson, who'd bought a new Cadillac *and* a five-thousand-dollar watch.

"And what about you, Gum? Everybody else has something new."

"He's got a new girlfriend," said Johnson.

"Yeah," said Tronstad. "Old enough to be his mother."

"Ooooh," Heather teased. "An older woman? Is that true, Gum? What is she? Thirty?"

"A little older."

"I'm tellin' ya, she's old enough to be his mommy," said Tronstad. "She's fifty if she's a day."

"She's forty-five."

"What's she like?" Heather asked. "How old is she really?"

Heather Wynn had eight to ten years on me and had always dismissed me rather casually, I thought, until this news about an older woman, which seemed to intrigue her.

"Heather." Lieutenant Sears appeared in the doorway behind us. "I thought I heard your voice. Why didn't you come straight to my office?"

"The guys and I were having a chat, honey. Have you met Gum's new girlfriend?"

"I don't believe I have." Sears looked at me for a moment, then turned back to his wife. We knew they weren't happy together, that she'd talked of divorce and left him several times, but we also knew he clung to her like a nonswimmer clung to an overturned raft.

When we were alone again, I sat heavily at the table and looked at Johnson and Tronstad. "You *both* bought new cars? The cops are looking for Ghanet's money, and you bought new cars? You don't think anybody's going to connect that?"

"I didn't know Robert was buying one," said Tronstad, picking up the sports page from the morning's *PI*. "I'm the one who needed it. He didn't need that gold-plated watch, either."

"It's not plate. It's solid," Johnson said. "And I didn't know about Ghanet when I bought the Caddy. It didn't come out in the paper until the next day."

"You must have gone directly from my house to the dealer," I said.

"I can buy a car if I want," Johnson said.

"It's not like we called each other up and compared notes," said Tronstad. " 'Sides, I had a handful of the bonds, and I wanted to see if I could cash them."

"You cashed some bonds?" I cried.

"Just enough for a down payment on the truck."

"We're dead meat."

"Don't be silly," said Tronstad. "This is a matter of bluffing our way through. Stuff like this used to happen in the Air Force all the time. I always weaseled out of it."

Johnson sat next to Tronstad and propped his elbows on the table. His uniform shirt was immaculate and stiff from the cleaners. "What else did you buy, Tronstad?"

"I mighta bought some other shit." He leaned forward and whispered conspiratorially, "I'll tell you this. Those bonds are as good as gold. Maybe better, because they're easier to pack around. Especially the U.S. Treasury bearer bonds. People at the bank thought I was an oil sheik." He opened his wallet and showed us a hundred-dollar bill. "That's all I got left."

"You spend everything, don't you, Ted? Every red cent." Johnson glared at him.

"I just showed you a hundred bucks, didn't I? Look." Tronstad reached out and tapped the back of my hand. "Maybe after Sears leaves we can take the rig and pick them up, huh?"

"I'm not getting the bonds today. Not so you can spend them."

Tronstad smiled. "Who put you in charge?"

"You did."

"You did what?" Chief Abbott bustled into the room, grabbed a coffee cup, filled it, slopping some onto the floor, and pulled out a chair. Before he could sit down, his phone rang. "I'll get that in my office," he said, hustling down the corridor, his footsteps on the wooden floor like cannon shots, an aroma of black coffee and Aqua Velva aftershave wafting in his wake. I figured he was still jacked up from talking to Heather, on whom he had a crush. We'd heard them talking up the hall.

"Around here we gotta shut up about this," said Johnson.

"No shit," said Tronstad.

I didn't want the bonds, and I certainly didn't want the trouble they were dragging down on us, but the only escape I could see was a confession. What worked in my favor was that Tronstad and Johnson had both squandered money and I hadn't. What worked against me was the fact that they would both be pissed enough to tell lies about me and, worse yet, the truth about Arch Place. It didn't help my case that I was in possession of the bonds. In fact, it sort of made me look like the ringleader.

13. LAST CHANCE TO RESIGN

After Heather left the building, Lieutenant Sears came into the beanery and shut the door, sealing us off from Chief Abbott in the other room. He tossed the wrinkled Sierre Leone bank bond note onto the table. "Okay. One last chance. Tell me where this came from."

My heart began pounding in my ears. This was my opportunity to send Tronstad to jail and avoid it myself, my opportunity to make everything right, to take the pain in my gut and medicate it with truth and justice. The problem was, I wasn't sure I had the nerve to send a coworker to jail, somebody I'd worked with for two years, somebody who'd made me laugh, somebody who'd protected me when nobody else would. What made it even tougher was that he was sitting right next to me. I needed time to think.

The three of us sat at the table while Lieutenant Sears looked at each of us in turn.

Johnson scratched his chin. "Gee, I don't know."

"You don't know what?" Sears asked.

"He don't know what you're talking about, Lieut," said Tronstad. "None of us do. See, that piece of paper you got there? You're right. It came from—at least I think it came from—Ghanet's place. Musta had something sticky on my boot, because I found it in the rig on the floor. I was showin' it to Gum and Robert the other morning when you walked in and copped it. I wonder if it's worth anything."

"You don't expect me to believe that, do you?" Sears said.

"Is that an official fire department question?"

Sears eyeballed Tronstad and then me. He'd been looking at me more than the others, and I had the feeling I was his lie detector, as if something in my face confirmed or denied veracity. I didn't think I was quite that transparent, but perhaps I was. "I'm just asking," he said.

"Because if that's an official fire department question," said Tronstad, with a smirk, "I need to call my union rep."

"You're taking this pretty lightly."

"I'm not joking," Tronstad said.

"Neither am I."

"Trust me. You're all wet on this one, Lieut."

"I hope so."

A few minutes later, the detail from 32's showed up and Sears left. The detail was a man named Bob Oleson, one of those big-boned men who'd come into the department a few pounds overweight but who had recently ballooned to even larger dimensions. Later, when Oleson was out of earshot, Tronstad looked at me and chuckled. "Even if Sears gets somebody to listen, how's he going to explain he thought we were thieves and then left me in charge?"

Somehow I didn't believe Sears's foolishness nor Tronstad's reasoning was going to sway the FBI. We were in trouble here, and I didn't know what to do about it. I was beginning to feel like that flying pig, whizzing through the deep blue twilight, no way to slow myself, much less stop.

I had a lot to think about as we rode around the district taking care of the tasks Lieutenant Sears had left us: testing hydrants, doing a couple of building reinspections, visiting a preschool. He'd asked us to run three wet drills, too. Johnson, Oleson, and I were willing, but Tronstad sprinkled water on the hose bed so it would look as if we'd pumped water through it, saying, "The bastard drills us enough without *us* drilling us. It's like asking a kid to go out to the woodshed and paddle himself."

In the back of my mind was the thought that I might end up in prison over this. I didn't think so, but it was possible. Going to prison would keep me separated from my mother during her last year of life. After the way she'd dedicated her life to me, I couldn't do that to her.

Finding herself pregnant at seventeen, my mother left Spokane and centered her life around me. I never met my father. The official story is that my mother divorced him before I was born, but by the time I was ten I knew that was bogus.

Her parents were hard-line Christians and never forgave her for her out-of-wedlock pregnancy. Mother was the youngest of five siblings, raised after the others had left home, so she wasn't close to my aunts and uncles. My grandparents are in their eighties and now live in Spokane, a six-hour drive from Seattle, a couple of cold fish who for twenty-five years have treated my mother like an outcast. We rarely saw them when I was growing up, though I now visit on my own once or twice a year.

My mother has good days, as the last four had been, days where you almost wouldn't know she was sick, and then she has days where she gulps painkillers and gets a distant look in her eyes. All along she's been desirous of the same privacy in death she enjoyed in life and has refused to inform anybody in the family she's sick.

Thinking of my mother made me even angrier that Johnson and Tronstad had splurged on new cars. We might have given the money back anonymously, but our chances of that were dwindling by the minute. I had assumed that under all their silly pranks they were mature individuals, but now as I viewed them through the clarifying prism of their greed, I knew I couldn't have been more wrong.

I saw how weak Johnson was, how flighty and vain Tronstad was. Johnson, who didn't know his district and refused to study it, should never have been the driver on Engine 29. Anybody with a smidgeon of pride would have either learned his district or given up the post, yet he did neither. The department might have turned him out of the spot, but that wasn't how things worked. Johnson liked to palaver about the fact that he was a small cog in a big machine, that he didn't have control over his life, philosophizing endlessly without ever coming to any useful conclusions. Outwardly, he was jolly and always in a pleasant mood, but under the surface there was a layer of brooding most people didn't notice.

Tronstad was a different cat altogether; no deep thought there.

Nobody who worked with Ted Tronstad ever forgot the impromptu stand-up comedy routines he put on at the drop of a hat. He was funny in a Robin Williams way. Everybody said he should audition for *Saturday Night Live.* He was gregarious and championed his friends, as he had me after the incident at Arch Place, yet on the downside, he had money problems, women problems, and a bunch of long-haired, tattooed, Harley-riding buddies who'd spent more of their lives in taverns and prisons than I cared to think about.

One thing Tronstad didn't have that Johnson did was a kind heart. Johnson rarely spoke ill of anyone, while Tronstad rarely missed a chance to mock or denigrate just about everyone he met: every client, patient, and fellow firefighter he came into contact with. I'd always dismissed it as some sort of slanted attempt at black humor, but it was more; it was a cover-up of his basic insecurity. He had a negative outlook on life, and that outlook made him see the worst in people.

Even though he choked up when we were around injured kids and could be as empathetic as anyone with certain adult patients, there were times when I believed Tronstad's heart was made of chilled titanium. Perhaps the callousness came about because his father beat him when he was a child. Or because his mother did, too. Or because he'd left home at seventeen to join the Army, where he had a rough go of it, switching to the Air Force three years later.

After lunch Johnson came into the beanery stealthily, closing the door behind him with exaggerated care. Tronstad was reading the sports page and I was rereading the article on Charles Scott Ghanet, or whatever his name really was. The chief had been gone for hours.

"Oleson's on the other side sawing the z's in front of *Butch Cassidy and the Sundance Kid.* We need to talk. We gotta figure out what we're going to do," said Johnson. "To prove we're not guilty."

"We don't have to prove shit," said Tronstad. "That's the beauty of this country. *They* have to prove *we* are guilty. And they can't do it."

"The cops have the bond," I said. "Or they will when Sears gives it to them. And you both bought new vehicles, plus you've got that new watch. They'll trace your transactions at the bank. Don't say they've got nothing. We need to turn that stuff in now."

"No way. To start with, Sears is not exactly Columbo. He's not going to prove anything. Split three ways, those bonds should be worth four million each. I don't know about you, but I'm going to Costa Rica, where I'm going to have me a different chick for every day of the week. With that much bread, they'll probably make me *El Presidente.*"

I'd pretty much decided to come clean with Sears when he returned that evening. I wasn't guilty of theft, and I didn't want to be guilty of conspiracy, either. I should have done it that morning, but I hadn't yet steeled myself against these two. They weren't going to get away with this, and even if they were, I didn't want stolen money.

Johnson and I looked at each other, knowing that the only things keeping Tronstad in the fire department were the bi-weekly paychecks and the fact that he was behind in his rent, credit card payments, and other bills. He didn't know any other way to manage his life and bought ice cream by the pint because if he took home half a gallon he'd horse it down at one sitting and get sick. A bundle of money would be gone in months, perhaps weeks.

Johnson and I continued our conversation late that afternoon in the basement, where he lifted weights and I pedaled the stationary bicycle. "I'll tell you this," said Johnson. "If Tronstad gets his hands on a penny of that money, he'll spend it before we can blink."

"You didn't do such a bad job yourself."

"I didn't know Ghanet was famous when I went to that dealership and the jewelers."

"What kills me about this is, I didn't do anything wrong."

"You and I are in the same boat there." I glanced over to see whether Johnson was serious. I hadn't spent any money and I hadn't reneged on my promise to take the bonds back. In fact, I'd tried to take them back when I drove past Ghanet's place that next morning. If the cops hadn't been there, the bonds would be on his property now. I couldn't see how Johnson and I were in the same boat. Not at all.

Johnson said, "I may not be the brightest penny in the jar, but I'm not stupid. When the dust settles I might buy some jewelry for Paula, and I'm pretty sure I'll go out and get a new computer for LaQuisha, but other than that, I'm not going to do anything to attract notice. Oh, and there's a gun I want. A nine millimeter. I *was* thinking about putting money on some vacation property in North Carolina on the shore where my folks live, but I'm not going to do anything stupid."

"Robert, we have to give it back. All of it. There is no other option."

"I can't get out of the lease agreement on the car."

"I thought you said you were taking the car back."

"I signed papers, man."

"You can get out of a lease."

"Well, yeah, maybe. But that ride is sweet." Johnson grinned at me, and I knew right then that as soon as I got off work the following morning I would recover the sacks and hand them over to the FBI. If they wanted to arrest me, I would have to live with it. "*I* can be discreet with money," Johnson continued. "Our trouble will be reining in Ted."

Johnson did a set of bench presses, huffing loudly each time he pushed the bar up. It was demoralizing to realize I would be turning him in for theft along with Tronstad.

"I read about Lotto winners," he said, swinging his legs to one side of the bench as he sat up. "Interesting stuff. The money almost never makes them happier. In fact, for most people it flat out ruins their lives. They did a study of twenty past winners of our state's lottery, and eighteen of them came out worse than before, both financially and emotionally— bankruptcies, divorces, lost friends, alcoholism. Two suicides. But I know that won't happen to me. I'm smarter than that. I'm praying for us, Gum. I'm praying Sears forgets all about that bond, and I'm praying the cops don't come sniffing around. I'm praying they find some money Ghanet was hiding and that it's in the Cayman Islands or someplace and they stop looking here. I'm praying for you, too, Gum. I'm praying for your mother. I'm praying for all of us."

"Thanks, Robert."

"What's all this praying about?" Neither of us had heard Chief Abbott descend the wooden steps to the basement. In fact, I hadn't heard him drive into the station. "You weren't talking about this, were you?"

Chief Abbott pulled a slip of paper out of his waistband and stretched it between his pudgy fingers. It was either the bond Lieutenant Sears had been carrying or a duplicate.

14. THE SMOKE ROOM

I don't know that I've ever met anybody who wanted to be liked more than Russell Abbott, or who had fewer clues on how to go about it. Yet, under the tail-wagging, waiting-to-be-petted puppy display he put on, there lurked a surly mongrel that snapped without warning.

Today he was wearing new sneakers, freshly laundered shorts that stretched halfway up his round torso, and an ironed fire department T-shirt. He held the bearer bond with a look on his round face that approached glee.

"Where'd you get that?" Johnson asked.

"The bigger question is, where did you get it?"

"Sears gave it to you?" Johnson asked.

"Or an investigator."

"What do you mean *an investigator*?" Johnson was unable to conceal his growing panic. The more nervous he got, the tighter his smile became and the shinier his black cheeks. "Are you talking about a fire department investigator? Or are you talking about the police?"

"I don't know. Which would be worse for you?"

"Don't have nothing to do with me." Johnson flattened his back against the weight bench and reached for the bar. He'd been bench-pressing his body weight, 240 pounds. I continued pedaling. When it became obvious we weren't going to beg for information, the chief stood in front of the full-length mirror and began waving his arms in small circles. His practice was to do light calisthenics for exactly twenty minutes, no more, no less, then take a half-hour shower, all of which he called his fifty-minute workout. Without prompting, you could get Tronstad to do a hilarious spoof of the workout, which had made Sweeney Sears laugh so hard one evening, he cried.

After several more minutes of torturous silence, Johnson went upstairs and left me alone in the basement with the chief.

"You boys concoct a story to tell Sears when he gets back tonight?" Abbott asked when we were alone.

"Sir?"

"What kind of story are you going to tell your lieutenant?"

I shrugged.

"Oh, come on, now. You tell me where the bond came

from, and I'll make sure you're not included in the fallout. I know those other jerks got you into it. How many of these bonds did you boys steal?"

I would tell Sears later, but I wasn't going to tell this bastard. "Tronstad thinks he brought it out of Charles Scott's stuck to his boot."

"But *you* were on the call. You were inside Ghanet's house. You helped find the body."

"I was there."

"And you didn't see any bearer bonds? Oh, come on, now, sweet cheeks. I find that hard to believe." He'd never used "sweet cheeks" on me before, although I'd heard him use it on others, and the condescension made me angrier than I thought it would. "What would you say if I told you I took this to a bank today and they told me it's as real as a Saturday night headache, that they were going to hand over a thousand smackeroos, no questions asked. You believe that, Gum?"

"If you say so."

"You trying to tell me you haven't cashed any yourself?"

"There's only the one."

"It gets deeper and deeper, doesn't it?"

"What?"

"Go ahead and play dumb. It's all going to come out soon enough." He gave me a self-satisfied smile. "By the way. I've scheduled a drill for your crew this evening. Sears called and won't be back until around ten. I thought we'd go down to Station Fourteen and see what sort of props they have set up. How would you like that?"

"Great."

"I thought that's what you'd say."

Drilling for Chief Abbott, who wielded practice sessions more as a form of punishment than as a learning tool, was always a contest of wills. Tronstad had it right when he said, "Abbot likes to see you smile while he's fucking you in the ass."

In the beginning, I thought surely Abbott's tales of his own prowess on the fire ground were at least partly true, that years ago he'd been stronger, fleeter, and trimmer and had fought fire with the best. But the old-timers at Station 32, where Russell Abbott had worked as a firefighter and then ten years later as a lieutenant, told us he'd been worse than useless on the fire ground—that he'd been downright dangerous. Over the years he'd been the cause of several firefighter injuries, unsafe with a chainsaw and dangerous with a hose line, and after a fire, when confronted, he always denied his inappropriate actions.

What confused me in the beginning was how sensible and calm he seemed around the station. His stories, mostly of others screwing up at fires, were detailed, witty, and often displayed an impressive store of firefighting tactics and strategy.

There were other clues, though. Once while responding on an alarm on Admiral Way in the battalion chief's red Suburban, Abbott got cut off in traffic. When he pulled alongside the dilapidated Buick that had cut him off, the driver, a steel-mill worker on his way home from work, gave Abbott the bone. Abbott, by now code-greened on the original alarm, began chasing the Buick, something he was not trained or authorized to do. He radioed the dispatcher to send the cops, updating his location and direction of travel every minute or so, his exclamations growing more shrill as the chase lengthened. Abbott ended up ambushing the Buick at a stoplight and holding the incredulous driver for the police.

During the commotion, Abbott began to feel chest pains and called for a medic unit. When the medics arrived and told him his heart was healthy, that he was only hyperventilating, he threw a temper tantrum that got him into such a state, they put oxygen on him and transported him to Harborview Medical Center. A year later he found himself in another dispute with a civilian, this time at the scene of an accident, after which he called the medics and told them he thought he was having "another" heart attack. Nobody bothered to remind him that he'd never had a first one.

Battalion chiefs drilled engine companies at their discretion, and in our battalion everybody knew if you crossed Abbott, you drilled. There was some speculation that perhaps he also drilled his wife and eight children when they got out of hand.

We made enchiladas, and the five of us—Abbott, myself, Tronstad, Johnson, and Oleson—enjoyed a meal that was so pleasant, we were taken aback when afterward Chief Abbott pushed himself away from the table and said, "Well, boys. You ready to do it?"

"Shit, Chief," said Tronstad. "You're not still thinking about taking us out, are you?"

"I'll meet you at Fourteen's."

"That stinks, Chief," said Tronstad. "We had a busy day. Besides, we did three wet drills this morning."

"Then you'll be especially sharp, won't you? Of course, we *could* sit around and talk about that bearer bond," Abbott said, leaning his thick arms on the dinner table, drumming the tabletop with his fingertips. Bob Oleson was the only one in the room who didn't know what he was talking about.

"I must have tracked it out of that place without knowing it," said Tronstad.

"Sure. Great," said Abbott, standing. "By the way, I'll call the dispatcher and put you out of service. And I'll swing by Thirty-two's and drop off Oleson. No point in drilling *him,* is there? Or would you like to drill with them, Bobby?"

Oleson said, "Uh, actually, I tweaked my back earlier."

"That's what I thought. Just the three of you, then. Station Fourteen. Half an hour."

Bob Oleson transferred his equipment from our crew cab to the chief's Suburban, and we all left the station.

Fire Station 14 sat on the reclaimed tide flats in the industrial area just south of downtown Seattle and was a working fire house as well as the training center for the department. Drill schools were conducted in the classroom inside the station and on the court in back. As we drove, I could hear Johnson and Tronstad griping that it was getting dark, and that Abbott wasn't drilling any other companies. That this was some sort of revenge. That Abbott was a butthole.

"Where did he even get that bond?" Tronstad asked.

Johnson said, "There isn't any chance he got one of the

bags, is there, Gum? You didn't do something stupid like hide them in the hose tower?"

"Of course not."

"Shit," said Tronstad. "Sears promised he'd keep this between him and us. I can't see him breaking a confidence. He's too buttoned-down for that."

"I think it's weird that Abbott took Oleson back to Thirty-two's," said Johnson. "After he drills us, how's he going to get us back in service with only three guys? Are we going to go pick up Oleson again? Why not include Oleson in the drill?"

"He doesn't want witnesses," said Tronstad. I couldn't tell if he was kidding or not.

Station 14 was an off-pink building with red barn doors and a tile roof that looked as if it belonged in Southern California. While Fourth Avenue in front of the station was busy with truck traffic, Horton Street along the south side of the station was a dead end that provided a wide access to the drill court behind the station. I'd driven there every weekday for twelve weeks of drill school, where I had marched and worked and fallen on that drill court in the rain and heat until I thought I couldn't stand up any longer. I'd put up hundreds of ladders to the seven-story training tower and hooked up to the hydrants too many times to count.

When we pulled into the parking area behind the station, it was just after seven in the evening, so we'd missed the ongoing recruit class by an hour. The pavement was still damp from the hose drills they'd been doing all day. Off to the side, three reserve rigs were parked and tarped for the weekend.

Behind Station 14 was a wide-open parking area maybe 200 feet by 150, bordered on the west by the rear of the fire station, on the north by a fence and a tin-walled manufacturing facility of some sort, on the east by railroad tracks and a Metro bus route, on the south by Horton Street, and across that a pest control facility. Beside the door stood a seven-story tower with no glass in the windows and a fire escape on one side; the tower rose eighty feet.

You could smell the pungent odor of smoke as we drove

up, a smell that brought back sharp memories of my first twelve weeks in the department. The smoke room. In my recruit school we'd done it five weeks in a row, always on a Friday so recruits would have Saturdays and Sundays to recover.

Situated at the bottom of the tower, the smoke room was a small, concrete-walled room that always reeked. After the third or fourth week of recruit school the instructors would haul a burn barrel into the room, set a fire in it, then, after the fire got hot, stoke it down in order to produce as much smoke as possible. The windows would be shuttered. The door sealed. An instructor in full self-contained breathing apparatus, SCBA, would tend the fire. In groups at first, and then alone, recruits would be herded into the room, the door shut behind them.

The first exposure would be a minute. In later weeks it would be two minutes. In order to make certain recruits weren't holding their breath, they would be forced to answer questions and perform tasks such as looking for a bolt on the floor. You quickly learned the best air was low, maybe an inch off the concrete floor, and you just as quickly learned to crawl with your face on the floor, even if somebody in front of you had puked. The rules were simple. If you couldn't handle the smoke room, you were dismissed. In my class two recruits had been given the boot because they failed this bizarre job hurdle.

Even though we wore SCBAs at fires, there was always the possibility the SCBA would fail or you would get lost or trapped and your air would run out. The department needed to know you weren't going to panic when the smoke got thick. *You* needed to know you weren't going to panic. Your partners needed to know.

I couldn't help thinking about my drill school experiences as Johnson parked the rig and the three of us walked to the back door of Station 14. "They must be on a run," Johnson said, glancing at the empty beanery windows.

"I didn't hear them on the radio," I said.

Tronstad ducked into the tower while Johnson thumbed the combination lock on the back door. A moment later Tronstad stuck his head out the second-floor window of the tower and said, "Hey, guys. Check it out. They left the burn barrel going."

"They're supposed to clean all that up," I said. "*We* always did."

"The guys on Ladder Seven are going to be pissed when they get back," said Johnson. "The last thing they want to do is come out here and clean up after a bunch of recruits."

The other two went to the TV room on the first floor while I walked to the watch desk at the front of the station and learned from the day book that Ladder 7 and Aid 14 were attending a first-aid class at Station 25. They would be gone for hours.

In the TV room, Tronstad flipped through the channels with the remote while Johnson and I speculated on what drills Abbott would throw at us. The department had a whole roster of preprogrammed drills, much like football plays, in which each member on the apparatus played a specific role.

"Hell," said Tronstad, tuning in a lingerie show on one of the cable channels, "there's only seven or eight basic hose lays. How can you forget 'em?"

"You should be going over these with us," said Johnson.

"Not me. I'm a millionaire. Or I will be tomorrow when Doublemint hands over those bags."

It was almost fifteen minutes later when the back door to the station opened and Chief Abbott popped his head into the TV room. "Okay. Let's go."

Like convicts behind a guard, we followed him down the dark hallway and outside, where smoke was drifting out the lower tower windows and spreading across the twilight-dampened drill court. In the eastern sky the last of the day's sun reflected off the high clouds.

"Just coats, helmets, and gloves," said the chief.

The three of us walked over to Engine 29 and put on our gear, then walked back to where Chief Abbott stood with his hands behind his back. He wore his bunking coat and helmet as if he were going to perform along with us, although we knew he wasn't. He rocked back on his heels and then up on his toes, eyeballing us each in turn, his gray eyes bulging like grapes.

He stared at us for a few seconds. "I've got something new here. I had Training leave that burn barrel for us."

"Really?" said Johnson. "We thought somebody was in trouble."

"Somebody is in trouble," I whispered. "Us."

"Okay. Upstairs," said Abbott.

When I headed for the stairs at the base of the tower, Johnson said, "We have to know what drill we're doing, don't we?"

Tronstad touched him lightly on the shoulder. "Figure it out, Robert."

Johnson and Abbott stared at each other until it became clear to Johnson. "I ain't doin' it," he said. "You can't make us."

"I can make you do up and overs," said Abbott. "I can make you lay every foot of goddamn hose you've got on that rig, and then I can make you lay it again. I can keep you here all night long! That's what I can do!"

In drill school an "up and over" meant running up the stairs of the seven-story tower and down the fire escape, a steel ladder that dropped straight to the ground—or, if the instructors felt peevish, up the fire escape and down the stairs. It was an evolution where a mistake could drop a recruit eighty feet onto concrete. In drill school up and overs were done three times a day and were frequently used for punishment. It got so that scrambling down a seven-story fire escape at full speed meant nothing. But then, that was the point.

"You don't mind, Chief, I'll do the up and overs. Tell me when to stop," Tronstad said, heading up the stairs at a jog-trot.

Abbott barked after him, "Run, buddy. We don't *walk* our up and overs."

Johnson gave me a long look. I knew how much heights disagreed with him, how he'd forced himself to deal with it during drill school, and how he swore he would never get on a roof or climb a fire escape again if he could avoid it. It was one of the reasons he'd chosen to work at Station 29, where most of our fires were in single-story residences.

"Chief?" Johnson said. "I don't ever recall any firefighter past probation being asked to go in the smoke room."

"You don't think it's legal?"

"*I* never heard of it."

"You can step into the room with the kid here, or you can call your union rep after I write charges on you. Your choice."

Like a couple of reluctant adolescents trudging into the gym teacher's office for a paddling, we marched up the stairs to the smoke room, which was situated between floors one and two, Abbott on our heels. Outside the closed door Abbott pulled out a stopwatch on a knotted shoestring. Holding his breath, he opened the heavy metal door with one hand and said, "It's only one minute. Get in quick. I don't want to let that smoke out."

I stepped into the small concrete room and turned to the chief. "I'll do the up and overs."

"Too late," said Abbott, pushing Johnson into me. "Too damn late."

The door closed with a metallic *clank,* and we were submerged in darkness and smoke. It was as if we'd been put in a dungeon. Straining not to inhale, I turned on my flashlight but couldn't see much except grayness. When I finally took a breath, I felt that old familiar feeling that I was being smothered with a dirty pillow, as if my lungs had been stuffed with wool gloves.

15. PUSHED IN, SEALED UP, FUCKED OVER

Anybody who's been on the wrong side of a campfire when the wind switches directions has a hint of what the first two or three seconds in the smoke room are like. After those first few seconds, though, things grow exponentially worse in a way that is almost impossible to explain to someone who hasn't lived through it. The moment you realize you're not getting out is the moment you begin to think you're dying. Thirty seconds seem like half an hour, and a minute seems like a week.

You choke and your eyes water and your nose runs, and if you're not smart, you cough, and when you do that you inhale quickly and take in more smoke, which makes you cough again, and then you get into a cycle where it feels as if someone's taken a chainsaw to your lungs.

Some say it's as bad as being forced to breathe underwater. You crawl around on your stomach searching for that one good, clean patch of air that hasn't been saturated with carbon monoxide and soot. You try to move to the doorway to get the scant fresh air oozing in under the crack, but there's always somebody in front of you, somebody with his face pressed up against the door. Tonight that somebody was Robert Johnson.

The worst part isn't that you think you're dying. The worst part is that you *are* dying, that you are in the first stages of death by CO poisoning.

It becomes a test of will. You hold on because others before you have held on. Because the instructors and other recruits are waiting for you to crack, and you're determined not to give them that satisfaction. You hold on because your career depends on it. Strangest of all, you hold on because you know it's good for you. You know that someday as a firefighter you may end up in a situation where you're trapped in smoke and where you'll grasp on to that hairsbreadth of difference between surviving and dying, that you'll survive because this experience gave you the framework, the reference point to persevere instead of panic. You do it because it's necessary. But that was in drill school. We'd already proved ourselves, every one of us.

"This is bullshit," said Johnson as soon as the door closed. "We're not recruits." When I joined him on the floor, I pressed the light button on my watch and took note of the second hand.

I took a quick circuit of the ten-by-twelve-foot room and rejoined Johnson at the door, trying not to inhale. "How long?" Johnson asked, strangling on the words.

"Twenty seconds."

"Fuck."

We knew every time we took smoke we were shortening our lives, dumping poisons into our lungs, liver, and kidneys, increasing our chances of heart disease and cancer. This *was* bullshit. Abbott had exceeded his authority, and it pissed me off, too.

Outside the door, we heard Tronstad run past, calling out the floors as he passed each, as was the custom. You could tell from the amount of air he had behind his voice that he was dogging it.

I glanced at my watch again. We'd been inside a minute now, and even though we were "cheating" by scooping up what little fresh air filtered in under the door, we were also dying, especially Johnson, who was beginning to breathe in small gulping hiccups. "One minute," I announced.

"Okay. That's enough," Johnson said loudly. "We're coming out now!"

Without removing his face from the sweet spot at the base of the door, Johnson reached up and fumbled for the knob. When he continued to fumble, I sat up and pulled hard on the door. It didn't budge.

"It's stuck."

"It's stuck, Chief," Johnson shouted. "Let us out. The door's stuck!"

I was sure Abbott could hear the panic in Robert Johnson's voice. Maybe this was easier for me because I'd been through drill school more recently. Or because I was younger.

It was then that the minimal quantities of fresh air that had been flowing under the door were shut off. When I turned on my flashlight I could see Chief Abbott had blocked the crack under the door with a rag or his coat.

"You boys getting a good taste of it?" Abbott asked from the other side of the metal door.

"Chief! Chief?" Johnson pounded on the door, his blows

thunderous in my ears, which were close to the door. "Chief. Let us out of here. Damn it, let us out!"

"Maybe now you'll tell me where you got that bearer bond?" Abbott asked.

"Wha—?"

"That bearer bond. And all the other bearer bonds. How many *do* you have?"

"Chief?"

"Talk to me, boys. You're in there. I'm out here. It's going to stay this way until you tell me about the bonds."

Johnson started crying.

"Think it over. I've got all night. Your time may be limited."

I looked at my watch. "It's been two minutes, Chief."

"You pussies aren't going to wimp out on me, are you?"

"Let us out," gasped Johnson.

"Not until you tell me what I want to know."

"This is crazy!" Johnson wailed. The panic lacing his voice would only encourage Abbott. "Let us out of here. We didn't have anything to do with it."

"Tell me about it."

"Tronstad took them bonds." The talking was too much for Johnson, who erupted into a series of loud, wracking coughs. My lungs were like sandpaper, and I was pretty close to coughing myself. I'd been trying to conserve energy, but the fact that we were locked in created a panic I'd never felt in drill school, where you could cry uncle whenever you wanted, then afterward go upstairs to the training chief's office and sign a resignation form. There had always been a way out. Tonight the only way out was past Abbott.

I tried the knob again, but the door was frozen.

We were going on three and a half minutes. The longest I'd ever stayed in the smoke room was two minutes, and that had kicked my butt. I began pounding on the door, hoping Tronstad would hear it when he ran past.

Johnson managed to suppress his coughing long enough to say, "Tronstad was the one. Tronstad—" I shouldered him hard, knocking him over, leaning into him with all my weight.

"Shut up," I whispered. "We're not going to tell him a thing."

"He's killing us, Gum. I got to."

"Not like this."

After a twenty-second silence, Abbott said, "You guys still in there?"

Neither of us moved or spoke.

"Gum? Johnson? You guys okay?"

Moments later the door opened slowly. I scooted out onto the concrete landing while Johnson piled out on top of me. The concrete hurt my knees, but I scrambled to the stairs, where a light breeze from the north kept the smoke off us. Suddenly we were breathing the cool Seattle night air again.

Hacking and slobbering as if he'd been Maced, Johnson sat on the concrete step beside me. I could hear the asthma acting up in his lungs. I didn't feel so hot myself. We'd been inside just under five minutes.

Chief Abbott had secured the inward-opening door with a rope, one end around the handle, the other around his waist.

The look of delight in his eyes made me want to knock him down. "So. Let's hear about the bonds."

Johnson coughed. I remained teary-eyed, snot-nosed, and silent.

"We made a deal, men. I let you out. You talk."

The effects of carbon monoxide don't hit you all at once. My first month out in the company, we had a fire victim with CO poisoning who was talking to us, said he felt fine, and died ten hours later in the hospital. It remained to be seen how sick we were.

Tronstad climbed down the last few rungs of the fire escape on the outside of the building, then jogged up to where we were blocking the steps, a look of incredulity on his face. "Jesus fucking Christ. How long were they in there, Chief?"

"Five minutes," I said.

"It was more like a minute and a half," said Abbott. "Anybody can't take a minute and a half should go join the Girl Scouts. When I came through drill school, they kept us in there five, ten minutes at a pop. They made us recite pump procedures. They made us do push-ups. I had to, I could sit in there for a half hour and play cards. And you pussies are crying about a minute and a half."

"Five minutes," I repeated.

Standing behind and above me, Abbott prodded my back lightly with the toe of his uniform boot. "I'm holding a stopwatch here, son. Let's see where I stopped it. Right. Just like I said. One minute, thirty-five seconds. Look for yourself if you don't believe me."

"Shit, Chief," said Tronstad. "You tryin' to kill these boys?"

"Now that we got the trial run over with," said Abbott, "I'm going to ask you each to go in for two minutes. Alone this time. Don't worry, Gum. Your friends'll be outside to make sure of the time in case your brain starts playing tricks on you again. After that, we're through for the night. Simple as that. Everybody in the battalion has to do it. You guys just happened to draw first straw."

"Two minutes?" Johnson asked, a note of hope in his voice. Hard to tell what he was thinking. I wasn't going back in. Nor was I planning to argue with Abbott about it. I'd taken enough smoke. My head was spinning, my legs felt heavy, and my lungs were like blisters.

"I'll stoke up the burn barrel, and then we'll begin. You, too, Tronstad. No shirkers this time. We're all going to do it."

Abbott didn't notice the look Tronstad gave him. If he had, he wouldn't have stepped into the smoke room alone.

As the chief went in to tend the fire, carefully sealing but not latching the door behind him to preserve the smoke buildup, Tronstad whipped out his body loop and connected it to the rope Abbott had tied to the door handle, pulling on the rope, closing the door, effectively locking Abbott inside.

Tronstad gave us a devilish grin and bobbed his eyebrows up and down. "He said *we*. That means him, too. Right?"

"Geez, that's the chief," Johnson said.

"Come on. Give me your body loop, Gum. I'll tie them together."

There was an eye bolt sunk into the concrete just below the window, and it was through this eye bolt that he secured the connected body loops—a three-foot-long piece of webbing sewn into a loop that every SFD firefighter carried—cinching the end so the simple friction of the arrangement held the door closed.

"You can't do this," I whispered.

"Watch me. He's not supposed to be pulling this shit and he knows it. Don't look so shocked, Gum. What, you think I'm going to do to him what he just did to you guys? Don't worry, I'll let him out after a minute, but he deserves a taste of his own medicine. If you don't like it, get out of here."

Abbott tried the door handle, then began banging on the metal door with his fists. He banged as if his life depended on it, then screamed at the top of his lungs. He kicked the door. Of all the recruits I'd seen go through the smoke room, I'd never heard anything like it.

Johnson pulled on my coat sleeve and said, "Come on, let's go. We don't want to be here when he comes out."

Reluctantly, I followed Johnson down the stairs and into the bowels of Station 14, into the beanery, where the windows overlooked the drill court and where if you stuck your head out, you could see the tower off to the right.

Johnson washed his face in the sink, then swigged down a glass of water. When he was finished, he parked himself far enough away from the windows that he couldn't hear Abbott's pleas. "Tronstad's in big trouble."

"No shit."

"You don't lock a battalion chief in the smoke room and walk away from it."

"No shit."

"I guess thinking about all that money's making him a little cocky."

"No shit." We looked at each other for several beats and then, inexplicably, began laughing. I reached out and closed the swing-out window so our laughter wouldn't drift outside.

"What do you think they're doing?" I said after we'd sobered up.

"Probably Abbott made Tronstad go in."

"Tronstad wouldn't do it without us there."

"Maybe after getting a dose himself, Abbott reconsidered."

As I looked at my own reflection in the beanery window, a Metro bus whizzed past a hundred yards away on the east side of the drill court, the windows filled with Friday night commuters.

In the past month I'd become a different person. Where I'd once been the greenhorn recruit, I was now a man of some experience, boinking a woman years older, messing up an alarm that resulted in civilian deaths, facing my mother's impending demise, and fighting off bouts of depression over the way my life was tanking.

In the reflection of the window, I saw the tidy little brown-eyed boy I'd always been. I still felt like a boy. I couldn't even honestly say I felt like a boy in a man's body, because I felt like a boy in a boy's body. I suppose that was part of my attraction to Iola Pederson, who treated me like a boy most of the time.

When a face appeared in the window beside mine, it took half a second to realize he was outside in the drill court. Tronstad pulled the window open and inserted his head in the opening. "You two better get out here. We got trouble."

"Oh, shit," said Johnson.

"Just kidding. Just kidding. What's on TV?"

"What do you mean, what's on TV?" I asked. "What did the chief say when you let him out?" Tronstad looked at me blankly. "Didn't you hear me? What did the chief say?"

Johnson and I considered Tronstad for a few seconds and then ran through the beanery and out of the building. The sudden movement made my legs feel heavy and uncoordinated. I marveled at how much devastation a few minutes of carbon monoxide could wreak on the human body. When we got outside, Tronstad was still next to the beanery window, the deviltry gone, his face a mask. The smoke-room door was closed, the rope and body loop arrangement intact, still wrapped around the eye bolt. "Where's the chief?" Johnson asked.

Tronstad stared at us without expression.

"Are you crazy?" I said, sprinting up the half flight of steps, fumbling with the rope and loops and pushing the door open.

As a tidal wave of hot smoke slapped my face, the door jammed against a body.

16. THREE-LEGGED DOG IN A CAGE

"Jesus Christ," I said. "Help me get him out of here. What the hell were you thinking, Ted? He's unconscious."

"He can't be. He was talking to me until I went to get you guys. I didn't even jam up the crack under the door."

"I don't think he's breathing."

"Of course he's breathing."

"This is a joke, right, Gum?" Johnson said.

Abbott was even heavier than he looked, and he looked heavy, so I wasn't going to move him far on my own. "Help me get him out of here."

Johnson turned to Tronstad, who said, "Don't look at me. You've seen how much he eats. The man was a heart attack waiting for a place to land." He made the face of a man having a heart attack, which might have been funny under different circumstances.

"Come on, guys," I said, sticking my head into the smoke. "Every second counts."

It's difficult enough to move a limp body out of a tight space, but trying to haul Abbott's rotund and cumbersome bulk out of this smoky atmosphere after already having taken a previous dose was practically impossible. The three of us struggled, and as we did, I couldn't help noticing Tronstad was less willing to eat smoke than Johnson or I, lollygagging at the doorway before vanishing altogether, even though he should have been fresh.

"Get back in here," I snapped. "What the hell?"

Tronstad took a deep gulp of clean air and ducked back into the room, holding his breath. We grabbed Abbott's arms and dragged him out of the smoke room and onto the landing and down the stairs into the open drill court, his feet and shoes skidding down the concrete steps and along the tarmac.

"He said we were all doing it," Tronstad stammered. "The worst I thought would happen was he'd shit his pants."

"How long was he in there?" Johnson asked.

"You guys were in longer."

I knew that was a lie. By my calculations Abbott had been in the smoke room just shy of ten minutes.

After we laid him down and rolled him over, I checked his breathing a second time, then placed two fingers across his carotid artery. "No pulse. No breathing. We gotta do CPR."

"It was a heart attack," Tronstad said. "Hell, he could have had it on the shitter. It wasn't my fault, guys. A harmless practical joke, that's all it was."

"We gotta work on him," I said. "Call the medics."

"We gotta get our story straight first." Tronstad's hard eyes were black in the evening light.

"Why do we need a story?" Johnson asked. "Why don't we just tell the truth?"

"Tell the whole fuckin' world we locked our battalion chief in the smoke room and killed him?" Tronstad said. "Are you shitting me? You want to go to jail?"

"He locked us in longer," Johnson replied.

"That's not true," I said. "And you're the one who locked him in, Tronstad. Why should we lie about it?"

"Because you helped."

Johnson and I looked at each other, and I wondered if he saw the same doubt and dread in my eyes that I saw in his. The truth here was an anchor being thrown overboard, and while the line was wrapped around Tronstad's feet, it was also wrapped around Johnson's and mine. If Tronstad went overboard, Johnson and I would follow.

"He's right," I said. "I gave him my body loop, and neither one of us let Abbott out."

"We were pissed," Johnson said, "because he locked us in."

Johnson and I *were* part of this. There was no use pretending we weren't. Either one of us could have pulled Abbott out when he banged on the door, or stuck around to ensure he was freed after a minute.

"Okay. What's the story?" I said, unsnapping the chief's bunking coat, removing his helmet, tearing open his shirt, and scissoring his undershirt down the middle with my Buck knife.

Tronstad paced beside me. "When we arrived, he wasn't here yet, so we went inside to wait. After a while, I came out to see what was up and found him in the smoke room. I called you two."

I found my landmarks on the chief's bare chest and began compressions, a hundred a minute.

"Fuck it. I'm not telling any more lies," I said, pumping on Abbott's chest.

"Then I'm not helping."

"Come on," Johnson pleaded with me. "Do what he wants."

"Talk to *him*," I said.

"You know how stubborn Tronstad is. If we have a chance of bringing the chief back, it has to be you."

"I want a promise," Tronstad said. "Otherwise I let him go. You rat on me, I'll tell everything. Arch Place. The bearer bonds. I'll drag you both in."

"Okay. I won't say anything *tonight*. After that I'll have to think about it."

They ran to the rig, where I heard Tronstad on the apparatus radio. "Dispatch from Engine Twenty-nine. We're on the drill court at Station Fourteen. Ongoing CPR. Give us a medic unit."

"Okay, Engine Twenty-nine. One medic unit to Station

Fourteen. Engine Twenty-nine? Is that a still alarm at Station Fourteen?"

"No. We have a firefighter down."

They secured the ventilation kit and Lifepak, and we hooked the Lifepak leads to Abbott's chest, all three of us aware that once the Lifepak lid was open, everything we said would be recorded.

We'd been pumping on Abbott several minutes when Medic 10 arrived from downtown, carrying two medics, a male and a female, plus two paramedic students. Johnson was bag-masking; I was doing the chest compressions. Abbott was naked from the waist up, diaphoretic and even sloppier and rounder than I thought he'd be. I'd never seen him with his shirt off before, and his pink nipples and the paleness of his naked skin were strangely disconcerting.

The medics hooked up their twelve-lead system, and the female medic scanned the screen on her machine. "He's asystole." She turned to her partner. "Want to keep working?"

"He's one of ours. We keep working."

A person generally didn't come back from cardiac arrest unless his heart was in defibrillation. A patient whose heart was asystole, or a straight line on the graph, did not come back. Less than a one percent chance.

We slid a wooden backboard under Abbott, moved him onto Medic 10's gurney, and put him in the back of their vehicle, where we continued CPR. Seattle medics normally would have left this to the students while they supervised, but these two did everything themselves, put lines into Abbott's arm, called the Medic 1 duty doctor, and got permission to inject drugs. Bicarbonate. Epinephrine. They moved rapidly and efficiently.

We worked on him for twenty-seven minutes, but in the end, he was just another dead man in the back of a medic unit, with a plastic airway jammed down his throat and taped across his mouth. In the end, he was dead and I'd helped kill him.

When I stepped out of the back of the medic unit, Sweeney

Sears greeted me with a melancholy look. If he'd been watching our resuscitation attempt, I hadn't seen him. I wanted to look around for my crew in the deepening darkness of the courtyard but couldn't rip my eyes off Sears long enough to locate them.

"You okay?" Sears asked.

"Yeah. Sure. I guess."

"You look kind of pale. Like you're going to faint."

"I'll be okay."

"What happened?"

"I don't know. "

"Is that the smoke room? The recruits forget to clean it up?"

This was my chance to confess. I needed a moment or two to think this through. There were clearly two options here: go along with Tronstad or tell the truth. Our critical error had been leaving Tronstad in charge. Yet at the time I'd been so irritated from the smoke and so pissed off, I didn't care what happened.

If I told the truth, Tronstad would go to jail. Tonight. He would be in jail, and the authorities would find out—if not from him then from Sears—about the bearer bonds. Once behind bars, Tronstad would implicate Johnson and me in the bonds, as well as in Abbott's death.

"Hell, Lieut," Tronstad said, appearing out of the darkness. "Give the kid a break, would you? He's taking this pretty hard."

"Were you with Abbott when it happened?"

"We were all inside."

"I know you must be in shock," Sears said, taking me by my shoulders, "but I need details here. The chief of the department's on his way. We need to know exactly what happened."

"I . . . I'm not sure."

"Well, yeah . . ." Sears took me by the elbow and walked me over to the sideboard of Engine 29 to sit me down next to Robert Johnson. Tronstad followed. "You need something to drink?" Sears asked.

"I'm okay."

"You don't look okay."

Tronstad's story was succinct. I listened without comment, as did Johnson, who I could see was entertaining the same doubts I was about whether or not to blurt out the truth. He must have known there was a possibility Ted had deliberately killed the chief to keep him from pursuing the bearer bond as doggedly as we knew he would.

I told myself that in all probability Abbott got overexcited, the way he always did around smoke, and had an MI—a myocardial infarction. It could have happened anyway, and if he'd gone down while all three of us were in the smoke room with the rope tied to his waist, he would have sealed us in and we'd all be dead. Suddenly I was pissed at how close he'd come to killing the three of us.

As Tronstad recounted the story, his voice grew subdued with dummied-up grief—humble, almost quivery. Like a lot of stand-up comics, he was an excellent dramatic actor when he needed to be. "The chief called us down here to drill. We smelled smoke, but knowing it was Friday and there was a recruit school in session, we figured it was residue from the smoke room. We went inside to wait for Abbott, and then after fifteen minutes or so we noticed the Battalion Five Suburban parked out on the court. It was Gum who found him behind the door in the smoke room."

Not the story we'd agreed on, but close.

"What the devil was he doing in the smoke room?" Lieutenant Sears asked, turning to me.

"Probably investigating that burn barrel," Johnson said.

"It's true," Tronstad said. "There's still a fire in the barrel."

Sears looked at me. "He was in the smoke room?"

"Yes, sir. On the floor behind the door."

"Holy Mother of Mary," said Sears.

"That's exactly what we said," replied Tronstad.

"The only thing I can think of," said Sears, "is they left the burn barrel smoldering by accident. Abbott went up to investigate and had a heart attack. When he fell, his body closed the door."

"Hmmm. Could have happened that way," said Tronstad.

When the safety chief showed up, Tronstad repeated his fable. A few minutes later he repeated it again to the chief of the department, Hiram Smith, who'd arrived with a small entourage, including the public information officer for the department, Joyce Judge. Later we heard Smith repeating the story word for word to a television news interviewer. By that time, Medic 10 had taken Abbott's body downtown to the King County Medical Examiner's office in the basement of Harborview Medical Center, where it would undergo an autopsy in the morning.

I wandered over to the base of the tower to escape the hubbub and was appalled to see the rope and the two body loops still attached to the smoke-room door handle, Tronstad's four-digit SFD ID number written plainly on his body loop in black grease pen, my own number on the second loop. When I saw Lieutenant Sears hoofing it in my direction, I dashed up the stairs, slipped the rope off the door handle, and stuffed it and the body loops into my large bunking-coat pocket just before he arrived.

"Right behind the door here?" he asked, peering into the smoke room.

"Yes, sir."

"Can I borrow your light?"

I detached the small department-issued flashlight from my bunking coat and handed it to him. He poked around in the concrete room longer than I would have, considering it was still full of smoke, then emerged, ever the stoic, refusing to gasp for air, pretending he was tougher than snot. Maybe he was.

Hours later, after the lights were out in the bunk room and Johnson and I were lying in the darkness, Johnson's voice floated from the other end of the room, "Gum? You awake?"

"Yeah."

"You think we did the right thing?"

"I don't know. I'm really worried about it. Tronstad blackmailed me into lying."

"He sure did. But what choice did we have?"

"We could go over and tell Sears right now."

"But it was an accident, right?"

"Ten minutes in the smoke room? I don't think so."

"We better stick to the story we told. Otherwise they're going to want to know why we lied. Tronstad's right. A guy's going to have a heart attack, he's going to have it. What difference is there if he has it tonight or tomorrow night? Hell, we gave him the best care anybody could give, didn't we? Gum?"

"Ten minutes in the smoke room for a guy with a heart condition is not the best care in the world, Robert."

I thought about it for a couple of hours that night and eventually fell into a fitful sleep, waking at five, only to relive the night's events for another two hours. In the morning the *Seattle Post-Intelligencer* carried an article in the second section. *Seattle Fire Battalion Chief Succumbs on Drill Court.*

After the oncoming shift relieved us that morning, the three of us congregated on the west side of the station, where Johnson patted his new Cadillac SRX as if it were a horse. "What the heck. Paula and I can afford this."

"I'm nervous as a three-legged dog in the pound," I said, borrowing one of Tronstad's sayings.

"You saw the paper," snapped Tronstad. "Fucker had a heart attack. Shit happens."

"I'm praying," said Johnson, solemnly. "I think we should all pray for him. And we should pray for ourselves."

"What are we praying for?" Tronstad said, flippantly.

"That maybe the FBI doesn't come around and want to know what we did with those bearer bonds," I said. "Or that the medical examiner doesn't decide Abbott died of smoke inhalation instead of a heart attack. Or that the medical examiner doesn't find that bond on Abbott and turn it over to the cops."

"Jesus. Where is the bond?" Johnson asked. "Where's the bond Abbott had?"

"I don't know."

"Shit," said Tronstad.

"I'm praying," Johnson said. "For Abbott's family and for

our families. I know the Lord is looking down on us, and I know he's going to give us guidance so we'll know to do the right thing."

"The right thing," I said, "would have been to sit down on those steps last night when Abbott asked us to go into the smoke room and wait for union representation."

"Let's all just put our trust in the Lord Jesus," Johnson said.

"The Lord helps them who help themselves," said Tronstad, heading for his new truck.

17. IF HE ONLY HAD A HEART

Sunday evening I was doing laundry when somebody knocked at the front door.

Iola blew in past me and moved from room to room in rapid strides. "You've got another woman, right?"

"How could I have another woman? You show up whenever you want. I'm always alone."

"Where were you yesterday? And last week?"

"Sometimes I have places to go."

"For days on end?"

After racing through my house and finding no one but me, she approached slowly, a drowsy look in her amazing blue eyes, a look I'd seen before. At times like this she was like a dog in heat.

Tonight, though, I had other business on my mind. I'd taken my mother up to Snoqualmie Pass for a hike to Franklin Falls, which was one of the shortest and easiest hikes in the Cascades, intersecting the historical Snoqualmie wagon trail and ending at the base of a seventy-foot waterfall after only one mile. I worried that it would be too much for her and tried to talk her into a movie instead, but my mother was determined to ignore her illness until it struck her down—she was more than determined. On the drive home from Denny Creek she had been so ill, we'd stopped in North Bend and spent an hour in the McDonald's while she rested and sipped from a paper cup of ice water.

"There's no point in being alive unless you stretch your limits," she said.

Throughout the weekend, I worried about my mother and about how Chief Abbott died. I'd promised Tronstad I'd go along with his story, but only to get him helping with the CPR. Later, I began to think maybe I was more culpable than I'd imagined. On the other hand, everybody knew Abbott thought there was something wrong with his heart and had called the paramedics on himself twice in the past eighteen months. Maybe everything would be okay. Or maybe I was fooling myself. Hard to know, because since the bonds showed up, I'd become a virtuoso at fooling myself.

Iola wore jeans and a sleeveless sweater vest, her auburn hair loose and windblown. We were going to have sex. She knew it and I knew it. When we kissed, her skin smelled of onions and pipe smoke, the latter probably from her father. We ended up making love in the dark on the couch without bothering to close the living-room drapes. This was just the sort of licentiousness that made Iola exciting to me.

Afterward, we lay cheek to cheek, our perspiring bellies stuck together. I said, "My battalion chief died Friday."

Her voice was mocking. "That was so great, Iola. You're fantastic in the sack. Oh, why, thank you, Gum. So are you."

"I'm sorry."

"Is that why you were gone all weekend? Because your chief died?"

"If you would ever let me phone you, I could have told you I'd be gone."

"Where were you?"

"Up at the pass. Hiking." The one time I mentioned my mother she'd ridiculed me—this from a woman who lived with her father and still called him *Daddy*.

She didn't want to hear about me or my problems. What she wanted was a roll in the hay and to have that be the end of it. Once in a while she would grumble about goings on at her work or complain about a driver on the road or some cretin of a cashier she'd run into, but she didn't want to hear about *my* problems. Not today. Or the last time we met. Nor the next time.

Iola pushed me off and began dressing, balancing on one foot while she put on her panties, then her jeans, leaving her top for last, not looking directly at me but well aware I was watching.

"By the way," she said. "You didn't get a visit from anybody, did you?"

"Who would that be?"

"Oh, nobody."

Though she'd obviously gotten wind of the fact her stepdaughter had been to see me, we were going to ignore it the way we ignored so many other aspects of our relationship.

"You want to stay? I haven't had dinner. There's that place up on California Avenue—"

"You know I'm not going out with you, sweetie. Besides, I only came over because I thought maybe you were sick or something. Don't look like that. You know I care, don't you, darling?" She kissed the top of my head and was out the door before I could gather my wits.

Her precipitous exits always annoyed me, but tonight more so than ever. Tonight was the one night I needed somebody to be with me, and for some crackbrained reason I had thought Iola might be that person.

For reasons nobody seemed able to elucidate—but probably because Seattle's mayor was scheduled to leave for a vacation in Mexico on Tuesday—the department funeral for Russell Louis Abbott took place on Monday at noon. A bagpipe team from Canada showed up, along with fire crews from our and a dozen other departments, an honor guard, and hundreds of firefighters in their black wool dress uniforms.

Monday coincidentally happened to also be our next working shift. The first thing I noticed when I arrived at the firehouse in the morning was that neither of my coworkers had returned their new vehicles to the dealer. In addition, Johnson was still wearing his five-thousand-dollar watch. "Geez, Gum," he said. "What if they ask one of us to say something at the funeral?"

"For years he treated us like dirt," said Tronstad. "I'm not going to lie and say I'm sorry he's tits up."

"Ted, you can't attend a funeral with that attitude," Johnson said. "Today's the day you have to dig deep and go to the wizard and ask for a heart."

Tronstad laughed. "That was a good one."

The ceremony was slated for noon, but we were tapped out of service at eight thirty so we could help handle the minutiae that precede any fire department funeral. Sears was to be one of the orators, as well as a pallbearer.

We helped a team of officers from the chief's union who came by to drape the Battalion 7 Suburban and Engine 29 with black bunting. We were given black armbands and black tape to place across our badges. Tronstad disappeared for long periods that morning, using an old firefighter's trick to get out of work, sitting on the crapper reading a magazine.

Midmorning I heard Tronstad talking to Lieutenant Sears. "So what was the official ruling on the cause of death?"

"I haven't seen the report, but from what I gather, he died of smoke inhalation. They're assuming he went into the smoke and had a syncopal episode. Kirsten says he's had a couple of episodes in the past year. Apparently he didn't want the department to know. They figure he fainted and his body closed the door when he fell against it. After that he just took in too much smoke."

"What a shame."

"Kirsten's inconsolable."

"Nothing sadder than a bunch of rugrats without a father," said Tronstad. "It's not like she's Miss America or anything. They're never going to have another father. I mean, who would marry a blimp like her?"

"Jesus, Ted. Give it a rest."

"You're right. I'm sorry."

We got to the church an hour early and took up the slack time chatting with other Seattle firefighters as they arrived, some on rigs, some in private vehicles, all in class-A uniforms with uniform hats, looking sharp in the crisp October air.

I'd always thought Abbott was a pompous buffoon, but listening to one speaker after another tell heartwarming narratives about his career and good deeds, I wanted to cry. Despite eight kids of his own, he'd been part of the Big Brother program, had worked at the Rotary, had volunteered at his children's schools, and was an assistant football coach at the local junior high. The list of accolades and accomplishments went on and on.

I was stunned when Robert Johnson approached the podium and told a series of touching vignettes about Abbott. Tronstad remained next to me on the church pew, maintaining a military bearing throughout the service, his face expressionless. When he bumped into Kirsten in the foyer after the service, surrounded by her kids, he kissed her on the cheek and whispered something in her ear that made her weep.

Sears went to the cemetery in Bellevue with the cortege while Johnson, Tronstad, and I took Engine 29 back to the station and removed the black bunting. Later, Tronstad said, "You guys see what she did?"

"What?" Johnson asked.

"Kissed me on the friggin' lips."

"Come on, Tronstad," I said. "Give her a break."

"On the lips!"

For supper that night Johnson prepared spaghetti and meatballs, a tossed salad, and garlic bread on the side. Sears tended to paperwork in his office while the interim chief went downtown to a meeting. Tronstad hid out on the other side of the apparatus bay, in the firefighters' bunk room, playing video games on the Internet. I did a light workout in the basement—lifted some weights and rode the exercycle—unable to stop thinking about the blue floor mat Chief Abbott had brought in for his sit-ups, marked, *Private property. R. Abbott.* The rest of his belongings had been gathered up

Saturday morning and packed off to his widow, but we'd be looking at that mat in the basement for years.

At dinner we were a crew again, the four of us: Sears, Johnson, Tronstad, and myself. We ate in front of the evening news, waiting for funeral shots on each of the local channels.

After dinner, Sears pulled the Sierre Leone bank bond out of his breast pocket and said, "We need to talk about this. There was only the one, right, guys?"

Tronstad came around the table, took the bond from Sears, and held it to the light. "Yeah. This is the one I found on my boot that night. You see on the news where they've been tearing apart Ghanet's house? The cops might want to know about this."

"They might want to know how it got in Chief Abbott's bunking-coat pocket, too, huh? Because that's where I found it."

"What?"

"This is the bond I left in my drawer the other day. How did Abbott get it?" We all shrugged. Tronstad did the thing he always did with his eyebrows, raising and lowering them in rapid succession. The officers' desk drawers didn't have locks, so Abbott had no doubt been in Sears's drawer looking for something else and discovered it, then started putting two and two together. "Did Abbott talk to you guys about this?"

"Heck, no," Tronstad blurted. "It's weird that he had it, though. Don't you think?"

After he'd looked at us each in turn, Sears said, "Okay. I promised I would talk to you." Sears stood up and walked to the doorway. "You first, Robert."

"What?" Tronstad asked. "What are you doing?"

"I'm taking Robert into my office to ask some questions. Then I'm going to ask you the same questions. And then Gum."

"I thought you were going to talk to us all at once. We don't have any secrets, do we, guys? What are you trying to do, Lieut? Turn this into an interrogation?"

"My office." Sears cocked his head at Johnson and

marched down the corridor, his back and shoulders ramrod stiff.

Tronstad whispered, "He wants to get three different versions so he can compare. It's an old cop trick. Look, Gum, just say what we agreed on. No more, no less. We stick to the story, we'll be copacetic. Got it?"

"Yeah."

The truth was, I couldn't remember what we'd agreed on. All I knew was that I'd contributed to Abbott's death, that I was covering up evidence in a criminal investigation, and that I had over twelve million dollars' worth of stolen bearer bonds salted away.

18. UNTIL I OPENED MY BIG MOUTH

While we waited in the beanery, Tronstad told a story I'd heard before about the afternoon he had sex with a woman in his recruit school—a woman who was now a captain and who by the looks of things would end up a battalion chief. Tronstad related in loving detail how they'd been studying for the midterm at her house and how he took hold of her and kissed her and then had sex with her on the kitchen floor. As far as anybody knew, the captain was an unabashed lesbian. Johnson joked she'd been straight until she met Tronstad.

All in all, if you were a woman, you wanted to avoid Tronstad. Not only would he do everything in his considerable power to seduce you—and maybe turn you into a lesbian— but he would brag about it to his friends for years afterward. No liaison was spared, not fiancées, ex-wives, or the babysitter he claims he screwed in sixth grade. Everything was a conquest with bragging rights.

When Johnson came out of the lieutenant's office, he wore his standard smiley face, his cheeks hard and shiny as rocks in a creek. Looking at the potpourri of pain, triumph, and resolution in his eyes, I had a hard time figuring out what might have transpired.

Tronstad went in next, rushing down the corridor as if he couldn't wait, a prizefighter catapulted into the center of the ring by fury and adrenaline. After the door closed on them, I turned to Robert. "What'd you say?"

"We prayed."

"You what?"

He grinned. "We prayed for Abbott's family. The lieut's not a bad guy when you get to know him."

"What'd you tell him about the bond?"

"He's not any smarter now than when I went in." Maybe not, but he was still a heck of a lot smarter than Johnson. Or Tronstad. Or probably me. Even if Robert hadn't told him anything, I knew Sears would puzzle this out before he was finished.

Tronstad's interview lasted less than a minute. Just before the door burst open, we heard Tronstad's voice, loud and petulant. "You know what your problem is? You've never been sued for defamation of character! That's your problem. Well, hang on to your hat, Lieutenant, because I'll be seeing my attorney in the morning."

"I *will* get to the bottom of this," Sears yelled.

"You know what this is? This is a goddamn witch hunt. You've had a hard-on for me since the minute you walked through the door." Tronstad stalked out onto the apparatus floor.

Sears stared after him for a few moments, then turned and signaled me with a glance. I walked down the corridor with a sense of foreboding. In his office he flung himself into the swivel chair, while I sat carefully in the straight-backed chair next to his bunk. It was a small room, cramped and intimate, with a tall window in the corner on the west wall. The light coming through the window was the same pinkish hue as it had been the evening we killed Abbott. Thank God he wasn't questioning me about that. I would have folded like a garage-sale pup tent. In fact, thinking about it made my hands sweat.

Stroking his thick mustache with two fingers of one hand,

Sears stared at me. It was chilly in the station, but Sears was wearing his immaculately pressed short-sleeved uniform shirt.

"I don't know if this bond is worth anything or if it's play money, but you three gave me a story a couple of shifts ago about how you came to have it. Frankly, after talking with Robert and Ted, I don't believe you." He stared at me.

"You don't?"

"No. For beginners, when I asked him about it, Robert went into a song and dance about the Lord and a bunch of other peripheral issues to put me off the scent. Tronstad pretended to be enraged over the insult to his integrity, as if Tronstad has any integrity. I've seen both guys use those same defense mechanisms before when they were feeling uncomfortable about a situation. What I want from you, before I turn this over to the police, is for you to tell me what really happened."

"You're turning it over to the police?"

"As soon as we're finished talking. But right now I want you to be as honest and forthright as I know you can be. Make me proud, Gum. I don't want to see you go down on a sinking ship with those other two." He'd chosen an apt metaphor. A sinking ship was exactly what it was.

Sears, who'd been tilting back in his chair with his hirsute arms folded across his chest, leaned forward and placed both elbows on his knees, his face three feet from mine. "Tell me what happened," he said, "and don't try to pass off that bull about Tronstad finding the bearer bond on the floor of the crew cab. I know that didn't happen."

I inhaled deeply. There were a lot of paths to take, and for a split second I wasn't certain which would have my footprints.

"The other night," I began, "at Ghanet's place, while you were talking to the neighbor, Tronstad brought three garbage sacks out of the house. I told him to put them back, but he said all they had in them was useless paper. At the station I found out they were full of bearer bonds. I didn't even know what a bearer bond was. Robert wanted to take them back, too, but by morning Tronstad persuaded him they might be worth something. That was when things got complicated."

"Three bags? Are you sure you don't mean three bearer bonds?"

"No, sir. Three bags. Stuffed full."

"Holy shit. Where are the bags now?"

"I hid them."

"*You* hid them?"

"It was only until we figured out what to do. We were planning to give them back." I could tell by his tone of voice, the look on his face, and the way he scrunched his bushy eyebrows downward that my level of involvement disappointed him.

"It's been two shifts, Gum. You could have given them back a hundred times over."

"I know. But a lot has happened."

"Gum, you've let me down. I figured those two were a bad influence, but I never thought they would drag you into something like this."

"It isn't what you think. They were going to get into a fistfight over them, so I agreed to hold the bonds, but only so we could give them back at a later date. That's all I was doing. Heck, they were only in my possession a couple of hours. I didn't think they were worth anything."

"But you hid them away somewhere?"

"Yeah."

"Gum, you're as guilty as they are."

"I would have turned them in if I could have figured out how to do it without Tronstad losing his job. I didn't want to see him flush everything away because of one mistake."

"You know as well as I do that Tronstad hasn't made just *one* mistake. He makes a mistake every time he turns around. The first thing Abbott told me when I got here was that there was a thief in the station and he thought it was one of you three."

"What?"

"Oh, yeah. A bunch of stolen items."

I was flabbergasted. If station members were losing personal articles, I had not heard of it. In fact, although Sears obviously did, I didn't believe it. It was typical of the sort of unverified gossip Abbott had been in the habit of spreading.

"I'm afraid this little escapade is going to send you to the calaboose."

"I know I should have come to you right away, but you were out of town and then at that meeting all day. And then Abbott died. Maybe those are lame excuses, but can't you see the bind I was in?"

"Who has the bonds now?"

"I do."

"Jesus, Gum."

"Lieut, they wanted to fight. That was the only reason I took the bags. We were going to give them back."

"And that's why you guys all bought new vehicles?"

"I didn't. Listen, I'm not a thief."

He swiveled around in his squeaky chair and picked up a pen and legal pad from his desk. "Okay. What I need from you are details. When exactly did Tronstad remove these three bags? And who saw him do it? Was it just you, or did Robert see him, too? Or did Robert help?"

"There's gotta be a way we can work this out. You said we were going to work this out. They're *your* friends, too."

"Gum, this isn't a game of tiddlywinks where you got caught cheating and everybody starts over. This is the real world. You men took something that might be worth thousands of dollars from a private residence. Don't be naïve, Gum. You're going to prison. The whole lot of you. You knew that."

"I drove past Ghanet's house the next day looking for a way to put them back!"

"I really should tap us out of service," Sears said, more to himself than me. Tronstad was right. Sears would hang us all and do it with gusto. "I should get the chief in here. This is going to be on the news. In fact, given Ghanet's history, it'll be big news."

"Can't you see I'm trying to make this right?"

"What I see is that the three of you lied to me when I asked where this bond came from. That you stole bonds and hid them, and you've been hiding them for over a week despite knowing the authorities were combing Ghanet's place for stolen money. What I want you to do now is tell me where the bags are. And by the way, what else have you stolen?"

"I've never stolen anything."

"Oh, come on. I know the three of you have been stealing on aid runs."

Dropping my head into my hands, it was all I could do to keep from crying. Maybe Tronstad was right. Sears *was* the enemy. Why couldn't he understand that I'd never stolen anything in my life, and that making this right was as simple as fetching the bags and returning them?

Of course, there was more than just the bearer bonds to think about. At the funeral I'd agonized over the events surrounding Abbott's death until I thought I'd go mad. Abbott had the bond and was asking questions, and because of that Tronstad killed him. The more I looked at it in that light, the more I knew this was going to get uglier than a high school football team mooning a choir bus.

Lieutenant Sears picked up the phone and called the dispatcher. "Hey, this is Sears on Engine Twenty-nine. Can you put us out of service here? We've got a personnel situation." He listened for a few seconds and said, "No, we've still got four men on board if you need us. It's just—" He listened again. "Okay. Yeah. Well, we can stay in service if that's what's going on. No problem." He racked the phone and looked at me. "They've got a four-eleven downtown. They're going to send us."

"They *never* send us downtown."

"I know, but there was a house fire earlier up in Thirty-seven's district, so everything's all screwed up." Even as Sears spoke, the house bells hit and the overhead lights came on. "Oh, and by the way, Gum?"

"Sir?"

"Don't tell the others what you told me, okay? It'll make things easier at the fire. I want your word on that."

"You call me a liar and a thief, but you want me to do you a favor?"

"Yes, I do."

"But I'm not a thief. I've never taken anything that didn't belong to me."

"Except for those bonds."

As we headed east down the hill on Admiral Way, we could see the glow in the sky on the far side of Elliott Bay, the black thermal column rising to three or four times the height of the Space Needle. It was a warehouse fire not far from the Seattle Center, and it was impressive, to say the least. I could tell from the way he was driving that Johnson was as nervous as a tick in gasoline.

I'd been to one other fire this large, so I knew this would be what we called a *surround and drown,* a defensive fire. Instead of going inside, we would sit in the street and pour hundreds of thousands of gallons of water into the conflagration.

I felt sick to my stomach. It was hard to tell whether it was from the pall of smoke hanging over downtown or my mishandling of the interview with Sears.

"You asshole," Tronstad whispered.

"What?"

"You told him, didn't you?"

"I . . ."

"Jesus Christ, Gum!"

We were entering the smoke zone, which encompassed most of downtown Seattle south of the fire. "I couldn't help it."

"You stupid asshole."

"I'm not going to argue with that."

19. WEARING YOUR ASS FOR A HATBAND

Sitting in the crew cab facing backward, it was hard to see what was going on, but every time we caught a glimpse to the north, the thermal column was thicker, the smoke rising faster. It was hard to worry too much about the fire when I knew I was probably headed for jail, that at the very least I would soon be out of a job. Still, you see a fire that large and know you're about to tackle it, there's a lump in your throat. Anybody who says there isn't is lying. The bigger the fire, the greater the chance of getting killed.

As we got closer and the smoke thickened, we gradually came to a crawl behind Ladder 3, which was headed the same place we were. Stationed in the Central District, where they got a lot of fires, Ladder 3 was probably taking this in stride, while in our crew even Sears was jacked up, having all but forgotten he was riding with three villains.

Drifting smoke in the street slowed us to five miles an hour. We'd smelled the toxic smoke a mile earlier, but as we drew closer, it began to take on a hellish taste. Eyes watering, we proceeded in tandem with Ladder 3 until we both parked behind a long line of fire rigs.

When Sears turned around and spoke through the open window into our crew cab, he sounded angry, an emotion I'd noticed some fire officers using to displace fear. "Okay, men. Get your masks on and report to staging with spare bottles. I'm going to talk to the IC. I'll meet you in staging. And carry a spare bottle up there for me."

"Oh, and carry a bottle for me, would you?" Tronstad mocked after Sears departed. "He's such a goddamn kiss-butt. '*I'm* going to talk to the incident commander. Everybody else reports to staging, but *I'll* go straight to the head of the line.' Shit! I don't even know why we're here. We'd be

better off hailing a cab. Get our money and a good head
start."

What I found odd was that Sears was calling us *men* for
the first time in memory. Ironic that we were *men* now that he
was sending us off to the slammer. Maybe that was his way
of distancing us, or of setting it firmly in his mind that we
were the masters of our own fate, that *we'd* chosen our downward path, not him. I'd been nuts to tell him. I still didn't
know quite why I did. Maybe it came from having a mother
who'd raised me to believe there was nothing more dear than
a clear conscience.

We began walking north alongside a long line of parked
fire apparatus, and as we got closer I could see 40-foot-high
flames leaping from the roof of a wooden building maybe
150 feet wide and two stories tall. Every once in a while a
barrage of smoke rolled down the street into our faces.

There were over a hundred firefighters, even more civilians, and scads of newspeople present. Many of the firefighters were visibly nervous, faces pale, glances fleeting
and edgy. The fire building occupied half a city block, and a
good third of the middle part of the structure was alight. It
was more than hellish, I thought, as an interior wall collapsed and the implosion ushered a flurry of sparks toward
the sky. It was also astonishingly beautiful.

"Jesus, we're in some deep shit," Tronstad sputtered.

"I wouldn't be worried," Johnson said. "A fire like this, all
you do is squirt water from the sidewalk. We might not even
get out of staging."

"I'm not talking about the fire. I'm talking about jail."

"Jail? You said yourself, we keep quiet and there's not a
thing anybody can do."

"Nice plan," Tronstad said. "Except for *big mouth* here."

"You're kidding, right?" Johnson asked, grinning at me.
"What? You accidentally let something out? He guessed?
What?"

"Tell him, Dubble Bubble. Go ahead. Tell him how you
fucked us."

We'd stopped in the dark in the middle of the closed-off

street, so Johnson couldn't see me clearly. Even though they'd initiated the crime, I felt as if I were solely to blame for our predicament.

"My Lord, Gum. Tell me you didn't tell Sears the three of us are sitting on all them bearer bonds. Jesus, Lord, have mercy on my poor black ass. Why the fuck did you go and do a fool thing like that? What were you thinking?"

"I honestly thought he would help us."

"You mean you thought he would help *you*," Tronstad said, punching me in the shoulder. "Jesus, you friggin' idiot." His blow didn't hurt through the thick bunking coat, but it was the first time he'd ever hit me, even in jest, and I took note of it. "You're a fuckin' squealer, is what you are. Nobody would have known if you'd kept your mouth shut."

"He was going for the cops before I said a word."

"Sure he was."

"He was."

Johnson put his hand on my shoulder where Ted had socked me. "We're in this together, but lordy, Gum, that was a dumb move. That was just plain dumb."

"Maybe if we get an attorney, we could make a deal. They don't prosecute and we keep our jobs."

"Dream on, peckerwood," Tronstad said.

Johnson's eyes were locked on the flames a block away. "We're not going to get the money, and we're going to lose our jobs. I didn't have anything to do with it, but I'm still going to have to explain why I bought that Cadillac SRX."

"I know this." Tronstad faced Johnson squarely as if I weren't there. "Somebody besides Sears, maybe we could cut him in. Split it four ways instead of three. But you can't reason with Sears."

Tronstad turned to me. "And you . . . I oughta wring your fucking neck."

"We're going to be here a couple of hours," Johnson said. "We've got that long to plan."

"I don't know about you guys," said Tronstad, "but I'm going to bug out of here."

"Like hell," Johnson said. "You leave, and we're no longer

a crew. He'll have us arrested the minute he sees you're gone. I see you make a move, I'm yelling for a cop."

"Then let's *all* go."

"No. We need to think it through."

"This is bullshit! We should all go!"

"And how long before Sears notices all three of us are missing?" Johnson asked. "If you weren't wearing your ass for a hatband you might be able to help us puzzle our way out of this."

"Sears is going to hang us," Tronstad said.

"He's doing what he has to do," I said.

"You're a dumbass if you believe that. He's been trying to bone us from the first day."

We were in staging now, an area set aside in a parking lot two hundred yards south of the fire building, where incoming crews reported while waiting for assignments. Including us, there were maybe thirty-five extra firefighters milling about. Most of the smoke boiled over our heads, but every once in a while a cloud rumbled down the street like a herd of black elephants through the massed firefighters.

As always, I was struck by how large the average firefighter was, most well over six feet, many over 250 pounds. This was before adding the 45 to 50 pounds of protective gear, MSA backpacks, and the compressed air bottles we all wore. I always tried to make up for my lack of bulk by working twice as hard as the next man, and I wanted to be especially diligent tonight, for this would be my last fire.

The mood in staging was subdued. If they weren't thinking about the fire in front of us, people were thinking about Abbott's funeral eight hours earlier. Across the street behind Battalion 2's Suburban, a cluster of chiefs in white helmets conferred. Every other company officer had followed protocol and gone to staging with his or her men, while Sears waited beside the chiefs like a lapdog expecting treats.

"We should make that fucker disappear," Tronstad said. "This would be the perfect place to make him disappear."

"You say another word, I'm going for a cop," I said. "I'd

rather spend the rest of my life in a box of dirt than see somebody else get hurt."

Tronstad stared daggers at me. "You didn't tell him about Abbott, did you?"

"No."

"You sure?"

"It didn't even come up. I'm not telling anybody about that."

"He make any calls after you spilled your guts?"

"To the dispatcher. They told him we were coming here."

"There's a coupla deputy chiefs over there," said Johnson. "Maybe he's telling them right now."

Tronstad looked across the street. "Not bloody likely. He tells them, they tap us out of service. He's not going to do anything to get shuffled out of here. He sees a fire like this, he gets a woody. We either get rid of him or we split and grab the bonds, divide them, and blow town. Those are our choices. Maybe you should tell us where you hid the merchandise, Gum." Tronstad bobbled his black eyebrows as if this were a joke, as if he were my friend again, as if I hadn't ratted him out and he hadn't hit me. "Your mother's place?"

"No way I would hide anything at my mother's."

"I can't blow town." Johnson looked at me beseechingly. "I've got a wife and a little girl."

"They're bearer bonds, Robert. Use your noggin." Amazed at our lack of imagination, Tronstad's brown eyes were large and wet now, cow eyes. "They're good anywhere. Take your family to Brazil and live like a king. In Brazil you could have a girlfriend on the side, put her up in a condo, buy her a little convertible, get her a boob job, all for just pennies a day. Hell, you could go ten years and barely touch those bonds. You could have *two* girlfriends on the side, one on each end of town. The women are beautiful down there, and they're all poor as church mice. Fuck you for a smile and a used bus ticket."

"You know I'm not like that," Johnson said.

"Goddamn it, Gum! Tell us where they are!"

Johnson looked at me. "We get there first, we'll only take our share, right, Tronstad?"

"Right as rain."

Now that I'd given up my next few years of freedom, I was even more reluctant to abandon the single piece of leverage I had. Or maybe I was sick of seeing people around me doing the wrong thing. I knew this much: I didn't want the two of them blundering through Iola's property in the middle of the night. If Iola or her father came out and confronted them, I couldn't be sure what Tronstad might do.

"So where's the booty?" Tronstad asked, feigning gaiety. "Tell us so we'll all know. That's only fair."

"Not tonight."

Tronstad's lugubrious mien morphed into a vision of pure evil. From the moment I took possession of those bonds, our relationship had changed. I'd felt it that morning and again when he showed up at my house and every minute since. In the past we'd been mentor and student, seasoned firefighter and tyro, but now we were antagonists. I'd seen the sea change in some of Tronstad's other relationships; Tronstad tended to love you or hate you, never a lot of ground in between.

"Know what Sears told me tonight after we prayed?" Johnson said. "He said Abbott brought him in to clean house."

"Motherfucker," said Tronstad, staring across the road at Sears.

"What do you mean by 'clean house'?" I said.

"Abbott didn't want us at Twenty-nine's. He told Sears to find some excuse to transfer us."

"That can't be right," I said. "Sears told us he was going to turn us into the best crew in the city."

"What he actually said was that I was worthless as a driver and didn't have the brainpower to learn my district. He said Tronstad took drugs off shift and had more than once come to work doped up, although he couldn't prove it."

I didn't know how to respond. Robert *was* the worst driver I'd ever worked with. And whatever the reason, he did not know his district. We all knew his wrong turns and zigzag routes would eventually cost a life, if they hadn't already. And from things Tronstad said, I was fairly certain he *was* taking drugs. As far as I was concerned, Sears had portrayed the two of them with uncanny accuracy.

"Know what he said about you?" Johnson asked.

"Me?"

"He said you were a natural-born fuckup. Said you could fuck up a wet dream. That he thought you should have been terminated in drill school. He said his goal from the first was to get rid of all three of us and bring in a crew that could do the job, but once he got there, he decided you would be first."

"He's an asshole," Tronstad muttered.

I was a fuckup? Sure, I'd made some mistakes, a few more when Abbott or Sears happened to be watching, but they made me nervous and I was new.

"You thought that dickhead was your friend?" Tronstad said. "I can see now we weren't doing you any favors holding this back. You want to know what he said about you? He was asking if we knew anybody who wanted your spot after he bumped you to another station. Isn't that right, Robert?"

"He mentioned it a *couple* of times."

None of this was fair. I hadn't stolen anything. I wasn't a thief. I hadn't bought a new car, nor had I made plans to move to Rio de Janeiro and take a string of mistresses. At least now I knew, perhaps, the reason Sears had turned against me so quickly: it wasn't a novel posture he'd adopted today, but rather an attitude he'd been entertaining and concealing from me for months. All along I thought Sears had favored me above the others. When he approached a few minutes later, I was still stunned by the revelations.

"Come on, guys," Sears said, happily. "I got us an assignment. Get up, Gum. You can sit on your butt some other time."

"We're not due up," Tronstad said. "Some crews here have been waiting half an hour."

"I jumped the line. Sue me." Sears walked ahead of us, carrying his portable radio in one hand, a six-volt battle lantern in the other.

"What're you going to do?" Johnson asked Tronstad.

"Fuck if I know."

"You're not going to do anything," I said. "I'll be watching."

Wearing our MSA bottles and backpacks, the three of us headed toward the fire building, Sears marching in front like a duck leading his sullen brood.

20. HEY, LADY, QUIT SMOOCHING ON THAT OLD FART

The fire buildings sat between Aurora Avenue and Dexter Avenue, both arterials. Another arterial, Mercer, ran along the south side, near the fire complex, and it was on this road that a task force of six engines from regional fire districts south of Seattle was waiting in a long line, black smoke smothering their vehicles and personnel. I couldn't think of a worse place to post them.

Knowing this was the last night I would wear turnout gear or be part of this army of hose jockeys, I tried to hardwire it all into my memory, soaking in the ethos, color, and sensibility of my firefighting life. After two years I was only just getting used to all this, and tomorrow it would be gone.

I felt a wave of melancholy over the fact that I'd let my mother down. Just as surely as she'd devoted her life to making certain I got a solid foundation, I'd devoted the past month to bankrupting her efforts. Worst of all, her last days would dwindle away in isolation.

City Light workers had killed the power to the fire building and the nearby streetlights, but on Dexter the flames along the face of the building provided so much light that a hundred feet away you could read a newspaper by it. I counted six teams of firefighters spaced on the street outside the building wall, most of them holding down two-and-a-half-inch hose lines or hunkered on monitors. The two-and-a-half-inch nozzles dispensed three hundred gallons per minute, the monitors eight hundred gallons per minute, and the back pressure from these appliances was such that at least one firefighter, and sometimes two, had to babysit them to keep them from kicking back or sliding around.

At the far corner of the building, firefighters had strung lines out of every conceivable port on two pumpers, until the hose in the street looked like a plate of spaghetti. There were spots in the roadway where the layers of cylindrical hose were two or three feet deep, where you had to step over the hardened hose the way you stepped over a fence, and where water got trapped inside the twisted stacks and formed pools a child could dog-paddle in.

In the dark along the south side of the building, a crew from Engine 6 dragged hose to a point at the southeast corner of the fire building, where they'd been told to set up a monitor for us. Sears informed us we were to man this monitor as soon as Engine 6 got water to it.

Johnson and I dragged hose while Tronstad traipsed alongside griping, occasionally filming us with the small video camera he sometimes carried. It was vintage Tronstad: all mouth, no work. "Jesus. Why don't *they* man it?"

"They've got other jobs," snapped Sears. "We don't." You could tell he'd about had it with Tronstad, too frustrated to even try to make him help.

When you thought about it, this was a bizarre situation. Any other officer in the city would have turned us in back at the station, but our lieutenant couldn't stand the thought of missing out on a 4-11.

Micromanaging each phase of our task, Sears gave a series of unnecessary instructions but studiously ignored Tronstad's lack of cooperation. When the monitor was set up, he watched for a few minutes as we poured water into the flames, then lost interest and wandered off, moving up the line of heavy appliances, chatting with the other crews. There was a time when he would have been pulling hose alongside us, when our sweat was his sweat, but we were lepers now. It was hard to blame him. I had no wish to be associated with this triumvirate of greed and folly, either.

After thirty minutes of holding down the monitor along-side Robert Johnson, I approached Tronstad, who was forty feet away, and asked if he needed help with the two-and-a-half-inch line he was manning.

"Fuck you, ya little snitch." He put the video camera on me and began taping. He'd been taping us on and off all day.

"Okay. Yeah. Sure."

"No. I mean it. Get the fuck out of here. I can't stand to look at your face. Move."

He continued to film me as I walked back to the monitor, where Johnson was adjusting the stream, taking his job con-scientiously, in contrast to Tronstad, who hadn't moved his nozzle once.

The fire continued to burn unobstructed, and in fact to grow, while we pumped half of the Cedar River Watershed into it. One way or another, most of the water we poured in flowed back out of the building, flooding the street and send-ing waves of lukewarm water up into our bunking pants and boots as we sat on the hose. My socks were sopping. At the hour mark we saw no signs that the water was having any salutary effect other than to keep nearby buildings from ig-niting. From time to time Sears showed up, gave more un-necessary instructions, watched for a minute or two, then rambled away as if he had another task on the other side of the building, which he didn't.

"He's like a flea, ain't he?" Johnson said, his face glowing sepia in the orange-yellow light from the flames. "You ever notice how he can't sit still? It's almost as if he thinks he's in charge of the whole fire, you know. He talks about Tronstad having Attention Deficit Disorder, but he's got it worse. Can you imagine being in a cell with him? He'd drive you nuts." Johnson laughed dismally. " 'Course, he's not going to be in a cell. We are."

"I blew it. I'm sorry."

Johnson sighed. "We both blew it. We never should have let Tronstad keep those bags. I guess if I've learned one thing in life, it's that you make your choices and you take your consequences. We threw the dice, and they came up snake eyes. "

"Speak for yourself. I didn't roll any dice."

"Sure you did, Gum. You knew the right thing was to turn us in, but you didn't do it, did you?"

"You didn't do the right thing, either."

"We're not talking about me. We're talking about *you*."

"I shouldn't even be part of this."

"Now you're whining. You hid those bags. You covered up a crime. Then you came back from our four-off and found out the government was looking for Ghanet's money. You had another opportunity to make a phone call. You didn't, did you?"

"I couldn't throw you guys in the clink. Not after you saved my bacon at Arch Place."

"I appreciate that, but people don't get fired for missing a single alarm. You should know that. We didn't save you from anything but a spanking."

Much as I hated to admit it, Johnson was right. Failing to override my own timidity and taking the easiest path was my biggest flaw, and this time it had been fatal.

After another half hour sitting on the appliances, it became apparent the other crews on the street were being rotated out and *we* weren't. "He volunteered us to skip the normal rest periods, didn't he?" I said.

"Would you expect anything less?" Johnson said.

"This bottle's killing my back."

Flames curled high and licked the night sky, alternating colors in a myriad of hues as diverse types of materials in the structure were consumed. "Sure is pretty. You kind of wish we could have a fire like this about once a week. People forget how splendiferous a tragedy can be," said Johnson.

I was in so much trouble. I was in as much trouble as if I'd taken a gun and robbed a branch of the Treasury. Once, years ago on my skates, after I zipped out into the street on Alki without looking carefully, a car struck me and I went tumbling over the hood. The feeling I'd had for those few seconds as I flew through the air was a lot like the feeling I'd been having for the last hour tonight—acute disbelief. A feeling that it couldn't be happening. That it couldn't be real. That this couldn't be *my* life. Maybe somebody else's life, but not mine.

Even if I managed to talk my way out of a jail term for the bonds, there was still Chief Abbott's death to worry about.

As the hours passed, the puddles in the street grew deeper and broader, and as happened sometimes at big fires, the water runoff itself became one of the problems.

"You know, Gum, I'll be seeing my attorney, J. P. Gibbs, first thing in the morning. You should see yourself an attorney, too."

"No shit."

By ten o'clock the fire hadn't diminished. In fact, shortly before we were relieved, another interior wall collapsed and prompted a flare-up that shot over a hundred feet into the night sky. We oohed and aahed like schoolboys and then carefully redirected our streams to tamp down the hot spots, though our water was about as effective as a BB gun against a charging moose.

Toward the end, I went back to Tronstad, who was getting weary and didn't refuse my help this time, although after a moment he said, "You are just the biggest friggin' jackass I've ever known. You never should have said a word to Sears."

"You're right. I should have turned you in that first night, at Ghanet's house."

Tronstad held my eyes for a few seconds, then burst into anguished laughter. "That's right. That's exactly what you should have done."

After the crew of Engine 11 relieved us, the four of us trudged over to the rest area and took off our MSA backpacks and bottles. Sears crossed the street to the command post and began communing with a chief he knew. Johnson sidled up to another black firefighter and began talking in low tones, while Tronstad downed Twinkies and a Coke. I wasn't able to force down anything but a cup of Gatorade. Afterward, I stood off by myself in a funk. I was angry with myself. With Sears. Tronstad. At my dumb luck for having been assigned to Station 29 out of drill school.

We were in the rest area fifteen minutes before I spotted someone I recognized in the crowd on the other side of the yellow fire-scene tape.

I walked over and stood in front of her for a nanosecond before her eyes came to rest on mine. When she realized who I was, she gave a little jump. The old guy she'd wrapped herself around wore a disheveled suit, his tie unknotted. He was maybe sixty or seventy. Hard to tell. I'd only seen him once before, the afternoon the pig fell through their roof, and his eyes looked dead then, too. They were black and flat tonight and never looked at you directly, always surveying some object in the distance. Bernard Pederson. Daddy.

Iola wore tight designer jeans, high-heeled boots, and a fancy coat.

When she spotted me, Iola whispered something into Bernard's ear, sending him on an errand, and as he turned and lumbered gracelessly through the crowd, she gave him a pat on the butt. I was pretty sure he hadn't recognized me.

After he was gone, Iola turned to me, stepping forward until she was pushing against the yellow ribbon.

"Firefighter Gum. How nice to see you in all your gear." She whispered, "You know how hot that gets me."

"What are you doing?"

"We came to see the fire. We were on our way home from Carmelita's. A little celebration."

"What's all the smoochin' on the old guy?"

"The old guy? That's funny. I suppose from your perspective, he does look old. Surely you remember Bernard."

"Bernard's not . . . but you call him *Daddy*."

Stepping forward, she cupped my face in her cool palms. "A lot of wives call their husbands that. Don't be upset. I think it's sweet that you didn't realize he's my husband. I mean, that's what I liked about you from the beginning. Your naïveté. I suppose it's only fair to tell you I'm tired of it now."

"You mean you're tired of me?"

"That's right, sweetie."

"You're ending our relationship?"

"Is that what it was? A relationship? Yes, I suppose I am ending it."

"If I'd known you were married, I never would have had anything to do with you."

"I wear a ring, sweetie."

"I thought that was from your first marriage."

"This *is* my first marriage. It was a lark, sweetie. Something to fill my afternoons. Don't look so shocked. I was mad at Bernard, so I had an affair. If you weren't such a bumpkin, you'd understand. It was a hoot. I won't forget you anytime soon. I've always wanted my own little fireman."

I watched the flashing red lights flicker across Iola's face. "Were you going to tell me, or were you just going to stop showing up?"

"Oh, you *are* hurt."

"I just want to know if you were going to tell me."

"I suppose I probably wasn't. But, hey, men do it to women all the time."

"Not me."

"Don't be so sensitive. It was a simple little flirtation. Now it's time for you to find a girlfriend your own age. Hush now. He'll be back soon, and I'd rather you two didn't meet."

Frankly, I was struck dumb. Not because I'd been a mere flirtation. Or because she'd dumped me. I'd been on the verge of doing the same to her for weeks. What bothered me was that I'd seen anything at all in this woman, who was about as shallow as a puddle of milk in a house full of cats.

"You'll live, sweetie. These things can be so messy. Bernard had a little friend once who called the house for months after he was finished with her. It was *so* tawdry. You don't want to be like that."

"There is one thing, though."

"What is that?"

"I left something at your place. I'll need to come by and pick it up. Maybe later tonight."

"Don't even think about it. Since that pig fell through our

roof, Bernard's been worse than ever. He gets up a couple of times in the middle of the night and checks the yard. He takes a gun to bed with him. I'm not joking."

"Maybe I could swing by tomorrow morning when he's not there."

"What could you possibly have left at our place? A jacket or something? Tell me what it is, and I'll bring it to you."

"That won't work."

"You'll have to write it off, then, because this is the last time we're going to see each other. Now shoo, before Daddy comes back. Shoo."

"It will just take a second."

"You show up, I'll call the police." It was an ironic threat, because by morning I would most likely already be in the hands of the police.

I watched her float away through the bystanders.

After a while, I felt a tap on my shoulder. "There you are," said Lieutenant Sears. "Come on. We've got another assignment. Let's go do something good for a change."

21. FULL TILT BOOGIE

Sears switched on the heavy-duty orange battle lantern he'd been carrying all night, peering momentarily into the cone of light, so that his face took on a curiously impish look. Every once in a while he did something that amused me, and staring into flashlights was one of my favorites.

"Come on," he said. "We're going to check the water damage down the road. I sent Ted and Robert ahead."

"Can we at least take off these backpacks?"

"The backpacks stay."

On top of all my other problems, I couldn't help obsessing about the way Iola had blown me off. What made me sore was how much of an ego massage it had been for her. I had the feeling jilting me had been on the program from the beginning, that she'd planned and choreographed the finale during those first minutes of sex at Station 29, that I'd been a pawn in a twisted marriage rite she and Bernard had been playing out for years.

It was hard to believe I could feel such gnawing emotional wounds when I was on my way to the slammer, but even a man walking to the gallows can step on a thorn.

Sears continued on while I stopped and bent over, hands on my knees, thinking I was going to vomit. When I caught up he was talking as if I'd been beside him all along. "We're going to track down all this water, Gum. Make sure it's not doing any property damage. Water can be as damaging as fire. There's a lesson in that."

"Yes, sir. I want to keep learning lessons. I'm probably going to be a firefighter for another couple of hours."

Ignoring my sarcasm, he nodded at a photographer who'd set up a tripod on the sidewalk.

"How long do you think before you guys put it out?" the photographer asked.

"We're not going to tap this one, sir," Sears said. "It'll burn itself down, but if you want a time line, I'd say another hour, hour and a half."

Sears led me down a quiet street that ran east and west and terminated at the south end of Lake Union several blocks away. The streetlights were out, and the roadway was vacant. The police had cordoned off the entire neighborhood. Here and there, sawhorse construction signs with flashing orange beacons stood like sentinels to warn people of an ongoing storm drain project that had left temporary holes in the street, some as large as bomb craters.

The farther downslope we proceeded, the deeper the water got as tributaries fed in from thoroughfares, all of it murky runoff from our fire. By the time we'd walked a block and a half, the heavy black water was deep enough that we were in danger of being swept off our feet. We picked our path carefully, hiking the center of the empty roadway, where the flow was shallower.

"Looks like it's headed for the lake," Sears said. "We're

flowing over ten thousand gallons a minute, most of it straight out of that building. I wonder if this is causing traffic problems on Westlake. What do you think?"

I said nothing.

The street was a ghost town, dark and empty, just us and the black water. We used our lights to keep from stepping into holes.

I kept thinking that now that we were a few blocks from the fire, I might make a run for it. Maybe if I got to the Pedersons' place in West Seattle before Iola and Bernard did, I could retrieve the bags and escape. I had no idea what I would do with the bonds, for I had no intention of spending stolen money, but I knew I couldn't leave twelve million dollars in bearer bonds lying around.

It was the closest to hope I'd been in hours. It wouldn't be as if I were running from the police, because the police didn't know about me yet. I wouldn't be running from anybody but Sweeney Sears, followed in a few hours by the full force of the federal government, of course. The feds would figure out right away that we had some or all of Ghanet's money. Flight would keep me out of jail momentarily, and like every fugitive, I had already begun planning my life minute by minute instead of week by week or year by year. Postponement was not the same as exoneration, but it was beginning to feel as if it was the only goal I had a shot at.

Knowing I wouldn't have more than a few minutes to stuff a sleeping bag and a knapsack with essentials, I rehearsed what to pack when I got home. It went without saying that my Subaru WRX would be useless. They would put an APB out on the car first thing.

"Ten thousand gallons a minute, and every drop is headed for the same place," said Sears. "We should have looked into this a long time ago. What do you think, Gum? You want credit for averting a disaster?"

"Will it get me a lighter sentence?"

Again, Sears pretended he hadn't heard me.

Tronstad and Johnson were right. Sending the three of us to jail meant nothing more to Sears than another line in his résumé; three more rungs to scrape his boots on as he climbed up through the department infrastructure.

"You know, Gum, there was a period when I believed I could make you into a good firefighter."

"Being a good firefighter isn't all there is to life."

My statement stopped him cold. He actually stopped walking. I knew why. Being a good firefighter *was* all there was to his life. "Gum," he said angrily, "if you're a good firefighter, you're also a good human being. The two go hand in hand."

"So if you're *not* a good firefighter, you're *not* a good human being? I know a lot of people who aren't capable of doing this job who are marvelous human beings."

"You're distorting my meaning."

"I know exactly what you mean. You really do think being a good firefighter is the point of life. It makes you nervous, doesn't it? That I know about you."

"I'm just committed to my job. Listen, Gum. I know you're angry, but you have to believe me when I say I feel bad about this."

"I don't have to believe shit."

Sears looked at me hard. "What did Ted tell you anyway?"

"He said you asked them who might want to come up to Twenty-nine's to replace me."

"I admit I might have thought about some manpower switches. It didn't have anything to do with you personally."

"Sorry to be such a disappointment."

He turned and once again began walking downslope toward Lake Union. By now, even in the shallows, the rushing water was well past our ankles. Had we stepped into the gutter, the stream would have eddied up over the tops of our tall boots.

"Where the hell are they?" Sears asked. "I told them not to scout too far ahead . . . Jesus, you don't think they took a flyer, do you?"

I looked him in the eye for the first time during our walk. "I have no idea how bad they want to stay out of jail, sir."

"I can't believe I sent them down here alone. Oh, shit. That was a—" When he grabbed my arm to make certain I didn't escape, too, I jerked it out of his grasp. He tried to grab me again, and I pulled away a second time, as we approached a side street that was wall-to-wall water. The water on this street was flat and black and lumbering instead of shallow and racing. Half a block away on the side street, I spotted Tronstad crouched in the center of the roadway, next to a couple of flatbed trucks and a backhoe. From where we stood, it looked as if Tronstad was ankle deep in a long, black mirror. Johnson was several hundred feet beyond Tronstad.

This area was darker and quieter than the other streets in the neighborhood, bordered by windowless two-story parking garages and what appeared to be a manufacturing building, also windowless.

Still in a crouch, Tronstad skimmed the water's surface with his fingertips. "What do you have?" Sears shouted. "You got something?"

"You gotta see this."

"What is it?"

"You gotta see it."

Holding to the shallowest part of the stream, we headed down the center of the street, and as we drew closer I noticed Robert Johnson running toward us in what he would have termed a full-tilt boogie, splashing in the water, yelling something I couldn't make out. I'd never seen him run like that, certainly not in full gear.

"What is it?" Sears shouted.

"You gotta see it! It's unbelievable," Tronstad replied.

Once again Johnson shouted something unintelligible. Sears began jogging toward Tronstad, his equipment jangling, his boots splashing.

It took a few seconds to realize what was happening.

I began sprinting, hollering for Sears to stop, but by the time I closed the gap and put my hand on his shoulder, it was too late for both of us.

"It's a trap," I said, as the two of us plunged into the sinkhole at the same time.

At first all I knew was that water had rushed up my nose

and was bogging down my turnout clothing. My helmet hit the water like a mini-parachute, and the chin strap wrenched my neck. Then I was under the surface, maybe three or four feet under. My boots filled quickly. I tried to swim, and kicked and splashed and attained the surface, caught a momentary glimpse of Johnson and Tronstad thirty feet away before I was dragged under. I gulped some air. Just enough.

Water rushed into my face again, and I swam with my arms, kicked, tried my best to resurface, yet the more I strained to reach the surface, the deeper I was pushed. Sears was holding me. Grasping my helmet from above, using me as a stepping stone, using my buoyancy to supplement his own.

It was only then that I remembered Sears couldn't swim.

I tried to breaststroke in the direction of Tronstad and Johnson, but Sears was keeping himself above the surface by holding me under. I'd become his personal flotation device. His panic was needless, because our equipment trapped enough air that it would have kept him afloat for a good little while. Had he relaxed for a few seconds, he would have seen that.

Without control of my head, I couldn't swim, and not being able to swim, I couldn't resurface. Nor could I dive under to escape, the way I'd been taught in Red Cross lifesaving. Through the water I could hear Sears shouting for help.

For a few seconds I relaxed and took stock of my situation, straining to reach out with my feet, hoping to find the bottom and push off, but the water was simply too deep.

When I turned on my flashlight, I was able to see a surprising distance underwater. It was maybe eight or ten feet deep here, deeper at the end of the pool where Tronstad and Johnson were standing.

Somewhere in the depths, right about where my light lost its effectiveness, I spotted a whirlpool—near the bottom of the pit—spiraling like a gigantic bathtub drain, an underwater tornado. It was what had dragged us down at first, and it frightened me more than the man riding me. It frightened me more than anything I'd seen in a long while.

22. THRILL ME, KILL ME

We'd been poor when I was growing up. Eat-the-crusts poor. One of the few things my mother could afford to do for me in the summers was to take me to a public swimming pool for inexpensive lessons. We used to hitch rides with the neighbors to Colman Pool below Lincoln Park. When I got older I walked three miles each way, or we'd ride the bus up to the YMCA pool across from Station 32. My mother, who had never learned to swim, was terrified about living in a city where there was a body of cold water in every direction, afraid I would drown the way a neighbor's child had. Consequently, I had lessons from the time I could walk, swam like a dolphin by the time I was eight, then went through life-saving courses and worked as a lifeguard during my last two summers of high school.

Had the two of us been in swimming trunks, slipping away from Sears and hauling him to safety would have been easy. A drowning man won't ride his flotation device under the surface, so I would have dived out of his grasp and swum around behind him, grasping him across the chest from behind and towing him to safety.

All of this was made difficult if not impossible by the fact that we were both wearing our complete complement of fire-fighting gear: fifty pounds of crap—nineteen pounds of compressed air cylinder and backpack, in addition to helmet, turnout trousers and turnout coat, knives and tools in our pockets, and portable radios. Plus rubber boots that came almost to our knees and were rapidly filling with water, which would soon turn into anchors.

Before I could consciously think of what to do, I slipped my thumbs under my chin strap and let Sears have the helmet, then ducked low and began swimming forward. It wasn't easy making headway with all that gear on. A lot of the problem was that I bobbed to the surface almost immediately, giving Sears another opportunity to grab me, which he did, his dogged tenacity outstripping even his first effort.

Sputtering, choking, gasping for air, he rode me. He climbed onto my backpack, pushing me under. I let him push and then went as deep as I could, and this time he released me.

Underwater, I fumbled with my MSA backpack, unfastening the waist belt, taking longer to loosen the chest strap, and dropping the cylinder, which bobbed to the surface. When I surfaced beside it, Sears began moving toward me like an eggbeater, intent on riding me one more time. I kicked once and moved away, keeping just out of reach. He was dangerous now, having lost, as does any drowning man, all sense of honor and purpose beyond keeping his head above water.

Without warning, something jerked me under.

Before I knew it, I was so far down I couldn't see any light. Spinning in circles. It took me a while to realize the whirlpool I'd seen earlier was sucking me deeper and deeper, until I didn't know east from west, up from down.

I stretched out my hands and feet, trying to stop, and found myself gripping a piece of rebar that jutted from one of the walls of the pit, holding on fiercely until I stopped spinning, though the water continued to suck at me. Eventually I was able to bring my waterproof flashlight around and orient myself.

Above were other flashlights. Below was a large black opening: a pipe. It was from this pipe that the whirlpool was originating. A drain at the bottom of this pit was sucking down great masses of water, and trying to suck me through it. If I let go of the rebar and headed for the surface, the suction would seize me again. Next time I might not be lucky enough to grasp something. Next time I might go straight into the pipe.

For the first time since we hit the water, I thought about dying.

The pipe below me was the diameter of a standard garbage

can, and the suction took all my strength to resist. I couldn't hold my breath forever, and I couldn't swim to the surface, so for half a minute I thought I was going to drown. Unable to let go, I was like a bird stuck on a wire in a windstorm. Then, for no reason that I could discern, the funnel-shaped whirlpool, which had been drifting like a spinning top, slowly released me.

Placing my feet on the concrete, I gave a mighty shove upward. I'd been under for well over a minute and barely had enough air left to reach the surface. Once I felt the cold air on my face, I took in as much oxygen as I could, gasping, then stroked toward Tronstad and Johnson. Though they were both within easy reach, neither stuck out a hand to help.

Behind me, Sears, who'd obviously swallowed some water, was in even more trouble than before.

"Help us, you bastards," I said.

Johnson made a move as if to reach out, but Tronstad put his arm across his chest and stopped him, then, as insane as it seems, picked up his camcorder and aimed it at me. I could visualize him replaying our deaths for the troops at the firehouse at some future date, the way he'd played the tape of him screwing his ex-wife.

When I reached the wall under Tronstad's feet, I got both elbows on the lip and began to lift myself laboriously out of the water. My waterlogged turnouts must have weighed five times what they weighed dry.

Before I could clear the pool, two things happened.

First, Robert Johnson stepped around Tronstad and grabbed my collar to help me. Then Sears caught me from behind and pulled me back into the pool.

Sears was in a worse panic than before, if that was possible, grabbing my head each time I resurfaced, pushing me under again and again. At one point his bottle hit me in the mouth. His fingernails raked my face.

I went limp, let him push me under, lower, and was finally out of his grasp. I swam deeper, hoping the whirlpool wouldn't snatch me again, ascertained which way he was facing, and came up behind him, trying to reach around his chest, but the bottle on his back made him too bulky to handle.

Still in a panic, he thrashed, twisted around, and reached out for me.

I grabbed his forehead and gave a mighty shove, pushing him away. Now, without his harassment, I swam to the ledge and launched myself up beside Johnson, then turned around on my hands and knees and reached out to give Sears a helping hand.

He was gone.

Nothing but a froth of bubbles populated the surface of the pool.

"Shit," I said. "Help me. Shit. Shit."

Tronstad was still filming with the camcorder, while Johnson, who stared dumbly at the water, said, "You know I can't swim."

I reached into the water blindly, moving my arm to and fro, then put my face in, although the last thing I wanted to do was submerge myself again. After a few seconds my eyes adjusted and I spotted a light, the battle lantern Sears still carried. He was doing a slow rotation six feet below me, caught in the whirlpool, tucked into a ball, spinning around as if his waist were curled around a bar.

I took another breath at the surface and again plunged my face into the cold water. He was deeper now, and there wasn't a thing I could do to help him. The whirlpool had him, and if I went in, it would grab me, too.

I watched the pinpoint of light from his battle lantern descend deeper. I watched until I could barely see the light. Suddenly it came heading back toward the surface like a torpedo, and before I could move, it smacked me in the face.

Tasting blood on my lips, I pulled my head out of the water and picked up the battle lantern.

"Where is he?" Johnson asked.

Tronstad knelt beside us, still filming.

"There's a pipe down there. I think he got sucked into it."

"That's not possible."

I stood and stripped my bunking coat off, then began peeling my suspenders and bunking trousers down to the boots, which were heavy with water. "Come on, you guys. Help me. We can get him out."

"Count me out," said Johnson. "I can't swim, and you know as well as I do that in a rescue situation sixty percent of the fatalities are rescuers."

"Tronstad?"

"Fuck him." Tronstad had turned the camcorder off. "That bastard was going to do us."

"Jesus! You *knew* that was a pit. You planned this." I looked around at the street. "You moved all the signs."

"You guys fell in. Not my fault."

"You set us up," I said. I pushed Tronstad, who pushed me back. Because my bunking trousers were around my knees, I fell hard on my backside.

I rolled over and put my head back in the water. The whirlpool was gone. So was Sears. There was nothing but darkness. Taking the occasional breath above the surface, I watched and waited. One minute. Two. When four minutes had passed and he still hadn't resurfaced, I knew he was gone. I knew it for certain when, a moment later, one of his gloves floated up to me.

"Jesus," I said, fishing the glove out of the water. "You lousy fuckin' bastard. You killed the lieutenant."

"*You* killed him. I got it right here on tape. You pushed him under, and he never came back up."

"What?"

"I got it right here on tape."

Grinning, Tronstad turned his recorder to playback and held it in front of me. He had captured twenty-five seconds of me and Sears thrashing in the water, the part where I grabbed his head and pushed him away. Unbeknownst to me, he'd gone straight under from my push. He'd been trying to climb up over me, was drowning both of us in his panic, but anyone who viewed the videotape would think I was the one in a panic, that I'd pushed him under, that I'd deliberately drowned my lieutenant. "So don't be blaming other people, Doublemint. Otherwise I'll have to show this around."

Warm blood coursed down my face and chin. My palms were bleeding from the rebar. My face stung where Sears had raked me with his fingernails. My upper lip was swollen. "You stupid bastards. You murdered him."

"I didn't do nothing," Johnson said.

"*You* murdered him," Tronstad said, smiling. "You drowned the fucker. I got it right here on tape."

23. HEATHER, ME, HIM, AND HIM

When they released me from Harborview at four in the morning, the safety chief drove me to Station 29, where I picked up my car and drove home. I slept until almost eleven, then lay in bed for a long time staring at the same ceiling I'd stared at all those times making love with Iola, who preferred to be on top, running the show.

I was in a state of shock that was hard to explain. I'd thought long and hard at the hospital about turning Tronstad in, but each time I tried to make the decision, I thought about that videotape of me shoving Sears underwater. It was clear on the tape he hadn't come back up after I shoved him. It looked like murder even to me. Me murdering Sears. Or manslaughter. Or whatever you call it. It scared me enough to keep my mouth shut.

At four in the afternoon, I put a Modest Mouse CD in and drove past Iola Pederson's home. Bernard's truck was in the drive, so I didn't stop. The next two days passed in a fog. Trying to cajole me into retrieving the bonds, Tronstad phoned me every two hours. Johnson called, too, more concerned with whether or not I was planning to blab about Sears's death than about laying his hands on the bonds, though he did mention the money in his third and fourth calls. And then again somewhere around his ninth call.

I scanned the local newspapers. One headline said, *Fire*

Officer Dies in Freak Mishap. Another said, *Firefighter Hero Narrowly Escapes Drowning.*

Late Thursday afternoon the three of us attended Sears's funeral at the same Catholic church on Capitol Hill where Abbott got his send-off. Before, during, and after the service I spoke to no one, a large bandage concealing the scratches on my face. Every time I caught someone staring, I was reminded of how much the white bandage stood out in a sea of black hats and black uniforms.

Parts of the two-hour funeral passed in a blur, while others dragged. It was a gut-wrenching affair. There were bagpipers and hundreds of uniformed personnel, the mourners from other departments, Heather's rugby teammates, and assorted citizens who'd gone to school with the dead man, had been on committees with him, or had skied with him.

People were beginning to call Station 29 the department's bad luck station. Ted Tronstad encouraged that line of chatter, possibly because it kept speculation centered around luck instead of the actions or inactions of our crew.

When you don't like a guy and he dies, in some ways it's a worst-case scenario. Perhaps because of this, Robert Johnson blathered on at length to anybody who would listen about how hard we'd tried to save Sears. I wanted to tell him to shut up, that he might as well have blurted a confession, but once he got rolling he was impossible to derail. According to Johnson, he'd almost gone into the drink himself trying to fish Sears out, and he didn't swim any better than Sears. He said the whirlpool would have sucked down a Volkswagen.

Tronstad came at it from a different angle, explaining that the stress of handling the funeral arrangements for Abbott and of losing a friend had warped the lieutenant's judgment and dampened his reflexes, that these were the reasons he'd stumbled into the pool and hadn't been able to extricate himself.

I didn't talk to anybody. Any conjecture about my lieutenant's death brought up images of the videotape. Us struggling. Me grabbing his face and ramming him under the surface. The camera lingering on the spot long enough for the viewer to realize he wasn't going to bob back up, lingering on me as I put my face in the water to survey the damage I'd done.

On Tuesday morning, instead of waking up in an orange King County Jail jumpsuit, I woke up cloaked in the mantle of celebrity, just as I had after bringing Susan and Fred Rankler's dead and dying bodies out of their burning home. It was the second time in a month I'd fraudulently sideslipped ignominy to become a hero. If Arch Place was my pedestal to fraud, surviving the water that vacuumed Sears to his death was my monument. Once again I'd become something of the department paladin.

For reasons I couldn't begin to understand, firefighters looked at me with renewed respect and deference. The groupthink seemed to be that if you wanted somebody you could count on, Jason Gum was your man—even though Sears had counted on me, and Sears was dead. The Ranklers had counted on me, and they were dead. How did these events make me a hero in anyone's eyes? It was tempting to bask in the respect of my peers, but I knew I didn't deserve their esteem, and the conceit sickened me.

Under police questioning, Johnson wept. I never knew whether it was artifice or genuine, though Tronstad swore it was the former. But then, Ted thought I was faking, too.

The police weren't happy with any of it, yet I could tell from their questions they didn't suspect murder. To complicate matters, the first street officer on the scene drove into the pool and high-centered her squad car on the edge of the hole, barely managing to climb out of the vehicle without drowning in the sinkhole herself.

At five the next morning, engineering crews recovered Sears's mangled body, which had been wedged into a culvert a block east of the pool. Most of the bones in his face had been broken during his ride through the concrete pipes. The condition and location of his corpse, my hospitalization, and the false sincerity Tronstad and Johnson displayed under questioning convinced investigators it was an accident.

I realized Tronstad had let me out of the pool only because I was the one who knew where the bonds were. The bonds, which had been such a burden to me over the past week, had ended up saving my life. From Tronstad's point of view, it had all come off without a hitch. Sears wasn't around to put us in jail, I was still alive to tell him where the bonds were, and he had a videotape with which to blackmail me.

At four-thirty Thursday afternoon the three of us were in Station 29's bunk room changing out of our class-A uniforms. We were the only people in the station. I was morose to the point of paralysis. In fact, while Johnson and Tronstad changed into civilian clothing, I stood like a wooden Indian in front of my clothing locker: numb, speechless, and more convinced than ever I was damned. The worst part was that I couldn't think of a thing I could do to make things right.

If I started talking to the authorities, there was a remote possibility Johnson's conscience would kick in and he would back me, but there was a greater chance he wouldn't, and that I would be charged in Sears's death. It was one thing to report events to the police, and quite another to turn yourself in for a murder you didn't commit.

"What's the problem, Juicy Fruit?" Tronstad asked, smirking. "Don't look so down in the mouth. Relax. We're free and clear. You, me, and Robert."

"That was a better funeral than Abbott's," Johnson said. "Don't you think, Gum?"

"You killed him," I said, staring pointedly at Tronstad.

"You read the paper. The man drowned. You'd think a guy who knew as much as he did would learn how to swim. Dumb fucker."

"Don't talk about Sears like that."

"Oh, he's your buddy now? He was going to send you to jail, pal."

"You moved those warning signs. You turned that hole into a trap."

"I didn't touch any signs. Did I, Robert?"

Johnson turned away.

"I know you saw him moving those signs," I said to Johnson. "You probably helped."

"I didn't help."

"You saw him."

"It was just a hole full of water. We didn't even know how deep it was. We didn't know there was an outlet at the bottom."

"Shut up, Robert," Tronstad said.

I pressed Johnson. "There is no neutral ground here. You're either a murderer or you're not. Which is it?"

"Gum, can't we just let this be? You're getting way too emotional."

"A man's dead! Two men! You cocksuckers."

"You're turning into a foul bird, Jason boy," Tronstad said.

I was convinced now that Tronstad had locked Abbott in the smoke room with the intention of leaving him there until he died. Until now I'd been willing to think it was a vicious prank gone haywire, but no longer.

"Come, come, Mr. Gum. You need to step back and look at the big picture. You don't want to go to jail. Robert and I wouldn't get our bonds, would we?"

"Hello?" A woman rapped lightly on the bunk-room door. "Hello?"

To my astonishment, Sears's widow, Heather Wynn, stepped into the bunk room, moving awkwardly in a skirt and heels.

"Hey, Heather," said Tronstad.

"I didn't know if it was okay to come in."

"Oh, for gosh sakes," said Johnson, closing the space between them and giving her an energetic hug. "We feel so miserable about this." Robert looked around at me. "We were just talking about it, in fact."

"You were changing. I'll leave."

"No. Tronstad and I are done. Gum can wait."

"You've all been so nice."

"I thought you would still be at the cemetery," Johnson said.

"I have a tough enough time around Sweeney's parents on

a good day, but they're driving me insane today. They think they're the only ones who ever loved him."

We were quiet for half a minute. Finally, Heather stepped across the space between us and touched my face above the bandage, her cold hand lingering on my skin. It was oddly personal and not a little erotic. "You're taking this harder than anyone, Gum. I can tell."

We stood like that until Tronstad said, "Maybe you want to have some coffee? We can go to the other side and see if they made any."

"I came here to talk to you three."

"Us?" Johnson asked.

"There was something going on here at work. Sweeney said it involved the three of you."

Johnson smiled. "Us? Me, him, and him?"

"The crew, he said. I assume it meant you three."

Tronstad said, "Did Sweeney talk much about his work to you?"

"All I want to know is what was going on."

Johnson stammered, "I, uh, don't know what to say. Do you, Gum?"

"Don't drag me into this."

"Why not?" Heather turned to me. "Why shouldn't he drag you into this?"

"Because I was the last person to speak to your husband. Because I feel like shit."

My statement startled Heather, who stepped back half a pace. She was one of those people who was always in your face, violating your personal territory, and she'd been too close since she touched my face.

"Jesus, Gum," Tronstad said. "Go easy on Heather, would you?"

"Maybe we better adjourn to the beanery," Johnson said. "Let Gum change his uniform. Maybe get him something to drink. I think he might be dehydrated."

"Fuck you."

Heather took another step back, while Tronstad moved in and draped his arm across my shoulders. "Maybe we should drag out that old videotape, huh, Gum? Play it for Ms. Wynn."

"What videotape?" Heather asked.

"Oh, just some snippets I saved over the months we worked with your husband. Shots of us drilling. Some clowning around in the beanery. I wasn't sure now was the time, but we could do it now."

"I'd like to see those," Heather said.

"What do you think, Gum?" Tronstad squeezed my shoulders so hard, it hurt.

"Not just now."

Tronstad bobbled his eyebrows. "Maybe I'll let Heather see it later."

"I'd like that," Heather said. "Maybe at the same time, you could look at some notes my husband left."

"Don't tell me he kept a diary?"

"A journal. It was the mention of money that kind of threw me."

"Money?" Tronstad looked at me.

If this was a fishing expedition, I couldn't see it in her eyes, which were puffy from crying. As always, she gave the impression of being a strong woman, both physically and mentally, but she also gave off the aura of a woman who wasn't quite centered. From our talks with Sears, we knew she'd left him several times over the past couple of years, leapfrogged from one fad diet to another with a devotion bordering on madness, and had sleep problems so severe she'd been to specialists. Tronstad opined that she needed to get rattled by a good man, but he said that about all women. To my mind Heather was easy to talk to and fun to be with. I could understand what Sears saw in her.

"What money are you talking about?" Johnson asked. "Like his paycheck was screwed up or something?"

"He said you guys had come into a lot of money. He said he thought you were going to give some to him."

My stomach sank through the floor. Had Sears been jobbing us all along? Was it possible he'd had no intention of turning us in, that he'd been toying with us so he could get a share of Ghanet's loot? Was that why he'd taken us to the fire instead of calling the police from the firehouse? If so, it was ironic he hadn't revealed his plans sooner, because if he'd asked for a quarter of the bonds, I don't think it would have occurred to Tronstad to drown him.

"He thought *we* came into some money?" Tronstad asked. *"Us?"*

"You got new cars. Two of you did."

"I'm going to get changed." I pulled my jeans off the hook in my locker and looked at Heather, who stared back guilelessly, her long face and blue eyes framed in a wash of dirty-blond curls. I unbuckled my trousers, but she made no move to leave.

"Maybe we should have a look at those notes," Tronstad said. "I bet we could figure out what he meant by them."

"I don't know what it could have been," said Johnson. "Do you, Gum?"

"Sure I do." My words froze the room. "He helped Kirsten Abbott handle her affairs. He'd just totaled up the insurance and the state and federal awards for an on-the-job fatality. She came into a good chunk of change. Maybe he had a premonition the same thing was going to happen to him, that he was going to die and you were going to come into some money."

"Jesus, Gum," Tronstad said. "For a minute there I didn't know where you were headed. I bet you're right. The lieutenant had a premonition. Weird."

My hypothesis gave Heather pause. She didn't believe it, but she couldn't discount it without going back over the words Sears had penned in his journal. On a crew of liars, I'd turned into the ace prevaricator.

"Think I hear somebody at the front door," Johnson said, although I didn't hear a thing. "Probably some of the neighbors. I'll go get it."

Heather must have been holding back the whole time, because as soon as Johnson left, the floodgates opened and she wept like a three-year-old—her hands at her sides, tears flowing until her cheeks and chin were slippery, distorted stars of grief splashing her chest. Tronstad snaked an arm around her shoulder, motioning for me to do the same from the other side. There was nothing I wanted less than to console Heather alongside her husband's killer, but I did it anyway.

We stood in that awkward posture for several minutes. I kept trying to think of something comforting to say. Surely a man in the bowels of hell couldn't be suffering more than I was at that minute.

24. MR. AND MRS. BROWN

Over the watch office intercom we heard Johnson's voice. "Ow. Damn it, let go."

"Who are you talking to?" asked another male voice. Then, with a loud snap, the intercom shut off.

I stepped away from our ménage à trois of heartbreak and guilt and caught Tronstad's eye through a tangle of Heather's curls. With a flick of his head he motioned for me to go see what was going on.

"I was trying to be so strong," Heather said, weeping onto Tronstad's shoulder, her arms around his neck now, his around her waist, palms poised over her ass as if about to clasp it. I didn't like leaving her alone with him, but I didn't like what I was hearing on the other side of the station, either.

"Just let it out," Tronstad said, parroting some bad movie he'd seen. "Let it out."

I walked across the empty apparatus bay, my footsteps echoing off the walls. The apparatus bay, watch office, and chief's office were overflowing with flowers and cards from concerned neighbors and other fire stations. When I opened the door to the watch office, a man in his late sixties or early seventies was nose to nose with Robert Johnson, whose spine was pressed against the high watch desk attached to the wall.

When he saw me, the old man moved back alongside an older woman I assumed was his wife. Johnson straightened himself and stepped beside me. The woman, her hair in a tidy bun, feet encased in hose and heels, was wearing what appeared to be a real fox coat. She looked as if she'd been raised with money, or had spent her life pretending she had. The old man was ramrod straight, with a Marine's haircut and a glint of steel in his gray eyes, dressed in a sharp, if outdated, suit and dress shoes buffed so that a blind man could have seen them.

"What's going on?" I asked.

"I've never been in a firehouse before," said the woman, her words clipped and birdlike. "Where do you cook?"

"Just a minute, Mother," said the old man. "We'll take a tour when I've finished my business." He stepped forward. "Who are you?"

Although he had the overgrown eyebrows of an old man, he was tall and lean and moved with the fire and confidence of someone much younger.

"Gum, this is Agent Brown," Johnson said, his voice shaky.

"Agent?"

"FBI," said Brown. "I'm here to ask about the man you knew as Charles Scott Ghanet." He looked past me at Johnson. "Your friend here was giving me the runaround."

"Yes, sir. Maybe a little, sir. It won't happen again," Johnson said. I thought he might be mocking the old guy, but he wasn't. He was scared.

Brown turned to me with a look of disgust on his face. "You part of the crew found Ghanet's body?"

"Yes."

"What can you tell me about it? Was anybody else there when he died?"

"The house was locked when we got there."

"You see anybody hanging around?"

"Just the neighbor who called us."

"I understand you'd been to his place before."

"Everybody in the station has been there."

"What's your name?"

I tried to turn my head to see how Robert was taking this, but before I could do so the old guy grabbed my jaw, digging his fingers into my cheeks so hard, I could feel his nails, could feel the adhesive on the bandage pulling at my skin. I made an effort to shrug out of his grip, but his fingers were like a vise.

"Don't be looking at your friend for answers," Brown said. "I see somebody turning to their friends for answers, I get the feeling they're lying." He looked at my name tag. "Gum. You a junior firefighter cadet or something, Gum?"

"I—I'd like to see your ID."

"That's a good idea," Johnson added, timidly. "I didn't see no ID, either."

The old man dug his fingers deeper into my face, holding me the way you'd grasp a half-flat volleyball. "You going to answer me, Sweet Pea?"

"Not like this, I'm not."

Brown squeezed my face until I thought his nails would make me bleed, until, without thinking about it, I raised my arms and knocked his hand away. "You're not with the FBI."

"Sonny, you're beginning to try my patience. I *was* FBI. I'm retired now. But I'm still looking for eight million dollars stolen from the U.S. of A."

"You better see my attorney, J.P. Gibbs," said Johnson.

Before either of us knew it, Johnson was on his knees on the floor. I didn't understand how it happened until Brown grasped my thumb with his other hand, and levered me to the floor in a similar fashion, the two of us on our knees, side by side, controlled by the old man, who had my thumb in one fist, Johnson's in the other. "Jesus," said Johnson. "Ease up. You're going to break it."

"All you have to do is answer the questions."

"Where's the fire truck?" asked the woman. "Isn't there supposed to be a fire truck?"

"It's still at the funeral," I said.

"What funeral?"

"Ma, you just stay out of it." He looked at me. "Name, rank, and serial number."

"Jason Gum. I work here on Engine Twenty-nine."

"You're just a punk. Sure you're not a cadet or a Boy Scout or something?"

"No."

"What do you know about that money?"

"What I read in the papers."

The pressure on my thumb increased until I yelped. Johnson started to say something, then yelped, too. "Jesse," said the woman. "Ask them where the pole is. I thought fire stations were supposed to have a fire pole."

It had been a long time since I'd felt this much pain. "The station's all on one level," I managed. "We don't have a pole."

"Where do you sleep?"

"On the other side."

"Tell me about the man you knew as Ghanet," Brown said. "He used to have a fondness for women. You ever see any women at his place?"

"No."

"The night he died? What happened?"

"The night who died?" Tronstad asked, coming into the room. "How come you guys are on the floor?"

Now that there were three of us, Brown let Johnson and me get up. Tronstad was a loose cannon, a fact that was instantly apparent to anyone who looked into the wild blackness of his eyes, or saw his manic gestures, or the bobbing and bouncing around even when he was standing still, his movements like those of a methamphetamine freak. In fact, the thought occurred to me that maybe he *was* a methamphetamine addict. It would explain a lot.

"I'm here as a representative of the United States government," Brown said. "Who are you?"

"Bond. James Bond," Tronstad said, in a perfect imitation of Sean Connery.

"Glad to meet you, Mr. Bond," Brown said, extending his hand. Tronstad reached out to shake and was quickly brought to his knees with the same judo or jujitsu that had taken us down.

"Goddamn it!" Tronstad shouted. "Let go, motherfucker."

"Watch the mouth. There's a lady present."

"You fucker!"

"Keep mouthing off, I'll break it."

"Okay, okay. Just give the digits a rest, huh?"

Brown eased the pressure enough so Tronstad, who'd had the back of his head almost on the floor, was able to get back on both knees. Johnson and I looked at each other, and I knew we were thinking the same thing. There were three of us, and he was an old man.

Neither of us budged.

"What'd you find at Ghanet's place the night he died?" Brown asked.

"A dead body and a shitload of flies."

"I told you to watch your mouth."

"And junk. You ever seen that place? You drop a five-year-old in there, you wouldn't find him for a week."

"Was it locked when you got there?"

"Fuck you," said Tronstad. "Fuck you and the horse you rode in on."

As Brown applied more pressure, Tronstad grew silent, sucking air through his clenched teeth.

"It was locked," I said. "He had security locks on everything. Even the bedrooms."

"But you broke them open, didn't you?" Brown asked.

"We were looking for the body," Johnson said.

"Shut up, assholes!" Tronstad shouted. "Can't you see this guy's a treasure hunter?"

"I've done some research on you three," Brown said, exposing his long front teeth and their yellow stains. "Seems you've come up with some extra spending money lately. What's that all about?"

At that moment the door from the apparatus bay opened and Heather Wynn walked in, eyes awash in tears. "What's going on here?"

"Who are you?" Brown asked.

Sizing up the situation, she said, "I'm the person who's going to call the police. I mean it. My brother's a Seattle detective."

Realizing the interview was over, Brown let go of Tronstad and moved to the outside door. Tronstad crawled across the floor and struggled to his feet.

"I'm Linda Brown," said the old woman. "This is my husband, Jesse. I was wondering if you might give us a tour of the fire station . . . as long as we're here and all."

"You better leave," I said. Maybe it was the sheer weight of numbers, or the fact that Heather's brother was a Seattle cop, but Brown opened the door and stepped outside.

"You coming, Mother?"

"We're not going to get a tour, are we?"

"Not today, Mother."

In a free-for-all, Brown could have handled all three of us and Heather thrown in for good measure. You could only guess what he'd been like in his prime.

"I shoulda bitch-slapped him," said Tronstad, after they were gone.

"Nobody was stopping you," Johnson said.

"Who was he?" Heather asked.

"Some crazy old gummer claiming to be with the FBI."

"He's going to get his ass kicked," Tronstad said. "Come in here bustin' our chops."

"We should call the police," Heather said, moving to the phone on the watch desk.

"I don't think that's a good idea." Tronstad put his hand over hers.

Johnson said, "I didn't know you had a brother in the police department."

"I made that up. I thought it might scare him."

After Heather left, Tronstad and Johnson caught me in the bunk room in my underwear as I was changing. "Things are starting to get hot," Tronstad said. "This place is going to be crawling with treasure hunters. We need to pick up the money tonight."

"And do what?" I asked.

"I'll tell you one thing. You're not giving it back. You give it back, you'll go to the big house for what happened to Sears."

"You show the tape, I'll tell the cops about the bonds."

"You tell the cops about the bonds, I'll fuck up your mother."

"What?"

"You heard me. I know she's dying, and I feel for you, Jason. I feel for you both. But if you mess with me, I swear . . ."

"There's no need to get rough here," Johnson said. "Give us the bonds and everything will work out. You'll see."

I tugged my jeans on and stood in my socks, trying to think. "I'll need some time."

"Tomorrow night," Tronstad said, handing us each a folded real estate flier. "Beach Drive down by the Fauntleroy Ferry Terminal. Place has been vacant for weeks. The old woman got killed in her kayak by a speed boat out in the Sound, and the old guy moved to Thailand or someplace. Tomorrow night, eight o'clock. You're not there, I'm going to your mother's."

"You do, and I'll kill you."

"Hey, guys," Johnson said. "Calm down."

"Just get the shit."

"I'll get it."

25. I BEEN PRAYIN'

Ten minutes later Robert Johnson and I left the building together. I walked to my sweet little WRX and wondered idly what would become of it when I was in prison. My mother couldn't drive a stick . . . What was I thinking? She wouldn't even be around to store it.

Johnson followed me to my car, smiling bashfully. "Don't worry about it, Gum. I have a feeling everything is going to work out."

"You fucker."

"Hey. Don't—"

"Tronstad killed Sears, and you helped. And Abbott. He killed him, too."

"Don't be like this, Gum. Sure, we're in a little bit of a mess here, but I'm with the Lord now, and I'm not going to make any more mistakes."

"He moved those signs, didn't he?"

"By the time I figured out what he was doing, it was too late."

"It's not too late to go to the police."

"How can I? He goes to prison, I go, too. And you? He'll show that video and *you'll* go to prison. He'll go for Abbott, and you'll go for Sears."

"Not if you tell the truth."

"And the bonds will go back to the government. I didn't want to be a party to murder, Gum, but it wasn't my fault. If I knew how to swim it might have been different."

"Don't kid yourself. I've been using the same kind of half-assed logic all through this. If I hadn't been screwing Iola in the basement the night of Arch Place, none of this would have happened. I wouldn't have missed the rig, and Tronstad and I would have gone inside together, and we would have brought those people out, and they would have lived. I wouldn't have owed Tronstad, and I would have ratted him out on those bonds."

"You were porking a woman in the station? Where? Out back in your car?"

"The basement."

"Where in the basement?"

"All I'm saying is, if it hadn't been for my screwup and the fact that you guys covered for me, I wouldn't have had to keep my mouth shut when Tronstad took those bonds. And if I'd turned him in, he wouldn't have been around to lock Abbott in the smoke room. He wouldn't have drowned our lieutenant."

"Gum, you don't really think you would have saved those people at Arch Place?"

"He and I would have gone in together. That's the way it's supposed to work. The buddy system. He was forbidden to go in without a partner. That's why he was hanging out in the front hallway. He didn't want me to get in trouble, so he didn't tell Sears I was missing. Those people died because he was trying to save my ass."

"You don't know Tronstad very well. He was trying to save his own ass. He could have told Sears you weren't there and gone in with Sears. But Tronstad didn't want to go in with Sears because he plain didn't want to go in. Sears would have seen he couldn't face fire. Sears would have written him up. Tronstad wasn't going in under any circumstances, and you not being there was perfect for him. I watched his feet under the smoke in the doorway. He never moved. You don't get it, do you? Tronstad doesn't go into fires. He always has some kind of excuse. If you'd been there, you still would have been rescuing those people on your own."

"He was downstairs protecting my back with the hose line."

"He wasn't protecting anything. Hell, he was on the porch most of the time you were in there dragging those people out. Outside on the porch."

"I don't understand."

"At a good house fire Tronstad'll always back out on you. He's backed out on me a bunch of times. That's what he does, Gum. Tronstad looks out for Tronstad, and that doesn't include going into a fire building if he can figure a way out of it. He had plenty of time to crawl inside and tap that fire. *I* would have done it. *You* would have done it. Sears would have done it, too, if he'd known you weren't there. Tronstad didn't make the effort, because that's not what Tronstad's about."

"So you're saying—"

"I'm saying you didn't get those people dead. Tronstad did. I'm saying Tronstad cannot be trusted at a fire."

"If I'd been there earlier, they would have gotten out sooner."

"Maybe. But Tronstad wouldn't have been helping."

"Why didn't you tell me this before?"

"I figured you were on *his* side." It took me several seconds to realize what he was getting at. "That's right. The white guys against the brother. I half expected you to split the bonds with Tronstad and blow town."

"Geez, Robert. You should know me better than that."

"I do now." Johnson grinned. "Don't worry. I been prayin'. If we can go this far without getting nabbed, we can go the distance. I'm convinced of it."

Though I was thoroughly convinced of the opposite, I didn't argue. Let him have his delusions.

26. WRESTLING WITH WOMEN IN THE DARK

How could any of our lives turn out to be normal? Two men were dead, and Ted Tronstad was groping the recent widow like an inbred cousin at a clambake. I knew retrieving the bonds and handing them over to Tronstad would only make things immeasurably worse, but if I didn't, he'd blame Sears's death on me.

The fleeting thought occurred to me that he'd set up our meeting in a vacant house because it was a convenient spot for another murder, and that once he was in possession of the bonds, there would be nothing to keep him from silencing me. A conspiracy has no place for a man with a conscience, and Tronstad knew that. He knew I'd confessed to Sears and no doubt feared I would confess to others.

Any attempt on my life, or on Robert's, seemed a dumb move on Tronstad's part, but if you looked at everything else Tronstad had done since he found the bonds, he'd made a lot of dumb moves. Any sane person knew the police would focus on him if any more members of our crew died, but Tronstad's reality didn't always correspond to the real world.

When I got home, I found evidence that somebody had tried to force my back door: jimmy marks on the door next to the dead bolt. They hadn't gotten in. Mrs. Macklin, who lived in the other half of the duplex, was an older woman with acute emphysema, and because she was tied to an oxygen bottle, she was usually home. "I haven't seen nobody," she said when I asked her about it. "Been sick all week. Can barely get to the bathroom. Can you come in and help me with my garbage?"

"Maybe later."

I mowed Macklin's lawn, took out her garbage each week, and picked up items at the grocery store for her. Twice she'd overflowed her commode by stuffing in half a roll of toilet paper, and twice I'd cleaned it up for her. There were certain people, you gave them an inch, they took a mile.

The prowler could have been anybody, but I suspected Tronstad, or "Agent" Brown, the latter prospect infinitely more frightening than the former. While Tronstad was demented and dangerous, I figured as long as I had the bonds I could at least reason with him. Brown was an unknown quantity.

That evening I found my mother at the kitchen table in her tiny third-floor apartment on California Avenue, sitting in a chair she rarely moved from. She'd covered her bald head with a pink-and-white flower-print bandanna, a gift from me. She'd taken to wearing hoop earrings, which, along with the bandannas, lent her a vaguely exotic air, like a gypsy or a Caribbean fortune-teller. Her face was pale and drawn, dark circles under her eyes not unlike the chronic circles under Tronstad's eyes.

Though we didn't speak of it, I often wondered if suicide hadn't crossed her mind. Given my current circumstances, it was easy enough to understand why people in dire straits resorted to offing themselves. There was a sullen comfort to be had in knowing you wouldn't have to face the consequences of your actions. Chagrined that the thought had occurred to me, I did my best to put it out of my mind.

I sat on the worn sofa near the living-room window.

"What's the matter, Jason?"

"Nothing."

"You've been down for well over a week."

"Is it that obvious?"

"Yes."

"I'm sorry. I don't mean to bring any of this on you. It's just that I never in my wildest dreams thought I could be in this much trouble."

"Do you want to tell me about it?"

"I can't."

"Is it money trouble? You've been paying for so much around here lately. My rent. My prescriptions."

"Mom, it doesn't have anything to do with you."

"I wish you would talk about it."

I took my mother to dinner down the street from her apartment building, at a Chinese restaurant, where she barely touched her food and I barely touched mine. Even though we knew she wouldn't eat them later, we boxed up the leftovers and took them with us.

It was dark when we got home. We'd spent the meal discussing politics, which she followed ardently and believed had deteriorated to a dismal state over the course of her lifetime.

"You want to come up and keep me company?" she asked. "We could watch TV." Mother had been a reader her whole life, but the drugs wouldn't let her concentrate on the front page of a newspaper, much less a book. I knew she detested the fact that watching TV, catnaps, and looking out the window had become the primary staples of her day.

"Thanks, but I have errands."

"So late?"

"I love you, Mom."

"Love you, too." I kissed her brow and she gave me a long look before she closed the car door and walked across the sidewalk to her apartment building, dutifully carrying the plastic bag of pork fried rice and moo shu beef.

I waited for her to get inside, popped in a Built to Spill CD, and drove around West Seattle, shifting gears like a rally driver, taking corners as fast as the WRX allowed, using the familiar feel of the car and the long nervous minutes of insane driving in a fatuous attempt to restore my sanity. I drove past Ghanet's place and found it dark and quiet, with a sign I couldn't read from the street nailed to the front door.

Dropping down the hillside to Beach Drive, I revved the motor until I was traveling sixty-five miles an hour, then eighty, eighty-five, ninety, passing the rare car on the road, driving like a dead man—or a man who wanted to be dead. Working on Engine 29, I'd come down here and picked up bodies produced by precisely this sort of reckless motoring. For reasons I couldn't guess, I slowed to below the speed limit just seconds before a cop passed me headed in the opposite direction. He did a U-turn in the street and followed me for two miles, then abandoned the surveillance. No doubt some citizen with a cell phone had reported me, but once again, lady luck had thrown her hat into the ring on my behalf.

After twenty-five more minutes of aimless cruising, I drove back down to the water near the lighthouse and headed east with homes, apartment buildings, and condominiums occupying all the available land on the hillside to my right. On my left lay a sandy beach, and beyond that the dark Puget Sound. I turned onto Bonair Drive and headed up the hill. Passing Hobart Avenue slowly, I kept driving and parked two blocks away. Carrying my keys, a pair of wool gloves, and a small flashlight, I hiked down the hill.

Perched on the side of the wooded slope overlooking the Sound, the Pederson home lay in a small cul-de-sac that had been notched into the hillside. Above it, a small greenbelt was forested with elms and maples, the trees only just beginning to lose their green. To the right on an embankment sat a high apartment house and parking lot, so that the Pederson place appeared to sit in a flat-bottomed hole.

Although there was a Miata in the driveway, neither Bernard's truck nor Iola's Land Cruiser was in evidence. The nearest streetlight was burned out. Except for a light in the rear, the house was dark, the blinds drawn, and if anybody had taken note of my approach, I hadn't seen them. The garage was to the right of the house and separated by twenty yards of grass and old concrete driveway. I walked through the grass, listening carefully for any cars on the road and mentally marking a large rhododendron in the yard as a place of concealment should I need one. Not far away on the Sound, a ferry slid across the black water. Except for the engine of a car below on Alki Avenue and some muffled music from inside a nearby house, the neighborhood was as tranquil as a mausoleum.

Feeling my way across the uneven lawn, I kept the flashlight off until I was up against the garage. For the first time in a long while I got the feeling that this was going to work out, that I would retrieve the bags and clear the property without a problem, that Tronstad would disappear with his share and our troubles would be over. The flavor of success stuck with me until I found the door jammed—not locked, but binding on itself, as if humidity or the earth settling had kicked the door frame out of plumb.

It wasn't until I switched on my flashlight that I spotted the figure at the corner of the garage, a woman in jeans and a short-sleeved shirt. She was so still that at first I thought she was a mannikin. After a moment, I realized she had a gun, that it was pointed at my chest. "Hey there," I said, trying to sound friendly.

"Don't move, motherfucker."

"Jesus. You're not going to shoot me?"

"Give me one reason why I shouldn't."

"Is that you? You're, uh . . ." I shined my light on her. It was the young woman who'd told me to stop dating Iola; the woman who nearly broke my thumb in the same way Brown had nearly broken it at the firehouse.

"Who the hell are you? Step into the light."

"You're Sonja. Sonja Pederson. I should have recognized the Miata. Gum. Jason Gum."

"I know who you are. You're the pipsqueak who's been banging Iola. What are you doing here?"

"She's your mother, for God's sake. How can you talk about her like that?"

"She's my *step*mother. Bernard's my father." She lowered

the gun. "Bernard is due home any moment. He'll blow your balls off as soon as look at you."

"He doesn't know who I am."

"You think Iola doesn't tell him everything?"

"He *knows* who I am?"

"Maybe not by sight, but he knows more than you think. What are you doing sneaking around in the dark? You a Peeping Tom as well as having a Mommy fetish?"

"Don't be crude."

"I'm not the one banging a woman old enough to be my mother."

"She's not—"

"She's forty-five."

"I stopped seeing her."

"Good for you. Now tell me what you're doing here."

I knew if I told her I was here for something I left in the garage, she'd scare me off with the pistol and search for it herself. The odds of her packing the three bags into her Miata and delivering them to my place were about a zillion to one. I was better off if she thought I was a Peeping Tom.

She put the gun away, then walked over to me and grabbed my hand, twisting my wrist so the flashlight illumined my face instead of hers. She had a cigarette in her free hand, which explained what she'd been doing outside. "You spy on her? You go in the garage and masturbate?"

"Heck no."

She exerted more pressure on my wrist. "Then, what?"

"Let me go, and I won't come back."

Without letting go of my wrist, she inhaled off her cigarette and examined my face. Despite the fact that she'd already been outside some minutes in a T-shirt and jeans, her hand was incredibly warm. She held my wrist, staring into my eyes. Using the hand with the cigarette, she began patting down my pockets for weapons. When I tried to resist, she clamped my hand tighter, and before I knew it we were wrestling. Without releasing the cigarette, she tried to get me in an arm lock. When I fought that, she gouged me in the groin with her knee, doubling me over. Then she put me into the arm lock and turned me into the building until the rough boards were scraping my cheek.

"You're the second weakling to throw me around today," I said.

"Weakling? Maybe we should take a picture of this, so you can remember which one of us has a face full of garage."

She patted me down and released me. It was hard to know why I did what came next.

Like a lineman taking down a quarterback with a cheap shot, I fell on her. She hit the ground on her rump, and it knocked the wind out of her, while I struck my left knee on something hard, probably a rock in the lawn. The flashlight whirled off into the darkness, along with her cigarette. We rolled in a tangle. She was like a wildcat. Flipping her onto her back, I tried to hold her down while she struggled, but she was strong.

What happened next was as strange as anything else in the past weeks.

Without warning, I slipped into a near-catatonic state. I simply went limp. As soon as she felt me go slack, she rolled over onto me and sat on my chest, her skinny haunches stretched across my ribs, pinning my arms, her head inches from mine in the dark. "What's the matter?" she said. "You sick?"

"Yeah."

Letting go of my arms, she sat upright. "You going to throw up?"

"It's not that kind of sick."

"What's the matter?"

"Lots of things. My lieutenant died three days ago."

She felt like a bird of prey sitting on me. It was sexy, too. Her stepmother had ridden me the same way. I put the thought out of my head, but even so, I felt a twinge of sexual tension, a tension that almost supplanted the pain in my balls.

"You're the firefighter who almost drowned?"

"Yeah. Let me up, okay? You win."

She stood up, reached for my hand, and hoisted me to my

feet. Just as she did so, a pair of headlights washed over us and a vehicle pulled into the drive beside her Miata. "That's Bernard. Let me take the lead on this. If he knows you're here to see Iola, he'll kill you. Just let me—" Before she could finish, he was on us, having slammed his truck door and rambled over to the garage like a grizzly. He stood now in the glow from his headlights, having produced a gun twice the size of the weapon Sonja carried.

"Who the hell is this?"

Sonja wrapped her free arm around my waist. "Daddy, this is Jason Gum."

"Who the freakin' hell is Jason Gum?"

"I was just—"

"He's my friend. We were talking."

"Out here?" I followed his eyes as he glanced at my flashlight on the ground, Sonja's smoldering cigarette in the grass, tendrils of smoke rising into the cockeyed beam of my light. "What the hell's going on?"

"I told you, Daddy. We're talking." With that, she laid her head on my shoulder. Her hair smelled of lavender shampoo, and I could feel her bony hip pressing against my leg, her arm tightening around my waist, a small, hard breast snug against my ribs.

"Jesus H. motherfrickin' Christ," he said. His truck headlights limned him, so I couldn't see his features, just the bulk of him, and the beard. And the Howitzer. He was larger than I remembered. His voice boomed, "Why weren't you in the house?"

"I had a cigarette. You told me not to smoke inside."

"I thought you quit."

"Just one."

He looked at me. "You sneaking a smoke, too?"

"No sir. I don't smoke, sir."

"You lying, son? Because I can smell a liar a mile off."

"No, sir. I'm not."

He laughed. "You scared?"

"I'm scared that gun'll go off by accident."

"Goes off, it won't be an accident." He raised the gun and

pushed the barrel forward until it was six inches from my brainpan; I could almost feel the bullet scorching my bones and flesh. "I shoot you, it will be deliberate."

"For God's sake, Daddy. No wonder my friends don't like coming around."

Lowering the gun, he laughed again, then stumped back to his truck, shut off the motor, locked it, and headed for the house. "Iola around?" he shouted.

"Haven't seen her," Sonja replied.

After he was inside, she let go of me, picked up the flashlight, and stubbed out her cigarette with the toe of her sneaker. "Six years ago at our cabin on Lake Roosevelt, he shot and killed a man. Shot him five times and got away with it. They said the man was a burglar."

"Good grief."

"A year ago, after she had too much wine, Iola told me the man he shot hadn't been a burglar at all. He'd been her lover. After she sobered up, she denied it, said it was just the alcohol talking. To this day I'm not sure if she was lying or not."

"He would have known that? That the man was her lover?"

"I assume so. I don't pretend to understand even half of what goes on between the two of them, but I wasn't going to stand around and watch him shoot you down."

"What happened to your real mother?"

"She moved to Wichita. Married a man from the old neighborhood—our real estate agent, in fact. My father tends to attract faithless wives. Iola's his third."

She walked me up the street to my Subaru and seemed reluctant to let me go, engaging in small talk for five minutes after I unlocked my car. "You seeing anybody?" I asked finally.

She stiffened and stepped back. "Not that you would notice."

Before I could say anything else, she turned on her heel and went back down the hill. Like two small nations threatened by a larger entity, we'd established an uneasy truce after her father showed up, but a truce was all it was.

27. BITCH DRIVE SOUTHWEST

Friday, I arrived at seven-thirty, a full half hour before the appointed time, and was surprised to see Tronstad's new orange truck already parked in the long drive, and beside it, Johnson's shiny new Cadillac.

The house was on Beach Drive—or Bitch Drive according to Tronstad—a scenic, winding road stretching along the Puget Sound from the Alki Point Lighthouse south to Lincoln Park. As the name suggested, it followed the beach on the western side of the peninsula that comprised West Seattle. With its barnacle- and seaweed-strewn rocks, it wasn't much of a beach, not compared to Alki north of the point. From time to time as I drove, I spotted the wreckage of the sunset through the trees and houses.

I loved this part of town, so full of wealth and privilege, as well as teenagers speeding around in Porsches or Infinitis. I would have given almost anything to have grown up here. It was ironic how much I'd craved money my whole life and how revolted I was now with the twelve million dollars in my possession.

This was an area of West Seattle the hoi polloi rarely saw, houses your average peasant like me never visited, not unless you showed up to install a sprinkler system, clip grass, pick up dog shit, or help tote in a piano with rags tied around your shoes. I'd done that in high school. It was such a contrast to the housing where I lived on the other side of the promontory: shacks left over from when the steel mills had been going gangbusters, little more than two or three rooms and a toilet.

Tronstad's real estate license gave him access to almost any house for sale in the area, a privilege he abused at will. He'd had his license for two years, but lethargy and indolence limited his sales to the infrequent stroke of good luck or an acquaintance in the fire department who hadn't been warned about him. His commissions were always gone within days.

I parked behind them, noticing that the bed of Tronstad's Ford was crammed full of belongings, including his motorcycle, which he'd roped down securely. I squinted through the darkness to where a single porch light burned over a utility-door entrance. As far as I could tell, it was the only light on in the house.

"Hey, man!"

"Jesus," I said. "You scared me out of my boots." Robert Johnson had been sitting inside his dark car as I walked past.

"Tronstad was already here at seven. Think he's setting a trap? You give him the bonds and he eliminates the last two witnesses?"

"You don't really think that, do you, Robert?"

"Why not?"

"I just don't believe it."

Johnson climbed out of his Caddy and closed the door quietly. "Tronstad's a loose cannon. There's no telling what he'll do." He pulled his jacket back until I saw the butt of a semiautomatic pistol in a shiny holster on his belt.

"Oh, no, Robert. What are you planning?"

He brushed past me and walked toward the house. "The question is, what is *he* planning?"

"I'm not going in if you're carrying a weapon."

"You think Tronstad doesn't have a gun? You think I won't be protecting you as well as myself?"

"I think . . . Oh, heck."

As we walked side by side to the house, I took some comfort in the fact that Robert distrusted Tronstad even more than I did, and that he and I had formed an alliance of sorts. There was no overestimating the maniacal thinking of a man like Tronstad, no overstating how fast a man with no conscience could move when you put the squeeze on him.

"You should get yourself a weapon," Johnson said. "Pick up a rock or something."

"I'm not very good with rocks."

Just outside the door, Johnson said, "By the way, where are the bags?"

"Inside."

"In the house?"

"I'll tell you inside."

He wasn't happy with that, but there wasn't much he could do.

The house was a two-story Georgian, white with dark green trim. The estate grounds comprised half an acre, all of it carefully groomed and maintained. The door was unlocked when Johnson tried it, pushing it open with the pads of his fingertips. "Hello? Tronstad?"

We went inside, proceeding toward a source of illumination at the rear of the house, Robert switching on lights as we entered each room. The house was furnished, though sparsely, as if raiders had taken favorite pieces, an open space here, an empty room there. On the walls were squares of lighter paint where artwork had been removed.

As we headed toward a light at the back of the house, I looked through the living-room windows and scanned the last of the pink-and-purple sunset over the Olympic Mountains. Puget Sound stretched out below the house, and at the end of the lawn a small dock jutted into the inky water.

"Took you so long?" Tronstad was in a chair at the head of the dining-room table, sitting in the dark, a bottle of Seagram's on one side, a half-filled cut-glass tumbler on the other. He was slumped, so his head was almost below the level of the table, sipping from the glass, handling it with the familiarity of a man who was already half-tanked.

"I don't see the bags. You didn't leave them out in your car, did you?"

"They're not here."

"You didn't get them?" Tronstad didn't even raise his voice. He was in a semi-stupor. "You didn't fucking get them?"

"No, and I'm glad I didn't."

"Why?"

"Because you're drunk."

"I ain't that drunk."

"The bonds are safe. I just can't lay my hands on them tonight."

"You trying to buy more time? Is that what this is about? So you can think through the ethical implications of your measly little life? Because if that's what you're up to, I got news for you. You're already on the wrong side of the fence."

"I couldn't get on the property."

"What do you mean you couldn't get on the property?" Johnson asked. Although he kept his voice calm, I'd been around him long enough to know he was pissed.

"They're on somebody else's property."

"Go back for them now," said Tronstad, calmly. "We'll wait. Better yet, we'll come with you."

"Not tonight. I almost got shot."

"You put them on somebody else's property?" Johnson was growing more and more indignant. "Why would you do a fool thing like that?"

"If you haven't noticed, I don't own any property of my own. Besides, somebody already tried to break into my rental. If I'd kept them at home, they might be gone now."

"Who tried to break in?" Tronstad asked.

"I thought it was you." I stared at Tronstad. "One of you guys."

"I didn't do it. Swear to God."

Johnson pushed a button on the wall and a dim overhead chandelier came on. Tronstad's face looked yellow, the circles under his eyes dark, as if he'd been made up like a pirate. His red shirt contributed to the effect.

"Hell, I knew you weren't dumb enough to keep the stuff at home," Tronstad said, laughing. "You're not the sharpest pencil in the box, Gum, but you're not that stupid, either."

"Who tried to break in?" Johnson asked. "Who else knows?"

"Brown knows," I said.

"If he doesn't," said Tronstad, "he sure as hell suspects. And then, of course, there's Heather. And whoever else she told, probably that whole lesbian rugby team."

"They're not lesbians," I said.

"Carpet munchers," said Tronstad. "All of 'em. Take my word for it."

"Brown's the one worries me," I said. "And whoever comes after him."

"We're getting off topic." Tronstad remained implacable. The times I'd seen him drunk, he'd been like this, sluggish, unconcerned, agreeable. "So we don't have the stuff tonight. When do we get it?"

"Like I said. I'll try tomorrow."

"We're working tomorrow."

"I'll take the day off."

"Great. I already called in sick."

"I called in sick, too," said Johnson.

"Jesus, you guys. Don't you think that's going to look funny? The whole crew out sick?"

"Fuck, they shoulda given us merits off," said Tronstad. "We went through some major trauma. Our lieutenant. Our chief." He sipped, poured himself more booze, then laughed. "Yeah, man. We been through minor-league hell, us three. And you, Doublemint. You're a fuckin' hero again. Surviving the whirlpool that got Sears. Every time I turn around you're a hero. Go ahead. Take the day off, you'll probably rescue a baby on the way home. The mother'll be a producer of the evening news. She'll give you a blow job and put you on national television. Afterward, they'll run you for senator. You're golden, man. The only thing you gotta worry about is when they accidentally prick your tittie pinning all those medals on your chest."

"Brown will be back," I said. "If not him, then the next guy."

"I'll take care of the geezer," Tronstad said. "Just give us the bonds."

"You're going to have to give me another day or two."

Tronstad waved his hand in the air. The lids of his eyes had become heavy. "I guess if you were going to run out on us, you'd be somewhere else by now. South America or wherever."

"I like it here."

"My question to you, Tronstad," Johnson said, "is why is your truck packed full of stuff?"

"Moving my girlfriend."

"You don't have a girlfriend," Johnson said.

"Fuck you. Fuck you both. I got into a beef with the landlord. Is that okay with you?"

"Why lie about it?" I asked.

"Because I knew how you two anal retentives would react."

"You're leaving town as soon as you get your share," Johnson said. "Aren't you?"

"I don't even know why you care."

"Because it'll point the finger at us," I said. "Once you vanish, they'll start looking more closely at us."

"Why would they look for me? I lost my lieutenant and resigned. That's not so strange."

"Bullshit," said Johnson.

After it was decided all three of us would show up for work in the morning, Johnson and I walked back to our vehicles in the dark. I said, "I hope he doesn't kill himself with booze and drugs."

"Maybe you should hope he does."

28. KISSABLE

I let Johnson leave first, then reversed onto Beach Drive and backed into the neighbor's driveway, where I shut off my lights and engine and took my foot off the brake. Except for the pinging of my aluminum engine block as it cooled, the neighborhood was hushed.

Something about the way he'd sent us off made me wonder about Tronstad's intentions. The whole time we'd been inside he'd made no effort to get up from the dining-room table. For someone as nervous as he habitually was, that in itself was noteworthy.

Although we were going about our business as if everything were hunky-dory, I knew nothing would be the same between the three of us. Once you were involved in another man's death, you thought about it when you woke up, when you waited at a stoplight, in line at the grocery store, and at night brushing your teeth. Not a day would go by that I wouldn't think about Fred and Susan Rankler, Russell Abbott, and Sweeney Sears—and what I might have done to keep them alive.

The most depressing aspect of it all was that I was aware of the magnitude of our collective folly, while the other two saw only dollar signs. Flash a few million in front of your average Joe-Blow Americano, and all electrical impulses to the nut shut off.

I waited in the car until well after eight o'clock. I couldn't help thinking people had been hidden in the house when Johnson and I were inside—Tronstad's biker buddies with rusty pipe wrenches—and that if I waited long enough, I might see them leave.

At a quarter to nine, a vehicle on Beach Drive stopped directly in front of me in the street. At first I thought it was somebody who wanted the driveway I was in, but the lights moved on and the vehicle pulled in next door.

The vehicle was a black SUV, a Nissan Pathfinder, dirty from a recent road trip. A minute later I walked to the property and spotted, barely visible through the muck on the truck windows, a red IAFF union sticker: International Association of Fire Fighters. The Pathfinder was vacant, the door unlocked, so I got in, picked up some of the papers on the seat, shuffled them, and found the words to the hymn we'd sung at Sears's funeral yesterday afternoon. *He will guide my pathway, e'er I trust his staff.*

The Pathfinder had belonged to Sweeney Sears. I detected the faint aroma of perfume, the fragrance Heather Wynn wore.

Feeling the guilt that comes with pawing through a dead

man's belongings, I went back to my car and watched the house through the wrought-iron fence. Fifteen minutes passed. Twenty. Surely, once she saw how potted he was, she would bail out.

When she still hadn't come out by nine-fifteen, I fired up the Subaru and left.

Five minutes later I found myself parked on Alki Avenue, across the road from the bike shop. I was only blocks from the Pederson place up on the hill. After a few minutes I went around to the back of my car, took out my in-line skates and helmet, and was soon relishing the hard sound of the plastic wheels on concrete as I launched onto the path along the beach. Because Alki Avenue was lit up like a circus ramp, you could skate there all night without bringing your own light.

I skated east to the viewpoint across from downtown Seattle, then rounded the point and headed south toward Salty's. Across the water, the high-rises were lit up and looked stark and clean against the dark horizon. Even though the path extended another mile or so, I turned around at Salty's in order to avoid Friday night drunks in pickup trucks crossing the trail as they came out of the restaurant parking lot.

On my second lap, I stopped at my car, doffed my jacket, swigged half a bottle of green Gatorade, and resumed skating. I hadn't gotten any exercise in a couple of days, and my pent-up energy propelled me to speeds that made my legs ache and my lungs feel as if they were bringing up blood. I skated for an hour. I wanted to skate all night. I wanted to skate for the rest of my life.

The weather was cool, and the stars winked in black patches of sky where the clouds separated. I saw a pair of heavyset women on the path. An old man wearing so much body armor he looked like something out of a Monty Python movie. A few other skaters.

There were people who skated everywhere with one arm behind their backs. There were those who refused to lift their feet. Those who picked up their feet as if walking through deep snow. Some skated upright. Others in a racing crouch. Others took on an odd rhythm with their hips. All of that was fine for a recreational skater, but economy of movement was key for speed, and most of an individual's identifying characteristics were imperfections of style. Ten expert skaters, it was hard to tell them apart.

A slight tailwind had boosted my speed just before I spotted a woman skating a quarter mile in front of me. I closed the gap, watching her move, thinking I knew who she was.

She was headed the same direction I was, and as was her habit, she wore wrist protectors but no knee pads and no helmet. I pulled alongside, dragging a skate with a rattling noise that startled her. "You?"

"You, too," I said.

She wore the same short-sleeved shirt she'd had on at the house a couple of hours earlier with grass stains on the knees of her jeans. If you looked only at her face with her wind-tousled bangs, she appeared to be around ten years old, yet she had a woman's wide hips to go with that bony frame and a good rhythm to accompany the coltish movement of her arms.

She sped up as if to skate away from me, but I paced alongside her easily, then behind her, on the other side, in front. I did a hop and a twist and skated backward ten feet in front. Showing off.

"You down here for the exercise, or are you following me?" I said.

"I didn't have anything else to do."

"No hot date? It's Friday night. I would think you would have a hot date."

"I *had* a date. I whipped his ass and sent him home."

"Ouch. That hurts." We skated in silence for half a minute. "What do you do?"

"I'm a cop for the City of Seattle."

"Funny, I work for the city, too."

"I know. You're a fireman." She accentuated the "fire" as if it were hilarious.

"You really a cop?"

"One thing I'm not is a liar."

A liar was the least of what I'd become in the last month. Maybe in the end Sonja Pederson would be the one to arrest me. Why not? She'd already beaten me up.

I flipped around so that we were facing the same direction. Skating side by side, we reached the end of the path a few blocks from the lighthouse and turned around, heading northeast toward the city again, forging into the breeze. We glided along for a minute or two without speaking. When we passed my car, I noticed her Miata parked next to my WRX. She said, "I didn't come here because you were here. I came despite the fact that you were here."

I didn't know if I believed her. I flipped around and began skating backward again, did a couple of backward crossovers. It occurred to me that she couldn't hate me too awfully much or she wouldn't be here.

"How'm I doing?" I asked, just as a skate hit a rock and I almost went down.

"Nice recovery." She increased her cadence, trying once again to pull away.

She got up a good head of steam and held it while I turned around and skated alongside. She wasn't breathing that hard, but then, she didn't appear to have any reserves, either. "You're in good shape," I said.

"Not good enough, obviously."

"You have slow wheels. I could switch the bearings out for you. I've got a faster set in the car. They'd be a lot nicer to skate on."

"Fast enough to get away from you?"

"Oh, you'd never get away from me."

"Maybe some other time."

"Your father get pissed at you for having me there?"

"No. It's just that I don't bring people around very often."

"Your dad sticks a gun in their faces, I can see why. I don't remember you from the day the pig went through the roof."

"I only stay over once in a while. I have a house out in Maple Valley. Funny you should mention it, though, because my dad told me he was so shook up after the pig incident he couldn't remember if I was in the house or not."

We were moving along at a pretty good clip now; not as fast as I'd been traveling on my own, but a steady pace. We passed an old man limping alongside a dog that appeared to be as old as he was. Sonja looked at me. "Would you answer a question?"

"Of course."

"What do you want out of life?"

"That's a strange question."

"It's the first thing people should ask each other. You find out a lot."

"Why ask me?"

"Because when I told Iola I knew about you two, she said something I haven't been able to get out of my mind. She said you were *sweet*."

"As in, maple syrup sweet?"

"And as in stupid sweet. I think she was profoundly disappointed in you because you were a nice guy."

"Let's not talk about her."

"Fine. Tell me what you want out of life."

We skated for half a minute before I said, "I want my life to be what it was a month ago."

"And what was that?"

"Simple. Wonderful. I had a job that allowed me to help people. I had my car, my skating. Friends. We didn't climb mountains or race yachts, but it was a life I felt comfortable with."

"So you had a near-perfect life a month ago and you want it back?"

"I had an *ordinary* life a month ago. I didn't realize what it was until I lost it."

"What happened?"

"You don't want to know."

She thought about that. "Was she right? Iola? Are you sweet?"

"She told *me* I was naïve."

"I think sweet's a better fit." Even though she'd tried to

skate away from me and had beat me up twice, I took her words as a compliment. I couldn't help thinking we had an easy manner between us that I hadn't encountered with a lot of other women and wondered if she had it with everybody, or just me.

As we headed around the point, I got in front of Sonja and told her to keep close. She'd never drafted before, but after a few miscues, she picked up the technique. In skating, most of the work involves pushing the wind out of the way, so that a skater following close on another skater's heels uses significantly less energy. I caught her hand and rested it on my hip so she could maintain balance and position more easily. "Watch out for cracks in the pavement. I'll point them out to you." We got going fast enough that I heard her breathing increase. After a minute, I said, "Want me to slow down?"

"No."

"You sure?"

"I've never gone this fast. It's incredible."

We worked hard for twenty minutes before I felt her flagging.

We took it easy on the stretch back to the cars, and she rolled to a stop against her Miata. She unlocked it and sat in the passenger side, unbuckling her skates while I did miniature backward figure eights.

We talked about city politics, global warming, and a recent police shooting in downtown Seattle that had caused a stir in the media but which I hadn't paid much attention to. She told me she'd once applied for a position with the fire department and been accepted but had changed her mind at the last minute. "Why?" I asked.

"I guess I found something I liked better."

At that moment I would have given anything not to have screwed her stepmother into delirium so many times. I'd run into Sonja three times now, but because of my relationship with Iola, the odds of another meeting were negligible.

"Why'd you stop here tonight?" I asked.

"I told you. I needed some exercise. Beating up guys is just not that taxing."

"You saw my car parked down here and wanted to see me again."

"Don't put words in my mouth."

"I'm glad you showed up. I was in a pretty sour mood until you got here."

"What were you looking for at my father's place?"

"My sanity."

Seated in her low-slung car, she looked up at my face for a good long while. I stopped the figure eights and held her look. "What the hell were you thinking with Iola?"

"I don't know."

"Was it just sex? Was it . . . What the hell were you thinking?"

I shook my head.

I'd been thinking it was a lark. A sexual romp. An escapade. I'd been thinking there wouldn't be any consequences. That Iola wasn't married. That she wasn't damaging me with her sharp tongue and derogatory comments. That she hadn't been treating me alternately like a sex toy and a doormat. Someday I would look back on it with disbelief, knowing the only thing I'd accomplished with Iola was to bollix my chances with this woman.

Sonja's face was flushed from exercise, her hair combed roughly by the wind. I'd never seen anyone more kissable. She walked around to her driver's-side door and got in. I skated behind her, my throat so dry, I nearly choked on my words. "Can I see you again?"

She laced up her sneakers. "Sonja Pederson. Maple Valley. It's in the book."

It wasn't as if I had a future. Sonja Pederson was a glimpse through a window I would never enter again, a world I'd stepped out of when I agreed to hide the bearer bonds. If my affair with Sonja's stepmother failed to obliterate my chances with her, getting arrested in a high-profile federal case and being carted off to prison would probably do the trick.

29. WE'RE BUFFOONS

Robert Johnson, Ted Tronstad, and I were waxing Engine 29 in the sunshine behind the station, a David Byrne tune blaring through the open apparatus bay as we took advantage of what we suspected would be one of the last sunny afternoons of the year. Just three multimillionaire murderers polishing a rig for the city.

Johnson was up to his old tricks, playing a joke on Tronstad by waxing his helmet while Tronstad worked on the other side of the rig. A dirty, battle-scarred helmet is a point of pride to any firefighter, so it was a testament to Tronstad's state of mind that he didn't react or comment at seeing his helmet, now shiny and clean, in Johnson's hands, looking as though it had never seen any action. Not being able to get his hands on the bonds had put Tronstad in a foul mood; he'd been hectoring me about it all day.

There wasn't much conversation, partially because the music was so loud—an infraction Tronstad committed to deliberately nettle the irascible neighbors—and because we were about talked out.

So far our shift had been relatively quiet, all the excitement and nightmares occurring in other people's lives, which was the way it was supposed to be when you were a firefighter. You went to other people's excitement and remained calm and unruffled because the trouble wasn't yours, and because you'd been trained to handle it dispassionately.

As expected, Tronstad came in hung over and throughout the day took catnaps when he thought he wouldn't be missed. The only reason Tronstad had come to work was to make sure I didn't blow town with the bonds.

One way or another, we wouldn't be working together again, and we all knew it. Tronstad would take his money and abscond. Johnson still hadn't made up his mind whether to run or to stick around and attempt to fake normalcy. Me? I was going to get arrested. Whatever else happened, whatever I decided to do, they would be coming for me. Sometimes you just knew when the jig was up, and I'd lived with this premonition for some time now.

Our temporary company officer, Lieutenant Covington, was a dull man with a bald head and a passion for growing roses and breeding Scottish terriers. Covington had been with the department twenty-two years and spent most of his free time at work in front of the television.

It was almost three in the afternoon, and some of the neighborhood kids were walking past the station with a soccer ball. I tried to savor what was probably my last day on the job.

"We meet again," came the booming voice.

I was alone on the officer's side of the engine, feeling the sun warm my dark blue uniform shirt. Standing in front of me was the ex–FBI agent, Brown, his wife lingering behind him in the apparatus bay. As before, he wore a dapper suit and polished shoes. He didn't stand close, the way he had the other day, but kept a good ten feet off. For reasons I couldn't understand, it was just as intimidating. "I may have intruded the other day," Brown said, squinting in the sunshine. "You men just coming back from a funeral and all. Thought I'd make my apologies and get the truth this time."

"The truth about what?"

"Son, I've put away more snot-nosed ass-wipes like you than you could count in a month of Sundays." He stepped closer, seven feet away now. "You just tell me what I want to know, and we won't have any problems."

"What would you like to know?"

"For starters, what time do you get off?"

"Tomorrow morning at seven-thirty."

"Jesus. Don't tell him that," Tronstad said, coming around the front of the tall fire engine. "You're just going to tell him whatever he wants? This guy's an asshole." Then to Brown, "Fuck you. And fuck that old bag." Brown made a move toward him, but Tronstad began dancing backward like a bantamweight fighter in the ring, retreating until he disappeared through the bunk-room door. "Don't tell him nothin'!"

I smiled a crooked smile at Brown. Funny how even when a man was trying to steal your life you wanted to be civil.

"You just tell me everything you know about Charles Scott Ghanet. Everything about that last night you were at his place. Everything you might know about whatever sparked your two buddies here to buy new vehicles shortly after."

"You'd have to ask them."

"Right now I'm asking you. Speak up, boy."

In the apparatus bay, Brown's wife began nosing into our supply locker, only to be intercepted by Lieutenant Covington, who said something I couldn't hear over the music, then escorted her into our living quarters.

"Holy cow," Johnson said, as he came around the rear of Engine 29 and spotted the old man. "Where did you come from?"

"Straight from the Federal Building downtown, son. And I'm here to tell you buffoons that if you don't tell me what I need to know, you'll be going there, in steel bracelets."

"You're not even official," Johnson said, uncertainly. "You're retired."

"I can arrest you both. Oh, you bet I can."

"I want to see my lawyer," Johnson said.

"What about you?" Brown's voice softened as if gentling a horse. "You willing to talk to the FBI?"

"I thought you were retired."

"We're not talking about me, son. We're talking about some righteous fellas I know who pee battery acid and sleep with women got brass wire growing out of their cunts. Four of the toughest sons of bitches you'll ever meet. They're downtown right now, and if I give them the say-so, they'll want to see you. Trust me, you'll be sorry you met them."

"I'm sorry I met you."

Brown moved forward, five feet away now. "Don't be sassing me, son."

"Leave him alone," Johnson said, stepping alongside.

"If you want to come back with your friends," I said, "come back with your friends. For all I know, you're a bank robber yourself."

"Bank robber yourself," Johnson repeated.

As we spoke, Tronstad, carrying a brown paper sack in his arms, opened the far door leading from the bunk room and sneaked across the front of the apparatus bay and outside through the open doors. I had no idea where he was headed, but I could tell he didn't want Brown spotting him. Knowing Tronstad, he was going to egg the old man's car.

"Just tell me what you three took out of that house. You do that and I'll let you go."

"Don't say anything, Gum. He can't arrest us. He doesn't have that authority."

"What'd you boys take out of Ghanet's?"

Robert was beginning to get that deer-in-the-headlights look he took on when he went wrong on an address or when you tried to talk to him about it afterward.

Brown said, "I knew you sons of bitches had done something. It just wasn't possible our people could ransack that house and come up with nada."

"It was a standard welfare check," I said. "A neighbor or relative gets concerned, and we investigate. If the place is locked and we think there's sufficient cause, we break in."

"You broke in *three* doors, son."

"We couldn't find him."

"I saw your place. Down there off Genesee Playfield. Saw *your* place, Mr. Johnson, over off Seward Park Drive. Got yourself a nice little homestead. Nice little family. Nice little girl."

"Are you threatening me?" Johnson asked. "Because if you're threatening—"

Brown stepped forward, smelling of licorice and mothballs and something that might have been booze. "I don't have to threaten you. You got the U.S. government on your tail."

"We haven't seen any U.S. government," I said. "So far all we've seen is you."

"I want that money back, son."

"If you're legit," I said, "get the real FBI up here." Brown glared at me. "I mean, if you think we did something. Which we didn't."

"We didn't," Johnson repeated.

Without taking his eyes off me, Brown said, "You got any idea what it's like in a federal prison, son? You think about that when you're congratulating one another on how you dusted me off, because that's where you're headed. Lompoc ain't going to be pretty."

"I don't happen to think *you're* pretty," Johnson said.

"We'll be in touch." Brown pivoted and walked to his wife, who'd just stepped back into the apparatus bay, took her arm, and escorted her out of the station through the front doors.

"What was all that about?" Lieutenant Covington asked, after they were out of earshot.

"He's just some weirdo," Johnson said.

"His wife told me he was with the federal government. She said he used to be postal inspector before he joined the FBI. She also said she was a ballerina with the Joffrey. You believe that?"

"He *could* have been with the FBI," I said.

"No, I meant the Joffrey. She's kind of wide in the beam for a ballerina."

"Maybe she gained weight after she quit," Johnson said.

"She was a nice woman. Wanted to know everything there was to know about you three. You're twenty-two, aren't you, Gum?"

"Twenty-four."

Covington was still talking when Brown's Lincoln appeared at the front of the station, the power steering squealing as he motored through the apparatus bay. For half a second I thought he was going to run us down, but at the last moment he veered to the right and screeched to a halt.

"I'll see you two again," Brown said through his open driver's window.

"You're going to have to remove that vehicle," Covington

said, stepping toward the Town Car. "You're on fire department property."

Brown sped off, and Covington went back inside to watch TV. After a while, Johnson said, "That old fart's been spying on us."

"I bet he's the one who tried to break into my place."

"What are we going to do?"

"I'm thinking he's after that money himself."

"Brown knows Tronstad and I bought new vehicles after we found Ghanet. In retrospect, that doesn't seem like such a great move."

"You think?"

When Tronstad showed up with a broad smile on his face, Johnson's voice was steeped in sarcasm. "Thanks for the help. At least with three of us we might have had a chance if he jumped us."

"You afraid of an old man?"

"I'm afraid of *that* old man."

Tronstad only grinned.

30. EDITED FOR BITTERNESS

As we left the station on an alarm, I spotted the black thermal column five or six blocks away, smoke rising into the cobalt sky with incredible rapidity, racing to the heavens as if pouring out of a deep fissure in the earth in a rapid series of interconnected bubbles.

In my two years in the department, we'd responded to any number of vehicle fires, and they'd all been like this, the smoke so thick that it looked like you could surf on it. A couple of hundred pounds of petroleum-based plastics lining the interior made it a fait accompli that almost nothing burned quite as hot as a car fire.

The dispatcher had sent Engine 29 on a single. Just the four of us. Before Tronstad even got to the apparatus, I had my heavy coat snapped tight, the collar up, and had pulled my Nomex hood around my neck for later deployment over my head. Though he was hyperactive in every other area of life, and as a kid had spent years on Ritalin, until Sears showed up and coached us Tronstad had been slower than ketchup getting onto the rig. Today he was back to his old habits.

When he finally climbed into the crew cab beside me, he was carrying his bunking coat instead of wearing it. He smiled as if we shared some delightful secret. I hated this sudden chumminess he was determined to inflict on me, as if now that we were killing officers together, we were *especially* good friends. I hated that he'd turned me into a co-conspirator and an accessory to murder, and despised myself for not being able to find a way out of this labyrinth. I didn't want to be in the same city with him, and I certainly did not want him thinking we were buddies.

"Yahoo!" Covington said, as we sped up California Avenue toward the intersection with Admiral Way, the key intersection in this end of West Seattle. "Would you look at that?"

It was a large American car sitting askew in the center of the intersection, as if the driver had lost control at the last moment. Oily rafts of smoke and orange balls of flame boiled out of every orifice and roared out of the radiator, shooting so high the flames were melting the lenses in the stoplight above the car. Shards of window glass glittered on the street around the vehicle.

The intersection was jammed up in all directions, most of the occupants of the nearby vehicles standing next to their car doors so they could gawk. As we rolled up, a pair of elderly women made a dash for the sidewalk and two big-bellied men in T-shirts danced around the periphery, dumping portable extinguishers ineffectually. The heat was so intense, the men couldn't get close enough to make their handheld extinguishers do anything but lay down a white film of chemical dust over the broken glass surrounding the car.

Before we stopped rolling, Covington turned around. "Preconnect, boys. Make sure you mask up tight. Earflaps down. I'll get a bar for the hood."

Tronstad should have been masked, covered, and gloved up when we came to a stop, but he wasn't anywhere close, so I was on my own.

The preconnect was a two-hundred-foot section of hose, preplumbed, so that all we had to do was pull it out of the hose bed at the rear of the rig, stretch it out, and kick the kinks out of it so water would flow freely. A good driver would fill the hose line while you were still running, nudging flakes off your shoulder with the water pressure.

The Task Force nozzle gave us 165 gallons per minute, and the tank on Engine 29 held 500 gallons. That meant, discounting the water it took to fill two hundred feet of inch-and-three-quarters line as well as the plumbing inside the rig, we would have just under three minutes wide open. In theory it would give Johnson plenty of time to connect to a hydrant while I tapped the fire.

As we rolled to a stop, Covington gave a radio report while Johnson did his in-cab procedures and jumped out. Outside he would set the wheel blocks, give me water on the preconnect, then go to the hydrant with one end of a supply hose and hydrant wrenches.

Even though I was fifty feet away, I could feel the heat as I climbed down from the crew cab. I had my mask on, my gloves, my Nomex hood over my face piece, and my helmet: enough gear that I could walk through flame if I had to, at least for a few seconds. As I approached the car with the hose line, a front tire melted and blew out with a muffled *thump*.

I heard the pump revving behind me, heard the sound of water under pressure as it filled the hose line, then took a good a grip on the heavy nozzle, ready to buck the pressure when I pulled back on the bale.

I opened the nozzle and moved in, getting closer than I probably should have, feeling the heat on my neck through the Nomex hood. The whooshing water made the burning materials inside the car crackle and turned the black smoke white. I kept at it, moving closer, waving the water stream in circles, bouncing water under the vehicle to put out the burning oil and gasoline on the pavement, and angling the stream in the windows.

In the backseat I saw something hunkered next to the door. It startled me because for some reason I'd assumed the car was empty. It was a body in semi-repose, arms upraised as if posing for a boxing photo. I recalled from training that burn victims frequently curled into a pugilistic pose after the fire shortened and tightened the tendons in their arms.

It was a female, hair and clothing burned off, charred beyond recognition. I couldn't figure out what was on the left side of her torso until I realized she had one silicone breast that had boiled over and dripped down her front like a raw egg. A cancer survivor, I thought. To survive cancer and die here . . . The rest of her was all char and grimacing teeth and wisps of smoke.

Covington still hadn't gotten the hood up, so I hit the flames through the radiator, then screwed the nozzle to straight stream and bounced water off the street under the car one more time.

Tronstad was behind me now, pulling the heavy hose line so I could move freely around the car. I couldn't help noting he still wasn't covered, his MSA face piece dangling off his chest, which meant as soon as we got near any smoke he would vanish.

The predominant winds were from the north, so as I moved around to the south side of the car and cooled the tires, I found myself in a wash of hot, oily smoke that permeated my clothing. In the smoke and steam, I could barely see the car. Not surprisingly, the driver's door was open, a second body half in and half out, having apparently gotten tangled in his seat belt, possibly as he turned around to help the woman. He was burned, though not as badly as the woman. His hair was gone, his face blackened and unrecognizable.

A wave of depression swept over me. Perhaps because I'd already been depressed all week, or because I didn't have enough years in the department to handle so many deaths in rapid succession. Life was supposed to be simple. You were conceived and born. You suckled and grew. You lived your life, and if you were lucky you left others behind who could take over where you left off. At the end of it all, and sometimes before the end of it all, you died.

Humans participated in this natural and inevitable progression, yet we spent our lifetimes trying to protect ourselves from the reality of it, society having worked out 1001 ways to buffer us from the truth: the quest for possessions, the lust for big houses, extravagant vacations, sex, big cars, stocks and bonds, gold, religion, spiritualism, yoga, belief in flying saucers, you name it. Five months ago I'd come up against the ugly bluntness of life when my mother told me she had less than a year to live. She was forty-one. I was twenty-four, and the last thing I wanted to think about was her death.

One of the first things you learn as a firefighter is to divorce yourself from sentiments you'd normally entertain in the presence of a dying man or woman or child. In that sense, we were like doctors and nurses, and maybe like executioners. The more death we saw, the easier it became, and until this past week I thought I was immune to death. Now, looking at these two corpses, I realized I was a child in a man's job. I was a tyro. A ninny. I wasn't immune to anything.

Tugging the door wide, I opened the nozzle in short bursts, watering down all the nooks and crannies I hadn't reached earlier. When the driver rolled over, I couldn't tell whether the movement was because I'd bumped him or because he was still alive. For a few seconds I studied him for signs of breathing, listening to the residual crackling of steel and glass cooling. I checked his carotid artery with a bare finger. His skin was hot and stiff.

When Covington was finished under the hood, I said, "You know we got a coupla DOAs here?"

"We what?"

"You didn't see them?"

Covington walked around to the driver's door, stopping six

feet shy of the first corpse. "Fuck," he said into his mask. "Fuck this shit."

When the lieutenant told Tronstad to get a couple of yellow disposable blankets to cover the corpses, Tronstad got the blankets but handed them to me. I dropped the nozzle on the street and wrapped the driver, accidentally touching his face through the blanket as I tried to secure the material against a breeze that was ripping along the street, the same breeze that had fanned the flames and helped make the fire so hot. I couldn't reach into the backseat, but I stuffed the second blanket through the window and more or less concealed the woman from gapers.

When I stepped back from the car, Tronstad said, "He don't look so tough now, does he?"

"What are you talking about?"

"That asshole from the FBI."

I looked at the car again. It was a Lincoln Town Car, the same vintage and color Brown and his wife owned. And the shoes on the driver. One was burned, but the other was outside on the ground, polished all to hell. The dead driver was Agent Brown; the passenger, his wife.

"You gave me a look when we left the station. You knew who it was before we left. That's why you weren't helping."

"Don't be stupid. I just now recognized him."

"How?"

"It smelled like a burning asshole."

"You bastard!"

"It sure was hot," Covington said, coming up alongside us.

"Hotter'n a whoopee cushion at a farting contest," Tronstad said.

Covington gave him a look and might have said something in the way of a reprimand, when a police officer spotted Covington and summoned him across the street.

After he left, Tronstad said, "Now, don't be accusing me of this."

"Why not? You did it."

"You accuse me, I'll have to release that videotape. And

nobody can prove I did anything. We start accusing each other, chances are you'll go to prison and I'll fly like a birdie. You wouldn't like that."

"You lousy bastard. You put some sort of incendiary timing device in their car. Jesus, he was FBI. You don't think his friends are going to be on us like white on rice?"

"*Was* he FBI? Did he act like FBI? Does the FBI go around twisting people's digits?"

"Jesus, Tronstad. What about his wife?"

"You want to save her? Go ahead. Drag her out and initiate CPR."

"She didn't do anything."

"She shouldn't have been hanging out with an asshole."

Tronstad couldn't have seen it coming, because I didn't see it myself. Even though the nozzle was turned off, the water pressure made the end of the hose stiff as a board.

Swinging the hose and nozzle with all my might, I whacked him across the side of the head, knocking his helmet off and sending him to the pavement.

"Jesus, you fucker!" he yelled.

He got almost to his feet, his hands still in the glass on the street, when I turned the nozzle on and knocked him down, holding it on straight stream. The intense water pressure pushed him backward and washed him up against the car. He held his hands up to protect his face, then yelped and rolled away from the still-hot sheet metal of the car, turning his face away from me now to protect himself, curling into a ball, trying and failing to get up or to crawl away while I bombarded him with the water stream.

He screamed as if in a great deal of pain, but I knew it couldn't possibly hurt as much as I wanted it to.

"You motherfucker!" he screamed while I walked behind him, never once letting up. Each time he tried to scramble away from me, the stream knocked him off his hands and knees.

Then they shut the water off on me. When the hose went limp, Tronstad picked himself up, limped away, and said,

"You goddamned motherfucking butt fucker." I stepped forward to punch him, but a pair of burly cops came up behind me and restrained my arms. "You pimply cheese ass! You're going to be sorry you did that. God. I think you took my eye out."

While one police officer escorted Tronstad across the street, towing him by the sleeve of his wet bunking coat, two others held me. "You okay now?" Covington asked.

I removed my helmet, peeled off the Nomex hood, released the face straps, and popped off my face piece. "Yeah."

"What was that about?"

When I didn't reply, one of the police officers said, "You going to handle this in-house, or you want us to take over?"

Covington looked across the street to where Johnson and a couple of concerned civilians were attending Tronstad's injuries. Dropping his hand on my shoulder, Covington said, "Why don't we hold on for a minute? I'll go see how bad it is."

31. ALL THE THINGS YOU CAN NEVER SAY TO ANYONE—EVER

They ended up calling a medic unit for Tronstad while I awaited the verdict across the street, next to a blue-and-white SPD cruiser. Meanwhile, the SPD had cordoned off the intersection for the inevitable accident investigation, taking statements from witnesses and directing cars out of the chaos.

We waited while the burned-out hulk steamed in the center of the street, while the two bodies cooled under their yellow disposable blankets. The half-melted traffic light blinked uselessly, and civilians watched from nearby shop windows. The marquee on the movie theater a few doors down advertised *Cold Mountain*. I'd seen it there with my mother.

Johnson picked up the wet hose, eyeing me quietly as he

walked past. I could tell he thought I was insane. Medic 32 showed up from Station 32 up the road, and while they worked on Tronstad, Covington huddled with them, presumably to verify the extent of Tronstad's injuries. The burned-out car continued to cool, every once in a while letting off small snapping sounds. A team of detectives from the police department showed up. The fire department's investigators arrived. On the far side of the intersection somebody put a large white patch across one of Tronstad's eyes. I knew Tronstad did not want me in jail, where I might be tempted to talk to the authorities, and where I wouldn't be around to retrieve the bonds for him.

The cop who'd spoken to Covington earlier was an older man with a graying crew cut who'd looked at me in a kindly way. I knew I appeared young enough that he no doubt assumed these were the first dead people I'd seen. Hell, I was up to my neck in dead people.

The medics finished with Tronstad and left on another call at about the same time I noticed a female police officer five feet in front of me. She may have been there all along, intermingling with the other officers on traffic duty, though I didn't recognize her until that moment.

She looked different; yet even in her bulky bulletproof vest and Sam Browne belt, fully loaded with 9 millimeter Glock, nightstick, flashlight, handcuffs, and Mace, she was as thin and reedy as ever. Drawing close, Sonja spoke in a low voice. "You seem to have gotten yourself in a jam."

"They're not going to arrest me."

"People who act like you shouldn't get cocky."

I inhaled slowly. Except for those hours skating last night, it might have been the first full breath I'd taken all week. Despite the fact that I'd seen her three times previously, and she'd beaten me up two of those times, she had a calming influence on me.

Standing close, she said, "You're right. He's not going to press charges. Why did you do it?"

"Long story."

"What's going on, Gum? You want to talk?"

Oh, how I wanted to talk. I was bursting with secrets. I wanted to tell her about the bonds and my complicity, and I wanted to tell her about Chief Abbott and the smoke room, and how he'd tried to torture information out of us. I wanted to explain how I hadn't had anything to do with Sears's death even though, if things went south, I might get convicted of it. Trouble was, if I told her any of these things it would be the last time I'd see her. Or daylight.

When a minute passed and I still hadn't replied, she said, "I guess the firefighter you hurt wrote a letter to the chief of the department about you."

"Complaining? Already?"

"No, before. He wants you to get an award for trying to save your lieutenant."

"I didn't save him."

"For trying." She looked me over. I knew that just as she looked different in her uniform, I looked different with my helmet and my collar turned up, sweating from the body heat my turnout gear captured. "You're a surprise a minute, Gum."

"So are you, Pederson." For a fraction of a second, I thought I saw her blush. Maybe it was the touch of vulnerability that made me blurt it out. Maybe I was coming to the end of my rope. "I think Tronstad set fire to that car."

"The guy you just knocked down? Wasn't he at the station with you when it started?"

"These people were visiting our station. They left, and then this happened."

"Are you all right, Gum?"

"I'm serious."

"I know you are. Do you realize you just accused a fireman you work with of a double homicide? Did he know those people? Did he have something against them?"

"He met them once before."

"Why would he want to kill two people he met only twice?" She'd been giving me the look she would have given a favorite crazy brother right before she was forced to commit him to the loony bin. "It doesn't make sense."

"Maybe you can go over and put the bug in the detective's

ear? Maybe if they put some pressure on him, he'll say something incriminating. Could you do that without telling the detectives it was me who put you on to it?"

"They're going to want to talk to *you*."

"I can't."

"Why not?"

"Maybe a police dog could sniff out explosives in his locker . . . This sounds crazy, doesn't it?"

"Just a little."

"The driver roughed him up."

"They're saying he was sixty-eight. How could he rough up anybody?"

I was trying to think of a way to explain without getting dragged into it, but of course, that was impossible. "Okay. Off the record. Can you talk to me off the record?"

"No. I don't know what you're going to say."

"Okay. Forget I said any of this."

"Now you're telling me your friend didn't set that fire?"

"I'm saying I must have been delusional. Duress. Can you accept that?"

"I suppose."

I turned to walk away. "One last thing?"

"What is it?"

"I hate to bring this up again, but I left something at your stepmother's—"

"Anything between you and her stays between you and her. Leave me out of it."

In addition to the rest of it, there could be little doubt in her mind now that I was obsessed with Iola.

32. FINDING JESUS AND KILLING YOUR FRIENDS

Oddly enough, we got another car fire at a little after five in the morning, another plume of royal black smoke arching into the sky in billowing coils. This one was in an area of apartment houses near the Alki Point Lighthouse. In my mind I could still feel the stiff and crinkly charred pelts of the two dead bodies earlier.

Four of us responded to the second car fire: me, Johnson, Lieutenant Covington, and a firefighter called in on overtime, whose name I forgot as soon as she told me. Tronstad had been sent home on disability, his eye injury chalked up to an accidental splash of water at the first fire.

Considering the crimes I'd been associated with, I was beginning to wonder if there was *anything* I could do that would land me in jail. I had stolen millions, been involved in four murders, lied to one and all, not been believed the one time I told the truth—to Sonja—yet remained free as a bird. Could I be bulletproof?

The afternoon after the first car fire, Tronstad found me just before he left the station. I was slumped in front of the television in the firefighters' quarters.

"You fuckin' murderer," I mumbled, without taking my eyes off the tube.

"You're getting a nasty mouth in your old age."

"Fuck you. You just burned two people to death."

"First of all, you can't prove shit. Second of all, like I already told you, you say a word to the cops, you're the one who'll end up in jail."

"Fuck you."

"You got my cell number. Tomorrow noon at the latest. Call when you get them. You don't, you'll wish you had. And by the way, I'm cutting your share down for all this stalling."

"I don't want a share. I never did." But he was gone. I felt like a coward for not going to the police. I was afraid he was right, that they wouldn't be able to prove he'd done anything and that I'd end up in jail because of the videotape. I needed time to think. I could always turn him in later, but I wasn't going to accomplish anything sitting in a cell.

The second car fire went smoother than the first, perhaps because I was working alongside the overtimer, a tough, brown-eyed woman who usually worked on a downtown company. We hit it with a semi-fog pattern, and by the time

Covington met us with the five-foot pry bar, the fire was knocked down.

As far as I could tell there were no witnesses. Nobody in any apartment windows. No bystanders. Just us and a 1999 Toyota some poor boob of an owner was going to find burned out and half-filled with dirty water.

As we were picking up the hose, Johnson and I found ourselves separated from the others. "It was Tronstad," I said.

"What was Tronstad?"

"This fire. And the first one. He lit Brown's car. Tronstad killed those two people."

"Oh, come on . . ."

"No. Listen to me. When we were talking to Brown I saw him sneak out front with something in his hands. He rigged their car."

"He could have been doing anything out there."

"When the alarm came in he gave me a funny look."

"Oh, now you're beginning to sound like—"

"He did that eyebrow thing. You've seen it. Like we had this secret together."

"The eyebrow thing?"

"Yeah."

"Oh, man! That's why you knocked him down. You really think . . . ? Jesus. They *said* it was an incendiary device. That's what Marshal Five came up with. Covington said when they found out he was ex-FBI they figured maybe somebody he sent to prison came back with a grudge."

"He actually *was* ex-FBI? I didn't hear that."

"But if Tronstad set fire to Brown's car, why would he come back and do this one?"

"He's giving us a message. He's mean and he's dangerous and he lights things and we better toe the line or he's going to make us wish we had."

"You might be right."

After we got back to the station, I found myself alone with Johnson in the bunk room. "You awake, Gum?"

"I'm awake."

"I'm glad I have Jesus on my side, because this whole thing is getting too weird. You been saved, Gum?"

"Not recently."

"Don't you think it's about time? Gum, I'd feel a lot better if you'd accept Jesus Christ as your personal Lord and Savior. Can you tell me you know Jesus loves you and you're going to dedicate your life to the gospel?"

Other firefighters and one former girlfriend had saved me before, and each time I'd found it relatively painless. If it made him happy, undergoing another religious conversion was no skin off my butt. "There *are* a lot of answers I've been needing lately."

"Accept the Lord. It would mean a lot to me. Tronstad's never going to find Jesus, but you're a horse of a different color. If you were a partner with the Lord, you'd be a partner with me, too."

"What do I have to do?"

"Accept the Lord Jesus Christ as your personal Savior."

"That's it?"

"There's more later, but that's it for now."

"Okay."

"You have to say it. I accept the Lord Jesus Christ as my personal Savior."

"I accept the Lord Jesus Christ as my personal Savior."

"Gum, that's great. Will you come to church with me?"

"If I'm not in jail."

"You don't know how happy it makes me, Gum, that you've accepted the Lord."

"No problem. It should make prison easier."

"It won't be easy to live up to."

"I know what to do."

"What's that?"

"Refrain from stealing anything else and don't kill any more people."

There was a long silence in the darkness before I heard Johnson coming toward me, sitting heavily on the foot of my bunk, the thick material of his turnout trousers crinkling. "You making fun of me?"

"You don't really think you're going to heaven?"

"Gum, are you making fun of me?"

"It's just that I don't know how to square up Bible-thumping with what we've done."

"What have we done?"

"To start off with, we stole twelve million dollars."

"I didn't steal anything."

"Split hairs all you want, but Jesus isn't going to look at it that way."

"Okay. What else?"

"What do you mean, what else? How about Chief Abbott's death?"

"Abbott died of smoke inhalation because he fainted."

"Is that why we lied about it?"

"We can't do anything about the people who are dead. Him or Sears. Or them old people. It's best to forget them."

"And just go on our merry way?"

"No. I've been thinking, and I think you and I should do something about Tronstad."

"Christ, Robert. Are you . . . are you telling me—"

"I been thinking about it for a while, but these car fires clinched it. You got a gun, Gum?"

"Don't say anything else."

"Gum, you—"

"Not another word. I know he's unhinged now, but he was my friend once. He stood up for me."

"He didn't stand up for jack shit."

"At Arch Place."

"Man, didn't I already tell you he never wanted you to show up at Arch Place? He told the lieutenant you guys were on the rig, that you were both ready. That's why we left the station without you. Don't you see? He was in a win-win situation. He goes inside, but he can hide. You can't tell on him because you're not there to know about it, and Sears can't tell on him because he doesn't go in with him, and if anybody asks what he was doing, he was looking for you. *You* would have taken the rap for everything that happened there."

"I *should* have taken the rap."

"You know what else? He told me the old man was alive when he got there. That he heard him calling for help. But he just stayed in that hallway. There wasn't even that much fire when we got there. He could have marched right down that hallway and got that old man, but he didn't move from the doorway."

"Why did *you* stand up for me?"

"I seen you go in there and I thought . . . well, I thought that was really something. First you come out with the old man. Then you come out with the woman. I thought that was really something. Besides, we all done things might have cost us our jobs."

"I never did. Not until that. It seems to be an everyday occurrence now. I've made so many mistakes. Sometimes I think I'm the unluckiest bastard on the planet."

In the darkness I could see Johnson's teeth as he smiled, trying hard to convince himself that Tronstad's operating principle was one we should adopt, doing something wrong to make something right.

33. A MAJOR CLUE FOR ALL YOU THIEVES, MURDERERS, ARSONISTS, TURD-DROPPERS, AND MOTHER-BEATERS

Two uneventful days passed, where I didn't see or hear from Tronstad. Then Tuesday's shift came and went, also uneventfully. By Wednesday morning, when I got in my car, I was getting pretty nervous.

As soon as I rounded the corner, I downshifted and pushed the accelerator to the floor. As the turbocharger kicked in, the forward momentum pinned me against the seat back. I loved rowing through the WRX's gearbox, working the clutch and shifter with split-second precision.

I tore through the quiet streets, making a right turn at

speed, zipping onto California Avenue and into the residential streets, racing down the hill on narrow Ferry Avenue until my tires were screeching, then cruising south on Harbor Avenue along the West Seattle waterfront while "Something Vicious for Tomorrow" by Built to Spill played in the background.

I might have gone past Iola Pederson's place, except I knew on the days she worked she didn't leave until just before nine, and on the days she didn't work she hung around even longer. In either case she would be home, and I couldn't retrieve the bonds while she was guarding the place.

On Genesee I parked in front of my rental. Because I was frequently gone twenty-four hours at a pop, I left the living-room drapes cracked open to give the place a lived-in look. This morning the drapes were tighter than a freshly dug clam.

Somebody had been inside.

The place was a mess, pictures on the wall askew or thrown to the floor, the sofa upside down, panels ripped open with what appeared to be a sharp knife, the television on its face, glass shards everywhere, and a dirty boot print outlined in blue toothpaste depressing the service panel on the back. The rooms were uncharacteristically cold, and in addition, there was a stench I could not identify at first.

As I picked my way through the rooms, stepping over items and clothing strewn on the carpet, I found the lock broken on the back door, the door wide, as were the doors on the refrigerator and freezer. Nothing had been stolen that I could tell, but plenty had been destroyed: my VCR, the DVD player, a small audio system I bought during my first six months in the department.

As I explored the rooms, I located a turd on the carpet next to my bed. If I suspected Tronstad, the signature giveaway was the etching on the bathroom mirror that said, *ass wipe,* one of Tronstad's favorite verbalisms.

He'd pulled everything out of every cabinet, dumped every drawer, and walked over most of it in his motorcycle boots. In the garage he'd climbed up through the attic scuttle and put his foot through the ceiling from above several times, leaving ragged holes with insulation poking through like pinched underwear.

What frightened me more than the wanton destruction was the fact that I could not ignore this the way I'd been ignoring everything else. The affront here was entirely too personal. Funny how my brain worked. I stood mute while Tronstad murdered people, but when he stepped on my toothpaste and took a crap on my carpet, things had gone too far.

Panic didn't set in until I realized my address book was missing. When I punched her number into my cell phone, she answered on the second ring. "If he's there, just say, 'Yes, I think so.' "

"He's left."

"You sure?"

"Positive. I've had the neighbors in helping to clean things up. We're just about finished."

"Did he hurt you?"

"No."

"Do you know who he was?"

"One of the men you work with. I saw him at your station. I don't recall his name."

"He have a patch over his eye?"

"How did you know?"

"You sure he didn't hurt you?"

"I'm okay."

"Did you call the police?"

"A very nice man took a report and said to call if I saw him again."

"I'll be right there. Don't let anybody else in."

"Don't worry about it. He was like a rooster, all strut and no bite. You'd be surprised how insignificant this is in the grand scheme of things."

If I could ever see the grand scheme of things, I'm sure I would have agreed with her. "I'll be there in half an hour."

Hurriedly, I nailed my back door shut, cleaned the carpet,

and performed a perfunctory search for the cat, Abraham, an old white tabby who'd been roaming the neighborhood when I moved in and who'd adopted me. I expected I'd seen the last of him for a few days.

Tronstad hadn't made nearly the mess in my mother's apartment he had in mine. "You all right, Mom?" I asked, kissing her forehead.

"I'm fine."

"Sure?"

"Just fine."

"Did he touch you?"

"He didn't mean to. He told me to stand in the corner." My mother was a small woman, barely five feet tall, and had been under a hundred pounds when she was healthy. I hated to think what she weighed now.

"He said all he wanted was some money you hid. I gave him thirty dollars and some coins. It was all I had."

"Did he hit you?"

"He did a lot of yelling was what he did."

"But did he hit you?"

"He might have slapped me."

I could tell she'd been crying before I got there and clearly had been terrified during the break-in. Her hands were still shaking, her face paler than I'd seen it since her last trip to the hospital. My mother was forty-one, but since her diagnosis she'd been hanging out with people much older, perhaps because they were closer to death than the other forty-somethings she knew.

"He said he was from the fire department. He said he was president of Local Twenty-seven. That there'd been an accident. I thought you were hurt, so I let him in."

"Did you tell the cops you knew the guy?"

"I didn't know what you'd want me to do."

"He's dangerous, Mom. Tell them."

"But what do *you* want me to do?"

"His name is Theodore Tronstad. I'll write it down for you. You can call as soon as I leave."

"Are you sure that's what you want me to do?"

"Do it."

She sat at the kitchen table and considered me. Nobody looks at a person in quite the proprietary way a mother does, and I basked under her gaze as if she were a second sun in the sky. "He said he owes money to some bad people and he can't pay them until you pay him."

"I wouldn't be surprised if he was in the hole for a good little bit."

"Seventy-five thousand, he said."

"Jesus. Listen, I've got some cleaning to do at my place. Then I've got an errand to run. After that I'm free till Sunday. Think about where you want to go."

"You don't need to spend all your time with your mother."

"That is *exactly* what I need to do. I'll put gas in the car, get some cash at the bank, and be back in an hour. How's that?"

"It's still warm east of the mountains."

"Good. You navigate and I'll pilot."

I filled the tank with premium, checked all the fluids and the pressure in the tires, then drove to the other end of West Seattle. I eased down the hill to Hobart Avenue and cruised past the Pederson homestead for one last attempt at retrieving the bonds.

Fortunately, neither Iola nor Bernard looked out at the road, the epitome of blissful matrimony as they soaped and washed her Land Cruiser in the driveway. It was all very convivial and sudsy and no doubt postcoital, and they looked as if they were settled in for the day. He must have taken today off.

On the drive back to my place, I made a call on the cell phone. "Robert?"

"Hey. I wasn't really trying to follow you this morning. You know that, don't you? I was horsing around."

"You followed me?"

"I couldn't keep up. That car of yours moves like stink."

"Tronstad broke into my place. He broke into my mother's, too. He roughed her up."

"Now are you ready to do something about him?"

"Not what you have in mind."

The line was silent for a few seconds. "You got the bags yet?"

"There's bound to be a window of opportunity, but not today."

"Tonight?"

"I'm leaving town. I'll be back after our four-off."

"Tronstad's going to be pissed."

"I hope he is."

I tidied up two rooms so I wouldn't be coming home to a complete piggery, asked Mrs. Macklin to feed the cat, then packed a small bag and called Tronstad on my cell phone. No answer. I called his house, but the phone had been disconnected.

Later, as I was driving up the hill toward my mother's apartment, my cell rang. Tronstad sounded either sleepy or drunk, his voice thick, guttural, and surprisingly friendly. "Hey, peckerwood. You got my stash yet?"

"I should kill you, you bastard!"

"Now, hold your horses."

"She knows you, Tronstad. She's been to the station."

"Who knows me? What are you talking about?"

"My mother. And you *know* what I'm talking about." There was a long pause while Tronstad tried to remember if he'd actually met my mother. "I kicked the crap out of you once. I can do it again."

Tronstad laughed, and I could feel rage coursing through my bloodstream like an illegal drug cut with cleanser.

I drove two blocks with the phone pressed to my ear, the line silent except for static. Finally Tronstad said, "You're treading on thin ice, buddy. You get those bonds and put an end to this shit. That's all you gotta do. Just go get 'em, and we'll divvy them up."

"You shouldn't have gone to my mother's."

"Don't fuck with me, Gum. Try turning me in, I'll swear you were in on it. Every last bit of it, including the car fire.

You fuck with me, I'll burn your place down. I'll burn your mother's place down."

"I wouldn't be setting too many fires. Those bonds are paper."

The line was silent for a few moments while he considered the prospect of accidentally destroying twelve million dollars. "Gum, I gotta get the money today. They're going to hurt me. God, we never should have turned it over to you. I'm sleeping in my truck. I got cheated gambling. All I got is twenty bucks cash."

"What happened to the other ten my mother gave you?" I asked, breaking the connection.

I found my mother upstairs at the kitchen table, packed and dressed for travel, the morning newspaper in front of her, sipping tea from a china cup and looking about as content with life as a sassy sparrow in a tree. The only remaining trace of Tronstad's visit was a picture frame on the kitchen counter waiting to heal, held together with glue and a congregation of rubber bands. The photo in the frame was of me standing alongside my mother at my fire department drill school graduation, sunlight glinting off the silver buttons on my black wool uniform, my mother looking ten years younger and fifteen pounds heavier. She'd wanted me to finish school and become a teacher or an attorney, but in the photo she was just as proud as if I'd been elected President.

I packed my mother's bags into the back of the WRX and belted her in. A block south of my mother's apartment house, I spotted Tronstad's orange pickup truck. Maintaining a block gap, Tronstad followed us through traffic. Just a clue for all you thieves, murderers, arsonists, turd-droppers, and mother-beaters: you want to tail somebody surreptitiously, don't do it in a bright orange pickup truck jacked up so high you can run over stray dogs without getting dirt in their ears.

I went through a yellow at Thirty-fifth, and he caught the red as we headed down the hill to the West Seattle viaduct. I knew he'd be thinking he could hotfoot it down the hill and quickly catch up, and it might have worked, too, except that once we were over the crest of the hill, where he couldn't see us, I gassed the WRX and hit speeds that made my mother's knuckles go white on the door handle, weaving in and out of traffic, doing everything but running over the tops of vehicles in my way.

He was nowhere in sight by the time we were on I-5 heading south to the Albro exit. I turned north and used surface streets on the east side of the freeway until we hit Rainier Avenue. From there we crossed Lake Washington on the floating bridge and headed toward the Cascade Mountains.

"I suppose there was a reason for driving like an idiot," my mother said.

"I think I've pretty much turned into an idiot."

34. DECISION BY PARALYSIS

The highway traversing Snoqualmie Pass rose only three thousand feet above the level of the ocean, but no road bisecting the Swiss Alps could have been more magnificent. Mom asked me to stop at the summit so she could spend a few minutes in the sunshine. It sounds macabre, but I'd come to the conclusion that the whole point of these trips was so she could get in touch with the earth before rejoining it.

She sat on a rock in the sun watching a group of mountain bikers unload their bikes from the back of a huge SUV. When she asked why they had different styles of bicycles, she was offered a lengthy explanation on mountain-bike design and told the differences between standard and downhill bikes. She had so much to be inward about, and yet every aspect of her life was threaded outward, each day spent learning as much as was humanly possible about the creatures around her and how they interacted with the world.

As we rolled down the slopes of the Cascade Mountains into Eastern Washington, cattle grazed in fields scorched brown from the hot summer. Horses stood like statues under the sun. The second mountain pass, Blewett, was a twisty, two-lane highway for most of the route, and once on it I passed slower vehicles at will, letting the turbo kick in as we climbed again into the cool mountain air.

It was late afternoon when we pulled into Winthrop, a dusty little Old West movie set of a town in the Methow Valley of north-central Washington. In keeping with the theme, the buildings lining the short main street all had false fronts of clapboard siding and sidewalks constructed of rough-hewn wood planks. When the snow flew, Winthrop metamorphosed into a mecca for cross-country skiers and snowmobilers; in the summers it attracted hikers, rock climbers, mountain bikers, equestrians, fly fishermen, and anybody else looking to get away from the clouds and rain on the west side of the mountains. It was just the sort of backwater bucket of humanity my mother loved to soak up, the chatty locals and atmosphere acting like Epsom salts on her woes.

We ended up staying at the Rio Vista, smack on the main drag in Winthrop. The hotel had burned to the ground a few years earlier but had been rebuilt. Mom got the story when she asked about a color photo of the fire that was hanging in a frame on the wall. Since I had entered the fire department she'd been fascinated by fires, car wrecks, air crashes—anything in which my job might involve me.

Our room at the Rio Vista looked west out over the Chewuch River, which had dwindled to a trickle under the October sun. After opening the patio slider and spotting a bald eagle in a tree forty yards away, my mother got out her binoculars and I lay down on the second bed. I'd worked the night before, and that combined with the five-hour drive and my current situation had put me under enough stress to bend steel.

I woke up an hour and a half later, and by then my mother was asleep on the other bed. I'd noticed lately her naps were getting more frequent and longer, and that she was slower than Christmas waking up. It was one of those observations I didn't speak about and was sorry I'd made.

She'd never really told me the details of her illness, only that she had breast cancer, that it had spread long before they found it. After a recent miserable course of chemotherapy, she told her doctors she would rather live the rest of her life taking painkillers in front of sunsets than undergoing expensive and ultimately ineffective medical procedures in windowless rooms.

In reviewing statements she made over the years, most of which seemed inconsequential at the time, I came to the conclusion that my mother had always been comfortable with the thought of death, comfortable in the same way that many old people get comfortable with it.

The four days we spent in the Methow were in the eighties, with a high overcast and some sun, and I wore shorts, though my mother bundled her frail torso in khakis and a fleece vest. We stayed three nights, taking short early-morning hikes each day before returning to the hotel for a nap. For the first time, she'd begun taking a second nap during the day, often inadvertently while reading in the afternoon on our room's patio, or while I was out in the hills on a rented mountain bike.

It became our custom to eat dinner at the Duck Brand Cantina across the street from the Rio Vista, where we eschewed the popular multilevel wooden decks outdoors in favor of eating amid a riot of ever-present Christmas lights in the back of the restaurant, beneath the Texas longhorn trophy. For breakfast each morning we walked down the street to the main intersection of town to eat at a place called Three Fingered Jack's, billed as the oldest legal saloon in the State of Washington. The Old West atmosphere there was slightly tarnished by the big-screen TV blaring in the corner, but I guess that was part of the fun.

Mom spent time talking to the locals, forming a particularly close attachment to a heavy-bottomed waitress named Doris at Three Fingered Jack's. They promised to write, and I believed Doris actually would. My mother carried on a humongous e-mail correspondence, spending hours each day keeping up with various friends and acquaintances and, in some cases, people she'd met and knew only through the Internet, from as far away as Australia and South Africa.

On our final morning, after we'd paid our bill at Three Fingered Jack's, she was sipping tea as I read a hundred-year-old ad on the wall for a single-cylinder automobile that cost two thousand dollars. She leaned across the table and fixed me with her steely gray gaze. Her scarf was pulled tight across her forehead. Once or twice on trips I'd caught her banging around our hotel room without her scarf, and seeing her bald head was as much of a shock as if I'd caught her nude.

The hardest part of her illness for me was acting normal, acting as if I didn't notice, and if I did notice, pretending I didn't care. She needed that from me during these last few months, to know it wasn't bothering me. Above all else, she craved normalcy.

"I know you're in trouble, Jason. And I know you don't think you have any way out."

"You're not going to tell me to have faith in God, not after what He's done to you?" We'd spent so much time avoiding talk of religion and any discussion of her impending death that I was almost as embarrassed by my statement as she was.

Even though we both knew I was lashing out at her in order to fend off inquiries about my own problems, she said, "What's God done to me? I've had a *wonderful* life."

"I love you, Mom, but you're forty-one years old, you've lived most of your life in poverty. You don't even own a car. You're dying of cancer. I don't call that being watched over by God. I just don't."

"Are you saying if I had a Mercedes, that would be a signal God was taking care of me? Don't be silly. My life with you was a miracle. I've been blessed."

"Your life with me was a struggle."

"Don't ever start feeling sorry for me or yourself, Jason. You were born in the wealthiest country in history. Most people on this earth survive on less than two dollars a day. Thousands of children starve to death each day, and we all march ahead as if it isn't happening. Don't ever feel sorry for yourself. And as far as me dying at forty-one? It's only been the last hundred years or so women even lived this long."

She stared at me, her gray eyes more earnest than ever. "Jason, don't ever feel sorry for me. *I* don't."

"Okay."

After checking out of the hotel, we drove to the Grand Coulee Dam and spent an hour at the visitors' center, then walked along the sidewalk on top of the dam and took the tour inside. Everything about the dam fascinated my mother: the immensity, the historical footnotes concerning the construction, the permanence. On the way home we explored Native American hieroglyphics in the boulders off the highway and hiked up into the caves with a smattering of other intrepid travelers. Later we had dinner in Wenatchee, a good-sized agricultural town just this side of Blewett Pass, where she ordered a salad but then had it boxed up on the pretext that she'd eat it later.

I'd taken this trip in the mistaken belief that travel might clear my head, but the longer we stayed away from home, the more antsy and chaotic my thoughts became, until I thought I was going mad. Four people—no, six people—were dead, and had I done things differently, they would all be alive still. My primary character trait these days seemed to be paralysis.

Ted Tronstad had gone from being a small-time prankster and troublemaker to being a thief, then from a possibly accidental killer to an intentional one. A smarter, more confident Jason Gum could have stopped every one of those deaths.

Mom didn't wake up until I was driving up the hill into West Seattle. "Going to be a nice evening," she said, sleepily. "The pollution always makes the sky pretty."

"Yes, it does."

The way I saw it, I had three choices.

I could turn the bonds over to Tronstad and Johnson and wait to see what transpired.

I could do something to stop Tronstad, either by myself or in conjunction with Robert Johnson.

I could go to the authorities.

Each alternative involved risk. If I turned the bonds over to Tronstad, the odds were he would try to get rid of me as an unwanted witness, maybe by firebombing my car or my house. If I *stopped* him, Johnson's euphemism for killing him, I would become what he'd become. I knew I couldn't live with that. If I went to the authorities, I would most likely end up in a cell.

I carried my mother's bags upstairs, made certain she was secure, kissed her brow, then went back out to my car, half expecting Tronstad to be lurking about, though he wasn't.

When I parked in the short driveway in front of my garage door, Mrs. Macklin was staring at me from her front doorway, one of her unshaven adult sons alongside. "Good evening, Mrs. Macklin. What's going on?"

I glanced to my right and saw what I should have seen when I pulled up.

My living-room window had a long crack running from bottom to top, and the drapes had been pulled off the wall.

35. MADE THEM SENSE OF NONE

"Harry took me to the fabric store to pick up some more green yarn for the Cottage Rose potholders I'm crocheting for Christmas presents," Mrs. Macklin said. "Then we stopped by the Safeway for some lima beans and raisins. Oh, and I had to get me some lottery tickets and cigarettes, too. But the line wasn't so long as usual. We couldn't have been gone more than an hour. When we got back . . ." She began weeping, her lower lip twitching.

"Somebody broke in?"

"They broke my back door. You should have been here. I can't watch this place all by myself. I have to go out *some-*

time, don't I? I don't even want to think what they would have done if I'd been home. A helpless woman all alone."

"When did this happen?"

Her son piped up, "A few hours ago. I have a case number if you want to call the officer who came out. She said you could call day or night. I didn't know whether to leave or not. You going to be around?"

"I'll be here."

"You sure?" Mrs. Macklin said.

"I'm sure."

Inside, the two rooms I'd cleaned after the first burglary were the worst, as if he wanted to break my spirit by destroying what I'd already tried to remedy. He'd shattered, bent, destroyed, stepped on, torn, shredded, peed on, or stolen everything of value. He'd taken each piece of silverware and bent it in half. My dresser drawers had been flattened.

In the garage the wallboard had been torn open with a shovel, a task that must have taken a good deal of time and made a lot of racket. Mrs. Macklin could hardly have thought I was remodeling, and she must have been home during some of it. There'd been a small fire in the center of the living room on the carpet, a calling card of sorts. He had tapped it with water from a pan, then collapsed the pan and left it on the charred carpet.

He'd apparently toyed with the idea of burning the place down, arrested no doubt by my remark about the bonds being flammable.

I formed a large pile of throwaways on the covered concrete patio out back. If I'd had any doubts this was Tronstad's handiwork, they were dispelled when I checked my in-line skate collection hanging on the wall in the garage and found he'd taken a cigarette lighter and melted a hole in the toe box on all four pairs. The garage still reeked of melted plastic.

I should have called the cops three days before, when he attacked my mother—she never did call them back. If I had, he might be in custody by now. I might be, too.

He'd scrawled filth on the walls with shoe polish, scattered clothing across the floors, and had even taken the time to write balloon captions on one high school photo of me and a girl named Pamela. The balloon over my head said, "Watch out for me, babe, I steal from my friends!" The balloon over hers said, "Such a tiny dick."

It was eight when I started cleaning. By ten-thirty I had the bedroom pretty much put back in place, though it would need a new carpet, dresser, and mattress. I found two sheets he'd neglected to slash and put them through Mrs. Macklin's washing machine; he'd cut the cord on mine. In fact, he'd cut the cord on every electrical appliance in the house.

Coming back from doing my laundry, I found Sonja Pederson's official SPD business card stuck in the back door. Considering how each had evolved, it was hard to explain why our few brief meetings had endeared Sonja Pederson to me, but they had. Then in one of those strange coincidences you don't think can be real even as it's happening, there was a knock at the front door. "You decent?"

Sonja Pederson stepped through the doorway. "This is bad. Somebody spent a lot of time here."

"Mrs. Macklin said she was only gone an hour, but I figure they were in here all afternoon, saw her leave, and then went over there."

"That's how we figured it, too. I'm sorry to barge in on you. I recognized the address when it came over the radio. The neighbor said you were out of town. If you don't mind, I thought I'd give you a hand."

"Really?"

"You are alone here, aren't you?"

"I'm alone."

"Your neighbor seems to think . . . well, she's under the impression this might have been done by one of the scores of older women you have wild orgies with at all hours of the day and night."

"You hate me, don't you?"

"Because of Iola? Don't be absurd. I never blamed you. Men are helpless when a woman wants something from them."

"Your stepmother ever do anything like this?"

"Once she beat on a guy's car with a tennis racket. Did quite a bit of damage, actually."

"What happened?"

"My father took care of it. Then he took Iola to Hawaii to patch things up. That's their routine. He makes her mad. She goes off with a guy. He scares the guy away. Then they patch things up."

"Why do they stay together?"

"I don't know why *he* stays. I assume *she* stays because he'll have money when Grandpa passes on."

"So you came because you think she did this?"

"She was at work. I checked. I came because I want to help. If you'll let me."

"I'll let you if you don't put me in any thumb locks and try not to kick me in the nuts."

She laughed.

She picked up a clock that had been stepped on until its innards were herniating out the sides. "So, where are we? What do you want me to do first?"

She was wearing her uniform, shirt, badge, gun belt, and, if I wasn't mistaken, a bulletproof vest underneath. When I told her she could use the bedroom to change, she went in and removed her vest, rebuttoning her shirt and strapping her gun back on.

"Thanks for coming," I said.

"You're welcome."

We worked together for half an hour. Little was said. At eleven-twenty a middle-aged African man showed up at the front door with a box of pizza.

"I hope you don't mind," Sonja said.

"At least let me pay."

When he'd gone, she carried the cardboard box to what was left of the sofa and said, "I ordered the biggest one. I didn't know how hungry you might be."

I wasn't hungry at all, but I sat next to her anyway.

She said, "When I was twelve my father took me to Japan on a business trip. The young people all wore these goofy

T-shirts with English writing on them, only none of them made any sense. They said things like 'All my life is a lovers.' Or 'Let's not throw; don't throw litters the way.' Every time I have pizza I think of one that said, 'We die mango pizza for.' " She laughed. "None of them made sense."

"Made them sense of none."

She laughed again, and while I couldn't laugh along with her, I liked it that she was trying to cheer me up by laughing at my anemic joke. Like a pair of hoboes at the city dump, we camped on the foam bleeding out the cushions and arms of my sofa. At least I felt like a hobo. With her uniform shirt and gun, she still looked very much like a Seattle cop, albeit a sexy Seattle cop.

36. GUM APPEARS TO BE A SIMPLETON

Like all humans, my psyche required intimacy—not mere physical intimacy, but intimacy in the realms emotional, spiritual, and moral. For me, right now, moral most of all, because I was floundering along the margins of corruption without a compass.

Although I desperately wanted to talk to somebody about my problems, the particulars kept me from it. I didn't know how to discuss my current situation without confessing to complicity, forced or otherwise, in a series of odious crimes.

I'd been about as close to obtaining emotional sustenance from Iola as a dog walking across a college campus was to obtaining a bachelor's degree. My time with Iola had provided nothing but short bruising periods of athletic sexual congress followed by long sessions of her blathering, which included unfounded and plain wrongheaded opinions on world politics as well as not-so-veiled references to her promiscuous sexual history, followed by a half hour or so of walking around the house in the nude while she commented freely on my lack of sophistication, and then, more often than not, a second session of sex, generally angrier, more vigorous, and more resigned than the first.

While these assignations had slaked my lust, they'd left me feeling emptier and more alone than I'd ever felt, like a man on a raft drinking seawater, which filled your stomach but left you thirstier than when you started. Sadly, my debauched enterprises with her stepmother had squelched any chance of romance with Sonja. I knew that.

Yet it was closing in on midnight, and here she was in my house, just her and me. I had a fleeting thought that maybe she was as batty as her stepmother and that she was the one who'd trashed my house, but I dismissed it.

Despite my yearning for companionship, I did not feel completely comfortable about her motives. First, there was the possibility that she was interested in me solely because her stepmother had been interested, and that Iola, Sonja, and myself were playing out some demented Olympian psychosexual family drama, that I was cannon fodder in a twisted scheme I would never fully comprehend. Even though I had no facts to support such a belief, it dogged me.

As we sat side by side on the sofa and gobbled pizza, another more likely and equally jaded vision began coursing through my brain. Sonja goes into her boss's office, and there are FBI agents huddled around a pile of notes and fact sheets. Sizing her up, they review her brief record with the SPD and ask her where she sees herself in ten years. She admits she has ambitions. They invite her to sit down. They ask if she knows a man named Gum. She admits she does. They ask if she can get close to Gum, if she believes she might coax him into saying things he would never admit in public. She says Gum appears to be a simpleton and she believes conning him might be possible. They ask if she is willing to wear a wire.

The whole idea of Sonja remaining in uniform as she bumped around my place made more sense when fitted into this whacked-out scenario. What a coup it would be in court when she testified that I'd confessed while she was in uniform—badge, gun belt, and nightstick in place.

Even though I wasn't hungry, I ate three slices of pizza, feeling my stomach grow tight, a pleasant and lusty feeling, one I didn't have often, as I watched my diet. I set my plate aside and straightened my legs, leaning back on the sofa. Sonja did the same, our legs splayed out like a couple of drunks in front of a football game. "Too bad about all this," she said.

"He got everything I own except that car out there."

"Renter's insurance?"

"Thanks for the tip. I'll sign up tomorrow."

"Sorry. You have any idea who might have done this?"

"I know exactly who did it."

She sat upright, pulled out a small notebook and a pen, then paused. "You're not going to tell me, are you."

"No."

The drapes were nailed up and closed now, the front door locked, the only light in the room emanating from a bare bulb I'd screwed into a lamp I'd rewired. The stark light cut across Sonja's face, accentuating her one dimple. Faintly, I could smell perfume mixing with the aroma from the pizza. "Let's get this cleaned up, then," she said. "At least so you can have somewhere to sleep."

As we started to get off the sofa, our heads moved closer, and in one of those split-second decisions that come back to haunt you when they go wrong but seem like utter wizardry when you think of them, I clasped her shoulders and kissed her. I could tell she wasn't surprised. She kissed me back, and despite my best intentions, all the purity of heart I'd been storing up for her vanished in a heartbeat as I began comparing her lips and body to her stepmother's. Her stepmother had been rapacious, greedy, all tongue, a pair of huge, spongy knockers thrusting against me, greedy hands diving for my belt buckle, while Sonja may as well have been a high-schooler on her first date.

When we parted I wanted to swim in the blue of her eyes. I wanted to tell her that, too, but it would have sounded as if

I'd lifted it from the Italian movie I'd heard it in, the one my mom and I watched our last night in Winthrop.

We went back to work, and from time to time she showed up in the doorway of the bedroom to show me a damaged utensil and ask if I wanted to keep it or pitch it. Unable to afford replacements immediately, I kept once-round pots now squashed into oblongs, forks with the tines bent, and knives doubled over like old men walking in the wind. I would reform them later.

It was almost two when I went into the kitchen and found her on her hands and knees scrubbing the floor with a wet rag. There had been no sound in the house, no music, just the euphony of our work: the tinkling and clinking of silverware, the splashing of water in the sinks, the scuffling vibrato as I dragged broken furniture out of the house. Except for a garbage bag full of broken dishes and a broken cabinet door, the kitchen looked almost new. I was bowled over by how much she'd accomplished.

"I'm going to have to stop for tonight," I said.

She sat up on her heels. She'd taken off her gun belt and uniform shirt. Underneath she wore an almond-colored camisole. "You look beat."

"I am."

She got up and walked with me into the living room, where we sat heavily on the ravaged couch in the approximate positions we'd taken up earlier. With the bare lightbulb behind her, she looked incredibly graceful, her neck long and swanlike.

"Do you have to work in the morning?" I asked.

"Not till noon."

She leaned toward me. "Maybe I should leave," she said.

I let her statement hang in the air, savoring the ambiguity. She hadn't said, "I need to get out of here." Nor had she said, "I'm going home now," or "I can't stay a minute longer." She had said, "Maybe I should leave." *Maybe.* I felt like a kid at Disneyland at the end of the day, worn to a frazzle and receiving an implied offer of one more ride. Maybe we still have time for Magic Mountain.

Without thinking, I leaned into her and we kissed for so long I lost track of time, our bodies molded against each other. And then she leaned back and began pushing up her camisole, and I was on top of her and she was kicking her shoes off and we were against each other, our bodies hot from the work and the electricity that had been humming between us all night.

It didn't take long to figure out nothing was going to happen. "What is it?" she asked.

"I can't do this. Not tonight."

"I don't mind that you and Iola . . . it doesn't bother me. It doesn't."

"It's not that."

It *was* that, but there was more, of course. There was the possibility I would turn myself in tomorrow, as I'd been contemplating all week, that I would be in a cell by tomorrow night. I wasn't in a position to give Sonja more than one night, and I didn't want to cheat her.

"Don't worry," she said. "I've been burned by guys before. I've had guys tell me I was too skinny. My nose was too big. I was too aggressive. If you want to head all that off at the pass, that's fine with me." She started to get up.

"No. You don't understand. I like you. I think I like you more than any woman I've ever . . . I really do. I just . . . this doesn't have anything to do with you. I know this sounds strange, but would you stay here tonight? Nothing else. Just stay with me?"

"Sure."

Five minutes later she crawled between the sheets I'd laundered next door and slid into my arms, her limbs cool, her stomach tight, her nose cold. Too tired to bother with a T-shirt, I wore only boxer shorts. Virtually all of my clothing had been shredded, so all I had left was what I had brought back from Winthrop and my uniforms in my locker at work.

Sonja gave me a tender kiss and settled in against me, her head under my chin. She giggled and said something, but I missed it, because I was already half asleep and kidnapped by a dream.

It was one of those nights when the moon could crash into the earth and it wouldn't wake me up. As I slept I was aware of a sense of well-being I hadn't enjoyed in weeks. At one point I shifted positions and felt a warm, lithe, half-naked body curl up against my backside, Sonja's hot breath on my bare shoulder.

Firefighters need to wake up quickly, but there are times when it is better for lovers to wake up slowly, and that is how it happened with us. I had a sense we were moving, that I was tangled in a web of limbs, and that I was embracing a naked woman—hard of tissue and muscle mass, leaner than any woman I'd ever pressed up against. I didn't fully awaken until I heard the slap of our bodies and realized she was as eager and libidinous as her stepmother.

"What's the matter?" she asked.

"I just had a thought."

"Don't think." She kissed me, and we began picking up the tempo, as she urged me on with her hands on my back. The bed was squeaking, and I wanted to stop because it was the same squeaking I'd heard all those weeks with her stepmother. I tried to put it out of my mind, but the more I tried the more it intruded, until I was pumping on both of them at once, this sinewy, athletic cop and her luxurious, big-titted stepmother, the two of them fused in my mind. And the more confounded I got, the more excited I became, until it was as if I were two people engaged in two sex acts at once.

After we were both spent and satisfied, I lay inside the firm meat of her thighs, my head draped over her left shoulder, feeling myself slowly shrink. I had a feeling she'd been thinking about her stepmother, as had I, thinking what a frightfully twisted act we were engaged in.

"What time do you have to leave for work?" she whispered.

"I don't want to go."

"I don't want you to. But what time?"

Reaching out, I located my watch on the floor beside the bed. "In just under an hour. I'll shower at work." When she pulled me back onto her, I added, "If I tell you something, can you keep it confidential?"

"You're going to tell me who broke in and why?"

"Yes, but it has to stay between you and me. You have to swear."

"Have you thought about an attorney?"

"What I would like," I said, deadly serious, "is to be able to talk to you freely and for you to keep my confidence."

"Okay."

"Promise?"

"I promise."

It was hard to know which was more foolhardy, her pledge or my confession.

37. HE WAS RIDING ME LIKE A MULE

"If a friend of yours steals something and gives it to you to hold, have you committed a crime? I mean, if you were holding it with the intent of giving it back to the original owner? If that was your intention all along?"

"You knew it was stolen?"

"Yes."

"This friend broke in? You had something he stole, and he came looking for it?"

"Yes."

"Are you going to tell me his name?"

"I don't want you going after him."

"Not unless you give the word."

"Theodore Tronstad. Until this, I didn't think he was a bad guy, really."

"He's the one you hit with the hose the other day?"

"Yes."

"Why don't you give it back to him? Whatever he stole?"

"It's not his."

"Then give it to the rightful owner."

"That's where it gets complicated. The night my lieutenant died, Tronstad filmed me and the lieutenant. He has a video clip of us in the water that makes it look as if it was my fault Sears drowned—as if I pushed him under on purpose."

I could feel her tense up in my arms the way a cat tenses up when it knows you're about to throw it out of bed. A couple of firefighters engaged in theft and personal squabbles was one thing, but a fire-ground death was something else.

"So he doctored the tape?"

"No. I did push him under. Sears didn't know how to swim and he panicked. He was riding me like a drunk on a mule. We were both getting mouthfuls of water, and . . . In life-saving you learn . . . once somebody panics, all they care about is breathing air instead of water. The technique is to sink and let them come under with you, because they'll let go of you and fight their way back to the surface, and that's how you get free. But with all that equipment on, all I could manage was to break loose and push *him* away. Instead of moving away from me, he went under. By the time I turned around to pull him out, he'd been sucked into that pipe."

"This is all on videotape?"

"Enough of it."

I was leaving out the deaths of Mr. and Mrs. Brown and Chief Abbott, but I couldn't see her keeping a confidence that involved three additional deaths. Nor did I have personal testimony on those. Sears was the only death I'd witnessed start to finish. Plus, if I told her the rest, I might as well put on a suit and go downtown.

"Were there other witnesses?"

"The other man on our crew. He and Tronstad are planning to split up what Tronstad stole."

"So he won't be testifying on your behalf?"

"I don't think so."

"This stolen item is worth money?"

"Enough to buy this duplex. And every house on the block. Maybe the next block over."

She thought about it a few moments. "It's the George S. David loot, isn't it? That guy who called himself Ghanet? You must have been on the crew who found his body. Who else have you told?"

"Nobody."

"Iola?"

"Nobody."

"That car fire the other day. The driver was a retired FBI field agent. You said your friend set that fire."

"I can't prove it."

"Maybe *we* can."

"Maybe."

She grew quiet. It was hard to know what she was thinking—that I was involved in these deaths. That I was a killer. That I was a thief. That she needed to get up and leave before the place got raided. Or before I told her anything else. I'd left so much out. If only she knew. "Jesus, Gum. You're in more trouble than anybody I've ever met."

"Even people you arrested?"

"Anybody."

38. THREE THINGS

That day at Station 29 two things happened—no, three things. The first was Robert Johnson began haranguing me about the bonds, becoming more belligerent as the day wore on, admitting finally he'd overextended himself and was in the process of buying vacation property in Palm Springs, and that he needed forty thousand dollars by the end of the week. "You got to give me my share today. I just want those bonds. Can't you see what sort of trouble I'm in?"

"I didn't tell you to buy property you don't need with money you don't have."

"Jesus, you're hardheaded, Gum. You used to be such an easygoing guy."

As the day wore on, I watched him grow angrier and more aloof. We had four alarms, and he went bad on three of them while I sat in back and let him take the wrong route to the wrong block. Our extra man for the day gave me a look that told me rumors of Johnson's ineptitude would be hotfooting it around the battalion for weeks to come.

Later, basking in the October sunshine, our arms folded against a chilly wind that portended winter's early arrival, we had another chat in the Safeway parking lot while Lieutenant Muir and Jim Snively, the detail from Station 32, went in to buy dinner. Considering the bitterness that had passed between us, it was curious that Johnson and I could chat like old friends, but we could.

"Robert?"

"Yeah?"

"If a woman's stepmother is having an affair with a guy and then her stepmother breaks it off, do you think there's any way that woman would be interested in the guy her step-mother was balling?"

"I don't see how. To start off with, he'd be too old for her."

"Supposing the stepmother has an affair with a younger guy."

"You ever see that movie *The Graduate*? Young guy is porking the mother, then runs off and marries the daughter? Wait a minute. This is you and the stepdaughter of that older babe you were banging, right?"

"Yeah."

"Whooo. That is weird, man." Johnson turned and looked at me, breaking into a broad smile. "A mother/daughter deal. Whooee. How many guys have dreamed about that?"

"I wish you wouldn't put it like that. I don't know if it could ever work out, but I like her a lot."

Johnson chuckled. "Gum, you got more surprises than anybody I know. I mean, there was the way you went into that fire at Arch Place. Two rescues all by your lone-some. Then there's the bonds. I never dreamed you wouldn't give them up the instant we asked. And then you beat the hell out of Tronstad with the hose line." He laughed. "Now you want to bang the daughter of the woman you were banging last week. Gum, you take the cake."

The second thing that happened was Ted Tronstad didn't show up. Since I'd attacked him, he'd broken into my house twice and my mother's once, so it stood to reason he was afraid I'd assault him again. Or sic the cops on him.

The third thing happened just before dinner. I walked into the beanery and found Sonja Pederson sitting at the table alongside Lieutenant Muir and Snively. Snively was reading the newspaper, oblivious of Sonja in the same way he'd been oblivious of us most of the day. Lieutenant Muir was making small talk while Sonja filled out a police department form she'd brought in.

Lieutenant Muir was a handsome man and reminded me of Sears in some respects, a fire nut who subscribed to *Fire Engineering* and frequently Xeroxed articles to pass around to firefighters who clearly didn't care as much as he did about the best way to disable the batteries on a fork lift, or how to dispatch units to an airplane crash in a train yard. He was a tall man, larger and thicker than Snively, who was large himself.

"Hey, Gum," Sonja said, standing and kissing my cheek. "I've been thinking about what you said this morning. We need to talk." Snively glanced up from the paper and raised his eyebrows, while Muir opened the station repair journal and pretended to make an entry.

The equipment on Sonja's Sam Browne belt jangled as she picked up her portable radio and the pad she'd been writing on and walked out of the room with me. I knew this story would fly round the battalion, a companion piece to the tale of Johnson's driving.

We went outside, where we stood on the grass next to her patrol car.

"You're not going to like this and you probably won't agree, but you have to turn yourself in."

"Spoken like a true law-enforcement officer."

"The Major Crimes Unit downtown would be the people to see."

"Turn myself in, or turn Tronstad in?"

She stared at me blankly, while a subtle breeze made her hair stand up in little spikes. The sky was blue to the north, overcast to the south. Her pale blue eyes searched mine. "Tronstad. You. Both. I'm serious. Listen, I'm not even supposed to be here. I left my sector just to see you. I'm worried about you. You have to make the decision."

"Do you hate me?"

"Of course I don't hate you. You know I don't." She stepped close and kissed my cheek. "I have to go now. If you want me to be there when you go in, call my cell phone. I'll talk to my sergeant and we'll go do it."

Turning in the bonds and telling the authorities the truth had been the right course of action from the start, even if it meant abandoning my mother to die alone. I was fairly certain I'd committed at least one crime and possibly dozens and that once my story saw the light of day they'd put me away like a rabid dog.

I had never been able to jump into a cold lake or swimming pool without dithering around the edges for a long time, but I'd been steeling myself to take this plunge for too long. Sonja was right. Even though it would feel as if I were stepping into the propeller blades of an airplane, I needed to step forward.

She kissed me again. "I'll be off tonight after eight. I'm staying with my folks for a couple of days, so I'll be close by. Call if you want some moral support."

She got into her cruiser and disappeared up Walker toward California Avenue, waving two fingers. I had a feeling it was the last time I would speak to her.

When I went back into the station, Robert Johnson, who had been watching us out the window, said, "That was her? She's a cop? No wonder you're turning into Dudley Do-Right."

39. HERO-SLASH-MADMAN

I stayed up late, watching a movie in the beanery the way a kid stays up late on the first night of a vacation, knowing there's nothing in particular to get up for in the morning. Nowhere to go. Nowhere but jail. For all useful purposes, my life was over.

"I suppose we're going to have a jet crash into the station tonight," Snively said at one-thirty, when he pulled himself up out of his chair to go to bed. We hadn't spoken in over an hour. Snively was a tall, saturnine firefighter who rarely smiled or conversed but, once started, could bellyache until the cows came home.

"Why do you say that?"

" 'Cause you guys are the bad-luck assholes of the department."

Several times during the day Snively had voiced misgivings about working with us, claiming the majority of the department believed there was a curse on our station and on us.

Snively began to list our bad luck. Abbott's death at Station 14. Sears's drowning at the Dexter Avenue fire. My own near-drowning. My assault with an inch-and-three-quarters hose stream and Tronstad's eye injury last week. All of which had become common knowledge in Battalion Seven. I'd noticed during the day that the interim chief, Lieutenant Muir, and Snively all treated me with the deference you might treat a celebrity, or maybe a legend. Until recently, I'd just been the new guy, the rookie, the inexperienced youth, so it was almost amusing to be perceived as the hero-slash-madman of Engine 29.

While cataloging our misfortunes, Snively added the fire deaths at Arch Place and the crispy critters in the Lincoln Town Car. "You could go your whole career without seeing somebody burned alive, but you seen four of 'em in a month."

"The first two weren't burned," I said. "At Arch Place it was smoke inhalation."

"Yeah, yeah. It all started when that pig fell out of the sky."

"That was the other shift," I said. "The pig."

"But you were there. And what worse luck is there than having a pig fall through your living-room roof? Twenty-nine's is supposed to be this sleepy little backwater where nothing ever happens, but you three guys—for you the sky caves in."

As much as his assessment irked me, I had to grudgingly give him credit for putting his finger on the pig, because that was what started it all.

"Weird shit happening up here," Snively said.

"If something happens tonight, it's your fault."

"How do you figure?"

"We already used up our bad luck."

"Bullshit."

We were the only ones awake in the station, the lieutenant and chief slumbering in their respective offices down the hall, Johnson in his bunk on the other side of the apparatus bay in the bunk room. I'd been assigned the night watch and had made up my bed and brushed my teeth but was too tired to drag myself away from a Mel Gibson movie about paranoia.

"We picked straws to see who would take this detail. No-body wants to work with you guys."

"You're not going to let it alone, are you?"

"I thought you should know. No, I mean it. You guys are bad news." He scratched his butt. "Anyway, six more hours and I'm outta here."

"We'll give you a door prize on the way out."

"You know, there's people saying the suicide almost a week ago was all part of the same bad luck."

"What suicide?"

"You know. Your lieutenant's wife."

"Muir?"

"The other lieutenant."

"Covington was only here one shift."

"Sears."

"Heather? I just saw her last week."

"She's dead, bud."

"She can't be."

"You didn't know that? Jumped off the Aurora Bridge."

"She wasn't . . ."

"They're callin' it a suicide. Depressed because of Sears's death and all. Didn't you hear about this? Everybody was talking about it at Thirty-two's this morning."

"Nobody was talking about it here."

"Yeah, well . . . I suppose you coulda missed it. It was just a little article, and her last name is—"

"I know her name."

"I forget the name she goes by."

"Wynn."

"Right. Fire boat pulled her out of the canal four days ago. They figure she jumped Friday night. Aurora Bridge. What's that? A hundred eighty feet?"

My mind couldn't help replaying the events on Beach Drive a week ago Friday. Tronstad had scheduled her arrival for half an hour after our visit.

I'd always admired Heather's independent spirit. Given her strong-willed temperament and her determination to find out what had been going on in the station before her husband died, suicide didn't seem a plausible prospect. It was more likely Tronstad had staged her death the way he'd staged the other deaths.

After Snively hit the sack, I sat alone in front of the movie. If I'd done the right thing at the beginning of this whole fiasco, none of this would have happened. It was all my fault. I was going to the authorities first thing in the morning.

At two A.M. I dragged myself to bed.

The station bells hit at 0315 hours, the tones signaling a fire rather than an aid call. I'd been sleeping so soundly, I

mistakenly thought it was the morning hitch, that the entire
night had elapsed, and that I'd been in bed five hours instead
of one. I was so exhausted I could barely pull myself out of
the bunk.

Our chief for the shift, a large woman named Cindy Polson, came out of her office in her black trousers, white
chief's shirt hanging out, pager beeping. "Where is it?"

"Beach Drive. Go down Admiral to Sixty-third and head
south. You can't miss it."

"Thanks."

By the time I came fully awake, the rig was roaring down
the hill on Admiral Way, the chief's Suburban behind us. I
was slinging the mask built into the seat back, cinching up
the shoulder straps and waist belt, getting ready to go into a
fire building with my reluctant partner, Snively.

"Goddamn fucking station," Snively repeated over and over.
"I knew this was going to happen. Goddamn fucking . . ."

The address was on Beach Drive SW. Engine 32's district,
or Engine 37's. It was the house where we'd met Tronstad the
other night, but I was too sleepy to run through all the men-
tal gymnastics required to figure out what that might mean.

As we arrived and parked behind Engine 32 and Ladder 11, we smelled smoke in the air. Chief Polson ordered
Engine 29 to take a line into the house to back up Engine 37's
crew, who were already inside looking for the seat of the fire.
In seconds Snively and I were carrying two hundred feet of
the same interconnected line, fifty pounds for each of us,
plus the fifty pounds of protective gear we were wearing. Muir
and Johnson would follow after they got their bottles on.

There was no doubt in my mind Tronstad had killed
Heather Wynn and was belatedly attempting to destroy the
scene of the crime.

"Goddamn it," Snively said, as we carried our hose bun-
dles up the dark driveway. "I knew something like this was
going to happen. I just fuckin' knew it."

"You don't want fires, you could transfer to the park department."

"Fuck you."

The driver on Engine 37 took our wye, attached it to a discharge port on his engine, and told us he'd give water when we called for it. The first line in the driveway was already hard and pulsing.

The front door to the house was wide open, the hose line running across the front step into the smoke. The outer walls of the house were blackened and wet where they'd already poured water, the burn pattern spreading horizontally along ten feet of outer wall. Fires didn't routinely spread horizontally. They went up, generally in a V pattern, so this indicated an arsonist.

But then, I already knew that.

Heavy black smoke rolled out the front door. Inside we heard glass breaking and the sound of a nozzle opening and shutting as firefighters endeavored to use only enough water to tap the fire.

"Oh, shit," Snively said. "Fuck! Fuck!"

"Water!" I yelled. Seconds later the hose line stiffened at my feet.

Snively had been in the flower bed putting his mask on, but now he was grabbing his wrist and spinning in circles as if trying to unwind himself. He grabbed his neck. For a moment I thought he'd stepped into a hornet's nest.

"Fuck, fuck, fuck."

"What is it? Come on, man. The other crews are going to run over us."

"Jesus! Fuck! Shit! Would you look at this?" He held up his left hand.

Switching on my helmet's flashlight, I spotted a fishhook through his glove, a line from the fishhook strung to the rhododendron he was standing beside. He was tethered to the bush by half a dozen sections of fish line. One hook had bit into his neck, others snagging his bunking coat.

"Just a minute," I said, pulling a small, folding knife out of the thigh pocket on my bunking trousers.

Just then, Lieutenant Muir and Robert Johnson arrived

and began masking up. "What're you doing?" Lieutenant Muir asked. "You're supposed to be inside."

"The place has been booby-trapped," I said. "Watch out for holes in the floor. That sort of thing."

"What?"

"Tronstad set traps," I said, tapping Johnson on the shoulder.

Muir and Johnson lowered themselves to their hands and knees and crawled through the front door, dragging our hose line with them.

In all, there were seven fish hooks in Snively or his gear. After I cut him loose and guided him to Medic 32, the medics took him into the back of their unit and began patching him up, though it turned out three of the fishhooks couldn't be removed until he got to the hospital. As the medics tended his wounds, he cursed a blue streak.

Chief Polson wore a concerned look when she met me at the medic unit. "What's going on?"

"Ted Tronstad is the one who did this. I bet he's around somewhere."

"Now, don't be accusing anybody without proof."

"He's here, isn't he?"

As we spoke, Engine 37 reported a tapped fire. The chief confirmed it and gave the news to the dispatcher before turning back to me. "I want you to stay calm. I know you have a grudge against him, but don't go making any wild accusations, okay? I'm on your side here, and I don't want to be up all night with union reps."

"Where is he?"

40. THE ONE-EYED MAN HAS A BLIND DATE

"Hey, Gumball," Tronstad said, grinning as if we were meeting at a train station to pick up a mutual friend. "What's goin' on?"

Tronstad was on the side of the road behind the medic unit, an aging bottle-blonde under his left arm. He wore motorcycle boots, leather pants, and a leather jacket, his long hair pulled into a ponytail. A black eye patch covered his injured eye, and he hadn't shaved in a few days. The guys on another shift had told us he'd come in to shit, shave, and shower, but he hadn't come in on our shift.

"You set fire to this house."

"Gum, you need to see a shrink. I was afraid something like this was going to happen."

Chief Polson moved beside me. "I don't know what's going on between you two, but be careful what you say here, Gum."

The blonde had her arms wrapped around Tronstad's waist and appeared to be drunk. I said, "Were you with him all night?"

" 'Cept maybe for when I hadda pee."

"Don't be interrogating my date, Chiclet. I'll ask the questions." He looked down at her. "Where's your husband, honey?" He laughed.

"Were you with him all night?" I persisted.

"I dunno. I fell asleep."

Beside me, Polson shuffled nervously. "Gum, let's get back to work."

"You set fire to this house. You put those fishhooks in the rhodie." The blonde leaned into him drowsily, and he kissed the top of her head. "You killed those two people last shift."

"Whoa. Whoa," said Chief Polson. "I thought we were talking about tonight."

"We are. But last shift we had a car fire. Two people died."

"Gum went berserk and attacked me," Tronstad said, addressing the chief. "I almost lost an eye. I didn't press charges, Chief, because I felt sorry for him. Just between you and me, I think he needs to go into Admin for a couple of weeks and get some rest."

"Did you see him set either of these fires?" Polson asked. "You have any proof?"

"No, but—"

"You tell the police?"

"No. Well, yes. One of them. I don't know if the . . . I'm not sure."

"Whoa, now. Whoa. If you go around accusing people of things you can't prove, you can be sued for slander. And you don't seem to have your story straight. Did you tell the police or didn't you?"

"Jah, you vouldn't vant to be sued, vould you?" Tronstad asked, slipping into his phony Scandinavian accent, which I'd always found hilarious until now. He thought it was funny that he'd fried the Browns. That he'd set this fire tonight. That he was getting away with it.

"You stupid bastard!" I said.

Before I could step forward and hit him, Polson wrapped her arms around me from behind. She was fifteen years older than me and I could have thrown her off easily enough, but too many people had been hurt already. Within moments, three other firefighters stepped out of nowhere and took my arms, pulling me away from the chief and holding me like I was some sort of lunatic.

"He set this fire. I think he killed Sears's wife, too. I'm almost sure he did. She came here to see him a week ago Friday night."

"Did you see her here?" one of the firefighters asked.

"I saw her truck. Sears's truck."

When I peered around at Chief Polson and the others, I could see this was more than a case of simple disbelief—they thought I'd gone insane.

"I believe he's having a nervous breakdown," Tronstad said.

"He killed Heather Wynn because she was looking for the money! And he set this fire. He was here—inside this house. Ask Johnson. He was with us."

Chief Polson said something to one of the firefighters, who then left.

"Listen to him," Tronstad said, perfectly at ease. "He's nuttier'n the cashew bin at Safeway."

Indeed, it sounded as if I were the Fruit Loop and Tronstad was the one talking common sense, but I was too tired to figure out how to turn it around.

"It was too much for him," Tronstad said. "First the chief and then our lieutenant. I told him to get help. I even told the department he needed counseling, but nobody listened to me."

"Calm down," Polson said.

"You think I'm going to come up with the bonds after this?" I said, staring at Tronstad.

"My dear boy, I don't know what you're talking about."

"Because you're not going to get those bonds. Not after breaking into my house and threatening my mother. Not after what you did to Sears and the Browns. And Abbott."

Tronstad looked at Chief Polson and raised his eyebrows, signaling that somebody better do something quickly. Polson said, "Are you all right? Are you really all right?"

"I'm trying to turn this fucker in. Don't you get it? I'm trying to turn this fucker in!"

"Don't swear at me." She turned to Lieutenant Muir, who'd just arrived with Robert Johnson. They'd taken their masks and backpacks off, had unbuttoned their bunking coats to let their wet T-shirts breathe. Both were carrying paper cups of Gatorade. "Has Gum been able to do his job today?"

"His job? Yeah. Sure. No problem. He's been good."

"He hasn't shown any signs of instability?"

We were in front of Ladder 11, the wigwags on so that the headlights alternated between high and low beam, casting an eerie syncopation over our discussion. I was sure it made me look even more insane.

Muir sized me up and said, "Instability? I don't think so. What's the problem?"

Polson looked at Johnson. "Were you ever at this house with these two?"

When he worked at it, nobody could look more innocent than Johnson. He was working at it now. "No."

Tronstad's laugh was like a rooster cackling.

"You're sure?"

"I never been here before."

"Do you know anything about Tronstad setting a car fire?"

"I know Gum thinks he did, but Gum's been having problems."

"Ask him how he even got here!" I screamed. "It's four in the morning. Tronstad doesn't live around here. How'd he know there was a fire? Because he set it."

For a moment I thought Polson was going to take me seriously. "How *did* you happen to be here?" Polson said, turning to Tronstad.

"Oh, now *you're* accusing me?" Tronstad grinned broadly, loving it, thinking he was invincible. "How did I get here? I was driving by Lincoln Park looking for Marci's house—she's staying with some people, and she sort of forgot where it was—and I heard the fire on my scanner. I knew my guys would be here, so I came down to watch."

"I don't know what to do with you two," Polson said.

"First thing is, you better keep him away from me," Tronstad said. "I almost lost the vision in one eye because of him, and I swear, he does anything else, I'm going to sue the department."

"I want him arrested," I said. "Start with arson, and we'll work our way up to murder."

Chief Polson looked at me for a long time and said, "Ted, could you make yourself scarce while we finish up with this fire?"

"You're not letting him go, are you?"

"I'm not a cop. I don't have the power to arrest anyone on your say-so."

"I'm telling you he set this. He killed Lieutenant Sears."

One of the firefighters from Ladder 11 said, "How? He dug the hole and filled it up with a garden hose?"

"He moved the traffic barricades. He waved us in there."

"You tell the police any of this?" Polson asked.

"No."

"Why not?"

"I . . . Goddamn it. He killed Heather Wynn. And Chief

Abbott." With the mention of Abbott, I could feel everyone around me sigh. There was no doubt I was demented.

"You're going to have to tell this to the police," Polson said. "There's an officer right over there."

While I glared at Tronstad, everybody else stared at me. Finally, Johnson came over and put his arm around my shoulder, extricated me from the group, and walked me away without saying anything. He and I'd both known things would come to a head sooner or later, and now that I'd publicly accused Tronstad of everything I could think of, I had a bad feeling it wouldn't make any difference with the police. Not without Johnson to corroborate.

"Hey, Doublemint?" Tronstad shouted after me. "One last thing. If you're planning to make off to Cabo San Lucas, forget it. I know you wanted to screw me, but it's too late." His grin was manic, his teeth white in his shadowy face.

"What are you talking about?"

"What do you think I'm talkin' about?"

"You found them?"

"It wasn't that hard once I put my mind to it."

At first I thought he was trying to trick me, but the look on his face was so smug, I began to have doubts. "When did you find them?"

"Just now."

Johnson whispered to me. "He's got them?"

"I doubt it."

"But is it possible?"

"Anything's possible."

"Shit!"

When Tronstad began to walk away, I yelled after him, "If you hurt anybody . . . If you hurt anybody . . . I swear . . ." He continued to guffaw as he and the blonde disappeared down the street.

"Are you going to back me up?" I said to Johnson. "When I talk to the cops?"

"I can't believe he's going to walk away with my share."

"Are you going to back me up about Sears and Abbott?"

"And go to jail myself? Not likely."

"He just robbed you."

"He'll give me my share. Tronstad and I are buddies."

"We have to tell the police."

"I am *not* going to prison. If you had any brains left, you wouldn't be, either. You're just going to get your own self in trouble. Nobody else. Just your own self."

41. I JUST CAME FROM MISSOURI

By accident or design, I was able to catch the blonde alone. I wasn't sure whether Tronstad left her alone on purpose— knowing I'd rush over to pump her for information—or if she'd gotten lost in the mix.

"Marci?"

"Uh."

"I thought that was what he called you. How long have you been with Tronstad? All night? What?"

"Who?"

"Ted Tronstad. The guy you're with."

"He's so funny. He's going to get the truck. He's going to pick me up in a minute. He's a sweetheart, ain't he?"

"Yeah. Tons of fun. You haven't been with him all night, have you?"

"We was at this party until a coupla hours ago."

"What about the last hour?"

"Just drivin'."

"Around here? Did you drive by here?"

"We're here, aren't we?"

"How about Alki Beach? Did you go by there?"

"I don't know this area. I just came from Missouri."

"Were you sleeping? Was that it?"

"Yeah. Part of the time. And we partied a little."

"Did he stop and get some bags?"

"Yeah. We scored some shit. Want some?" She began to reach into the top of her disheveled blouse.

"No. Three large garbage sacks?"

"I don't know nothin' about that. He wanted me to sleep with his friends, though. I told him I don't go in for chain bangs."

"Did he drive near the beach?"

"I just came from St. Louis two months ago. My ex is in prison here. Lotta nice people here in Warshington, though. I never knew that was how they pronounced it. War-shing-ton."

"Did Tronstad tell you where he was going tomorrow?"

"Yeah."

"Where?"

"He's taking me up to Monroe to visit my ex in the joint."

I knew that was a load of crap. Tronstad was the king of the one-night stand, and fake blondes like Marci were never around in the morning.

When I tried to organize my story to tell the police, I realized I was too exhausted to get my facts straight. I'd already tried and ended up sounding like a lunatic.

"You sure you don't want to swear out a complaint?" one of the officers asked me a few minutes later after Marci was gone. Chief Polson had sent them over. "I mean, if you think you know for sure this guy set this fire, we could talk to him."

"No thanks."

In the morning I would take my accusations and the bearer bonds into the prosecutor's office, where I would, with an attorney's help, explain the story in detail. It was going to take hours, and even then I would have trouble convincing them. Certainly all the firefighters on tonight's fire ground—where word spreads almost as quickly as smoke—thought I was a crank.

On the way back to the station, I talked Johnson into taking Bonair Drive up the hill, winding up the hillside through the deserted residential streets. I wanted a peek at Iola Pederson's house so that I could confirm that it hadn't been ransacked or looted or razed, that there weren't three dead people lying in the yard.

Lieutenant Muir didn't know our district well enough to

object, and the detail from Ladder 11 who'd joined our crew for the rest of the shift in place of Snively wasn't saying a word. Bob Oleson was a big guy, six-four, maybe 230 pounds, and was furious about being detailed to 29's without his sheets, bedding, or civilian clothes. We might have swung past 32's to fetch those items, but Lieutenant Muir, who wanted to grab another hour or two of shut-eye, nixed that. Though Chief Polson promised to drive Oleson back to Station 32 first thing in the morning, the promise did nothing to alleviate his mood.

Oleson was one of the men who'd restrained me when I went after Tronstad; I must have been holding a grudge, because when he tried to talk to me, I said, "Fuck off."

As we wound our way up the hill, I stood up in the crew cab and surveyed Hobart Avenue. The Pederson household was as quiet and dark as you'd expect a house to be at five in the morning. Bernard Pederson's truck, Iola's Land Cruiser, and Sonja's Miata all stood in the driveway like sleeping cattle. Except for the front porch light, the house was dark.

After I crawled back into my bunk in the watch office at the station, Johnson came to the door. I'd had one hour of sleep and maybe four hours the previous night. "What if he has the bonds?" Johnson whispered. "How're we going to get our share?"

"He doesn't," I said.

"How do you know?"

"Because if he had them he wouldn't have been jacking off at that fire. If he had those bonds he'd be out of here."

"Right. Yeah. You're right. Hey, Gum?"

"What?"

"Didja know Tronstad came and got his bunking clothes?"

"When was this?"

"Just before I went to bed. He took a mask and backpack off the reserve rig, too. I shouldn't have let him, should I?"

"No."

"Geez, what do you think he wants with his bunkers and a mask?"

"I have no idea."

Forty minutes later, at 0550, hours the station bell hit.

It was a single to Bonair Drive, "smoke in the vicinity."
Jesus.

42. LET'S ALL BE KILLERS NOW

Siren growling, we traverse the quiet, residential side streets
until we hit Bonair Drive, which erupts out of nowhere and
runs down an incline from Forty-seventh, wending down
along the side of the hill overlooking Puget Sound. The entrance to Bonair looks nondescript, almost like an alley
entrance, and strangers are unlikely to blunder into it by accident. It's a secret door into Narnia, where a pig fell through a
roof, where twelve million dollars are waiting for a claimant,
where a woman unlike any woman I've ever known is sleeping. Every time I drive this road I savor the view to the west:
the snow-capped peaks of the Olympic Mountains fronting
gauzy purple sunsets, the slate-colored plate of Puget Sound
stretching to the north until it marries the mist.

We were on a single, just our engine company. Most of the
rest of the battalion, our nearest engine companies and the
chief, were at a brush fire down the hill by the West Seattle
Golf Course, an alarm that came in ten minutes earlier.

"Smoke in the vicinity." Engine companies get these calls
every day. Sometimes they are fires, but more often they are
yokels arc-welding in their garages, kids setting off fire-
works, woodstoves running amok, you name it. Most of
Engine 29's "smoke in the vicinity" calls turn out to be smoldering beach fires.

Beside me, Oleson gets his gear on and twists the knob on
his compressed air bottle. I follow suit. All we have to do
now is pull our face pieces on and we are ready to rumble.

Halfway down Bonair and within a couple of blocks of
the Pederson house, we slow to a crawl. "You guys smell

anything?" Lieutenant Muir yells through the open crew-cab window.

"Nothing," says Oleson, peering out the side window next to his jump seat. Even though it is contrary to department policy, I stand in the crew cab and peer out over the top of the rig, past the light bar, a dangerous move at best because of the possibility of getting decapitated by a low-hanging branch or wire.

I pray this is something as silly as a beach fire, but deep in my gut I suspect otherwise.

We are two-thirds of the way down the hill when I spot an orange truck parked outside a duplex on the right-hand side of Bonair. "Stop!" I yell.

Johnson brakes while Lieutenant Muir turns around and speaks through the crew-cab window. "You see something? You got smoke?"

Without replying, I climb off the apparatus and leap to the ground before the engine stops moving.

Tronstad's pickup is partially hidden in a carport. Nobody else would have a license-plate holder that reads, "Dial 911. Make a firefighter come."

"Smoke? You see smoke?" Lieutenant Muir asks.

Wearing all my gear and my air bottle, I sidle between a carport wall and the truck. Inside the cab are empty beer bottles, greasy McDonald's wrappers, and soft-drink cups. Tronstad is not in the truck and I know he doesn't live here. We're about a block and a half from the Pedersons'. Before I can do anything else, I hear the sound of breaking glass farther down the hill.

Johnson and Lieutenant Muir have heard the sounds, too, because the engine begins rolling down the hill without me. I give chase, fifty pounds of air bottle and heavy turnout clothing weighing me down, my helmet almost four pounds by itself. The engine turns into Hobart Avenue, and as it completes the turn, it blocks my view. All in all, I run a block and a half before I see the Pederson house. I am breathing like a racehorse.

The front doorway is on fire. So is the large picture window to the right of the doorway. Hastily, I scan the house for signs of life, but except for the fire, it is as still as every other house in the neighborhood.

Johnson is climbing out of the apparatus to set the wheel blocks and run the pump. Lieutenant Muir is yelling something I can't understand. Oleson is stretching a hose line from the side of the engine toward the house. I assist him, still breathing heavily from my run, the two of us dragging two hundred feet of preconnected inch-and-three-quarters line to the front of the house.

We nudge the kinks out of the hose line with our boots so they won't lock up when the water flows, and Oleson shouts for water. We continue to draw closer to the house, and I see flame inside the living-room window, lots of flame. Much of the glass in the window is broken out.

It is Tronstad's work, of course—Tronstad, who's often bragged about the Molotov cocktails he made and tossed as a youth, mostly by the river in the woods near Redlands, California, but at least once into the mayor's convertible and, weeks later, the mayor's replacement convertible. He'd been an incorrigible teenager, hauled into juvenile court half a dozen times.

Oleson holds the nozzle firmly and rinses the area around the front door, then begins moving to his right, toward the window. He is wasting water, bouncing it off the siding, and I want to tell him to stop, but before I speak he aims through the living-room window and blasts away, knocking out window glass as he goes. The water stream knocks the blinds down, and Oleson swirls the water in circles, shooting into the living room, which by now is pretty much an inferno. The flames don't dampen one little bit. A hundred fifty gallons a minute, and it's as if we're not even there.

I've never seen a hose line so ineffectual. I smell raw gasoline and know immediately Tronstad has saturated the living room with his favorite Shell product. In addition, the living room has pine-wood paneling instead of the standard fire-resistant wallboard most modern houses contain, which gives it a colossal fire load even before the gasoline. I know also from my visit in August that the stairs to the bedrooms are directly behind the living room, and that Oleson is pushing the flames up the stairs and into the sleeping area on the second floor.

A large piece of the window that had been hanging on the top of the frame drops like a guillotine blade and narrowly misses cutting Oleson off at the wrists.

"The fire's in the front," I say. "We're pushing it up the stairs toward the bedrooms. Let's take the line around back and push it out here."

"Good idea."

He closes the bale on the nozzle, drops the hose line, and begins covering, as do I. I don't want to cover here, but I don't want to be out of sync with him, either. It will take thirty seconds to get our face pieces secure, get the air flowing, pull the Nomex hoods over our heads, and refasten our helmets.

I finish masking up before Oleson, pick up the nozzle, and begin tugging the end of the hose around the side of the house. With two hundred feet of line, we should have more than enough. Because of the intensity of the fire, this is the best way to keep the flames away from people inside.

Twenty feet behind me, Oleson drags hose and helps me get it around the corner of the house. From the outside, it is a simple structure, rectangular with a steep roof and one gable on the front and another gable in the back—a box, really, painted white with blue trim. I drag the hose around the house to the right, and as I peer down the side, I catch a glimpse of a figure in fire gear walking away from me into the backyard. No other units are on scene yet. From the way he moves, I know it's Tronstad.

When I get the hose line around the corner into the backyard, Tronstad is fifteen feet from the house, a greasy look of exuberance on his face. He wears full turnouts and one of our standard MSA bottle-and-backpack combos. He is ready for fire.

I am hoping to see three pajama-clad people in the backyard, but there's nobody but him and me.

He grins, then cocks his arm back and throws something at the house. I don't realize what it is until I see it in midair, whirring as it hurtles through the early-morning twilight. A Molotov cocktail disappears through a ground-floor window.

He turns back to me and grins again, as if there is something hugely amusing about firebombing a house with people inside. With Tronstad, everything is a joke.

"You stupid shit!" I say. "I know those people in there!"

"Oh, are there people inside? Gee whiz."

"Have you gone insane?"

"Come on, man. Let's get in there and get them bonds before they burn up. You better get your shit out while there's still time."

"What are you talking about?" I ask, yanking more hose into the backyard.

"The bonds, man. They're gonna burn."

The machinations of his plot become instantly clear.

"You followed us back from Beach Drive."

"You bet your ass I did."

"You never had the bonds at all."

"I will. Just as soon as you get them."

His earlier claim to have retrieved the bonds had been contrived in order to deceive me into leading him to them, which I'd foolishly done by having Johnson drive by here so I could check on the Pedersons. He and Johnson both knew about the pig—everybody on the West Coast did—but more than that, they knew where Iola lived and that I'd been bopping her. I hadn't spotted him following us, but it is easy enough to tail a fire engine by sound alone, especially when the streets are quiet and you know the two or three basic routes back up the hill.

"I knew you had 'em stashed somewhere in the district. I just couldn't figure out where until you swung by here to check on them."

"I wasn't checking on the bonds, asshole! I came by to make sure you hadn't hurt anyone."

"Hurt anyone? I'm not here to hurt anyone."

I spot three more gasoline-filled wine bottles in the grass, wet rags dripping from their necks like turkey wattles. He is going to continue pitching Molotov cocktails into the house unless I stop him.

It takes Tronstad a second to realize what I am doing, another second to reach for the gun jammed into the belt of his MSA backpack. He doesn't quite get a grip on the pistol before I slam into him at full speed, hitting him squarely in the chest with the gray composite forty-five-minute bottle on my back.

We both go down, but I roll in the grass and come up on my feet. He is on one knee, bloodied, cradling his arm as I walk over and heave the pistol into the darkness.

I kick him in the head with my steel-shanked rubber boot and manage to kick him once more before Oleson pushes me aside and stands between us.

Tronstad rolls to his hands and knees, heavy dollops of bright scarlet dribbling out of his mouth and dangling in thin chains. "Better go get your shit," he says, undeterred, looking up at me in the darkness.

"It's Ted Tronstad," Oleson says. "For God's sake, get a grip, man."

"I know who it is. He set this fire."

"What are you talking about?"

"Look at those bottles. How'd he get here? Why's he wearing his bunkers? He set it."

Oleson turns to the side in order not to expose his back to Tronstad. "You told everyone he set that other fire."

"He set both of them. I just now saw him throw a Molotov cocktail through that window."

Oleson looks past me toward the broken pebbled bathroom window. Behind the window is a room full of flickering orange.

When I turn back, Tronstad is running into the shadows near the Pederson garage. He's got one of the Molotov cocktails in his hands. Oleson gives chase. I fling the other two Molotovs, unlit, into the darkness of the yard and check my gear to make sure I don't have any bare skin showing. I key my radio and say, "Dispatch from Engine Twenty-nine. This is an occupied house. Flames showing front and back. We have three possible victims. At far as we can tell, nobody's out yet."

The dispatcher repeats my words, so I have the confidence that firefighters arriving on scene will know what to expect.

"Sir? Sir? Can you help me?"

When I look up, Iola Pederson is in the gabled window above the fire room in a baggy sweatshirt, hair disheveled. I hear burning wood crackling inside the house as the fire heats up on the first floor. She looks past me into the shadows, where Oleson and Tronstad are wrestling. It must be a bewildering sight, to spot two firefighters in full gear rolling in the darkness.

"I can't breathe."

"Keep your door closed."

"My husband said to open it."

"Close it. I'll be right up."

"The stairs are on fire. We can't get downstairs."

"I know. Stay there. I'll get a ladder. Is Sonja with you?"

"Sonja?"

"Your stepdaughter. Is she with you?"

Iola looks back into the room, as if uncertain just who is with her and who is not, then puts her head back out the window. "Do you know Sonja?"

"Stay there."

I jog around the side of the house, detach the heavy twenty-six-foot ladder from the side of Engine 29, and lug it on my right shoulder to the back of the house. It hurts my shoulder and is hard to balance. Generally, two people carry it, but tonight there is no one to help. Muir and Johnson are getting water. Oleson is wrestling with Tronstad.

The living room is burning pretty heavily now, flames from the window licking lazily up the outside wall of the house. I'm beginning to wonder if we've used the correct tactics. The fire in the living room looks amazing. It's startling what a little dab of flammable liquid will do.

Hustling around to the rear of the house, I dig the spurs into the sod and raise the ladder in one motion. I begin pulling on the halyard, raising the flies, then I let the ladder drop against the building with a metallic *clank*.

43. THE NEIGHBORHOOD CUCKOLD FIRES LIVE ROUNDS AT YOURS TRULY

I am halfway up the ladder when I feel somebody climbing behind me. Oleson. Behind him, jogging across the yard toward the base of the ladder, is Ted Tronstad. "Watch out," I say. "He's crazy."

"I figured that out." Oleson turns around in time to get pulled off the ladder by Tronstad. They fall with a clatter like a couple of knights in battle armor. I continue climbing. Oleson is heavier and taller than Tronstad, so I figure he can handle himself. Even if he can't, I have other priorities. We've already squandered too much time.

As far as I can tell, the fire hasn't moved off the first floor yet, but it will. The staircase will act as a chimney, conducting heat and flame upstairs. In no time the second floor will be hotter than the first.

We've been on scene maybe three minutes, and no other fire units have arrived.

I reach the window in the gable and peer inside using my flashlight. If the Pedersons make a habit of keeping their second-floor doors closed, the rooms will be relatively smoke free, but they don't and they aren't.

The room lights are on, the fixture on the ceiling glowing like a dull sun straining to burn through fog. Because the design of the gable and the slope of the roof don't allow room elsewhere, I've placed the tip of the ladder under the window. I climb over the sill and lever myself onto the floor, where the smoke is thinner. The room is crowded with furniture, a desk, bookcases laden with computer manuals, and several file cabinets.

The woman on the floor with her back in the corner is clad in sweatpants and a sweatshirt, knees tucked up against her chin. "Iola?" She looks up, striving to recognize me through the smoke and my face piece. "It's me. Gum."

She's been crying, a ring of soot around her nostrils, tea bags of loose skin under her eyes, hair in strings.

"No. Don't stand up. It's too hot. We'll crawl." When I start to move us toward the window, she doesn't budge, so I sit back on my heels, take off my gloves, and place my arm gently around her shoulders, urging her along. When she *does* move, she hobbles along like an old woman who's had too much to drink, and after thinking about it a few seconds, I realize she *has* had too much to drink. Over the weeks of our affair she made frequent references to polishing off a bottle of Chardonnay every evening.

What luck—to end up blind drunk the night a sociopath fire-bombs your house. But then, if you're drunk every night . . .

When she sags against me and stops moving, I urge her on, but quickly realize I've accidentally palmed one of her breasts under the sweatshirt. My intimate touch brings her back to life. "Oh? What? Who's that?" I readjust my grip and feel her stomach sag slightly as she crawls alongside me. Odd how different her body feels now than it did three weeks ago, when the feel of her torso as she moved thrilled me to the bone.

Tonight she is simply a woman in need of rescue.

She cries all the way across the floor to the window, where I say, "Time to climb out."

"I don't do heights," she replies, placing the top of her head against the wallboard. "I can't."

"I'll put you on the ladder."

She begins to stir. "Are you coming with me?"

"I have to get the others. Where are they?"

"My husband's in the other room."

"What about your stepdaughter?"

"I haven't seen her."

With some maneuvering on my part and a good deal of whimpering on hers, I assist her out the window and onto the ladder, where the rungs bite into her bare feet. Oleson comes up behind her, encapsulating her with his thick arms. Her knuckles are like white chocolate on the rungs, and as she descends, Oleson has to pry her hands loose from each one. It's like taking a terrified child out of a tree. Tronstad is below Oleson, in the grass. His face is bleeding.

I walk across the room and crack open the door. The smoke in the hallway is so hot, I drop to my hands and knees. I've already put my gloves back on.

Down the stairway I can hear the fire crackling. I know from my initial visit that a long hallway runs the length of the upstairs, with a bathroom at one end and a staircase leading down to the first floor at the other. The room I've laddered is closest to the stairs.

I head left, toward the bathroom at the opposite end of the hallway, feeling along the wall for doorways or bodies. I hear wood beams cracking on the floor below and feel the intense heat roaring up the staircase, rolling over my back, the racket coming at me like a freight train. I can feel the heat and heavy smoke through my thick turnout clothing. If it weren't for the fact that I'm breathing cool, compressed air, I might easily panic.

About where I expect to locate it, I find another doorway on my left. I crawl in. As was the case earlier, there is less smoke in the room. There are clothes on the floor: shoes, a boot. A pair of trousers, twisted and flat on the rug. A pillow. I reach up to flip the light switch on the wall, but it is already on and is having no effect in the smoke.

Using the flashlight on my helmet, I make my way to the bed, which takes up most of the width of the room. There is no window, a skylight instead. In the smoke the beam of my flashlight moves like a saber in front of me. What I want more than anything is for the beam to alight on Sonja Pederson's face.

I see something on the bed that I can't identify at first, but after focusing through the smoke, I realize it is a human arm, that there is a gun at the end of the arm, and that the muzzle is pointing at me. It is the man of the house, Bernard Pederson, gun-toting iconoclast. He is the proud American home-owner with the right to bear arms, and I am the intruder caught in the wrong place at the wrong time.

It occurs to me that I've cuckolded him repeatedly and that in some societies shooting me would be his right—in others, his obligation. How ironic that we should meet like this. It would be even more ironic if he killed me.

His eyes are bloodshot and teary from the smoke, snot trickling down to his beard from his wide nostrils. He wears trousers, one boot, and a shooting jacket. I figure he woke up to the smoke, and while his wife was dodging around looking for an escape route, he was in here girding himself for battle. Iola has told me how paranoid he's become after the kamikaze pig made its suicidal crash attack on their house.

For five seconds he stares, trying to figure out what I am doing in his bedroom at six in the morning. I try to figure out how nuts he has to be to have wasted time putting on a shooting jacket.

Working on intuition, I step to one side at the exact moment he fires. He fires twice more, the sounds deafening and the muzzle flash like sheet lightning in the smoke. He is as benumbed by our transaction as I am.

I've never been shot at before, and I am more pissed than scared, although I am plenty scared. I reach across and take the gun out of his hands. He grapples for it but gets only a handful of smoke. A man with a gun doesn't expect you to reach out and take it from him.

"Seattle Fire Department. Don't shoot." That last part coming too late, of course.

"Give that weapon back."

I toss the semiautomatic pistol onto the floor in the corner of the room and reach for him. "Come on, buddy. We're getting out of here."

"I musta left the flue closed," he says, as I pull him upright on the bed.

"Your house is on fire."

"That's absurd."

"Trust me."

"I've kept the wiring to code."

He is drunk. It is six in the morning, and he's drunker than his wife. Protesting every step of the way, he staggers to the door, at which point I force him to crawl into the hallway, where it is noticeably hotter than it had been a minute earlier, so hot that he complains. I sympathize, but this is his only chance to escape a grisly death.

"Can't do it," he says, and balks. "It's too smoky." His breath is coming in small gulps.

Still angry over the shooting, I prod him along the corridor and into the room with the laddered window. Although I made a point to close it earlier, the door is open, and a good deal of hot, black smoke from the corridor has found its way into the room and is blowing out the window past us.

Below, I spot Oleson hitting the fire through the back door with a straight stream, but it doesn't look as if it's going well. I can tell he's not coming inside.

I've heard nothing on the radio in my chest pocket for a good while, no sounds of incoming units receiving instructions or announcing their arrival, and no sounds of firefighters communicating with each other inside the structure. We are going to lose the house. The fire is already too entrenched.

I close the door behind us and the heat decreases as if I've closed an oven door. I don't want this room to flash over any sooner than it has to. It is the only route through which I can channel Sonja after I locate her. The stairs are untenable, a death trap.

I lead Bernard Pederson, still crawling—it is too hot for him to stand—to the window. When I stick my head outside, Oleson looks up from the hose line and rushes toward the base of the ladder. It is a strange fire, two of us doing the work of ten, the second occasion in six weeks where I find myself making rescues with no help.

"One more after this," I yell.

"Okay," he says, starting up the ladder. Without prompting, Bernard climbs out and touches the rungs with his feet, his eagerness to evacuate a welcome contrast to Iola's reluctance.

"My daughter," Pederson says, as he situates himself on the ladder. "Where's my daughter?"

"I'll get her. Don't worry."

"Oh, my God. Sonja. Sooonnnnja . . ." He tries to climb back inside, but I stiff-arm him. He is larger than me and charged with the superhuman strength of a man in desperation, but I have leverage, positioning, and even more desperation.

Bernard Pederson looks down as a huge sheet of bright orange flame roars out the bathroom window to his right, the flame shooting maybe eight feet into the air. We can both feel the heat.

"Holy shit," he says, and heads down the ladder past the flame.

I have seen no sign of Sonja inside the house. I can only hope she has not been sleeping with her bedroom door open, because if so, she has already taken too much carbon monoxide to survive. I'm also hoping she didn't go downstairs earlier when the stairs were tenable and find herself trapped by flames. I can hear the fire roaring down there, an express train of heat and violent death rolling through the rooms, waiting for the right moment to complete its assault up the stairs.

When I turn to leave the room, I am startled by a man, squatting under the heat in the same corner where I found Iola. The sight of him frightens me in a way I haven't been frightened all night.

"Hey, boy!"

"Tronstad. How did you get up here?"

"Same as you. You get 'em yet?"

"One more. She's down the hall. I think."

"You stupid fuck! The bonds. I'm talking about the bonds. Did you get the bonds? They're going to burn up if we don't get 'em out of the building pronto. Come on. Get going. Move along, buddy."

44. SONJA

I push the door into his face and dive into the hallway, where the heat is significantly hotter than it was a minute ago. Fires grow exponentially, not linearly, so I'm guessing it's probably forty percent hotter. I know it will only be a minute, perhaps two, before the hallway bursts into flames. It is being preheated now, and even with all my gear on it takes tremendous willpower and no small amount of perseverance for me to push down the hallway and mingle with the heat surging up the stairs. In an instant the heat penetrates my turnouts and I get small burns in half a dozen places—my wrists, my calves, the back of my neck.

Once again I turn left, moving as quickly as I can on my hands and knees. I fear the rest of these bedrooms don't have windows, that the only room available for escape is the one I've laddered. Not that there is anybody on the fire ground to throw another ladder up. Nor do we have another ladder. Engine 29 carries just the one.

It occurs to me that Tronstad will not follow me, that the sight of flames licking the high ceiling at the top of the stairs will convince him to retreat. If one thing has been written in concrete over the past weeks, it's that Tronstad doesn't do fires. At Arch Place he barely budged from the doorway, even with a hose line to protect himself; here, he has no line, and it's hotter than the front porch of Arch Place. It's hotter than the front porch of hell.

When you're a firefighter and you go into a fire building, you want two things. The first is protection from the fire, such as a hose line. The second is a means of escape you can return to, as well as a backup. What we have here is no hose line and a single exit, our pathway to the latter already compromised by flame.

To my surprise, Tronstad trails me. Tonight he is not risking his life for the lives of strangers or the respect of his fellow firefighters, or for cheap laurels the fire department might hand out in a ceremony virtually nobody will attend. Tonight he's scrambling to rescue twelve million dollars, money that has already resulted in the deaths of five human beings and converted him into a liar, burglar, arsonist, conspirator, murderer, and defecator.

"Gum?" He is trailing me, but I know by the amount of smoke, the lack of visibility, and the growing heat that he's in unknown territory, that he's counting on me to know what to do.

I push on the first door I come to and identify it as the room in which I found Bernard. My helmet light slices the smoke in front of me, but the swath of yellow extends a mere two feet. Beyond that, I see nothing but a solid wall of gray.

The heat in the hallway, spectacular to begin with, grows hotter by the second. Even on my hands and knees, I feel it creeping up the cuffs of my turnout trousers when I move, biting my wrists, creeping down my upturned collar to kiss my neck and scald my skin like a succubus.

If it's this dicey for me in my turnouts, it will be unbearable for Sonja.

I know I have only seconds to find her.

"Gum? Gum? Wait for me."

I am in the bathroom now, searching, reaching into the tub, turning around, bumping into Tronstad, who, inexplicably, now jams the doorway with his bulk. "Get out of the way."

"I ain't movin' until you tell me where them bonds are."

I smack the side of his head with a left hook, giving it all the strength I can muster. The blow is unexpected and knocks him flat. I crawl over him.

"You fuckin' bastard," I hear him say as my weight squeezes the breath out of him. "Gum? Quit fuckin' around. We gotta get those bonds out. This place is about to blow."

There is a bedroom door across the hallway from Bernard's room.

"Fire department," I say, as I reach up and open the door.

As soon as I enter the bedroom, it begins to fill with smoke the way a pit on the beach fills when the tide crawls in. From behind, Tronstad scampers across my legs and into the room, sprinting for the bonds, or so he believes.

I close the door, hoping to keep some of the heat out, but already the room is blacked out. I can barely see Sonja. She's on the floor, staying low, where the air is clearest. She wears only panties and a bra. I cannot tell whether she is alive or dead.

Although the sounds have been registering subconsciously for some time, it is only now that I realize the noises I've been listening to downstairs are the popping noises of ammunition heating up in the fire and exploding, one cartridge at a time. It is louder in the bedroom than in the hallway. Dozens of bullets are blowing apart in the fire downstairs. A round strikes the floor below us with a *thunk*. I can't tell whether the round has punctured the floor or stuck in the floorboards.

"Sonja. It's me. Gum." As I speak, my alarm bell goes off, signaling I am almost out of air. I sit up and disconnect the high-pressure hose line that attaches to my nose piece, silencing the alarm but leaving my face piece in place. I may need that last little bit of clean air. It won't last long. The room grows quiet as the smoke slides down my windpipe and sears my lungs like battery acid. I'm relieved to hear Sonja cough. It means she's alive. "It's Gum, Sonja."

"Gum?"

"Hey, Doublemint? You know this chick?"

"I woke up hearing shots across the hall."

"Your father took a couple of potshots at me." The thought flashes through my mind that Iola had neglected to wake her stepdaughter.

"We gotta get you out. Is there a window?"

"A skylight. It's way too high."

"Follow me. Keep low and you'll stay under most of the heat."

She coughs again. "I tried before, but it was too hot and smoky."

"The faster we move, the easier it'll be."

"Okay, let's go."

"Hey, wait a minute, Gum!" Tronstad says.

"Get out of the way."

"I'm not letting you out until—"

"They're outside in the garage."

"Bullshit!"

The smoke is hot and acrid enough to sting my eyes inside my mask. I guide Sonja past Tronstad.

Before we reach the doorway, she stops precipitously and flops onto her stomach. Tronstad is holding her bare ankle.

I turn off my helmet light and stand up, feeling a tremendous blast of heat that is almost incapacitating. Walking past Sonja, I kick Tronstad in the head. In the smoke, he doesn't see it coming, and the blow knocks him backward, dislodging his face piece momentarily. Air hisses out. I think I might have broken his neck.

Crawling forward, I steer Sonja out of the room and into the excruciating heat. In the minute or so I've been inside her bedroom, the corridor has become superheated to a degree I'm not sure I've ever felt before. I don't know how she is braving this in only bra and panties, but she is. I'm not sure she can make it to the ladder room. In fact, I'm almost certain she cannot.

Below us, ammunition is popping off at a furious pace, the house sounding like a gigantic popcorn popper run amok. More and more free-flying bullets lodge in the floor beneath us, making sounds like builders pounding on it from below.

In the hallway, Sonja grinds to a halt. "Keep moving," I tell her.

She squeezes the words out between shallow gasps. "I can't breathe."

The room we're trying to get to isn't more than twenty feet away, but it must seem like miles, for she balks and stalls, coughing like an asthmatic. She will be burned if we continue. She will be burned if we stay. She is being burned now.

I feel the pain from the smoke in my lungs, the same pain she feels.

The flame that had been crawling along the ceiling at the end of the corridor has run down the hallway and almost reached the door of the room we've just left, dark orange fingers showing through here and there in the black smoke.

There's no way a woman in a bra and panties can make it along the corridor now. Hell, there's no way *I* can make it in my gear. Not without two hundred gallons of water a minute at my fingertips, and maybe not even then.

She begins to crawl forward, but I stop her. "I can make it," she says.

"No."

Without a plan, I take her across the hall to Bernard and Iola's bedroom, sealing the door behind us. There is less smoke in here, although it is by no means clear. Much of the heat has been excluded from this room because the door has been closed. The problem is there's no window.

Downstairs they're applying water though the windows and doors from outside. With all that ammunition exploding, they will have declared a defensive fire. An exterior operation means the building is going to be a grounder. The fire simply has too deep a grip; there are too many nooks and crannies that cannot be reached with hose lines in the yard.

"If we're going to die, I'm glad I'm with you," Sonja says, moving toward me. I brush her aside, not wanting to hug her in my gear, which has been heated up now and will scorch her with contact burns.

"We're not going to die."

I rip off my face piece and give it to her to hold against her face, then hook up the high-pressure line so she can breathe whatever clean air is left in my bottle. Tethered to Sonja by the mask and line, I find the wall between this bedroom and the room next door and pull a dresser away from it. I keep her close and lie on my back on the floor, finding studs and kicking at the space between them, kicking hard enough to injure my heel. I continue kicking.

Fortunately it is wallboard and not the wood paneling

they've installed downstairs, which I wouldn't be able to break. I kick out a hole twenty-four inches wide, the standard wall-stud distance when this house was constructed. When I get through it, I begin to work on the wallboard in the room next door. I kick frantically, knowing it is only a matter of a minute or so before the room next door is compromised by flame, knowing also that the ladder might not be there, and that the firefighters below may have already given us up for dead.

I sit up and begin breaking out wallboard with my hands.

"Where's the other fireman?" Sonja says through the mask.

"He'll be here."

After enlarging the hole to a dimension she can squeeze through, I discover a desk up against the wall in the other room. I lie back and shove with my legs. Slowly, it begins to lurch forward. I grip the two-by-fours and push with added leverage. Sonja keeps close, the high-pressure air line and face mask feeding her confidence along with the compressed air. The desk moves slowly.

I've done all the work I can do and have taken all the smoke a man can take. I'm running on willpower and the desire to see a good woman go out and live the rest of her life. I don't care any longer if I make it. The engine driving me is running on the principle that it will be a damn shame if Sonja dies because I'm not enough of a firefighter to get her out of this.

Every microgram of adrenaline in my bloodstream has been used up. I feel nothing but weariness and an almost irresistible urge to close my eyes and surrender. Inside my sopping bunkers, the sweat competes with a dank, slippery kind of fear. I am as thirsty as I've ever been in my life, as if my mouth is full of desert sand.

"Sonja?" When I hear my voice, thick, hoarse, and threadbare, I realize how little time I have left in which to function. "Sonja?"

My bottle has run out of air now. She coughs, and mutters,

"Gum." She is curled up on the floor. Neither of us can see each other in the smoke, although she might be able to see the light on my helmet.

"Go through here. Through the wall. There's a ladder at the window."

She comes alongside and I guide her to the opening she can't see, usher her through, feeding her thin limbs through the ragged hole, her smooth, pale skin a stark contrast to the heavy firefighting gear I wear. In order to get through the wall she has to drop the mask, which is now useless but which she's been holding like a teddy bear. She wriggles through the hole, her bare feet disappearing into the other room, and I think how incongruous her pale feet and legs look in the smoke.

"Gum?" She is disoriented in the smoke, having ended up behind the desk.

I am about to follow her when I hear a noise behind me.

Tronstad.

He's got less than a minute—maybe two if he closes the door he's left open—to accompany us through the hole in the wall. It occurs to me that I can leave without him and let him die, and that it will be the end of my troubles.

As I consider this, something strikes me in the face, a board, a baseball bat, the butt of a rifle—I cannot tell. I see stars and fall backward into the wall, then slump to the floor.

Tronstad hits me again, across the helmet this time, and the force of the blow knocks me to the side. It is a glancing blow and does not sting as much as the first. My teeth on that side of my head are loosened, and a large section of my cheek is numb and beginning to swell. I can hear Sonja through the hole in the wall, calling my name. "Gum? It's over this way. Are you coming?"

It breaks my heart that I cannot go to her.

45. DISCONNECTING

Tronstad stands over me and rains blows across my helmet and shoulders, across the composite air bottle. I curl up like a sow bug, and he beats on the bottle for fifteen or twenty seconds, striking my shoulders and hips with every third or fourth blow. I know if it goes on much longer I will be useless to get Sonja out of the house. All he's thinking about is money. All I'm thinking about is Sonja. Over the past weeks I have messed up everything, but I am determined to get her out of this house.

I can tell by the sound it makes on my empty air bottle, by the sting of the blows striking my body through the multiple layers of protective gear, the vapor barriers, the liners, the Nomex outer shell, that he is probably using a baseball bat. The blows are slowly crippling me.

I reach out to grab one of his legs, but he is either moving too quickly or I am misjudging his position, because I grasp only smoke and then a corner of Iola's bed. My left ear is ringing and my face is swollen. He catches me on the hip, and I believe he may have damaged a nerve bundle, because I find my left leg next to useless.

Each time he hears the bat ringing on the composite cylinder, he moves the blows up or down, aiming for my legs or my head and hitting each with remarkable ease. He strikes my helmet two or three times more, and it makes my head ring and wrenches my neck. At least the helmet protects me from a disabling concussion.

I spin in tight circles, sweeping the carpet with my legs, hoping to touch him, to get some clue as to precisely where he is. The bat smacks my left thigh and I scream in pain. I am a tortoise hit by a truck on the highway, waiting for another vehicle to finish me off.

Finally I touch something, and without thinking, I lunge.

I make contact, and we are immediately rolling on the floor.

"You gonna tell me where the bonds are hidden? Because if you're not, you're—" He is on top of me, slapping my face with his gloved fists.

Letting him beat me, I strip off the glove on my right hand and reach up to find the small plastic lever on the nose of his MSA face piece, working the mechanism with the agility of someone who's practiced it hundreds of times.

Before he realizes what I'm doing, I pull his air hose off.

He is long overdue for this kind of unpleasantness.

Gulping his first lungful of smoke, he fights to locate the end of the air hose, swimming his arms in circles, slapping my face, my hands, my helmet. The smoke has spun him into a panic.

He coughs and inhales with an ugly sputtering sound, then gets even more frantic, riding me like a drunk on a bronc.

When he rolls off me, I hold on to the hose attached to his bottle, and as he struggles he begins to drag me like a man dragging a big dog on a leash. He coughs, and I can hear his inhalations grow shallower as his lungs spasm against the bitter smoke. Breathing is the most basic of human impulses, so it is a cruel twist of fate when those same inhalations draw death into our lungs.

"Fuckin' rookie. Fuckin' cunt. Give me that hose." He stands up, but I don't let go of the high-pressure hose that can give his life back.

When I look up at the ceiling, all is blackness and superheated smoke, but then for a split second, a flash of orange lights up the mixture. Like a clueless civilian, Tronstad's left the door wide open behind him, so superheated gases from downstairs have followed him into the room and are rolling across the ceiling above us.

With a low *whoomph* that hits me like a blow to the gut, the ceiling area near the door bursts into a bowl of orange. We're seconds from being incinerated.

"Goddamn it, Gum!" he wails.

It occurs to me that I've never seen Tronstad eat smoke.

Not at fires and not in the smoke room the night Chief Abbott ran us through our paces. Most people panic in smoke in the same way they panic underwater. Heavy smoke makes you feel as if you are drowning and smothering at the same time, makes you feel as if Lucifer and all his dark angels have just farted down your windpipe.

I hear Tronstad crashing into the wall, screaming in rage inside his face piece.

Stooping low, I let go of his high-pressure hose and squirm through the hole in the wall. For a few seconds I am stuck, and then on the other side, the temperature drops precipitously.

"Sonja?" It is dark in here. The light on my helmet is missing. "Sonja?"

She is directly under the window, in a stupor from the heat.

It doesn't take long to get her on the ladder. Oleson, who's been waiting at the bottom of the ladder, rushes to help, climbing, looking at me past Sonja's ass. "Anybody else in there?"

Pretending not to hear him, I turn away from the window to deal with Tronstad. This room is shielded from the fire in the hallway because the hollow-core door is closed. It's a simple thing, a closed door, but it can protect from 1200-degree temperatures. The protection won't last forever, but so far it's preferable to the room next to us. As most hollow-core bedroom doors, this one is rated at twenty minutes, though I doubt it will last that long.

Walking across the room, I drop to one knee and peer through the hole in the wall into the dense smoke in the next room. My hip hurts and my shoulders are bruised, and the smoke and exertion have wilted me like a flower. My legs feel as if I've climbed Everest.

Tronstad is thrashing around like a bull in a pen, making anguished and increasingly frightening sounds. Abject panic is what I'm hearing, as he bangs into walls and tramples furniture. He's not even crawling the perimeter of the room, seeking escape. He seems to be banging around aimlessly.

Because he's cheated on all his tests, has gone on disability to evade the more serious exercises, and is a master at finding reasons not to go inside a house that's on fire, Tronstad's eight years in the department have provided him with only the bare minimum in training.

As I wait, Tronstad steps close to the hole, close enough that I can reach out and touch his boot with my hand. I can save his life with a touch. He's two feet from salvation. Or I can let him move on, and become his executioner.

I sit on my haunches and let him walk past.

Watching his boots disappear in the smoke, I feel no emotion, only the wetness on my face and the knowledge that I'm weaving a major crime into the textile of my soul, mutilating my future as profoundly as if cutting off a limb. In a month surfeited with appalling moral choices, I've made the most appalling of the lot. Here, I do not even have the excuse of calling myself a hapless onlooker. Here, pure and simple, I am engineering a murder.

I tell myself Theodore Tronstad has been running loose long enough. That he's killed, burgled, set fires, assaulted my mother, blackmailed me, and crapped on my carpet. That he deserves this.

Below us, bullets pop off. Outside the window behind me, I hear men shouting. Fresh air gusts into the room and punches a hole in the smoke.

And then, in a moment of clarity, I realize I cannot do this. This is not in my nature. I cannot kill a man and walk away from it. I'll take him outside, and they'll arrest him for arson and maybe they'll arrest me, too, but that's the way it'll have to be.

"Tronstad. Tronstad. Over here."

"What?" he gasps. "Where are you?"

"Over on the other side of the wall. Come here. I'm in the room with the ladder."

And then he's in front of me, kneeling in the smoke. "You fucker. Where are the bonds?"

"I told you. The garage. They're outside."

"You're lying."

"I'm not lying."

"I looked in the damn garage. They're not there."

"You must have missed them."

"You liar. I know they're in here."

"Tronstad. The fire's on top of you. Get out."

"I'm going for the bonds. I know what I'm doing," he gasps, moving away from the opening.

"Come back."

"Fuck you."

I hear him exit the room, whimpering as he pushes past his limits, and for a split second, I contemplate squirming through the hole in the wall and chasing after him, but I know it would be suicide.

Feeling woozy, I walk to the open window and climb onto the fire department ladder, where I am able to draw in the first clean air I've had in ten minutes. I fill my lungs and begin to feel light-headed. My legs are heavy, and my arms barely have the strength to grip the ladder. I do not want to fall two stories, but I'm in danger of doing just that.

The house is roaring, flames leaping out every window except the one directly above, and then, as I descend, flame bursts out that window, too.

46. TWENTY-FOUR SECONDS

I scan the twilight until I spot Sonja in the corner of the yard being attended to by a medic, a sheet from the medic unit draped around her shoulders. "Gum?" she shouts across the yard. "Are you all right?"

I nod, although I'm far from all right.

At the bottom of the ladder, I stand motionless, my thoughts dull and unfocused, the heat from the windows warming me.

It seems like weeks since I had that ladder on my shoulder,

and I wonder vaguely where I got the strength to carry it. I can barely keep myself upright. In fact, my legs are trembling, as is my upper lip, my cheek, and a muscle running along my spine.

A firefighter in a yellow helmet stands in front of me with a hose line. The insignia on the helmet tells me he's from Ladder 7. "Fuckin' A. You made another rescue? Damn, did you make another rescue? Fuckin' A. I bet that's some sort of record. How many people have you brought out in the past couple months? We're going to have to retire your number."

As he speaks, a bullet breaks out a piece of the plate-glass window in the frame beside us. We move away from the house, and I stumble and fall on my face in the cool grass. I'm not asleep, but I'm not awake, either. I'm not unconscious, but neither do I have the willpower to get to my hands and knees.

After a while, somebody helps me out of the backpack. I feel like puking, but as long as I don't move, I'm okay. People carry me around the house to the medic unit on the street the way they might tote a dead dog, my head sagging.

On my back, I lie on the gurney listening to sounds of the fire ground outside the medic unit. They're putting a line into my arm. The veins are good, and they insert the needle without any problem. As they work, I zone out, able to talk but preferring not to. I hear Sonja's voice nearby. Then Iola's. Sonja is asking about me.

Unless a miracle happens, Tronstad is dead.

There are certain truths that will govern the next few days. I will tell lies designed to get the authorities off my back and dissuade Robert Johnson from resuming his hunt for the bonds. I know from experience that one lie begets another, that dishonesty will breed like fruit flies until a fierce swarm of fictions surges out of my mouth.

I might tell them about Tronstad now, but that would create a circus with a hundred or more people standing around waiting for the body recovery. With that many witnesses, I would be unable to retrieve the bonds until later. With that many people roaming the property, the bonds might get discovered by accident. I decide to keep mum. Right or wrong, I'm not killing him. He's already dead. It will make no difference whether they find his body now, in five hours, or in five days.

"You don't see one like this very often," says the medic who's working on me.

"Gum! Hey, Gum!"

"What?"

A firefighter in full gear climbs into the medic unit and sits beside me, Lieutenant Muir. "Where's your stuff? They want to know if you left your PASS device inside. The guys on the back of the building think they hear a PASS device."

"In the house?" I ask.

"In the house. There's a bunch of bullets firing off, too, but there's this sound like a PASS device. They think it's on the second floor."

"Is Oleson out?"

"Oleson's over in the rehab area."

"He was my partner."

A PASS device, about the size of a pack of cigarettes, is built into our MSA backpacks and gives off a high-decibel signal when the wearer stops moving for more than twenty-four seconds, the idea being to alert fellow firefighters that there's a man down.

Lieutenant Muir and one of the medics leave. A minute later the door opens and the medic climbs back inside.

"They going in?" I ask.

He is breathing heavily. "Are you kidding? The owner said he had five thousand rounds of ammunition in there. Plus, it's burning like a kiln."

"Crazy."

"It sure is."

47. THE KING OF NOT GETS KISSED AND SLAPPED

By seven A.M. the fire has mostly burned itself out, so they send Engine 29 back to the station to clean up and exchange crews. Even though the medics want to truck me up to Harborview for further evaluation, I refuse and return to the station with Lieutenant Muir, Robert Johnson, and Oleson. I am dizzy and a tad spaced out but have no intention of lying in a hospital bed with doctors and nurses hovering over me while I brood about my dead friend.

So far, nobody except me knows there's a body in the house. Oleson thinks Tronstad fled the scene and has said as much.

At the station I find the oncoming crew has put my bedding away, so I take a long, hot shower, hunkering under the spray until I've revived myself to the point where I can plan the rest of my morning. I am disoriented from the smoke and lack of sleep and from simple exhaustion.

I do not speak about the fire to anyone, not my crew, not the oncoming crew, and not the new chief, Mortimer, who tries to question me about the rescues. "It all happened pretty fast," I tell him from the shower stall, when he comes into the bathroom to question me. Embarrassed by my anemic responses and the flashes of nudity he has exposed himself to, he withdraws.

I stand under the hot shower for a long time and eventually sense the rumble in the floor when Engine 29 fires up and retires from the building. The fire is tapped, but Marshal 5 is investigating, and they will need fire crews to stand by with hose lines and strong backs as a precaution against a rekindle, and to help with the removal of debris, which comes up layer by layer as the investigators ply their trade. After Tronstad's body is discovered, they'll even more thorough. Engine 29 will be out all morning.

Under the hot spray, I hawk up gobs of gray phlegm, slimy souvenirs from my minutes in the smoke. My eyes are bloodshot, and when I screw a washcloth into my ear with one finger behind it, the cloth comes back sooty. Even after three shampoos, my hair reeks of smoke.

Johnson emerges from the restroom while I'm dressing and stands near my locker in flip-flops, a large white towel wrapped around his waist, with a puckered scar zigzagging the top of his chest. If he notices the bruises Tronstad has left on my shoulders and back, he doesn't mention them.

"Tronstad set that, didn't he?" Johnson said. "Just like he set Beach Drive. And the car the other night. And the Browns. Oleson said you saw him with a firebomb."

"Yeah."

"You don't want to talk about this?"

"I took a lot of smoke. I'm pretty sick."

"You should have gone to the hospital, man."

"I don't like hospitals."

"Your mother. I forgot about your mother. You know, they found an empty five-gallon gas can in the yard. They were guessing he broke that front window and poured a couple of gallons of gasoline into the living room before anybody could do anything about it. You think?"

"Maybe."

"No wonder it was burning so hot. I mean, you guys put that line into the living-room window, and it didn't seem to have any effect at all. It musta been hot upstairs. You see a lot of fire up there?"

"Mostly smoke."

"And all that ammunition. It sounded like the Fourth of July. You know, a bullet clipped our light bar. I thought I was going to get plugged. I'm surprised you didn't catch a bullet yourself, inside. The homeowner said he almost shot you by accident."

"Yeah."

"You sound tired."

"I am."

"So where did Tronstad go? You see him leave? Oleson

said they were fighting in the backyard. I wonder why Tronstad lit that particular house. That part has me stumped."

"It belongs to Iola Pederson."

"The house?"

"Yeah." My short replies, general reluctance, and lack of eye contact are beginning to dim Johnson's enthusiasm.

"Is that the woman you were banging? With the tits?"

"They all have tits, Robert."

He laughed. "You know what I mean. You think he was trying to get even with you? Break up your relationship?"

"I think we were supposed to get there sooner. I was supposed to run in and grab the bearer bonds. Tronstad would then take them from me."

"Are you saying the bonds were in that house?"

"That's what I'm saying."

"So who's got them now?"

"Jesus, Robert. You saw that fire. I was busy dragging people out."

"Tronstad got them?"

"Nobody got them."

"You burned up our bonds?"

"Tronstad did."

"Did you even tell him where they were?"

"I told him."

"And he didn't go in and get them out?"

"I lost track of him."

"Maybe he got them out."

"About the only thing I can tell you for sure is, that didn't happen."

"He sets the fire thinking the bonds are inside and we'll get there in time for you to go in and grab them? The timing . . . I bet when we stopped halfway down the hill, it threw everything off."

"The gasoline probably didn't help."

"No. But why the hell did you put the bonds in that woman's house? That was just plain stupid."

"That first day, he was following me. I had to ditch them.

It was the only place I could think of that wasn't my house. It only became a problem after Iola broke up with me."

"I don't want to hear this," Johnson said, grabbing his head. "This is too much. Sweet Jesus, Gum, tell me you got them out. Tell me you gave them to Tronstad and he's going to meet us in ten minutes. Tell me something that won't tear my gut in half." His voice is cracking. He is near tears.

"I can't say any of those things."

Johnson wanders across the bunk room in a daze. I've never seen him so low. As I finish dressing, he drifts into the shower room and begins flossing his teeth with the energy of an old man petting a dog. When I come in, our eyes meet in the mirror.

"Maybe this is better," he says. "I'll take that Caddy back to the dealer, and Paula won't be yelling at me anymore. Tronstad can come back, and the three of us will work together like old times."

"It'll never be like old times, Robert."

Each of my offenses has been birthed in passivity; each arrived through *not* doing something I should have done. Like everyone else, I have been of the belief that to be a criminal you need to be aggressive, violent, audacious, to pick up a gun and rob somebody, at the very least write a bad check. That you have to do something brassy. But becoming a criminal, I've found, is as uncomplicated as letting timidity overwhelm common sense. It's also *not* doing something you should do.

I am the king of *not.* Inaction is my throne.

Not getting on the rig when we were called to the Arch Place fire.

Not confessing to my officer that I'd missed the call.

Not betraying Tronstad over the bearer bonds.

Not telling the truth the night Chief Abbott died. Or the night Sears drowned.

I am the maestro of inaction, the king of *not,* my mouth zippered by reticence.

Outside, I throw my personal gear into the backseat of my

car, then fire up the engine and let it idle. After a few seconds, I realize Robert Johnson is standing beside my driver's window. "You know, it's probably just as well those bonds are gone," he says.

"Absolutely."

"If you want the truth, I was getting pretty unhappy."

"Not to mention all the dead people."

"Yeah." Johnson stares down the street as a couple of schoolchildren carrying colorful knapsacks yell and laugh. "At least we won't have to tell any more lies. That was the worst. Having to lie to my own wife. No more lying. Thank God."

"Yeah. At least the lying is over."

Instead of heading home, I hook a left on California and wend my way through the neighborhood to Bonair Drive, then coast down the hill to Hobart Avenue SW and the scene of our latest fire. Sunlight glints off the water in the Sound, dark clouds to the north, a high overcast beginning to squat on the city. The first inklings of winter are trickling into the region. I slow before reaching the carport where Tronstad's truck sits untouched.

Engine 29 and Ladder 11 are the only crews still on scene at what's left of the Pederson home. It is easy enough to see by the lassitude and the laughter among the firefighters that they haven't discovered Tronstad's corpse yet.

While the structural components of the first floor are largely intact, most of the second floor has collapsed onto itself. Tronstad's body will be under the collapsed section.

The gritty, acrid smell of smoke lingers everywhere, tendrils from the roof doing a slow dance in the sunlight. All three cars are in the driveway, where they'd been earlier.

I stand at the corner of the house and watch as the fire crews go about their work. There isn't much to do, and they seem in no rush to do it. The job now is to make sure the fire doesn't flare up again and to assist the Marshal 5 investigators as they dig through the rubble.

When a pair of firefighters from Ladder 11 carry the remains of a sofa out the front door and off the porch, I pull on a pair of goatskin work gloves I've brought along for this purpose and lend them a hand. Even though I am in civies, everybody in the department knows who I am by now. After we dump the sofa onto the debris pile in the yard, one of them says, "Gum. I heard you made another rescue. Jesus Christ, you have got to be the luckiest son of a bitch in department history."

I shrug. As I know better than anyone, luck is a matter of perspective.

"I think it's so cool," says Stanislow, who is working a debit shift on Ladder 11.

I know my answering smile is a sour miracle, a synthetic conglomeration of hypocrisy, deceit, and, as much as I detest myself for it, undeserved pride.

When somebody inside throws a handful of charred boards onto the front porch, I rush over and carry them to the debris pile. It is important to get people accustomed to seeing me carrying garbage away from the house.

"Gum. Hey, Gum." It is a fire investigator, a man named LaSalle, a heavyset man with dark, bushy eyebrows, whose claim to fame is that his father was once mayor of Seattle. Spotting LaSalle pumps ungodly amounts of adrenaline into my system. "I talked to Oleson. I thought you were going up to Harborview, or I would have spoken to you, too."

"I passed on the hospital."

"You think that's smart? You look like shit. At least get it documented on a Form 44."

"I'm okay."

LaSalle takes my arm and walks me out of earshot of the others. "We know this started with at least one Molotov cocktail. We got one of the bottles. Oleson said you saw Ted Tronstad throwing a bottle into the house. He said you guys had a tussle with him in the backyard."

"That's right."

"You saw Tronstad throw a Molotov cocktail into the house?"

"I did."

"You understand you might have to testify to that?"

"I'm ready."

"I heard you and him had some sort of scrap at a car fire. What was that about?"

"I thought he was disrespecting the dead."

"You sure that was all there was to it?"

"Ask him. He'll tell you."

"You have any idea why Tronstad would throw a Molotov cocktail? I mean, is this his ex-girlfriend's house or something?"

"It's my girlfriend's house. And my ex's."

"She's your girlfriend or she's your ex?"

"They're both here," I say, even as Iola Pederson strides across the yard from the garage. Her presence depresses me. It is going to be almost impossible to steal back those three garbage bags.

Iola wears a bulky ski coat, which I assume she's gotten from the garage.

She steps close to me and slaps me across the face like a slugger straining for a home run, hitting me so hard, it hurts her hand. Bernard Pederson has emerged from the garage, also in a ski jacket, in time to see her do it.

"What the hell are you doing here, you little bastard?" Iola says. "Do other people's misfortunes tickle your funny bone?" On the far side of the yard, Iola's stepdaughter exits the garage behind her father, sees what is happening, and starts toward us, only to be held back by Bernard, who grasps her ski coat from behind.

"You the girlfriend?" LaSalle asks, displaying his characteristic lack of tact.

"You say that again, I'll sue," Iola says.

"Funny way to treat the man who saved your life," LaSalle says.

"What are you talking about? You saved me?"

"This man here is the guy who brought you out of the house."

She turns to me. "You put me on that ladder?"

I nod.

"Crap!" Her eyes widen and I realize the startling blue I'd always admired is missing. "You really saved me?"

"Me and a man named Bob Oleson."

"Gum saved your husband's life, too. And that other gal over there."

"Sonja?"

"Right. If I were you, I'd think about an apology."

"The both of you can go fuck yourselves." Angrier than ever, she storms away. People who lose everything have a right to be angry. I remember how pissed I was after my place was burgled.

"That's not much of an apology," says LaSalle, displaying a silly grin.

"She's got reasons."

"So let's get back to business. Oleson told me Tronstad was here in full bunkers. Said he even had an MSA backpack and bottle."

"Robert Johnson told me he got it off the reserve rig last night."

"When was the last time you saw Tronstad?"

"He was in the backyard wrestling with Oleson." The lies flow out of my mouth like oil.

"Oleson says he went up the ladder sometime when you were inside. You didn't see him in the house?"

"No."

"Oleson says there was a gun."

"It should be back there in the grass somewhere."

"We'll look for it. You don't have any idea why Tronstad would torch this place?"

"No."

"That's all I've got for you now. Talk to me before you leave."

"Sure."

After a few minutes, Bernard crosses the yard behind Iola, taking special care to avoid the man his wife has just slapped. In the morning light it is easy to see why I'd thought he was her father.

Sonja approaches and takes my arm, kissing the same

cheek her stepmother just pasted. "They're a little upset," she says.

"Are you all right? Why aren't you at the hospital?"

"Why aren't *you*?"

"I'm fine."

"Good. I'm fine, too. I convinced them to let me leave."

But she isn't fine. Her voice sounds painfully hoarse; she has Silvadine cream on both ears, her nose and cheeks, and the back of her neck; her hair has been singed; and there are first degree burns on every visible part of her body, making her look badly sunburned. One hand is wrapped in gauze.

"You should have stayed at the hospital," I say.

"It's okay. I'm fine. Really."

"Hell of a way to wake up, huh?"

"Whew! My heart's still racing. From now on I'm sleeping in a full-body canvas suit with a hood and big rubber boots, just in case. Maybe I'll get me a pickax to keep by my bed, too." She grins and coughs, then gets serious. "I can't believe you do that all the time. I'm so grateful you were there."

"I don't do it all the time, and I'm glad I was there, too."

"It was your friend, wasn't it?"

"Yes." As we speak, Bernard signals Sonja from across the yard.

"We're going to get breakfast and some real clothes," she says, looking down at her out-of-season ski parka with a shrug.

"Sonja. Are you sure you're all right?"

"Yeah. Thanks."

"Drink lots of fluids. Keep it up for a couple of days."

"I will." She flashes her dimple. "You take care, too, Gum."

The three of them drive away in Bernard's truck. After the chief leaves, there are only the two fire investigators, the two crews, and me. I continue to carry crap from the front porch to the debris pile. The garage door remains open. From the yard I can see the Volvo, where I stashed the garbage bags. In front of the Volvo are six or eight lawn mowers, their handles tilting this way and that like drunken soldiers.

I find myself getting jumpier and jumpier as I contemplate what I need to do. Finally there comes a point at which both fire investigators and most of the firefighters are inside the house. Taking advantage of their absence and ignoring the two civilians watching from the street, I stalk over to the garage, step around the lawn mowers, and pop the back door of the Volvo. No wonder Tronstad didn't spot them. They are nearly invisible in the unlighted garage, the three black plastic garbage bags where I left them on the floor behind the front seats. Hoisting them out by the knots in the necks, I carry all three bags across the yard at an unhurried pace, walking to the street and down the block to my WRX.

Without turning back to see whether anybody is watching, I drop them onto the ground behind the car, unlock the rear hatch, hurl them in, and close it. As I lock the car, a large, black SUV with government plates rolls up the street, stops beside me, and reverses toward Hobart Avenue and the house fire. The passenger, a stern-looking man of about fifty, eyeballs me as if trying to match my face to a Wanted poster. I am pretty sure he's FBI.

48. I MISTAKENLY TELL THEM TO SEARCH MY CAR

After conferring with LaSalle and his partner, the two men from the government car walk purposely past the debris pile to the edge of the yard, where I stand. It feels like forever, but only a few minutes have passed since Sonja and her family left for breakfast. Less time since I placed twelve million dollars in stolen bonds in my car.

It seems as if the two government agents are walking in slow motion.

"Your name Gum?" Both agents wear suits. The older

man's temples are salted with gray, a bald spot glowing on top of his head. He's tall and lugubrious, his mouth has down-turned ridges at each end, and his sad, brown eyes make me think his life has been gloomy, that he's lived through one tedious tragedy after another. The younger man has plump cheeks that have gone rosy in the crisp morning air.

"I'm Gum."

"We want to talk to you about a burglary."

"A what?"

"You know what we're talking about."

"I guess . . . I guess I don't."

They stare at me. I stare at them. They've seen me with the bags. They probably have a confederate getting a warrant to search my car even as we speak.

"Your house get broken into this past week?"

"Sir?"

"The place you're renting," the older agent says, irritably. "It got broken into, right?"

When I still don't answer, they flash their IDs and identify themselves as Smith and Jones. "No jokes, please," says Jones. "Just tell us what was missing. The police report wasn't specific. We received some fingerprints from SPD taken from your back door, from a possible perp."

They give me penetrating looks. A month ago my life was an open book. Now there are a million things I don't want people to know—actually, twelve million.

"Man named Jesse Brown. Died in a car fire. His fingerprints were found on the outside of your back door. He ever visit you at home?"

"Not while I was there."

"Can you think of any reason he'd want to break into your house?"

"He was looking for some money he thought we might know about."

"Who's 'we'?"

"Me and the rest of the crew. This was at the station."

"What money would that be?"

"It had something to do with a patient we had."

"Go on."

"His name was Charles Scott Ghanet."

Both men raise their eyebrows. "And what did Brown think was going on between you and this patient?"

"He accused us of some sort of conspiracy to steal money Ghanet had. We had to practically throw Brown out of the station."

"And you had some of this money at your home?"

"God, no."

"What do you know about the car fire that killed Brown and his wife?"

"I know it happened after he left our station. And we were the ones who tapped it."

"What exactly did Brown want to know when he visited the station?"

"If we saw anything at Ghanet's place the night we found his body."

"Did you see anything?"

"You could barely walk through the place. He'd been collecting junk for years."

"How long were you in the house?"

"Long enough to find the body. When the lieutenant called for a C and C, we went out to the rig. Then the cops got there and we left."

"That was it?"

"Yeah."

"This happened in the middle of the night?"

"Right."

"What was the lieutenant's name?"

"Sweeney Sears."

"Where can we find him?"

"He died at that fire down on Dexter Avenue."

They stare at me for a long time. I get the feeling they hadn't believed what we did was as important as what they did until they learned Sears was dead. A newfound esteem blossoms behind their eyes as they digest the news. "Who else was on your crew that night?"

"Robert Johnson and Ted Tronstad."

"Where are they?"

Tronstad is about sixty feet behind them, lying in the charred remains of the Pederson house. As patient now as he'd been impatient his whole life, he will wait until we have the time or inclination to unearth him. I note he's died just about where the falling pig died, one story higher but in the same vicinity. It is ironic, because it all started and ended in the same spot. "Johnson just got off work. I don't know where Tronstad is. He might be in some trouble."

"Why is that?"

"He set this fire."

"This one here?" The younger agent is speaking for the first time. He's been eyeballing my yellow WRX over my shoulder in a manner that makes it hard for me to decide whether he's admiring it or checking it out for professional reasons. Perhaps I looked suspicious with those garbage bags in my hands. Or maybe I look suspicious now.

"That your car over there?" asks the younger agent.

"Yes."

"What's in it?"

"Bunch of old dirty laundry."

"You mind if we look inside?"

"Not at all."

This is just another of my choices that hardly seems like a choice at all. Had I said no outright, it would look suspicious, perhaps suspicious enough for them to hold me and try for a warrant. I might cite some minor misdemeanor drug violation and tell them I don't want the local gendarmes looking in my car, but I doubt that would work, either. There doesn't seem to be any right answer.

I am finished. I know it, and from the way he is fixating on me, the younger agent knows it, too.

Looking sober and grave, LaSalle joins us and says, "I thought you guys might want to know, we found a body on the second floor."

"There were four people inside?" I ask. "They told me there were only three."

"It's Tronstad."

"Jesus. Are you sure?"

"Yeah. The wallet in his hip pocket didn't take that much damage."

"This the guy you just told us about?" the older FBI agent asks. "The one who set this fire?"

"Yes, sir." I am dismayed at the use of the word *sir.* I know it makes me look suspicious to be overly submissive here.

"He's dead?"

LaSalle nods. "He was acting crazy last night. He set two fires that we know about."

LaSalle looks at the three of us in turn. We are quiet. I am because I know the jig is up, that I am going to jail in a few minutes, and later, after the trial, to prison. The two agents are because they are about to break the back of a major conspiracy. "You guys want to see the body?"

The agents nod and follow LaSalle toward the house. Before they've gone too far, LaSalle gestures in my direction and says, "You guys realize you were talking here to the man who's made the most single-handed rescues of any firefighter in department history?" Both agents turn back and ogle me while continuing to walk toward the house. Hard to know if I am looking guilty, heroic, or dim-witted, though I feel the latter more than anything.

Awaiting my fate, I loiter at the edge of the yard in the blinding sunshine while firefighters straggle out of the house in ones and twos, heads hung low. Tears streaking her broad cheeks and mingling with traces of soot, Stanislow comes over to me. The guys on her shift call her *pigpen* because of her uncanny ability to accumulate dirt just about anywhere.

She steps close and gives me a hug, snorting into my ear as she weeps. "He's gone, Gum. Tronstad's up there on his face. He's dead. There was so much debris stuck to his PASS, we couldn't hear it."

Chief Mortimer shows up before the FBI and our two fire investigators are out of the fire building, bustles over to the Ladder 11 crew, and exchanges a few words. "How the hell could we lose a firefighter and not even know it? This is un-acceptable! There's no excuse for this sort of incompetence." As if aware that the surest source of incompetence on the fire ground is me, he says, "Gum! What the hell went on here? How could you people lose a firefighter and not know it? Goddamn it! Answer me!"

"It's Ted Tronstad, sir. He wasn't working yesterday."

"What do you mean, he wasn't working? How the hell did he get in that house, all burned to shit, if he wasn't work-ing?"

"He set the fire."

Chief Mortimer grows quiet, then moves to the front door and waits until the two FBI agents come out, exchanges words with them, and then watches them walk purposefully to their vehicle, climb in, and drive away. They seem to have forgotten about me.

I remain in the yard, waiting to get handcuffed. Thirty minutes later I am still waiting when the chief of the depart-ment and his entourage show up. Shortly thereafter, the Ped-ersons come back and the police begin questioning Bernard and Iola. After a while, Sonja comes over to where I am standing.

"Gum."

"Sonja."

"Somebody died in there?"

"The man who set the fire."

"Bernard's telling them he thinks the dead man was some-body Iola jilted. Is that possible?"

"Anything's possible."

"That he came here for revenge. You knew him pretty well, didn't you?"

"You never know anybody very well."

"I think I know you."

"I wouldn't bet anything important on it."

"Bernard's going to get an attorney. Iola's pleading igno-rance. And I sure as hell don't know what's going on."

"Neither do I."

They say, when threatened, human beings react in one of five ways: fight, flight, freeze, fidget, or faint. I believe I found another F to add to the panoply of human reaction—falsehood. It has become my weapon of choice.

After another ten minutes elapse, I tell LaSalle I'm leaving. "Sure, man. You had a rough night. These guys are taking over. They have any questions, they know where to find you. It looks like we're going to tie this in with that car bombing last week, the house fire on Beach Drive, and about six grass fires last night. It's beginning to look like he just cracked. People do that."

"Yeah. They do."

Out of sight of Bernard and Iola, who are both on borrowed cell phones, I kiss Sonja good-bye and walk to my car. I drive up Bonair at speed, then wait at the top of the hill to see if anybody is following. They aren't.

I drive to my mother's apartment house on California Avenue, remove the three garbage sacks from the back of my Subaru, go inside, and knock on her apartment door.

"Jason?"

"Hi, Mom." I give her a kiss. "I need to store some stuff."

"Sure. Use the spare bedroom."

We talk for a while, and after I realize she's fallen asleep on the couch, I head back into the spare bedroom, where I open all three garbage sacks, my heart jumping in my chest like a frog on a hot sidewalk. Slowly and carefully, I spread out the bearer bonds and count them, making the tabulations in ink on the sweaty palm of my hand. Tronstad's arithmetic was spot-on. Just over twelve million dollars. It is small consolation, but at least all these people haven't died over three sacks of rubbish.

I tie the bags and hide them in the back of the closet.

49. TWELVE MILLION DOLLARS SPLIT ONE WAY

Six months after my mother's death, Sonja and I drive to Mount Rainier, where we scatter my mother's ashes along a portion of the Wonderland Trail Mom admired. There had been no request to have her ashes dispersed in the wilds. Her death, like virtually every minute of her life, includes no personal requests.

We never have that final chat you always believe you're going to have with your loved ones before they die, that Kodachrome moment when you clear the air and say how much you love each other, when a lifetime of secrets gets unraveled and spills across the floor like a ball of yarn. To this day I have no clue who my father is. My mother didn't speak of it in life and made no reference to it as she lay dying. She gave birth to me when she was seventeen and single, the same year she got kicked out of her parents' house in Yakima. She spent the rest of her life dedicated to making sure my days were happier than hers.

A guess tells me I am the result of a high school romance, but after the age of ten, I stopped quizzing her. I have no brothers, no sisters, no father, only a set of grandparents who keep their distance emotionally and geographically. The only family I have now is the woman who sleeps beside me in the darkness. As if reading my thoughts, she says, "You awake?"

"Yeah. But I didn't know you were."

"You were tossing and turning. Talking in your sleep again. You said something about money."

"I had that dream again."

"You have it a lot."

"Yeah."

"Get some rest. We're going to look at houses tomorrow."

"Sure."

You screw up and get somebody dead, you either get very

hard, go nuts, or you get so you can surgically separate the event from the rest of your life. What they don't let you know in murder school is how incredibly depressing it is to cause the death of another human being, or even to be involved in a death, and that the depression never entirely departs. The other thing they don't tell you is that you'll never be allowed to stop lying about it.

Perhaps because we are both accustomed to driving sports cars, we get carsick in tandem as we are chauffeured around in the expensive SUV our real estate agent drives just a smidgeon too aggressively. He's so vain about his prowess behind the wheel, no amount of polite hinting can get him to slow down, take corners on a firm line, or remove his left foot from the brake pedal as we bob and wobble across West Seattle looking at houses.

He spends the morning taking us to homes we can afford and some we clearly cannot, seeming to take pleasure in showing properties for which the monthly payments are greater than our total monthly income. One of them is the estate on Beach Drive SW where Robert Johnson and I met Tronstad so many months ago, cleaned up and back on the market. When the agent walks us through, I give no indication I've been inside before.

Next to the front door they've planted a wisteria that must have cost a fortune, because despite its newness, it is eight feet tall and in full bloom, a delicate purple.

Despite the fact that I continue to feel an underlying depression, my life is blooming too.

Sonja and I plan a quiet wedding in three months.

Though Sonja visits them on occasion, I see her father and stepmother only infrequently. There are times when I fear my sweaty history with her stepmother will be the unmaking of our relationship, but Sonja seems cool with it. If Bernard knows about my liaisons with his wife, he gives no hint; Iola treats me as if I've immigrated from another continent, as if I'm of the servant class, someone she can barely tolerate. It's hard to blame her, but I'm not giving up Sonja so Iola can be comfortable.

For the past year I've been driving Engine 29. I'm the youngest driver in the battalion.

Unwilling to place another firefighter's life, or a civilian's, under the crude hammer of my judgment, I've given up my dreams of taking promotional exams.

After Tronstad's funeral, Robert Johnson transfered to Station 28 in the Rainier Valley, giving up five percent driver's pay to relocate. Rumors surface that he's become a heavy drinker. From time to time I get concerned that his buddy Jesus will tell him to turn himself in, and me with him, but so far it hasn't happened, and we are fast arriving at the point at which it will be his word against mine.

Tronstad's funeral is massive, the third fire department funeral in a month. Exhibiting a familiar eagerness to conceal unpleasant facts, as well as an unwillingness to dig into the truth behind the catastrophes that have dogged Station 29 for so long, the fire department refuses to finger Ted Tronstad for anything more than the fire at the Pederson place. They don't reopen the investigations into the deaths of Sweeney Sears or Chief Abbott. I find the videotape of me in the water with Sears in Tronstad's station locker, and I destroy it. As usual, I keep my mouth shut.

The death of the Browns goes unsolved.

Although it is common knowledge inside the department that Tronstad had been behaving erratically and that he may have set at least one other fire, news of his string of possible felonies fails to reach the media or the general public. Nobody seems curious about why he set fire to the Pederson home, although there are fictitious reports in the department that he'd been seeing Iola Pederson.

Rumors have gone around in the fire department that Tronstad's death has traumatized me so badly, I cannot talk about it; consequently, few people press me for answers as to what happened that night or why I didn't see him inside the house while I was making the rescues.

Two days after the funeral, the FBI locates a bank deposit box in Ghanet's name with $546,000 in cash in it. After more weeks of poking around, they close the investigation, satisfied Ghanet either blew or lost the rest of his booty.

Waiting patiently for federal agents to show up at my door and arrest me, I sweat it out for weeks and then months, but by the first anniversary of our discovery of Ghanet's bearer bonds, I realize they are not coming, that they aren't going to question me about the money or about Tronstad's death. I'm not quite sure why I haven't turned the bonds in or run off to spend them, but I haven't. Actually, in the back of my mind, I believe I subconsciously *want* to be arrested.

Sonja talks about the fire sometimes, but if she suspects me of rat-holing Tronstad in her father's bedroom to die, she does not bring it up.

Sonja loves me. She is good to me. I love her, and I hope I'm good to her. Occasionally we argue, but we make up quickly and laugh about it later. It is easy to know we are going to be happy together for a very long time.

We share our first Thanksgiving with her stepmother and father and grandfather and a couple of aunts and uncles. Toward the end of the evening, when I am swollen with turkey and cranberries and pie, I begin to relax. Bernard corners me and gives me a lecture on how the U.S. government is protecting world peace with military might. Iola glares at us from across the room. Changing the subject to hybrid vehicles, he bends my ear for another twenty minutes, a man more concerned with machines and public policies than with the people around him. It is easy to see why Iola is drawn to serial affairs.

I've mistakenly believed my mother's funeral is going to be just her and me, Sonja, and a couple of Mom's elderly neighbors; but over 150 people attend: swimmers who'd worked out with her at the YMCA pool before she got sick, neighbors from her apartment house and the apartments where she'd lived in the past, co-workers from her last three jobs and the food bank where she'd volunteered, a doctor who cared for her, and the waitress we met at Three Fingered Jack's in Winthrop, a woman who has driven five hours in a broken-down Ford to be here.

Four days after my mother's death, I am in her apartment going through her things—she'd gotten rid of just about all her personal items to make it easier for me—and am shocked to discover a life insurance policy worth $900,000. I can't bear the thought of receiving money as a result of my mother's death.

I cash out the insurance policy and make donations to my mother's favorite charities. The American Cancer Society. Northwest Second Harvest. The Goodwill, where she did much of her shopping throughout her life. I retain an attorney and dump the rest into an investment account, to be reviewed once annually on the anniversary of my mother's death. Eventually the money will go into a trust for the children Sonja and I will have together.

I've had my mother's mail rerouted to my place, so every time she gets a package of coupons or a renewal notice from the Sierra Club or Amnesty International, I get sweet little reminders of a life lived well.

A little more than a year after Tronstad's death, Sonja takes a vacation to Hawaii with her three best friends, young women she's been close to all through school and beyond. "You don't mind, do you?" Sonja asks.

"Not at all. It'll give me a chance to spend some time at the titty bars."

"Quit it."

"If I get tired of boobs, and the weather cooperates, I might drive over to Eastern Washington and go hiking. Maybe even an overnighter."

"That sounds like fun."

After her plane leaves, I drive home, pack up the bearer bonds in a large cardboard box, wipe it clean of prints, and take it to an attorney, where I lay out the entire story. The attorney contacts the local federal prosecutor and hashes out a deal. I will turn in the bonds in return for blanket immunity to any crimes associated with the theft. I will guarantee I'm not holding anything back, and they will trust my guarantee. Twelve million in bonds is far more than they were looking for. I will keep the names of any confederates to myself. In return, the government will not name me publicly. They will get the bonds, and I will walk away with a clean slate. Everybody will be happy.

Sonja comes back from Maui, and a month later we buy a two-bedroom fixer-upper on Thirty-fifth Avenue SW, a main thoroughfare near Station 37. We are pounding nails and restoring it one room at a time. The work is satisfying, especially my chores in what will be the baby's room.

I strive to be a man who defines himself, rather than having his possessions define him. I do not wallow in luxury goods or run up tabs on credit cards.

It is ironic that in death my mother has given me what she could never provide in life, a surfeit of material wealth. Just as ironic is the fact that I cannot bring myself to touch it.

I ride Engine 29 and take pride in my duties. On alarms I deliver the goods, and when we have a fire, my crew gets water. We drill for the chief and I make no mistakes. Sonja and I talk about having babies, about her day in the patrol car, my day at the fire station, about national politics or the last movie we saw together. Whenever the weather allows, I skate. When she's not at work, Sonja skates with me. We listen to music. We read books. We take walks after dinner. We enjoy each other's company and the company of our friends.

Two weeks after I make the deal with the feds, my attorney calls. The government has flown experts from the Treasury Department to Seattle to examine the bonds and has learned they are fakes. Eventually the bank would have caught Tronstad for the bonds he cashed. The government bonds are counterfeit, and the private and foreign bank bonds are phoney, too. For twenty years Ghanet had been hoarding a treasure that is bogus.

It kills me to think about it. Three sacks of garbage propelled the runaway machine that chewed up my life and killed six people.

Once a day, sometimes more, black thoughts cross my mind, thoughts of pumping on Russell Abbott's chest, of the charred corpses at the intersection of California and Admiral Way, of the tiny article in the *Seattle Times* noting

Heather Wynn's death. Sears twisting in the grip of the whirl-pool. Tronstad choosing money over his very life. I lie to myself. I rationalize and I justify and I make the best of my part in all of it. I live my life and it is good, but underneath, I carry a secret that is as nasty as the cancer my mother walked around with.

These days, perhaps more than anybody around, I realize the value of law.

I do not trample rules. I do not roll through stop signs. I do not drive the interstate five miles over the speed limit. I do not hedge when filling out tax forms. I return my library books on time. I pocket my litter and that of the next man. Some-times my punctiliousness annoys Sonja, but I will not change.

I have to admit there are times when I am tempted by the money my mother left, but I know I'm happiest when I'm living a normal life like everybody around me. A life with simple pleasures.

Sonja loves me and I love her, and I've found that's more than enough.

Read on for an exciting preview of
Earl Emerson's new novel

FIRETRAP

Available in hardcover from
Ballantine Books

1. THE Z CLUB

Captain Trey Brown, Engine 28, C shift

I was seventeen the first time I stole India from my brother.

They say you never forget your first love, and I guess it's true, because even though I haven't laid eyes on her in almost two decades, I find my thoughts straying in India's direction often. But then, my life changed forever that summer, so why shouldn't my thoughts stray to that time? There were a lot of changes during the course of those months: our oldest brother dying in a car wreck, India's sister the victim of an assault that changed her life and mine forever, the dark evening I got myself blackballed out of the Carmichael family on what was essentially a hand vote.

Perhaps it is because memories of youth are so often marbled with yearning that I believed parts of our summer might one day be recovered. Memories of desire heated to the melting point dim slowly. The summer India and I cheated on my brother, I was seventeen and she had just turned eighteen. At the time I believed we were more in love than any other two people on Earth. Had events turned out differently, that feeling might have eased out of my soul of its own accord instead of being jerked out like a gaffed flounder. Oddly, her last name is Carmichael now, a detail that lends more angst to my recollections than anything else.

Being excommunicated from the family was only the beginning of my troubles. At seventeen I came as close as I ever would to a jail cell, and then had the stuffing beaten out of me by two ex–pro boxers while Barry Renfrow stood by and watched. Renfrow's back now, too, which shows how circular life can be.

Though I hadn't laid eyes on India during the intervening years, I'd seen pictures of her in the newspaper: at a Mariners game sitting with the president of the ball club and his wife; a wedding photo the week after she married Stone Carmichael; and more recently, functioning as the hostess at a charity ball attended by Puget Sound's hoity-toity, the odd software billionaire sprinkled in among the five-thousand-dollar gowns and designer tuxedos. For me the photos were freeze-frame glimpses of a life I'd been banished from.

Even now I remember our last night together, the silky feel of her breasts under my touch, the ultimate tension in my loins as her thighs tightened. Oddly enough, she married into the only family on this planet who held me in lower regard than her own family did. But that's a long story. Only weeks ago Seattle suffered its most devastating fire in recent history, and the irony that disaster can reunite us just as disaster once split us apart does not elude me. Today I am a lonely man of common tastes, who wonders occasionally not whether his lost love thinks of him as frequently as he thinks of her, but whether she thinks of him at all.

This morning I debated whether or not to take the Harley to work, but in the end decided the riots would probably be over by six forty-five when I left the house. The radio reported rock throwing in the Rainier Valley, random gunshots on Beacon Hill, bricks thrown at a fire station several blocks from my home. In the nine days I'd been out of town, the public outcry over the fire had snowballed from bitch sessions to rioting. If things continued in this vein, it was only a matter of time before more deaths were added to the fourteen at the Z Club—fifteen if you counted the witness who was murdered two blocks from the fire.

It was four weeks after the tragedy, a Friday morning, early October, and Seattle was sleepwalking through a typical fall of fog-shrouded mornings and hazy afternoons. The news said rain was moving in.

At the intersection of Martin Luther King and Jackson, a gaggle of black teenagers stood idly in the fog. I could tell from their body language that they'd been out all night, hunting up hassles and emboldening one another with tough talk and macho posturing. A small grocery store on the northwest corner revealed broken windows and graffiti streaming across the front door like cartoon captions. As I waited for the red light, one of the boys realized I was the only motorist at the intersection and threw a half-full beer bottle onto Jackson, where it burst twenty feet from my front tire. Several of them laughed, the others waiting for my reaction. I wanted to tell them that if this was a black-white revolution, perhaps they should go after a white guy instead of yours truly, but all I did was blip my throttle a couple of times and roar away when the light changed.

I'd been in a cocoon of my own making for the past nine days, having flown to Las Vegas on my annual trek with my mom and brother, my real family. I hadn't had time to catch up on all the news, but I knew the official fire department report had come out two days ago and yesterday the papers had unloaded a bombshell that made the report look like a pack of lies. Since then, all hell had broken loose. While my minor burns from the Z Club fire had healed, the community rebellion had grown worse.

This would be my first shift on Engine 28 in almost a month, and as much as I detested Las Vegas, making the trip each year specifically for my mother and brother, who couldn't get enough of it, the journey had been a respite from the angry speeches, department arm-twisting, and political diatribes prompted by the Z Club fire.

As did other papers in the country, the Las Vegas *Review-Journal* had carried daily updates on the unrest in Seattle. *USA Today* sported a photo of bodies under a large tarpaulin on the sidewalk outside the Z Club, and it was because of those bodies that last Friday and Saturday night African-American youth rioted in Seattle in a manner that hadn't been seen here since the late sixties. Monday morning, almost sixteen hundred marchers, black and white, forced the mayor to stand in the rain outside the municipal building and give a conciliatory speech about knitting the community back together. So far nobody had been killed in the riots, although one police officer received a broken shoulder when some moron dropped a cinder block from a roof. Each day there had been organized marches, and later, under cover of darkness, a different set of protesters staged miniriots, break-ins, and looting.

According to reports I heard on the radio, the vice president's visit this morning had forced the SPD to maintain an expansive presence on the streets. I was afraid my little brother Johnny, who had a penchant for lunacy and a compulsion to be part of any crowd, would get sucked into the maelstrom, so I had hoped the ruckus would have died down by the time we returned from Nevada. In fact, we had taken the Vegas trip a month early trusting in just such an eventuality. But instead of dying down, the turmoil had mushroomed.

Thirteen black civilians and one white firefighter had died at the Z Club fire. One version of the story had a mostly white fire department pouring water into the building in a cowardly style from the sidewalk, while frantic young blacks tried to escape the premises without any help. Another version painted a picture of firefighters so intent on saving one of their own that they ignored relatively easy civilian rescues, leaving more than a dozen African Americans to die. If I bought into either of those scenarios, I might have been tempted to march in the streets, too.

Yesterday afternoon the mayor's office issued its official reaction to the fire department's report on the Z Club fire and to the news stories yesterday morning which supposedly debunked that report. The TV news had been filled with cautiously worded affirmations from city administrators and fire department brass juxtaposed with statements from the outraged local NAACP chapter president, from angry black ministers, from family and friends of the victims, and from more fortunate partygoers who'd escaped the Z Club that night. Melinda Burns, the lieutenant I would be relieving on Engine 28 this morning, was interviewed during one newscast, announcing rather lamely that it was "always a shame when people had to die at a fire." From the department's perspective, the interview probably wasn't a great idea, since Melinda was white, the victims were black, and that distinction had been the number one topic of contention from the get-go.

Situated on Rainier Avenue, Station 28, my home away from home, was a stereotypical firehouse with three tall roll-up apparatus bay doors and hard tile floors throughout. Because of the institutional nature of our structure and furnishings, I often thought the building could serve as the living quarters for the staff in a state facility, most likely a nuthouse.

I shut off the Harley and rolled into the station without getting off, walking the bike quietly between the rigs to the rear of the station under the basketball hoop. It was seven A.M., and most of the firefighters from yesterday's shift were just climbing out of their bunks. In half an hour, today's crews would take over and hold the fort until seven thirty tomorrow morning: four firefighters on Ladder 12, three of us on Engine 28, and two paramedics on Medic 28.

Lieutenant Burns, who met me outside the engine officer's room, was thick through the middle—like someone who'd been drinking beer for too many years—but had been a star athlete in college: rugby and lacrosse. She was anxious about living up to department standards, even though as far as I could tell, she generally surpassed them.

"All heck's been breaking loose," she said.

"Oh, yeah?" I left the door open a few inches while I went into the small engine officer's room, tugged off my motorcycle boots, and stepped into a freshly laundered fire department uniform I'd carried to work in my saddlebags.

"We bunked four times last night," she said from the hallway. "Had two Dumpster fires down near Alaska. Got called to the South Precinct after they pepper-sprayed a couple of guys outside one of the holding cells. They must have had eighteen or twenty people under arrest for rioting. People are really bent out of shape over that report. Tonight might be more of the same."

"Yeah, it's Friday."

It was unexpected and a little sad to see the black community so angry at the fire department. Historically it was the police department that attracted our wrath, as it had not too long ago when police officers killed a mentally unstable black man who'd held two women hostage for ten hours. Although the guy had been armed only with a kitchen knife, the police shot him seven times, which did a grand job of stirring up righteous indignation. Four months later when the Z Club fire came along, the black community was still simmering.

"By the way, Melinda. I saw you on the news. You looked good."

"The chief called and chewed me out. They want either a chief or the PIO to be talking to the media. Nobody else."

"There was a memo to that effect before I left. You didn't see it?"

"I did, but they stuck a microphone in my face and asked me to say something, and I just went ahead and shot my mouth off. I don't know why."

"So what's going on around here?" I'd changed and was in the corridor, the two of us walking toward the beanery, which had begun to fill up with yawning firefighters from yesterday's shift. Somebody was grinding coffee beans in the kitchen alcove.

The kitchen, or the "beanery" in department parlance, was

a big room suffused with the odors of aftershave, yesterday's cooking, and the residue of smoke from last night's fires. A television sat in the far corner, and a long wooden table dominated the room. One corner had two refrigerators, a range, and a sink. Rank-and-file firefighters slept in the large bunk room on the other side of the apparatus bay, while the engine and truck officers slept in the offices behind us. The medic room was sandwiched between the officers' rooms.

Except for Melinda and one oncoming medic, everybody in the room was male. Two firefighters in the corner were discussing a bow-hunting trip. Other than that, all talk centered around the civil unrest. When the phone rang, I snapped it up. "Captain Brown. Station Twenty-eight."

"Cap? This is Garrison. I'm going to be late. I-5's a parking lot. I heard on the radio there's another protest south of the old Rainier Brewery. If it's like last week, it'll gum things up for hours."

"I'll tell Hannity," I said, picking up the remote off the table and switching the TV to the local news. A chopper was displaying a sky view of about a hundred fifty sign-waving marchers on Interstate 5. They had taken over all four of the northbound lanes, and the southbound lanes were stalled with gapers. "If Hannity can't stay over for you, I'm sure somebody else will."

"All they're doing is making people mad. There's going to be like six thousand people late for work."

"We'll cover for you."

Winston, one of the incoming medics, had been studying the TV images and said, "Gee, I wonder how they work that? Do they call their boss and say, 'I need to take a few hours of comp time so I can be on the freeway fucking up the morning for everybody else'? Or do they call in sick and scam a day off the company? Or maybe they all work the night shift? Maybe they're independent entrepreneurs and are planning to make up the lost time by working this evening. Jesus."

The ridicule in his voice was rich with the implication that none of the black marchers had jobs, thus were able to mess up the day for hardworking white people, who did. The secondary implication was an old one I was familiar with, that the marchers didn't have jobs because they didn't want to work for a living.

"The squeaky wheel gets the grease," said Lieutenant Black cheerfully.

"If you ask me, the squeaky wheel should get greased," growled Winston, making a gesture toward the TV with thumb and forefinger as if shooting someone.

"If I remember correctly, this is still America," I said. "A guy decides to march with a sign, you don't shoot him. That's banana-republic SOP. Besides, their goal isn't to foul up commuters. It's to stall the vice president, who's landing at Boeing Field at eight o'clock. They want to disrupt *his* schedule so they can make the national news. I'm not saying it's right. I'm just saying they're not out to make regular people late."

"Whatever it is, it's a load of crap!" Winston said.

Somebody else said, "You're right, Captain. If they can tie up the vice president on his way to see the mayor, it'll make national."

"The city blew it," Melinda said, "letting that report out without having all the facts. Then that nine-one-one call on the news. That recording: 'Help me. Help me. Please don't leave me here. The firemen keep walking past me.' They've been playing it every half hour. It doesn't sound good."

"It had to be a fake," said Smollen. "No firefighter would leave a victim."

"They got headlines, all right," said Lieutenant Black, who'd picked up the remote and switched to the *Today* Show on NBC. The same chopper pictures we'd been viewing locally were being broadcast nationally.

"Anybody read the SFD report?" I asked.

"It's not in the stations yet," said Melinda, "but on the news yesterday they said it absolved the fire department of all wrongdoing."

"As well it should have," said Winston. "I was at that fire. We worked our butts off. Somebody wants to torch a place, there's not a lot you can do to stop them. This is just another . . ." He looked up at me and stopped.

"Go ahead. Say it."

"This is just another case of the black community not being able to face the fact that their problems are of their own making. I'm sorry, but that's the way I feel."

"What about that nine-one-one tape?"

"I don't know about that. I'd like to see them identify those firefighters who supposedly passed that guy up. If they exist."

Most people in the fire department kept their thoughts on race, whatever those thoughts were, to themselves. Winston was one of the outspoken ones, and in some ways I appreciated his candor, if not his attitude. The room grew quiet. As a captain I was the ranking officer as well as the only black man in the room. "Opinions are like assholes," I said. "Everyone has one."

"Yeah, I know," Winston said. "But you don't agree?"

"You mean, do I agree the marchers should be shot?"

"I shouldn't have said that. I mean do you think that tape is legit?"

"It sounded real to me."

Somebody said, "Where'd that nine-one-one tape come from, anyway? Why didn't we have it the first day after the fire?"

"Maybe the dispatcher held it back from the city investigators so the fire department wouldn't look bad," I said.

"So who was bypassing victims?"

"God only knows," I said, although in the back of my mind I had an idea.

The most recent and inflammatory news report had been a clip from a dispatch tape reportedly made on the night of the Z Club fire, in which a man who claimed he was trapped in the fire called the 911 dispatchers on his cell phone to tell them that firemen were passing him by. Sounds of fire and even an MSA mask operating could be heard in the background. They were playing snippets of the tape on every newscast. The pleas had been heartrending, given the fact that the man had apparently died shortly thereafter. No survivors had admitted to making the call, and the phone had been found beside one of the victims on the second floor.

"Okay, they're saying we didn't try hard enough to get those people out because they were black," said Winston. "A lot of firefighters at the Z Club were black. They're trying to make it into this huge racial thing when it wasn't."

The worst part about the controversy for black firefighters was that when we defended the black community, we were looked on with suspicion by white firefighters, and when we stuck up for the fire department, the black community called us Uncle Toms. There was no way to win. But then, there never is.

"They just don't get it," Winston continued. "Not everything is racial."

I said, "That's just it. Everything *is* racial."

"How can you say that?"

"How can you deny it?"

"Because it isn't. Take you, for instance. You're a captain in the fire department. You got that position *because* you were black. Not in spite of it. How do you figure you've been hurt by racism?"

"You got about a year to listen?"

"Don't give me that. The type of racism these people are talking about doesn't exist in Seattle. I doubt it exists anywhere in the country anymore."

"You paint yourself black for a year and then I might give some thought to what you're saying."

"Walk in the other man's shoes? Is that what you're telling me? Why don't you paint yourself white?"

"I've already *been* white." The room grew quiet. One by one we focused on the TV and the vice president's motorcade heading onto the freeway. It was a little like watching the O.J. chase, excruciating in its slowness and in the inevitable knowledge that when the motorcade collided with the protesters, the outcome would be dismaying.

Twenty-five minutes later Clyde Garrison had just signed into the daybook when the bell hit, and Garrison, Kitty Acton, and I rushed out to the apparatus bay and climbed onto Engine 28. It was good to be back.